MISSING EVIDENCE

Ray was frantic now. Grunting, he tilted the Polaris, kicked beneath it with his boot. He let the machine down with a thud, then knelt and reached under the tarps. Thirty seconds later he stood up. Breathing hard, he stared incredulously at the disheveled contents of the shed and cursed.

"Lose something?" Leeland asked.

Ray swore again, more emphatically.

"What is it, Ray?" Billy Bob wondered, wide eyes looking out from his Plexiglas eye guards.

"The body," he panted. "It's gone."

ELEMENTS OF A KILL

AN INUPIAT ESKIMO MYSTERY

CHRISTOPHER LANE

AVON BOOKS ◆ NEW YORK

This is a work of fiction. Names, characters, places, and incidents are the product of the author's imagination. While some events, locales, and organizations in the story are real, they are used here fictitiously.

AVON BOOKS
A division of
The Hearst Corporation
1350 Avenue of the Americas
New York, New York 10019

First Avon Books Printing: April 1998

AVON TRADEMARK REG. U.S. PAT. OFF. AND IN OTHER COUNTRIES, MARCA REGISTRADA, HECHO EN U.S.A.

Printed in the U.S.A.

WCD   10   9   8   7   6   5   4   3   2   1

➤ AUTHOR'S NOTE ◄

I HAVE A confession to make: I am not a Native, a sour-dough, or an expert on Alaska. Originally from the South-west, my connection with the Last Frontier began in the mid-seventies when my father was transferred to Anchor-age by an oil service company. I attended high school and then college in the state's largest city. When I went Outside to finish my degree, I had no idea that I would not be returning, except as a tourist.

My wife is a true Alaskan. Though not a Native, she was nevertheless born at the Alaskan Native Hospital. Her fa-ther was stationed in Alaska in 1954 as a doctor with the Public Heath Service and was instrumental in the eradica-tion of tuberculosis from among the Native population.

Anyone who has ever visited Alaska will testify to its extraordinary grandeur and unsurpassable beauty. The peo-ple there and the mysterious, almost magical land they in-habit are both unique and unforgettable. Which is why *Elements of a Kill* was so enjoyable to write. It afforded me an opportunity to explore and experience, if only vi-cariously, the Great Land once again.

I relied on several sources in the creation of this adven-ture. First and foremost, my father. As manager of Alaskan operations for Halliburton Company from 1974 to 1980, he had the opportunity to travel the width and breadth of the state, making regular trips to the North Slope. He was an inexhaustible fount of information regarding Prudhoe

Bay and I am truly grateful for his assistance.

I also gleaned important research from a number of books, most notably, *The Alaska Almanac*, *The Native People of Alaska*, and Nick Jans's lyrical essays in, *The Last Light Breaking*. Those interested in delving into the subjects touched on in this novel may wish to hunt down these volumes.

I would like to thank Lyssa Keusch and the rest of the Avon Books staff for their hard work, encouragement, suggestions, and long-suffering over the course of this project. My wife, Melodie, is responsible for helping to hammer the manuscript into submittable shape. Without her support and inspiration, it never would have been written.

Any inaccuracies, errors, or mistakes in the portrayal of oil exploration on the National Petroleum Reserve, the traditions of the Inupiat Eskimo, or the North Slope in general are mine. I have taken artistic liberties at several points in the story, adding to and subtracting from the reality of Prudhoe Bay and the surrounding region in an effort to enhance the drama. These embellishments, along with the characters and companies presented in the plot, were derived wholly from my imagination.

Having issued that disclaimer, I hope that you will receive this novel as it is intended: a fictional blending of Alaska's natural majesty and noble people groups—with a mystery thrown in for good measure.

Enjoy.

Christopher A. Lane
1997

GLOSSARY

aarigaa!—wow!
aklaq—grizzly
anjatkut—shaman
Eskimo—"eaters of raw meat"
igloo—house of any type
Inupiaq—the language of the Inupiat Eskimo
Inupiat—"The Real People," Eskimos of northern Alaska
ivrulik—sod house
Ivisaapaatmiut—people of Invisaapaat or Ambler
kila—animal helping spirit
labret—a decorative shell or stone plug worn in the lower lip
mukluks—fur trimmed boots of seal skin and caribou
muktuk—whale skin
naluaqmiu—white person
naluaqmiut—white people
nigiluq—hunting ritual in which the throat of an animal is
     slit and the cartilage under the tongue removed in order to
     allow its spirit to escape and be reborn to be hunted again
Nunamiut—"people of the land"
piinjilak—ghosts
qaspeg—outer shell worn over a parka to keep it clean
taiku—thank you
Tareumiut—"people of the sea"
tukkuq—host
tuungak—spirits

vii

ulu—a razor sharp knife with a fan-shaped blade, traditionally used by Eskimo women for scraping and chopping
umialik—"captain of the umiak"; leader
umiak—large, open skin boat

⊱ PRELUDE ⊰

THE SPIRITS OF the night were a swirling guide, enlivening blind eyes to see past the curtain of darkness, empowering deaf ears to hear beyond the voice of the shouting wind. Beneath his boots—ice, four meters thick. Above his head—snow, ushered south on gray, frigid wings. Into the frozen void he went, each step confident, every movement calculated: a solitary hunter blessed by the gods.

Trotting . . . Slowing . . . Waiting . . . Listening . . . Heart tuned to the language of the Land . . .

It was out there, somewhere in the black, somewhere in the storm, hiding in winter's angry fist. The challenge was finding it.

Jogging . . . Pausing . . . Holding in breath . . . Eyes darting . . . Ears straining . . . Embracing the Land . . . Becoming a part of the Land . . .

And suddenly it was over. Disappointment became a weight that draped itself over his shoulders. The excitement of the chase, the accompanying flow of adrenaline, the expectation of the attack, the thirst for blood. Then this: a still form in the snow, a body curled into a fetal ball, a soul having relinquished itself willingly to the grave. No fight. No battle. The hunter's weapon still silent. It was almost shameful.

He took to the task mechanically, putting a bullet through the heart, bending to remove the worm from beneath the tongue, then working to sever the head, to set the poor, defeated creature's spirit free. Perhaps it would return as a car-

1

ibou or a bear, and the two would meet again, in a more engaging, provocative conflict.

The crescent-shaped blade had only just begun its journey through the stiff, cold flesh, toward the jugular, when he heard it: a dull crunch. He became a statue. There was another crunch. Another. Feet stomping across crusty, wind-packed snow. More footsteps. Fifty feet away . . . forty . . . thirty . . . Phantoms approaching.

The hunt over, the job basically completed, he hurriedly repacked the knife and began dragging the carcass across the ice, away from the prowlers. It was time to hide the kill, to stash it in a hole where it would not soon be discovered.

ONE

THE CABLE SLIPPED over the collar and around the icy gray neck like a giant hangman's noose. Two hooded figures labored in a pool of halogen light, long shadows performing an erratic dance as their clumsy, mitten-clad hands struggled to secure the load. Seconds later, one of them shouted something, his words quickly stolen by the howling wind. Forty feet away, obscured by blowing snow, the floorman knelt inside the rig enclosure and began wrapping rope around the cathead. A motor groaned from up above, gears grinding. The slack, three-quarter inch catline jinked once, twice . . . Suddenly it jerked taut, the loop shrinking to grip the pipe.

A thermometer on the outer wall read 57 degrees—below zero. The simple device failed to account for the chill factor, the thirty-mile-an-hour wind driving the temperature down to minus 134.

When the pipe had been pulled from the rack, up the wooden walk, and into the enclosure, a crew member hurried to shut the door against the cruel night.

Inside the rig, the pipe continued its journey, one end tipping skyward, following the cable up the derrick. Three stories up, perched on a monkey board, a small man in coveralls and a hard hat awaited its arrival. He would "stab" the pipe, guiding it into a similar piece of casing already seated in the ground.

When the pipe reached him, he took it in two gloved hands and aimed it at the hole thirty-five feet below. He quickly

3

lined it up and shouted, "Go!" his mind busy calculating the time it would take them to set the remaining 1300 feet of pipe. They were behind schedule, but if things went well today, they might be able to . . .

As the piped jiggled slightly and floated away from him, he noticed something.

"Hold it!"

Peering into the pipe, he swore.

"Swing it over!"

The crew did, two men pulling the pipe to one side. The man stepped across the monkey board and reached for a sledgehammer.

Still cursing the pipe, he warned the men below, "Got mud in it! I'm gonna give it a whack. Hang on!"

The steel cylinder rang like a chime with each tap. When that had no effect, he lifted the hammer and took a bigger swing. A gong echoed through the enclosure, but the interior of the pipe was still dark.

He cursed the black hole and swung at it as if it were his enemy. *Clang! Clang! Clang!* Nothing. Tossing the hammer aside, he examined his watch. An expletive escaped from his lips. Another delay. And all because the jerks back at the main camp didn't have the sense to check the pipes before sending them out to the location. He considered a hot, fiery resting place for the entire bunch. They were back in Prudhoe, residing in relative luxury, eating pastries and watching first-run movies, while he was here on a blasted ice island, sleeping in a crummy prefab building across the yard from the rig.

He retrieved a flashlight from his tool kit and took another look inside the pipe.

"Dang mud," he muttered.

"Did you get it?" a voice called from below.

"Heck no, I didn't get it!"

"What's the holdup?" The drilling foreman was aggravated.

"Some sort of obstruction," the man shouted back. "I can't tell what it is."

"What is it?" the foreman asked.

"I said, I can't tell!"

"What?"

"Probably mud!" the man answered.

He heard someone swear. "Can you get it loose?" the foreman wanted to know.

"I'm trying!"

"Use a sledge!"

"I did!"

"Use it again!"

The man took up the hammer and beat on the pipe with renewed energy, with vengeance. It teetered and swung away from him; the man chased it, whacked it, reared back and . . . missed—a full swing of air that nearly sent him off the monkey board. Regaining his balance, he told the pipe what it could do to itself.

"Any luck?" the foreman shouted up.

"No!"

"Then let's get it out of here. Bring in another section!"

On the floor of the rig the foreman climbed into his down parka, zipped up the hood and face mask, and pulled on a pair of gauntlet mittens. He followed the pipe back outside to its resting place on the rack. Waving to a man driving a forklift, he yelled, "Clear this thing!"

The roustabout hopped out of the lift and ran toward him. "What?" Two dark, almond-shaped eyes looked out from under the fur-lined hood, past the neoprene mask and clear goggles. Even with the cold weather disguise, it was obvious that he was a Native.

"Clear this thing! It's full of mud!"

The roustabout nodded. "Want us to finish this first?" He pointed to a stack of equipment crates that had been dumped unceremoniously near the center of the yard.

The foreman glanced at the crates, then back at the pipe rack. "Yeah. I think we've got enough casing to set the hole, but make sure it's clear before morning. Okay?"

"Okay."

The foreman trotted back to the rig enclosure, hunched against the wind, ice pellets assaulting his parka. When the roustabout reached his vehicle, he used the short-wave radio to contact his partner, another Native operating a lift just twenty yards away, somewhere behind the veil of snow.

"Hey, Sam, we got a pipe here we're supposed to clear."

There was a burst of static, then, "Tonight?"

"Yeah. After we get these crates into the hanger."

Sam swore through the static. "But Jim, the next shipment's due around three."

"Maybe we can finish this load and get the pipe cleared before the truck shows up."

"Maybe." Static crackled. "I really don't want anymore overtime. I haven't slept in two days. I feel like a zombie."

"Hey, man, me too. But the way we're gettin' paid, who cares?"

They both laughed at this.

"I'll bet we can move these crates, fix the pipe, and still have time to grab some coffee before the next shipment," Jim boasted.

"How much?"

"Twenty dollars."

"You're on." Both lifts grunted to action.

Two hours later, at 2:30 A.M., it looked like Jim was going to be twenty dollars richer. Having spread the equipment around the yard and stacked it into the sheds, they parked the lifts and approached the clogged pipe.

Jim shined a light inside. "What the heck's in there?"

"Huh? What's that?" The wind and their tight hoods made conversation almost impossible.

"I said . . ." he leaned toward his partner and shouted, "What the heck's in there?!"

"Mud?" Jim shrugged. "Stand back." He picked up a ten pound hammer and swung it as if he were splitting wood with an ax. The resulting clank was muffled, lost in a powerful, arctic gust.

"Hit it again!"

He took another half dozen swings at it, the smooth surface of the pipe refusing to wrinkle or scar. Sam sent the beam back into the pipe. "Still there. We need . . . um . . . a rod."

"A what?" Jim cupped his mittens over the spots on his hood where his ears would have been.

"Something long! To poke it out with!"

Across the yard, the crew emerged from the rig. Having finished one phase of their work, they were taking a break, trudging toward the camp building in search of food, warmth, nicotine, and caffeine. Faces toward the ground, shoulders slumped in exhaustion, they looked like prisoners of a Siberian gulag on a forced march.

The two roustabouts set out in the opposite direction, toward an equipment shed. Huddling against the far outer wall of the structure, they examined a pile of discarded junk in the beam of the flashlight: a carburetor from a pickup, oversized rubber hoses, a dented metal box, broken wrenches, empty fifty-five gallon drums, a cracked exhaust pipe off of a pump truck, a dozen shredded tires, a scattering of broken two-by-fours . . .

"Here." Sam wrestled a piece of steel rebar from the pile. "Too short."

He considered it, then tossed it back like an undersized fish. "How about this one?" He pulled on another. It was longer, almost ten feet with a crook in the end. Jim nodded.

They returned to the pipe. "Here goes nothing," Sam said. He commando crawled into the cramped space, pushing the rebar out in front of him. His torso, then his waist disappeared into the cavity. Only his legs were still visible when the rebar struck something.

"Got it!"

"What?"

Sam jabbed with the rebar. Whatever it was that was clogging the pipe, it was solid. Probably hardened, frozen mud. He continued jabbing, sweat matting his hair beneath the hood and mask. Winded and tired of fighting something he couldn't see, he decided it was time to make his escape from the pipe. Wiggling backward, he swore. "I'm stuck! Pull on my feet!"

"What?"

His shoulders rubbed the sides of the pipe as he worked himself out, clumsily, inch by inch. He bruised a knee, then an elbow before spilling to the ground. Righting himself, he realized that Jim was shaking, muffled laughter making it through his outfit.

"What's so funny?"

"Nothing," Jim promised, still snickering. "Just that . . . Well . . . I thought that steel snake was gonna eat you alive!"

"Shut up!" Sam brushed himself off and rubbed at his elbow. "Get one of the lifts. Let's tip this mother. Maybe I loosened it a little."

His partner vanished into the whiteout. A minute later Jim was back, piloting a forklift that belched trails of thin black smoke into the wind.

Sam guided him in, pointing to a good spot for the forks. "Okay. Up!"

The yellow lift coughed, the motor grunting as it strained to raise one end of the heavy pipe into the air.

"Anything?"

Sam shook his head. "Higher!"

The fork lurched up another two feet. When nothing came out of the pipe, Sam took the hammer and beat fiercely on the side. After ten swings, he swore and gave up. Abandoning the sledge in favor of the rebar, he was about to direct Jim to lower the lift so that he could climb back inside, when he noticed it: a thick, sticky substance oozing down the bar. It was dark red, almost black.

"What the heck?" Jim shouted.

Sam was in a trance, watching as thick globs of reddish black goo slowly dropped to the snow at his feet.

Jim hopped out of the lift. "Must be an animal in there."

"What?"

"A rabbit or a fox," he shouted, "in the pipe."

Sam shook his head and shoulders at this. "A rabbit or a fox wouldn't clog a twenty-incher!" he shouted back.

"Polar bear? They got 'em out here."

Sam studied the opening of the pipe thoughtfully. "Maybe. But I'm not sure a bear would fit."

They were standing at the foot of the tipped section, still gawking at the rebar, when something slid out of the pipe. It was round, about three inches in diameter, and shiny: a frost-encrusted jewel sparkling in the halogen spotlights.

"What is it?"

Sam bent and picked it up. Wiping it against his parka, he lifted it toward one of the lamps: gold band, round face with inset stones, gold hands . . . a watch! Letters on the face marked it as a Rolex.

He presented it to his partner.

"Hot dog!" Jim took it and tried it on over his mitten. "Perfect fit!"

"You know what this means?"

Jim's mask was twisted, thick lips grinning beneath the neoprene. "We're a couple of lucky guys?"

"No. It means that ain't no animal stuck in there." He gestured to the pipe, then held up the rebar. With gloved fingers, he rubbed at the blood. "And it ain't mud either."

➤ TWO ◀

"RAYMOND?"

Delilah was smiling at him from across the club: pearly teeth framed by full, pouty lips, bedroom eyes inviting him to approach. When he didn't, she began floating in his direction, a drink in one hand, hips swaying to the music. Wisps of long blond hair cascaded down over her bare shoulders, down upon her buxom . . .

"Raymond!"

Even atop six-inch spike heels, she was graceful . . . alluring . . . seductive . . . She arrived at his table, exuding sensuality, took his hand and . . .

"Ray-mond!"

Draping both arms over him, she giggled, then purred, "Let's dance." He just stood there, frozen, his heart pounding out a heavy, accelerated beat, as her fingers played at his shoulder, drifted down the buttons on his shirt, gripped the loops of his blue jeans . . .

"Raymond!"

The temptress pushed her body against his, let him breathe in her sweet perfume, then danced away, teasing him with a look. Long firm legs twirled, hips wriggled. Drawing near again, she whirled, a slow-motion blur of smooth skin and golden hair . . . and magically transformed herself into . . .

"Raymond! Wake up!"

. . . a petite brunette . . . Delilah had become . . . Margaret?
"Wake up!"

She was enraged. Her full, smooth cheeks were flushed, her brow furrowed into a scowl. She looked like she was going to bite his head off, to punish him severely for dancing with another woman—a *naluaqmiu* at that. And rightly so. Margaret was, after all, his fiancée, the lady he had promised to marry. Her fiery eyes glared at him. Then, without warning or explanation, her expression softened. She grinned, her face glowing. Leaning forward, she placed her lips against his and . . .

"Wake up!"

Suddenly the entire world was shaking, bouncing madly. Margaret flickered and vanished like a skittish ghost. He felt blankets, a pillow, cool air moving past his face.

"Wake up! Answer radio!" an irritated voice was saying.

Ray opened his eyes and blinked up at a pale yellow light washing across the sod ceiling. His groggy mind was trying to decide where he was when a shadow leaned over him. Deep-set brown eyes glared down from a leathery, wrinkled face.

"You wake up!"

He jerked to a sitting position. "Huh? What's the matter? What happened?"

"Radio wake me up!"

"What?" Disoriented, still under Margaret's spell, Ray stared at his grandfather. "What time is it?"

"Not matter. What matter, radio wake *me* up! I wake *you* up!" With that, the old man stumbled out of the room. A door slammed down the hall and the light retreated. Ray found himself sitting alone in complete darkness. From the corner, he heard the radio hissing and popping.

Depressing the Indiglo button on his watch, he squinted at the numbers. When they refused to come into focus, he let up on the button and sighed. It had to be early. Five. Maybe five-thirty, Saturday morning. He had left Barrow around four on Friday afternoon, driven hard on poorly maintained, snow-covered roads, and reached Nuiqsut around eleven. After abandoning his truck, it was another forty-five minutes on snow machine before he pulled up outside Grandfather's remote sod house. Then, as was the ritual, they had spent the next three hours chewing the fat, the old man complaining energetically about all things modern. That meant that Ray had managed a whopping two hours of sleep. No wonder he felt like whale dung.

After lighting the kerosene lamp next to the bed, he wrapped himself in a blanket and crouched on the dirt floor, next to the radio. The room was cold, his breath visible in the dim glow of the lantern.

The speaker on the radio flared to life, crackling with snatches of a faraway conversation.

From the other end of the house, a gruff voice muttered, "Adiii . . . kill radio . . ."

The light on the device was blinking, signaling an incoming call. It was supposed to beep an alert, to make him aware that someone was trying to reach him, but the thing was ten years old and had spent most of that time stored in subfreezing temperatures. As a result, it routinely self-activated, erupting like a popcorn cooker gone haywire whenever a call came in.

As he reached for the receiver, the device snapped with a fresh pulse of static. From down the hall he heard his grandfather offer an Inupiaq curse.

"This is Officer Attla. Over."

Waiting for a response, he tilted his watch toward the lantern: 3:42. Good grief! No wonder his eyes were burning, his head throbbing.

"Raymond? This is dispatch. Over."

"Betty? What are you doing up at this ungodly hour?"

"Same as you, honey. Workin'." Betty was Athabaskan, just under five foot, somewhere around 250 pounds. Even over the radio she sounded big, her weight taking the form of a deep, throaty voice.

"Didn't the captain tell you?" He paused to yawn. "I'm off till Tuesday."

"Not anymore."

He suppressed an expletive. "Why?" he groaned. "What's up?"

"Got a call from the Slope. They got a popsicle."

"Since when does Barrow PD care if an oil worker freezes to death?"

"Not that simple. The guy's inside a pipe."

"So? . . ." He sighed melodramatically into the mike.

"So the company called Anchorage and—"

"Good for them. Let the city cops fly in and take a look."

"Except the Deadhorse airport is closed. And according to the weather reports, it won't open again for a couple of days, maybe not till midweek. So the Anchorage PD can't get in."

"Oh, come on. Don't tell me it's that bad."

"Apparently even the Bush pilots are nervous about risking it. Not so much the cold as the wind. Gusting to fifty or sixty miles per hour at times. Pretty nasty stuff."

"Yeah. But I still don't understand why you're calling me, Betty."

"Captain wants you to go over and check it out." She sounded impatient now.

"What about Lewis? Or the sheriff over at Deadhorse? What's-his-name . . . ?"

"Lewis is here in Barrow. You're a hundred and fifty miles closer to the scene. As for the sheriff, his name's Mattheson . . ."

"Right. Let him—"

"And he's Outside. Went to Hawaii for a couple of weeks. He's got a deputy working for him, but—"

"Can't the deputy—"

"Apparently the kid is wet-behind-the-ears, can't even wipe his own nose without the sheriff being there to hold the tissue."

"Aw, geez . . . Betty . . . Come on!"

"Eh. . . . Shut up!" Grandfather urged from somewhere down the dark hallway.

"Captain's orders," Betty explained.

"Let me talk to him."

"He's not here."

"Well, where is he?"

"Where do you think he is at this time of night, Raymond? He's in bed."

"I have time off coming," he whined.

"I know."

He paused, listening as the random noise on the channel surged in time with the wind outside.

"What camp? ARCO? BP?"

"Davis Oil."

"Never heard of it."

"It's an independent. And it's not at their camp. It's at an ice rig. Number seventeen. Off Oliktok Point." She read him the map coordinates. "Got that?"

"Yeah . . ." He let up on the button, swore softly, pushed it again. "Please tell me it can wait until morning."

"Sorry, Raymond. You're supposed to meet the deputy out there ASAP. Guess they're still trying to get the guy out of the pipe. If you hurry, you can be there for the unveiling ceremony."

"Ha-ha," he groaned. "Officer Attla out."

"Dispatch out."

He switched off the radio and sat on the bed, clutching at the blanket as he considered his luck: the middle of January, in the middle of the night—the first night of a well deserved four-day vacation—a full half-hour of sleep, a violent storm raging outside, temperatures diving toward record lows . . . He listened as a gust approached, shook the sod house, then continued on, moaning across the frozen tundra.

"I can't think of anything I'd rather do than saddle up and go on a tour of the ice floes. . . ."

He carried the lantern to the mirror and examined himself. Yep. He looked about as good as he felt: lousy. That was one thrashed face staring back at him: eyes riddled with bright red veins, dark bags drooping toward gaunt, stubbly cheeks, a jet black mane that would have made Medusa jealous. No time to bathe or shave, not when both activities required going to the kitchen and heating a tub of water over the Coleman stove. It was times like this that he wished Grandfather had forsaken the traditions of the People. He was one of only a few Inupiats who still lived in *ivruliks*—primitive earthen structures with few modern conveniences. A little running water and electricity would come in handy right about now. Of course, there was no way to convince Grandfather of that.

Not only was he one of the elders, a keeper of the old ways, he was as stubborn as a fence post.

Gathering his long hair together with one hand, Ray used a leather band to tie the locks together, creating a ponytail that dangled down between his shoulder blades. He climbed into a second set of insulated underwear, then a flannel shirt and jeans before pulling on a RefrigiWear suit and a parka. Fishing a topographical map out of his pack, he studied the coordinates of the ice rig and plotted a course: across the frozen Colville Delta, northeast along the coast to a forsaken knob of land approximately thirty miles west of Prudhoe. He had just refolded the map and was in the process of breaking down the radio and stowing it in its waterproof pouch when Grandfather shuffled in.

"Where you go?"

"Gotta go to work."

"Work? Now?"

"Duty calls."

"Duty? Duty to People?"

"Not exactly." He was in no mood for another lecture about the debt he and every other Native owed to their ancestors.

"You take parka." The old man turned and disappeared, feet scraping the floor.

"No, Grandfather. Mine's fine."

The old man returned, heavy, halting steps scuffing across the dirt. He was carrying a caribou parka: thigh length, burnished brown fur, sleeves and hood decorated with beads.

"Really, Grandfather," Ray protested, adjusting his own jacket. "This one's fine."

His grandfather lifted the lantern and examined the parka skeptically. Fingering the down-filled Gor-Tex, he said, "This one crap. Who dis 'Eddee Bawa'?"

"That's who made the coat," he sighed, resisting the urge to remind the old man that he had given him an identical parka for Christmas. Ray wasn't sure whether Grandfather was forgetful, senile, or just ornery. Probably a combination of the three.

"Never hear dis Edee Bawa."

"Mmm . . ."

"Never hear him!" he repeated angrily.

"It's not a him, Grandfather. It's a company. In the lower forty-eight. Okay?"

"Hmph . . ." The old man frowned at this, his face a maze of stiff creases. "What he know 'bout make parka? It sixty minus—wind angry. You take mine."

"I gotta go Grandfather. I don't have time to . . ." The look on the old man's face stopped him. It was an odd, pained expression, as if he had just seen or felt something terrible. "What's the matter? Are you okay? Is it your heart?" Ray reached out to assist him. "Here, sit down on the bed. I'll get your medicine. Where is it?"

The old man pulled away from Ray's grasp. "My heart . . . yes. But not this one." He thumped his chest with a bony finger. "This one." Here he tapped his temple. "I see something, with my heart eyes. You no go tonight."

"What?"

"Bad. You no go." He was shaking his head, brown eyes wide.

"Grandfather, I have to. It's my job."

"No go. I see somethings."

"What?" Ray asked, growing irritated. "What do you see?"

Grandfather closed his eyes and let his head fall back. "Adiii . . . In my heart eye . . . I see *tuungak . . . piinjilak . . .* a *anjatkut . . .* evil . . . very power . . . but liar . . . very lying . . ."

Ray rolled his eyes, waiting for the old man to run out of steam. Spirits, ghosts, shamans. It was all very spooky, especially at this hour with the wind howling outside, but he was no longer a kid and he had work to do.

"*Taiku,*" Ray said, taking up his knapsack and the radio. He patted Grandfather affectionately on the shoulder. "Thank you. I appreciate your concern. Listen, I'll try to get this cleared up quickly. Be back by noon or so, hopefully. We can wait and make the trip to Barrow on Sunday."

"*We*? Why *I* go Barrow? I not go Barrow."

"The party, Grandfather. Remember?"

"Par-ty?" He grimaced, making it sound obscene.

"The Messenger Feast," Ray reminded. It wasn't a Messenger Feast. It was a wedding shower. But the term had helped to convince the old coot to make the trip.

"Ah! I practicing drum for feast."

"Yeah, I know. See you this afternoon."

Ray turned to leave, but the old man caught him, two gnarled hands gripping his shoulders like a vice. Grandfather took a deep breath, then began to chant in a raspy singsong voice. It was a blessing, something he had sung over Ray since he was just a child. Ray's mind automatically translated the phrases, anticipating and finding comfort in the familiar words.

> *Walk with strong legs, like those of the caribou calf.*
> *Walk with strong legs, like those of the little hare.*
> *Be careful not to go towards the dark*
> *Be careful to always go towards the day*

"Taiku," he responded when the old man had finished. Pulling away from his grip, Ray slipped on his gauntlet mittens and secured his face mask, hood, and goggles. "See you later."

Opening the door, he slid through and shut it behind him. As he loaded his sled and mounted the snow machine, he was struck by the irony. Grandfather had just advised him to steer clear of the dark, to seek the day, exactly the opposite of what he was doing. But the pithy bit of wisdom was obviously symbolic. Going toward the day meant practicing good, as opposed to evil. Didn't it?

Twisting the throttle, the machine shuddered under him, then shot forward, leading the sled down the short trail, into a featureless black sea of wind-packed drifts. With only the single headlight, a thin beam swallowed up in blowing snow, to guide him, the night seemed extraordinarily empty and dead: precisely the conditions that brought hostile *tuungak* and *piinjilak* up out of their hiding places to visit death and sickness on The People.

Or so the elders said.

⋙ THREE ⋘

THE POLARIS HAD been plowing along for nearly an hour, skating along icy, one-lane tracks, blasting through crusty snowbanks, when Ray stopped to orient himself. A quick check of his compass and map told him that he was traveling in the right direction, northeast into oblivion.

He had to stop two more times in the following twenty minutes, both times to free his trailing sled from deep powder drifts. The sled was his lifeline—a 14-foot-long wooden emergency basket on outrigger skis. It was piled high with spare snow machine parts, extra fuel and oil, tools, a shovel, a tent, a down sleeping bag, dry and canned food, a kerosene lantern, a first-aid kit, his 30.06 rifle. Without a sled, a trip like this one was worse than foolhardy. It was a death sentence.

He was eyeing the gas gauge, wondering if the rig had a supply of unleaded, when he noticed the miniature constellation twinkling on the horizon. Glinting lights formed an upside-down T. Support buildings formed the low crossbar, he decided. The tall stem had to be the derrick. The tiny, earthbound stars winked and disappeared in a gust of snow, then materialized again, surging brighter before vanishing completely.

Above, the sky was a black void. Beneath the runners of the Polaris, snow swirled on blue ice, a frantic dance in the beam of the headlight. Under the thick layer of cobalt lay the extreme, outer edge of North America. Either that or the

Beaufort Sea. It was difficult, if not impossible, to tell where the ground stopped and the ocean began. For nine months a year, the Arctic merged into a singular mass: salt-water, ice, and land becoming one.

While he watched, the drilling platform continued to play hide-and-seek, lights swelling, dimming, flickering out. Suddenly the Polaris lurched and dove away, abandoning Ray. He was thrown back, then forward, the padded seat ramming him between the legs. He gave the breaks an urgent squeeze and realized that he had dropped onto the haul road, a double-track trail that had been pounded into the ice by diesel trucks, four-wheel-drives, and the rubber feet of a Cat train. He followed it across the wide, flat expanse, maneuvering carefully through frozen potholes and ruts.

Five minutes later, the rig materialized for good, bathed in a wavering pool of halogen. On one side of the oval yard was a two-story, prefab building. *The camp*, Ray thought, where the workers ate, slept, and spent what little free time they had. There were a few other structures, probably equipment and vehicle hangers, but the main attraction was the derrick itself: 180 feet of steel, cable, and pulleys. The bottom quarter was boxed in by wood, the remaining section rising into the wind, lights decorating the tower at ten-foot increments.

The entire encampment was temporary, seated on ice. Every November, when the temperature fell to minus 30 or so and the surface of the coastal inlets froze, the companies came out and created these platforms. Sea water was drawn from holes in the ice and sprayed from high-pressure hoses until an island was formed: a manmade iceberg that rested firmly against the bottom of the Beaufort Sea, thirty feet below. When it was finished, the island would sustain the weight of a rig, trucks, support vehicles, equipment, and the camp itself.

Ray knew the rigs were out here, that the Reserve on the North Slope was the largest, most productive petroleum field in North America, but that was about the extent of his knowledge of oil exploration at Prudhoe Bay. That, and the fact that Grandfather considered the companies and their work an abomination. Of course, to Grandfather, nearly any form of change, especially that which concerned the Land, was anathema.

The concept of progress was lost on the old ones. To them living from the Land was the Inupiat way. They viewed the North Slope development as another in a long line of hostile intrusions upon their simple, even holy, lifestyle. The first intrusion had been the arrival of the Russians in the 1700s. Their presence had introduced the practice of trading, and with it, Grandfather contended, greed. The second intrusion took the form of miners, men obsessed with defacing the earth in their relentless quest for gold. The third was born on the shoulders of the missionaries. Representatives from the Friends Church, Quakers, journeyed north offering medicine, education, and an alternative religion. Whether intentional or not, the succeeding waves of invaders had effectively stripped the People of their unique identity. At least, that was what Grandfather claimed.

Of course, not all Natives shared Grandfather's hypercritical sentiments. Many of the People welcomed change. Diseases that had once wiped out entire villages in a single season had been eradicated by antibiotics and vaccines. Starvation was no longer a routine problem. Food stamps, federal welfare checks, Native corporation dividends, permanent fund shares, longevity bonus awards, and unemployment benefits had seen to that. Thanks to the Bureau of Indian Affairs and the Hootch consent decree, every village had a school, and most of the People were now literate. They could read and write, though not in their own language. As for the oil companies, some saw them as a boon. Oil money meant better schools, better homes, better food, better salaries, more financial assistance— a more prosperous life for the People.

Ray had mixed emotions about what was happening to the Inupiat and to Alaskan Natives in general. Orphaned at the age of three, he had been raised by his grandparents. Grandfather, an *umialik*, a skilled whaler and esteemed leader of the People, had brought Ray up to honor and value the old ways. Ray's childhood had been spent learning to harpoon bowhead, stalk game, seine for sheefish, hunt for seals. He had been trained in the art of the drum, taught the ritual dances, made to participate in the celebration of the seasonal festivals. Much of that had fallen away, though, when he left the village and started high school in Barrow. Most of the other teens he met there were more American than Native, reaching for the new ways as if they were a coveted prize.

The transition was solidified in college. Attending the University of Alaska in Anchorage, he was exposed to people, books, ideas, and philosophies that chipped away at his heritage. Over the course of his study, he found himself adopting a very different perspective from that of Grandfather's. It was broader, more modern . . . more white. When he returned to Barrow, he brought with him more than simply a degree in criminal justice. He brought a new worldview that challenged the ways of the elders.

In Grandfather's estimation, the last hundred years had been a curse. Ray wasn't so sure. Yes, there was something disturbing, even sad, about watching an alien culture swallow an entire people. And yet, there were so many benefits: though still linked to the Land, the Inupiat were quickly becoming high-tech hunter-gatherers. After harvesting a whale and celebrating the catch, village residents would return home in their 4x4s, to microwaves and cable-equipped televisions. It was an odd mix of new and old, a culture in process.

The transition wasn't over. Far from it. The two societies were still at war, a lopsided battle in which one was molding the other into its image.

What would be the fate of the Eskimo? Ray considered the question as the oil derrick rose before him. He didn't have an answer, but he did know one thing: survival at the close of the twentieth century meant accepting change, going with the flow, rather than fighting the current. It was a lesson Grandfather and his kind would never learn.

The thought chased him the final mile to the rig. As he approached, blue letters on a wide white sign proclaimed: Davis Oil. The colors matched the trim on the rig and the camp building. Slowing, he urged the Polaris up an eight foot embankment, onto the island, and pulled into the yard. A half dozen diesel trucks were lined up in a neat row, pickups and 4x4s parked next to the camp. The place was quiet. Ray began to wonder if everyone was in bed. Passing the shed, he spotted a crowd of men in blue RefrigiWear suits huddled next to the rig platform. They seemed to be watching something. Switching off the engine, he dismounted and joined them. It was then that he noticed the sparks: a shower of orange fire arching into the air before being scattered by the wind. A man wearing a welder's helmet was bent, one knee to the ice, his torch ripping a long, straight gap in a pipe.

The onlookers were entranced, audience to a taut suspense thriller.

Ray glanced at the pipe, then asked, "Can someone direct me to the supervisor?"

A trio of heads swiveled in his direction, six eyes giving him the once over through slits in the neoprene masks. "Who're you?" one of them asked.

"Officer Attla, Barrow PD."

A gust stole his words.

"Who?"

"Attla!" Ray repeated. He clumsily fished a badge out of his parka pocket with two fingerless mittens.

The man leaned to examine it. Satisfied, he grunted, "In there." The hood nodded toward the main building.

"Thanks." Ray left the men to their work and trotted across the yard, up the steps. Inside the metal modular, he paused in a mudroom and began undressing, slipping off his goggles, mask, parka. The air in the building felt uncomfortably warm, stifling, after an hour and a half of braving the unforgiving elements on the snow machine.

He looked for a hook on an overburdened coat rack. Additional parkas had been tossed over the backs of three folding chairs. Boots were scattered about the floor, each pair adrift in a shallow puddle of muddy, gray water. Ray pulled off his boots, opened the only other door, and padded down a hall into a cafeteria. Ten or twelve men were seated at long tables, a few of them eating breakfast, the rest meditating over steaming Styrofoam cups. Behind a waist-high partition, a trio of cooks were pacing back and forth in a narrow galley, clanking pots and attending to sizzling meat. Ray's stomach growled.

He was about to ask for the camp supervisor again, when

he noticed a handwritten sign attached to an open doorway just a few feet from the kitchen: OFFICE. Beneath the letters was a crude arrow. Ray followed it.

Voices met him in the hall as he approached a wide, window-like opening in the wall where fluorescent light spilled out over the tile floor. The office turned out to be nothing more than a small room into which six Formica desks had been wedged. File cabinets, stunted book shelves, and two printer stands consumed the remainder of the space. A woman was sitting at one of the desks, her back to the door as she tapped at a computer terminal. Ten feet away, a man stood facing Ray. He was short, heavy set, with wide shoulders. His face was bright pink: thick, fleshy cheeks; a broad, glowing forehead. A flattop of silver-white hair punctuated his cubic appearance, square body, square head. The man's parka was thawing, chips of ice tinkling to the floor as he engaged in an animated phone conversation. Behind him, the window blinds had been pulled.

"No. I don't know," the man was saying. He looked exhausted, tired eyes shifting from the woman, to the floor, to the window. "No. They're still working on it . . . Yeah . . . Well, that's why it's taking so long. Our welder's sick, so I had to call the main camp. They yanked some poor guy out of bed, fresh from a twenty-four-hour shift."

Ray stood there, waiting to be noticed.

"Oh . . . maybe an hour. Maybe sooner," the man said. "Depends. The deputy is around here somewhere." The man rolled his eyes and his voice dropped to a hoarse whisper. "Some green kid. Just out of school. But the good news is, the real cops haven't shown up yet. With any luck, maybe they won't. Maybe the storm will . . ."

Ray smiled at the man, waving his badge.

The man swore softly. "Scratch that. They're here." His expression was a mixture of irritation and weary resignation. "What a mess . . . Good question . . ."

Ray heard steps, dress shoes clattering on linoleum. He turned and saw a man in a gray felt Stetson and insulated police jacket, bearing two white cups. The guy was maybe 5'10" and rail thin, except for a slight paunch around his gut.

"You must be Officer Attla," the man drawled.

"I must be," Ray said.

After setting the cups on the ledge of the opening, the man extended his hand. "Deputy Cleaver."

"Cleaver? As in . . . ?"

He nodded enthusiastically, buck teeth protruding from thin lips. "Yep. As in Beaver Cleaver. 'Cept, my name ain't Beaver, a course."

"*A course,*" Ray said, shaking his hand. Cleaver's face looked so young that Ray wondered if the kid had skipped high school and gone straight into law enforcement.

"You a coffee drinker, Officer Attla?"

"Yeah. Thanks." Ray accepted one of the cups. "What do you have so far, Deputy?"

"Billy Bob. You can call me Billy Bob."

You've got to be kidding, Ray thought. "Okay," he sighed, "*Billy Bob* . . . what do you have? Dispatch in Barrow said something about a popsicle."

"A what?" The combination of Bugs Bunny teeth, innocent eyes, the name, and the accent made Billy Bob seem like something out of a cartoon, the stereotype of a dumb Texas hick.

"Popsicle. Somebody frozen to death."

"Aw . . . yep. I think so."

"You *think* so? Where's the body?"

"Out in the yard."

Ray nodded, frowning. What a waste of time this was turning out to be. Investigating a popsicle with a goat roper. He glanced down at Billy Bob's shoes: brown leather cowboy boots with an intricate pattern running up the sides. Just the right footwear . . . for Dallas. What a cheechako!

"You're not from around here, are you Bill?"

"No sir. I come from Monahans, Texas. That's oil country." He studied Ray for a moment. "You're an Eskimo, ain'tcha?" According to Billy Bob, the word was pronounced, *Ezkeemo.*

"Inupiat," Ray said with a nod.

"Wowie! I ain't never met a real Ezkeemo before. Not face-to-face." He squinted at Ray, curious eyes scanning from his feet to his head—as if he were some sort of museum exhibit. "Ain'tcha' kinda big for an Ezkeemo?"

"As a child I always ate all my Wheaties," Ray replied, looking down on the deputy. He had a good two or three inches on Cleaver.

"Do your people really live in igloos?"

Ray blinked at this. "How long you been up on the Slope, Bill?" *Thirty seconds?*

The deputy shrugged. "'Bout . . ." A tongue reached out to flick at his bunny teeth. "Waa-ell, I guess almost two weeks now."

Ray was about to ask ol' Billy how he had kept from frost-biting his toes in the leather clodhoppers when the man in the office hung up the phone.

"Jack Simpson," he said shaking Ray's hand. "Camp supervisor."

"Ray Attla, Barrow PD."

"And you've met Deputy Cleaver here."

"Yeah."

"He give you the lowdown on the situation?"

"Not yet."

"Not much to tell, really," Simpson said. "The crew was running pipe. One of the casing sections was clogged. They assumed it was mud. When they tried to clear it . . ." Simpson's face twisted into an odd expression, something between curiosity and surprise. "Is it just me, or are you tall? For a Native, I mean. What are you? Six two?"

"Six one," Ray replied. "About the body, I'd like to take a look."

"Still in the pipe," Simpson snorted. "Having a heck of a time gettin' it out." The phone rang and he answered it. "Simpson . . . yeah? . . . okay. Call me back." He replaced it and addressed the policemen. "Listen, whatever you boys need, you got it. Phones, computers . . ." He gestured about the office. "Houston says to give you whatever you want. We intend to cooperate fully. Get this business cleared up ASAP. Davis Oil is a company that operates on the up and up. We don't tolerate foul play on our projects. Course, we don't want a scandal either. If you take my meaning.'' Here he gave both of the officers a knowing look.

"Foul play?'' Ray asked.

Simpson's hands flew into the air. "If that's what it turns out to be.''

"Are you saying this body in the pipe . . . somebody put it there on purpose?''

The hands lifted higher, palms toward the cops. "I'm just covering the bases. Whatever happens, we're ready to cooperate, but the word here is speed. Houston wants this thing cleaned up posthaste.'' The phone rang again. "Simpson here . . . Sure, just a sec.'' Placing the receiver against his chest, he said, "You fellas go on out there and have a look around. I'll be with you in a few minutes.'' He returned his attention to the phone.

"Come on,'' Billy Bob said. "Let's see how they're doin'.''

Ray followed him, sniffing at grilled sausage links as they traversed the cafeteria. Through the fogged windows in the mudroom, they could see sparks whirling in the wind. In between gusts, the welder materialized. He was attending to the bottom of the pipe now, his slot running down four-fifths of its diameter.

"How did they find him?'' Ray asked, sipping at the coffee. It was lukewarm, a little thin, but he needed the caffeine to help him stay alert.

"Who?''

"The popsicle.''

"Oh. They was runnin' pipe,'' Billy Bob drawled.

"I caught that. What's it mean?''

"It's when the crew puts the pipe in the hole,'' the deputy explained. "Fella looked in, saw somethin'. They took the pipe back out, hit on it awhile. Finally, a couple roustabouts started pokin' in there with a rebar. Saw some blood . . .'' He paused, setting his coffee on the chair, and dug into the pocket of his jacket. "This fell outta the pipe.'' He handed Ray a gold watch.

"Nice.'' Ray examined it. "Still running.'' He gave it back. "What else?''

"That's it. I was thinkin' 'bout talkin' to the roustabouts when you showed up."

"Why does Mr. Simpson back there think it was murder?"

"*Murder?*" Billy Bob's eyes grew wide.

"He called it 'foul play'. But that's what he was thinking. When I got the call, I assumed somebody just froze to death. You know, got disoriented in the storm, crawled into the pipe to get warm or something. Happens out here."

"Maybe that is what happened," Billy Bob offered.

"Maybe," Ray nodded. "Sure would be nice. Then we could all go home and get some sleep."

Outside, the welder was flat on his back, torching the underside of the pipe. Blowing snow made the scene dull and undefined, like an impressionistic painting.

"We better get out there," Ray said. He pulled on his parka and mask, then stuffed his feet into two white bunny boots. Next to him, Billy Bob waited with a blank expression—a Texan lost in the Arctic.

"Do you have any *real* boots?" Ray asked.

The deputy shook his head.

"You have a real coat, don't you? And a hat?"

Another shake. Billy Bob pulled two thin leather gloves from his pocket.

"You're kidding? Those are your gloves?"

A nod.

"Didn't the Borough issue you any cold-weather gear?"

"Sure. I got a mess of it back at the office in Deadhorse. But . . . well . . . I don't go outside that much. Don't get much call to. The Slope's a quiet neighborhood. And when I patrol, I'm in my truck. It's a Ford. Got a good heater."

"Here." Ray selected a parka and a pair of mittens from the rack. "What size shoe do you wear?"

"Thirteen."

Ray blinked at him, glancing at his feet.

"They grow ever-thang big in Texas," Billy Bob announced proudly, a stupid grin pasted on his face.

Ray picked through the boots. "Well . . . twelves will have to do. Put 'em on."

Billy Bob sank into a metal chair and yanked at a cowboy

boot. When it finally slid off, he began to struggle with its partner. Shoeless, he worked his feet into a pair of heavy-duty Sorrels. Setting his Stetson aside, he climbed into the parka, zipped it up, and pulled the cord to snug the hood and built-in mask.

"Boy, howdy. This is comfy. I'm warm as toast!" his muffled voice declared.

Ray led him outside, into the darkness and the subzero wind, wishing with all his heart that he was back in Nuiqsut, sleeping peacefully in Grandfather's drafty *ivrulik*, instead of out here on the ice with Cowboy Bob.

⇒ FOUR ⇐

RAY AND BILLY Bob had just reached the pipe when the welder snuffed his torch. The man lifted his visor, cursed, added something about "going to bed," then waved the rest of the crew in. The group of bodies split up, four hustling to one end of the casing, three taking the other. The slit in the steel grew from an inch to two inches, to four inches, widening as the men used their weight to pull the two sections apart. It groaned and resisted before snapping in two.

Ray stepped forward and looked into the left section. It was empty. Turning to the other, he saw a tangle of boots and pants.

Simpson appeared next to Ray. Even cloaked in down and neoprene, the guy looked irritated, as if finding a dead body in a pipe was a royal pain in the neck. He swore loudly in a pretense of concern.

Ray nodded to Billy Bob. "Let's get him out." They each took a boot and started to pull. Nothing happened. They tried again. The body wouldn't budge. It was frozen into the steel cylinder. Finally, with two men assigned to each leg, the clump of rock-hard flesh slid out onto the ground. It landed with a clink, like an ice cube in a tumbler.

Simpson swore again, this time in genuine horror.

It was a man. Or at least, it had been at one time. The body was crumpled into a ball, legs against the chest, arms folded between the knees. Loosed from its confining quarters, the corpse remained rigid, in a fetal position—an oversized infant taking an eternal nap. Dark dress slacks and Sorrels covered the lower extremities. A parka zipped up above the neck provided unnecessary protection from the icy wind. No gloves. And no face mask. The hands and cheeks were purple-black from frostbite. The entire specimen was encrusted in a thick layer of dirty gray frost.

Popsicle, Ray thought, but chose not to say. "Anybody recognize him?" It was an unfair question, really. Even if the hood had been pulled back, the parka zipped down, identification would have been difficult.

"Anybody?" he repeated. Hoods shook from side to side. "Mr. Simpson?"

The supervisor stared down at the gnarled figure. "I don't think so." He knelt for a closer examination. "Hard to tell . . ."

Ray sighed at the body, then bent and gazed into the pipe. It was shiny with ice, but no blood, no gloves, no mask . . . nothing. *Popsicle*, he decided with growing certainty.

The dress slacks. The Rolex. That made John Doe an executive. Maybe. *Probably some dope from Outside*, Ray thought. Guy comes up from the Lower 48, visits the Slope, goes for a walk around the equipment yard, doesn't show the proper respect for the environment, like old Billy Bob here in his dung kickers. At minus 50, any exposed skin would frostbite almost immediately. The severe chill factor would only speed the process. The clown panics. Hypothermia sets in. The cold affects his brain. His judgment is impaired. He climbs into the pipe, presumably to get out of the wind. Thinks he can warm up and go back inside for a nice hot cup of joe. The lights go out.

It made sense. Sort of. Except for one thing: No one had seen him before.

"You had any folks up from Davis Oil's headquarters in Houston?"

"No. At the main camp in Prudhoe. But not here. Think he's management?"

Ray shrugged at this.

"How'd he get in there?" Billy Bob wondered aloud, squinting at the pipe.

"Heck if I know," Simpson said, frowning. He glared at the maimed piece of casing and shook his head.

"What're we gonna do with him?" Billy Bob asked.

"I called the medical emergency team in Deadhorse," Simpson said. "Guess they're socked in by the storm. Should've been here by now."

"Call them back. Tell them not to bother. This guy doesn't need a medic," Ray assured him. "Don't suppose you've got a coroner on staff?"

"Coroner?" Simpson shook his head, as if Ray had been serious. "No. We got a nurse. But she's off this week. Went to Anchorage." He paused, thinking.

"What about Jorge?" one of the men offered.

"Jorge?" Ray looked at the worker, then to Simpson. "Who's Jorge?"

"Mexican on the drilling crew. Went to med school for a while. Acts like he knows a lot. Did CPR on a roustabout one time. Turned out it wasn't the guy's heart though. Just a bad case of the flu."

Ray nodded. He was already planning his revenge on the captain for sending him on this tour of la-la land.

"I'll see if I can find him." Simpson marched toward the rig.

The cluster of blue suits began to disperse. "Hey, guys, help us carry him inside," Ray instructed. Hoods shook, profanities were grumbled, the figures turned and moved toward the camp.

Ray cursed under his breath, then looked to Billy Bob. "Grab his legs." The deputy hesitated. "Grab his legs!" Together they lugged the ice man into the building, through the mudroom, past weary diners consuming ham and eggs. When they reached the office, Ray puffed, "Where can we put this?"

The secretary typed something into the computer before swiveling in her chair. Her mouth fell open as she inspected their cargo.

"Is there a spare room someplace?" Ray asked.

"Geez . . . he's . . . heavy," Billy Bob panted.

The woman started to say something but gasped instead,

the blood draining from her face. A hand rose, a trembling finger pointing at the wall. "S—s—storage room."

They started down the hall, wet boots skating and slipping on the tile. After passing three closed doors, they came to a doorless rec room. It was deserted: two empty couches, an unused Ping-Pong table, a silent television set . . .

Ray cursed, losing his grip on the corpse. He used a knee to get a fresh hold. At the end of the corridor he could see a meeting room with a table and chairs and a stairwell.

"Where's the storage room?" Billy Bob whined. "My arms is fixin' to fall off."

Ahead of them, a janitor in blue coveralls rounded the corner, pushing a cart of cleaning supplies. He worked a door with an oversized key ring, then swung it open.

"Is that the storage room?" Ray asked, his biceps burning. The man's head swiveled toward them. He looked them over suspiciously, eyed the body, dropped his broom.

"Is that the storage room?" Ray demanded.

The man nodded in slow motion, mouth agape.

"Can we put him in there?"

He shrugged. "Be my guest." Moving his cart to one side, he backed away.

"We could shore use some help," Billy Bob grunted as they trudged past the man, into the room.

"I'll just bet you could," the janitor scoffed. The wheels of his cart sang as he hurried away.

"Down," Ray ordered, as if they were movers carrying in a sofa. They placed their load, as delicately as possible, on the floor. It clanked on the tile.

"We can't leave him here. We need something to put him on."

"How about this?" Billy Bob tapped one end of a long table that had been folded and was leaning against a row of shelves. Ray took the other end and they swung the legs down.

"We should cover it. When this guy thaws . . ." Ray made a face. Turning to inspect the shelves, he saw paper bags, toilet paper, a box of plastic garbage sacks, kitchen supplies . . . No tarps.

"This'll have to do for now." He spread three garbage sacks on the table. "Okay, on three," Ray said, bending to hoist the corpse. "One, two, three . . ."

The compact body rose into the air, sank to the table and slid halfway down the sacks, spinning slightly—a human hockey puck. Ray nudged it back to the center.

From behind them Simpson announced, "Jorge's on the rig, finishing up his shift."

"We'll need to speak with the men who found the body," Ray said.

Simpson examined his watch. "The crew will be off in . . . three hours."

"So?"

"So," Simpson explained with a thin smile, "you can talk to them then."

"Mr. Simpson," Ray said, unzipping his coat and pulling at his mittens. "A man is dead. In your camp. We need to figure out what happened."

"I realize that," Simpson replied with a nod. "But we can't just shut everything down."

"You can if I tell you to," Ray threatened.

"Listen," Simpson argued, "I'm not trying to be difficult. You have our full cooperation. It's just that we can't stop in the middle of an operation. Aside from losing me my job, it would be a disaster, financially speaking. We're talking thousands of dollars down the drain. Maybe more—if the hole is compromised.

"This has been a problem rig from the start. More problems and slowdowns than you can shake a stick at. I've been getting my butt chewed, long-distance, for three weeks. As of yesterday, we finally got things squared away. We're at a critical stage. We gotta get the pipe in, past the permafrost as quickly as possible. If we don't, it melts, and the hole goes soft on us. Might even soften the platform base."

Ray was about to debate the issue, to assert his authority, when Billy Bob stepped in. "He's right. It would really screw things up to just up and stop drillin'. They have to finish."

Great, Ray thought. Just great. Bronco Billy is on Simpson's side. Ray glared at the deputy, then at the supervisor.

He was exhausted, in no mood to play games with a couple of good old boys. "What are we supposed to do until the shift is up?"

Simpson adopted a victorious grin. "We've got beds right down the hall. You can get a little shut-eye. Cafeteria's open twenty-four hours. Drop in there, get some coffee and grub. Watch a little TV in the rec room . . ." His arms flailed in a gesture of unbridled hospitality. "Make yourselves at home."

Ray had to admit, the bed sounded good. He studied his watch: 5:43. Still too early to check in with Barrow. "Okay. We'll wait."

The smile grew. "Right this way, fellas." Simpson led them back toward the cafeteria, to a door directly across from the office. Fishing a key out of his pocket, he unlocked it. "Here we go."

The room looked like something you would find in a college dorm: 15 x 15 with short-nap beige carpet. A bookshelf, a narrow desk, and two chairs were arranged near the center. A pair of single beds was pushed up against the far wall. Another wall was taken up by a small window and a closet. Next to the entrance was a door connecting to a bathroom.

"It's occupied," Simpson explained, waving at the manuals on the desk and the poster of Shania Twain hanging over one of the beds. "But both of the men are off right now. One went back home to Tulsa. The other's . . . in Seattle, I think."

"Do the men usually leave the state on their days off?" Billy Bob asked.

"These guys work hard," Simpson explained. "Three seven-day weeks, twelve hours on. Some of them pull five weeks. Then they get a week off. With the money they make, and believe me, they earn it, they can afford to go where they please.

"Now, you fellas just relax. Catch a few Zs. Get a bite to eat. I'll be back when the crew is off-rig." Simpson wiggled his eyebrows at them before closing the door.

"You get the feeling he's giving us the bum's rush?" Ray asked. He stepped to the bed and tested the mattress with his fingers.

"Naw. He's just tryin' to do his job," Billy Bob replied.

After dumping his parka, and boots, he pulled off his insulated jacket and hopped onto the bed.

"I'm dead tired," Ray mumbled, sliding off his own gear.

"Me too." The deputy's eyes were already closed, arms crossed over his chest. "Don't usually work nights. eight to five. That's me."

Ray flipped off the light and crawled under the blanket.

"I'm a morning person, really," Billy Bob continued. "Not much fun in the evenings. Kinda a party pooper. After dinner, I don't waste much time afore hittin' the sack. Little music, a little readin', and I'm out."

"Uh-huh . . ." Ray felt his muscles relaxing. His breathing slowed, becoming deep and regular.

"I 'member when I was a boy . . . back in Pecos . . . before we moved to Monahans . . . I loved gettin' up in the mornin'. Sunshine. Birds singin' . . ."

"Mmm . . ."

The account went on and on, Billy Bob's lyrical southern drawl fading, wavering, growing distant. His words floated and dove in the darkness—night birds soaring gracefully on a warm summer evening down in Dixie. Under this spell, Ray's tired mind released his body and raced toward the horizon, toward the world of dreams.

➤ FIVE ◄

IT WAS LIKE a scene from a movie: vivid, convincing, disturbing—full-color action set to a quirky, tangential script. A command performance, and Ray was the star of the show. The boy on the screen was *him*.

It was autumn. They were in a dingy sod house. He and a woman. His mother. Except that it wasn't his mother. Not really, and somehow he knew that.

He was playing with an Eskimo yo-yo. Flinging it into the air, he lost his grip on the string and the two walrus-skin balls hurtled across the tiny room, knocking a pot from the fire. The woman swore at him and began kicking at the ground. Whirling, she reached down, took two handfuls of dirt, and pressed them into his eyes.

The boy cried out and began scratching at his face, drawing blood.

The scene dissolved like a mirage and it was winter. The house was cold. Their breath issued like smoke, gliding and then curling into the air. The woman looked angry, weary, a harsh expression on her haggard face. The boy sat in the corner, still and quiet. His eyes no longer seeing, his world black.

There was a noise outside, snow crunching beneath heavy feet. Suddenly an arm thrust through the door: white fur bearing a fan of black four-inch claws. There was a tremendous roar, a deep voice shaking the walls. The woman gasped and picked up the boy's bow and arrow. Handing it to him, she demanded that he kill the intruder.

Terrified, he aimed it blindly, with trembling hands. The mother assisted him, pointing the arrow toward the bear—at its heart. She shouted something at him and he let the gut string go. The missile took flight, striking the bull's-eye, entering the animal with a sickening whisk. The bear wobbled, then retreated, disappearing through the doorway with a groan.

Outside, it stumbled only a few feet before collapsing, life escaping from its lungs in a final, throaty sigh. The woman cautiously pulled back the skin that formed the door and studied the bear: motionless, blood flowing from its chest.

"You missed it," she lied to her son. She punctuated this with a curse, then kicked the boy in the stomach.

He felt the blow, bent in half, fought for breath. From his vantage point, Ray studied the woman, suddenly realizing that it was not the face of his mother or any mother. It was the face of . . . *Margaret?*

Ray woke with a start. He was panting, heart thumping in his chest, his hair damp with sweat. Swinging his legs over the edge of the bed, he sat up and rubbed his forehead, trying to calm himself. A stingy witch . . . a blind kid . . . a bear . . . Margaret . . . What a weird dream. What a *nightmare*! And somehow, it all seemed vaguely familiar. Had he dreamed it before?

Toggling the Indiglo button on his watch, he squinted at the face: SAT 6:41. He had been asleep for almost an hour, and he felt worse than when he lay down. Dripping with perspiration, the blanket still tangled around him like a serpent, he felt winded, as if he had just completed a ten-mile run.

A shower, he decided, would cure his ailment. Rising, he tiptoed to the bathroom, shut the door, and ran the water. It was hot right out of the faucet.

As the steam rose, spray massaging his skin, he realized why the dream had caused a sensation of déjà vu. He hadn't dreamed it before, but he had heard it. Many times. The storyline: the boy, the wicked mother, the polar bear . . . It was the first half of an old Eskimo fable Grandfather used to tell him.

The tale went on to describe how the mother used the bear for food all winter, refusing to share the abundance of the catch with her son. When spring came, an enchanted loon spoke to the boy, calling him to a nearby lake. He told the boy to climb on his back, and then dove into the water four times. After that, the boy was healed. He could see!

Returning home, the youngster saw the carcass of the polar bear. He also found that he had been sleeping in a squalor. He pretended that his eyes were still blind until his mother tried to serve him a bowl of rotten berries and fat. Throwing it down, he told her that he could see. In order to punish the woman for her selfishness, the boy took her out in their *umiak*. When a white whale surfaced, he threw a harpoon into its back and fastened the end of the line to his mother. The whale quickly pulled her into the icy water.

In the days to come, the boy, now a youth, spent much of his time hunting seals. And every so often, he would see his evil mother, still tied to the whale's back. He felt sorry for her and wished that she had not been so greedy and unkind.

It was a depressing story. Ray had never liked it. Having lost his mama at birth, he had always cringed at the idea of a boy seeking revenge on his own mother, no matter how cruel she was.

Stepping out of the shower, he considered the fable as he toweled off. Why had he dreamed about it? Better yet, why had Margaret shown up in it as the wicked mother, no less? Was his subconscious trying to tell him something? Did marrying Margaret represent the end of his freedom? Of his sight?

He dismissed the ridiculous ideas with a shake of his head. Having taken Psych 101 in college, he had just enough insight into dream interpretation to be dangerous. In actuality, it was probably nothing more than a combination of stress and fatigue.

He was in love with Margaret. He *wanted* to marry her. Didn't he?

After slipping into his clothes, Ray sat down at the desk

and picked up the phone. It was going on seven. Margaret would be up, getting ready to go to the office. She was a social worker with the Alaska Native Assistance Association.

Ray had met her in Anchorage, at the U. of A. It was clear from day one that they were soul mates. Both valued their heritage yet knew that the Inupiat must adapt to the rapidly evolving, modern world around them. To that end, they had returned to Barrow with the idealistic intention of leading the People into the new age. Ray's contribution was law enforcement: keeping the People from self-destructing, teaching them to observe white laws. Margaret's was economic: keeping the People from wasting away, making them aware of the vast resources of the Borough, State, and U.S. Government.

They were laudable, even altruistic goals, and they offered financial rewards. As a rookie cop, Ray's starting salary had been almost six figures. Margaret's position with the ANAA was even more lucrative. Of course, the cost of living in Barrow was astronomical. Housing was outrageous, the cost of fuel, clothing, and food almost prohibitive. Still, thanks to their education and degrees, they were comfortable, stable enough to get married without living in poverty. And yet, Ray had been putting off the union for the past five years, hemhawing, stalling, making up excuses, wavering on the brink of the great abyss: a lifetime commitment to one woman.

Two weeks earlier, he had finally taken leave of his senses and stepped off the ledge, asking for Margaret's hand in marriage. Since then, he had been doing a free fall: weightless, a man without a parachute watching as the ground raced toward him.

He dialed the number and waited. It rang twice, then, "Hello?"

Her voice had the curious effect of making him feel fully alive and hopelessly trapped at the same time. "Margaret?"

"Ray? Are you back already?"

"No. I'm on the Slope."

"The Slope? I thought you were going to your Grandfather's."

"Yeah. Well, I was there last night, for a little while."

"What's going on?"

"They had a problem up here. A popsicle. The captain wanted me to check it out."

"That's crummy. When are you coming back? You'll be here for the shower tomorrow, won't you?"

"Shower?" Ray swallowed hard. "Oh . . . yeah. Sure."

"You didn't forget, did you?"

"Uh . . . No. Of course not."

"Raymond Attla!" she admonished, pretending to be angry.

Plans for the wedding shower had begun the very evening that Ray had proposed. All of Margaret's family would be there: mother, sisters, aunts. It was going to be a gala affair, Barrow's answer to the society scene. Ray's attendance was non-negotiable.

"I can't believe you forgot."

"I didn't forget."

"Uh-huh . . ."

"I didn't forget," Ray argued.

After a long pause, she sighed. "I miss you."

"I miss you too," he agreed. "I was thinking of you last night, while I was shivering in Grandfather's old *ivrulik*. You're the only reason I didn't freeze to death."

She chuckled softly.

"I'm serious." This drew another laugh. It was a magical sound that made Ray's chest tingle. "Don't worry. Unless we hit a snag or something, I'll be back in plenty of time. Okay?"

"Okay."

"I love you," he told her.

"Not as much as I love you."

"Wanna bet? See you tomorrow evening."

"Be careful," she said.

"I will." He replaced the phone.

"I didn't know you was married."

Ray glared at Billy Bob. The cowboy was sitting upright in the bunk. "That was a private conversation."

Billy Bob shrugged. "Sorry. Didn't mean to eavesdrop."

Ray picked the phone back up and dialed Barrow PD.

"Got a picture?"

"Huh?"

"Of your wife."

"I'm not married . . . yet."

"Aw . . . engaged, huh? Well, congratulations."

"Yeah, thanks," he muttered. "Betty? Ray here. The captain in yet?" He cursed her answer under his breath. "Tell him I need to talk to him . . . No . . . Looks like a popsicle . . . No . . . But the problem is, I need to get back to Barrow. Because Sunday," he paused, glanced at Billy Bob, then whispered, "there's a shower for Margaret and me . . . a shower." When Betty insisted that he speak up, he nearly shouted, "A wedding shower!"

Billy Bob chuckled at this as he made his way to the bathroom. "Ain't women a hoot?"

"Any news about the Anchorage PD? . . . *Great* . . . What's the weatherman say?" Ray paused to swear. "Have the captain call as soon as he . . . Wait. He can't call me. The radio's out in the sled and I don't know exactly where I am—or what number I can be reached at. I'll just call him. Tell him I'm looking for him, though. Okay? . . . And Betty, this is important." He replaced the phone and stepped to the window. Outside the wind was blowing ferociously, driving powder pellets sideways. Snow devils churned away into the darkness. Even under the powerful halogens, it was a whiteout. They could have been aboard a ship or on an airliner and not known it.

Ray heard the toilet flush. The water ran for a few seconds, then the bathroom door swung open and yellow light glared across the room.

"I'm rarin' to get some vittles," Billy Bob declared with a lopsided smile. "How 'bout you, partner?"

Vittles? Ray thought. Was this guy for real? "Sure. Maybe by the time we finish eating, the crew will show up."

Ray slipped on his boots and they went down the hall, following the smell of eggs and bacon to the cafeteria. Despite the simple surroundings, the selection approached that of a Sunday brunch at a fine hotel: fried eggs, scrambled eggs, ham and mushroom omelets, bacon, sausage links, hash browns, toast, muffins, pancakes, juice, coffee. They fell into line behind a dozen hungry men in stained blue coveralls, and began inching their way along, filling their plates from the steaming chrome platters.

Billy Bob took a seat at the end of one of the folding tables and dove in, a blur of silver as utensils cut, pierced, and stabbed at his breakfast. Ray sat across from him, suddenly feeling as though he hadn't eaten in a week and was about to faint from starvation.

The room was quiet, jaws working steadily, forks and knives clinking on china. It was five minutes before Billy Bob spoke.

"Tell me about yer sweetie," he asked between bites.

Ray took a long swig of coffee. "My *sweetie*?"

"Yer fiancée. What's she like?"

Ray shrugged and picked up his muffin. What was Margaret like? A kitten? A tornado? A child? A wildfire? "She's . . . quite a lady," he finally answered.

Billy Bob nodded. "I'm gonna meet me somebody like that one a these days, yes sirree. There's a woman out there for me. Just gotta find her, that's all." He inhaled a mouthful of eggs. "When you gettin' hitched?"

"Next month."

"What day?"

Ray sighed. "The fourteenth." He was trying to think of a way to change the subject when Billy Bob sat up straight, his eyebrows reaching for the roof.

"Valentine's Day! No kiddin'?" His voiced seemed to boom across the room. Heads turned, eyes focusing on Ray.

"Yeah."

"Ain't that sweet. Marryin' yer sweetheart on Valentine's Day!"

"*Ain't* it. Tell me about Texas."

"Texas . . ." Billy Bob said dreamily. He began to gleam, pride exuding from every pore. "I miss her. 'Specially now. I ain't never seen nothin' like this." He shook his head and gestured toward the window. "It's night all the time. And colder than a witch's heart. How do you ever get used to that?"

"You just do."

"Does the sun *ever* come up out here?"

"It will along about . . . the end of February. Until then, well, in between storms, it'll get light for a few hours. That's about it, though. No sunshine."

"And I hear tell it's light all the time in the summer."

"Pretty much. For a couple of months—June/July—the sun never sets. It just runs around the horizon, kind of like a basketball caught in the rim."

"A toilet ringer. That's what we call that down south."

Ray finished off his pancake and wiped his lips. "Good food."

"Darn good! I was about to die I was so hungry." He stopped and gave Ray a quizzical look. "What sort of food do you eat where you come from?"

"Where I come from?"

"Back in the village, in yer igloo."

Ray stared at him. Surely he wasn't serious.

"You know, yer ice house."

"First of all," Ray began, struggling to mask his irritation, "most igloos aren't made of ice."

"They ain't?" Billy Bob's eyes grew wide, as if this were a startling revelation.

"They're sod. Second of all, I don't live in a village anymore. I live in Barrow. It's a town with thousands of people. That's why we need a police department."

"Huh . . ." He nodded before stuffing half of a muffin in his mouth.

"As for what I eat, it's pretty much the same thing you eat. When I was a boy, I lived with my grandfather. We'd hunt caribou, go whaling, do a lot of fishing. Those were our main meats. We had seal and walrus sometimes too. Many of our people still live by subsistence off the land, but in the bigger villages and towns, they get a lot of their food just like the folks in Texas do: by going to the grocery store."

"Is that right? Ezkeemos shop at Piggly Wiggly?"

Ray was still marveling at the deputy's ignorance when Simpson appeared with a short, dark-haired man in tow.

"Officers," Simpson said, "this here's Jorge."

The man rubbed an oily hand on his coveralls, then extended it toward them. "Jorge Rodriguez at your service. Hear you fellas have a body for me."

 **SIX**

ABANDONING THEIR TRAYS, they led Jorge to the storage room.

"He's in here," Ray said, reaching for the door. He twisted the knob, pushed it open . . . swore.

"Geez!" Billy Bob exclaimed.

Jorge agreed with the assessment, muttering a curse in Spanish.

In the warm air of the storage room the body had uncurled and slipped from its perch on the table, taking one of the garbage sacks with it. Limp arms and legs were splayed on the tile floor, as if the corpse was trying to swim away in the shallow pool of pink ice water. The sight was overwhelming.

Ray covered his mouth with one hand and surveyed the shelves with the other. He found a box of painting masks and a container of cleaning gloves and handed Billy Bob and Jorge a set. When their faces were safely hidden behind the white filters, their hands covered in yellow plastic, Ray sighed. "Let's get him back on the table."

The three of them waded into the shallow lake. Ray concentrated on his breathing, fighting off a wave of nausea. Next to him Billy Bob's thin frame was slipping and sliding in the pale red pond, arms waving in an effort to maintain his balance. Even with the mask, it was clear that the deputy found this chore repulsive.

Jorge didn't seem to mind. He stepped forward, bent, took

hold of a blood-soaked mitten, a wet Sorrel. "Okay, on my count . . . One, two, three . . ."

The body was more difficult to handle in its thawed form. It was heavier, the clothing soaked to many times its normal weight. And the limbs were rubbery, the torso flexing and twisting like putty. The head lolled back, to the side, then forward.

"Down," Jorge directed. The soggy corpse thumped onto the table, face-up, an arm flopping off the side.

Ray repositioned the stray arm, then noticed the front of his pants. They were stained with red blotches, as if they had been splatter painted.

"Hope this stuff washes out," Billy Bob was saying, brushing at his western shirt.

"I hope we don't get AIDS," Ray lamented.

Jorge ignored them. Slipping smoothly into the role of medical expert, the stubby oil worker examined the body with rapt concentration. He stared at the head, studied the torso, the legs. Finally, he examined the boots.

"What do you think?" Ray asked, feeling helpless. "Guy froze to death, right?"

Jorge shrugged. "Lot of blood. Help me roll him over." They did, the corpse slogging to its side, then face-down. The back of the parka was saturated. Just above waist level there was a tear in the fabric. Jorge pulled up the coat and underclothing to expose the skin of the back. The flesh was scarred by a jagged, inch-wide hole.

Jorge used a yellow finger to circle the cavity. "Puncture wound, lower lumbar region, just lateral to the spine."

"You sound like an ME," Ray noted.

"I almost was." He peered into the hole.

"Is that from a gunshot?" Billy Bob asked stupidly.

Jorge shook his head. "Jabbed with something. Might have struck an organ. Didn't kill him though. Not enough blood. I'd have to do tests, to conduct a real autopsy, but, well, I'd have to say this guy was already dead when this was made."

Ray blinked at this. "So he froze to death."

"I didn't say that. I said he didn't die from this wound. Can't imagine how he got it though. Somebody must have—"

"The rebar!" Billy Bob nearly shouted.

"What rebar?" Jorge wanted to know.

"Fellas who found him," Billy Bob explained, "they poked him with a piece a rebar. They was trying to unclog a pipe. Thought it was full of mud."

Jorge stared at the hole, obviously trying to picture this in his mind. Satisfied, he said, "Okay, roll him back over." He returned to the head, rolling it back and forth on the flimsy, lifeless neck before pulling back the hood and zipping down the parka.

"Uh . . ." Ray groaned, swearing loudly. Beside him, Billy Bob retched.

The face was purple, withered from frostbite. Not a pretty sight, but nothing to bring up your breakfast. The neck, however, was a different story. It had been cut from ear to ear, brittle gray skin curling back to reveal a deep channel of muscles and tendons.

"Subject's neck is lacerated," Jorge observed calmly. He began to investigate the trench with a steady hand. "Skin, infrahyoid muscles, larynx . . . all severed."

"Somebody slit his neck," Ray muttered, still grimacing.

"No," Jorge disagreed, gloved fingers pulling at the opening. "Somebody tried to chop his head off. Or rather, slice it off."

It was Ray's turn to retch. Thankfully, the contents of his breakfast stayed put.

Jorge pointed to the edges of the cut. "See how smooth the entry marks are. The blade was sharp. Except"—he squinted at the neck—"they didn't use a regular knife."

"What did they use?" Ray asked, trying to swallow.

"Something curved. Kind of like a scimitar . . . but shorter."

Breathing deeply, Ray returned his gaze to the corpse.

"But this didn't kill him either," Jorge continued. He seemed to be enjoying this.

"You're kidding," Ray muttered.

"Same problem as the puncture wound. Not enough blood."

"If cutting off his head off didn't do it, what did?"

"Good question." Jorge zipped the parka the rest of the way open and folded it back. Tracing the jacket with his hand, he stuck a yellow pinkie finger through a tiny hole. "Voila!"

"Bullet?"

Jorge nodded. "Pierced his jacket, went through the rest of the clothes . . ." He pulled up the sweater, unbuttoned a dress shirt—presumably bleach white in its original state but now dark red—and pushed the insulated underwear into a wad. "Entered the subject's thorax, struck the heart."

"What about an exit wound?" Ray wondered. "The bullet should have come out the guy's back."

"We may have missed it," Jorge said.

"Or maybe it was one a them Black Talons," Billy Bob threw in.

Ray nodded. Black Talons were slugs that expanded on entry and often didn't make it out. They caused such internal devastation that they had been outlawed shortly after their debut.

"Those babies bounce around like rodeo bulls," the deputy continued. "Make a real mess of yer insides."

"Get his clothes off," Jorge ordered. They slid off the wet, pungent parka, the drenched sweater, the shirts. With each piece, the sightless head rocked, its open neck emitting a silent scream.

"Now his boots and pants."

When the corpse was naked, they rolled it to its side. "Nope," Jorge said. "No exit. Must of hit a bone or something."

"Any idea what kind of gun?"

Jorge frowned at this. "I'm not much on ballistics." The frown intensified. "Small caliber rifle."

"Twenty-two?"

"Bigger than that. But nothing like a thirty-thirty or anything."

Ray looked down at the broken, mutilated form. "So that's what killed him?" He pointed to the gunshot wound.

"Yep. His heart was violated by a chunk of lead." Jorge continued his examination, lifting the arms, checking the hands, flexing the knees. Five minutes later he was back at the head. Pulling the lids up, he glanced at each eye, into the ears, ran a glove through the tangled, matted hair. He gazed into the nostrils, pulled open the jaw, stuck a finger in and wiggled the teeth. Then he took hold of the tongue.

"That's interesting."

Ray leaned in for a better look. Billy Bob kept his distance, eyes on the wall.

Jorge was actually smiling now, savoring his work. "How odd."

"What?"

"See here?" He stepped back and a gloved hand raised the stiff, pink lump of flesh. "The muscle from the underside of the tongue is gone."

"Gone?"

"Cut out. With a sharp, curved blade."

A shiver ran up and down Ray's spine. *"Nigiluq."*

"Huh?"

"That's what it's called."

"That's what *what's* called?" Jorge asked.

Ray sighed. "When I was a kid, my grandfather used to take me down into the Range, hunting for *aklaq,* for grizzly. If we got one, he would always make me remove the worm, the cartilage under the tongue, and chop off the head." Ray took a slow step back from the table before cursing at the mental image. "According to tradition, you're supposed to leave the worm and head in the field, bury them or impale them on a tree, to insure that the bear's *kila,* his spirit, won't haunt you but will go on to be reincarnated. The ritual is called *nigiluq.*"

The room was silent as the trio considered this.

"When we brought a bear home," Ray added, "Grandmother would prepare the meat with an *ulu.*"

After another minute, Billy Bob asked, "What's an ooloo?"

"A small knife with a curved blade. Usually a bone or

wood handle. Native women use them for just about everything, including cleaning a catch.''

"You think this here man was mistaken for a bear?" Billy
Bob wondered, a twisted expression on his face.

"I don't know what to think," Ray said. "It's . . . it's . . ."

"Creepy," Jorge said glibly. He paused, gingerly tugging
at his sleeve in an attempt to avoid soiling his shirt as he
looked at his watch. "Listen guys, if that's all, I need to get
some dinner and hit the sack. I'm on again in eight."

"Uh . . . yeah . . . thanks. I guess that's it for now." Ray
wondered how the guy could even think about food after conducting a guided tour through a fresh cadaver.

Jorge slid off his gloves, snapped the mask back, and
splashed his way toward the door.

"We can't leave this guy here," Ray noted. "Any suggestions?"

Jorge paused and shrugged at this. "I'd cover him back up
and put him out in the yard. Once he freezes, he won't stink
as much. Easier to transport too." With that, he left, his slick
boots squeaking away down the hall.

"I thought I'd seen ever-thang," Billy Bob said, frowning
at the shelves. He was being careful to keep his eyes away
from the body. "Why in heaven's name would somebody do
somethin' like this?"

"No idea." Ray looked to the face for an answer, studying
the features above the unconscionable damage.

"I tell you why. Cause they're depraved, wicked . . . downright evil. Immoral . . . Sinful . . ."

Ray was suddenly reminded of the evangelists he had seen
shouting and sweating through sermons on television.

"Whoever it was, they should be strung up."

Ray tended to agree but decided not to say so. "Maybe
somebody can ID him now."

Billy Bob glanced at the corpse. "Maybe." He swallowed
hard, his breathing uneven. Turning his back on the horrific
sight, he asked, "You ever investigate a murder before, Officer Attla?"

Ray nodded. "A few." But nothing like this, he failed to
add. Murders in Barrow were rare, and when they did occur,

they involved three major components: women, booze, and firearms. Usually in that order. Despite the fact that Barrow had been dry since '94, the scenario went something like this: guy sees his lady with another man, gets plastered on contraband liquor, goes home, loads his rifle, goes looking for trouble. Deciding who did the shooting was never much of a feat. You looked for the hotheaded drunk with the smoking gun. And there were always witnesses ready to fill you in on what happened. The crimes were not well planned, seldom premeditated, and never went unsolved for more than a few hours.

"What about you?" Ray asked.

Billy Bob scoffed at this. "Naw. Soon as I got out of the police academy, I come up here. Ain't never even stood this close to a dead person. Good thing you're takin' the ball on this one, Officer Attla."

"Yeah, well . . . I'm not exactly a homicide detective." He shook his head at the body. "And call me Ray. Looks like we'll be spending some quality time together."

►► SEVEN ◄◄

"NO, I'M SURE . . . Positive . . . Captain . . . Captain, listen . . . No, it was *not* an accident, believe me . . ."

Ray was standing in the hall, Simpson's cellular stuck to his ear, watching through the doorway as two janitors traded curses and sprayed down the empty table in the storage room with disinfectant. He and Billy Bob had taken Jorge's advice and put the body back out in the snow. It would freeze solid in no time.

"Captain, the guy took a bullet to the chest—the heart— and an *ulu* to the neck . . . Yeah, an *ulu* . . . That's what I'm trying to tell you. Whoever did this was . . . demented."

One of the janitors was using a sponge to wipe down the table legs. The other was pushing thin, watery blood with a mop, herding it in the general direction of the floor drain.

"Leads? Are you kidding? We haven't even IDed the body . . . No . . . Because I didn't bring a camera . . . Well, I sketched the face, but . . . I'm no Rembrandt." He glanced at the pad in his hand. Two sorrowful eyes stared up at him from the arrangement of pencil scratches: lumpy cheeks, over-sized ears, narrow nose . . . "Looks a little like him . . . sort of. Anyway, I'm gonna show it around, see what I can turn up . . . Yeah . . . Yeah . . . Okay. Any word on the Anchorage Police? . . ." His frown intensified. "I really need to get back to Barrow by . . . Yeah, I know . . . Right . . . I'll call in this afternoon."

He hung up the phone and watched as the janitors dabbed

at the last blotches of what looked like wet, red clay.

"They about got that mess cleaned up?"

Ray glanced up the hallway and saw Simpson and Billy Bob approaching. He handed the phone to Simpson. "Just about."

"What's next?" Simpson asked. "You fellas done? Ready to head on out of here now?" He was clearly anxious to be rid of them.

"Not quite," Ray sighed. "We need to ask a few more questions, talk to the guys who found the body."

Simpson nodded knowingly, then examined his watch. "They're all off-shift, either sleeping or eating." He gestured toward Ray's pad. "What's that?"

"Sketch of the victim," Ray answered. He presented it to Simpson. "Look familiar?"

A hand stroked his fuzzy flattop. "No . . . Don't think so. But it's a good drawing. You an artist or something?"

Ray smirked in response. "Wanna introduce us to the roustabouts?"

"Follow me."

Simpson led them back to the cafeteria. When they arrived, he paused and surveyed the tables. "Maybe they're sacked out . . . Hold on, there's Jim over on the end there." He pointed to a thin figure bent over a tray. The man's hair was long and wild, black locks twisting away in every direction.

Marching to the table, Simpson said, "Jim, these policemen want to have a talk with you."

Jim's head tilted up from his plate and two dark eyes examined them suspiciously.

Simpson's phone chimed. He answered it, then covered the receiver with a beefy hand. "You boys do what you need to do. I'll be in the office." With that he hurried away, jabbering into the cellular.

Billy Bob and Ray slid into seats directly across the table from Jim.

"Ray Attla, Barrow PD." He offered a badge. "Mind if we ask you a few questions?"

Jim shrugged and continued eating.

"Tell us what happened out there, when you found the body," Billy Bob said.

"Nothin' to tell."

"Nothing to tell?" Billy Bob blinked at this, confused. "But you were there when . . ."

Ray waved him off. "Why don't you go get us some coffee. I take mine black."

The cowboy nodded and left to attend to the chore.

Two minutes passed. Jim finished his eggs, sipped at his juice, studied Ray. When he had wiped his mouth and seemed ready to leave, Ray asked, "Where you from?"

"Ambler," Jim sniffed.

"Ambler . . . That's the Ivisaapaatmiut, right?"

Two black eyebrows shot up, the nonverbal, Inupiat cue for *yes*.

"Good people," Ray noted.

Jim's eyes widened, another affirmative cue. "The Real People."

"Got an uncle lives down there. Well, close to Ambler anyway. Village of Shungak. Ever heard of it?"

"Sure. Used to fish just a few miles down the Kobuk from there." Jim seemed to warm slightly. His brown eyes gave Ray the once over. "You full-blood?"

Ray answered with his eyebrows.

"Sure are tall."

His eyebrows rose again. Jim was right. Ray had a good three to six inches on most Inupiats. "My mother died when I was born," he explained. "My Grandfather says that's why I'm as big as I am. The *tuungak* blessed me with size in exchange for taking my mother." He decided not to add the bit of family trivia he had learned from an aunt: that his great-grandfather on his father's side had been a Friends missionary and that fact, not some superstitious tale about a spirit blessing, accounted for his height.

Jim seemed satisfied now.

"What brought you to the Slope, Jim?"

"Money."

Ray nodded at this. That was the single draw. The weather sucked, so did the landscape. The hunting wasn't very good anymore, not since the whites had shown up and started drilling for oil. The only reason anyone ventured to Prudhoe was for the money.

"How do you like working for *naluaqmiut*?"

Jim's lips pursed. "My partner, Sam . . . he hates it. Says they're all devils. Says they're just using us, you know, like slaves. Keeps talking about going out with a rifle and doing some *naluaqmiut* hunting."

"What about you?"

"I don't mind so much. Long as they pay us. Most of 'em are pretty decent."

"Most of them?"

"There's a few . . . you know . . . jerks. They got this attitude about *klooches*." He paused to denounce them with a curse. "But it's still better than Ambler."

"How's that?"

"I hated village life: being poor, not having enough to eat, living in those cold dumps they call houses." He swore again. "Here I got a room, board, all the food I can eat. Pulling down major bucks. And I'm saving it up."

"For what?"

"Buy a boat."

"A boat?"

Jim grinned for the first time, displaying a mouth full of yellow, chipped teeth. The eyebrows were animated again, rising into his forehead. "Me and my buddy Sam, we're gonna go down to Mexico. Be fishermen."

"Is that right?"

"Make a good living doing that. And it's warm down there. Warm and sunny." He seemed to bask in the light of this fantasy for a few seconds. Then, "I gotta get some sleep." He tossed his utensils into the center of his empty plate and put his juice glass back onto the tray.

"Where *is* your partner?"

"Sam? Already in bed. Where I should be."

"Why aren't you?"

Jim sighed. "Dang coffee. Drank a cup just about an hour before we finished up. Got to sleep okay. But I woke again. Starving. Happens a lot. Caffeine messes with my stomach."

He gripped his tray and shifted his weight, about to stand.

Ray stopped him with an outstretched hand and slid the sketch across the table. "Recognize this guy?"

Fingers flicked at a two-day growth of facial stubble, then his nose wrinkled: *no*.

"That's the man who was in the pipe," Ray told him.

"Oh, yeah?" Jim's disinterest was total.

"You've never seen him before?"

More furrows in the nose. "Nope."

Billy Bob returned with two Styrofoam cups and took his seat next to Ray. Jim was suddenly sullen, eyes darting from Ray to the goofy looking *naluaqmiu,* back to Ray.

"How about a couple of those buns?" Ray suggested, gesturing to a platter of cinnamon rolls. "See if they'll warm them for us in the microwave."

Billy Bob groaned, "Okay."

When he was out of earshot, Ray asked, "What happened out there, with the body?"

After a long, melodramatic sigh, Jim said, "We got done forking some crates around and started working on the pipe. The rig foreman said it was clogged."

"Foreman? What's his name?"

"Mr. Driscoll. Anyway, me and Sam, we figured it was full of mud. We banged around on it, Sam tried to work the clot loose with a stick of rebar . . . Didn't work. So we tipped it up with the lift. And a watch come out."

"The Rolex."

Rising eyebrows. Jim shrugged. "That's it. We told Mr. Driscoll, he took it from there."

Ray considered this. "Any idea how the body got into the pipe?"

The wrinkles in the nose were accentuated by Jim's frown.

"Doesn't someone check the pipe before it's taken into the rig house?"

"Supposed to, I guess."

"Who's responsible for that?"

One eyebrow rose, the other fell. "Guys at the main camp?" It was a question rather than a statement.

"Is that where the pipe comes from? Is it trucked up from Prudhoe?"

Jim's eyes grew wide. "Think so. Can I go now?"

"Yeah. But we need to speak with your friend, Sam. Have him look at this picture."

Jim's face pinched into a sour expression.

"It won't take long."

"I can guarantee he won't recognize the guy. Besides, he's sleeping. Sam doesn't like to be disturbed when he's sleeping," Jim warned.

"Maybe not, but we have to do it."

"Okay . . ." He rose and dumped his tray onto a conveyer belt on his way to the door. Ray followed, motioning to Billy Bob with a nod of his head. Discarding the two piping hot buns he had just acquired, the cowboy hurried to catch up.

In the corridor, they met a fresh crew: sleepy-eyed men shuffling toward the aroma of breakfast, parkas slung over their backs.

Jim took them up a stairwell and down a long corridor lined with doors. They went past another rec room: deserted Ping-Pong and pool tables, a big-screen TV. Stopping midway along the passage, Jim thrust a key into a lock and pushed the door open. The smell of damp clothing filtered into the hall.

After flipping on a lamp, he aimed a thumb at the bunk on the far wall. It contained a long lump shrouded in heavy blankets. "He won't be happy about this."

"Just wake him up," Ray said. "Please."

"Sam?" The lump didn't move. "Sam?" Jim reached his hand out and jiggled a shoulder. "Sam . . . Hey, man . . . Wake up." The bulge in the bedding grunted, twisted, then grew still again. It began to snore. "He sleeps like a log," Jim explained. He kicked the frame. When that had no effect, he took hold of the bed coverings and yanked them back. "Sam?"

The man in the bed, abruptly dislodged from his warm cocoon, swore angrily. Sitting up, he squinted at them, cursed again, then shouted, "What do you think you're doing?"

"Sam, these guys are cops and they want to talk to you."

Sam scowled at this. "Cops . . ." His inflection made the word sound profane. He rubbed his eyes on the back of a hand and muttered a crude sentiment. "What time is it?"

"Sorry about this, Sam," Ray apologized. "I'm Officer Attla, Barrow PD." He presented his badge.

Sam told him what he could do with it.

"Okay . . . Well, we need you to take a look at a sketch."

"A what?" He began to curse again, this time in Inupiat.

Ray leaned forward and held the drawing in front of Sam's face.

He squinted at it, blinked, told them all where they could go.

"Ever seen this guy?"

"No! Gimme back my covers!" He wrenched the blankets free from Jim's grip and dove beneath them.

"You sure?" Billy Bob asked the bedspread.

A head reappeared, brown eyes shooting fire at them. "Leave me alone before I have to hurt you!"

"This is the man who was found in the pipe," Ray explained.

Sam growled a curse, reached for a Sorrel and flung it across the room.

"Told you he was cranky," Jim said with a half-smile. "If that's all, I really need to get some sleep. I'm on again in six."

"Thanks for your help," Ray offered, only half serious.

When Jim had ushered them through the door and slammed it shut behind them, Billy Bob asked, "You suppose one a them fellas did it?"

"Did what?"

"Killed that man they found in the pipe."

Ray shook his head. "Doubt it." He started for the stairwell.

"They're . . . uh-uh . . . you know . . . They're . . ." Billy Bob stuttered.

"*What?*"

"Ezkeemos."

"So?"

"So . . . the way that fella was killed . . . You said it was like a Ezkeemo hunter."

"Yeah. But that doesn't mean those roustabouts did it. They lack something called motive." Ray considered sharing Jim's disclosure, that Sam had a twisted fantasy about mowing down whites with a rifle, but that would only fuel the deputy's simpleminded, even bigoted, "the Ezkeemos did it!" theory. "Why would they want to shoot and slice some suit and stuff him into a pipe?"

Billy Bob didn't have an answer, but seemed to be working on the question as they made the stairs, his features twisting into an expression that approached serious concentration. "What do we do now?"

"Keep asking questions. See if someone can place this face," Ray answered, lifting the sketch. "I'd like to talk to the guy who was fitting the pipe inside the rig."

"*Settin'* the pipe," Billy Bob submitted.

"Right."

They found Simpson at his desk, on the phone. His cheeks were red with anger.

"I don't care what the schedule says . . . No . . . No! Listen, we're fine . . . We'll be producing by . . . What? How in the heck am I supposed to know that?" He waved Ray and Billy Bob into the office, offering them a seat.

"I don't care what Houston says . . . Well, they're not up here having to deal with permafrost, equipment delays, dead bodies . . ." Simpson rolled his eyes at the two police officers. "I have to go . . . No . . . I'll call you back when it's firmed up." He snapped the phone shut and tossed it onto the desk. "Executives . . ." he muttered. "They go to college, get a degree in marketing, and then pretend to know something about the oil field." He punctuated this sentiment with a fitting expletive.

Ray nodded. Whatever. "Mr. Simpson, we need to speak with the pipe setter—"

"The derrick man," Billy Bob corrected.

"Right. The guy who first noticed that the pipe was clogged."

Simpson stared at them, obviously still annoyed at whomever he had been speaking with on the phone. His hand was back at his flattop, stroking the stiff silver hair as he mentally gnawed at the problem.

"Mr. Simpson . . . ?" Ray prodded.

"The derrick man . . . right." He nodded and considered this. "Let's see, that would be Ed. He's off-shift. I didn't see him in the cafeteria. Try the dayroom on the second floor. If he's not there, he's probably crashed in his room." Simpson scrawled a name and a room number on a piece of paper and handed it to Ray. "All the way to the south end."

Ray presented his sketch. "We need to make copies of this and have the crews take a look at it. Got a copier?"

The phone rang before Simpson could respond to the request. He swore, picked it up, pointed to a copy machine in the corner of the small office. "Help yourself."

"Thanks," Ray said. After fiddling with the controls, he ran off ten duplicates of his work of art. Setting one on Simpson's desk, he looked to Billy Bob. "Come on."

They took the south stairwell this time. Upstairs, the dayroom Simpson had mentioned was uninhabited, the dartboard, billiard table and television neglected. When they found room 28, Ray gave it a rap. Thirty seconds later, he tried again, harder this time.

"Yeah?" someone grunted from inside. In one word the speaker managed to convey extreme irritation.

"Ed Stewart?" Ray read from Simpson's note.

"Yeah?" the voice was still annoyed, but more wary now.

"Could we speak with you for a minute?"

"I'm busy."

"We need to ask you a few questions."

"Who the heck's *we*?" the voice growled.

"Po-lice," Billy Bob replied, accenting the long o. He smiled, clearly relishing the opportunity to assert his new-found authority.

"You got a warrant? 'Cause if you don't . . ." The unseen speaker went on to explain precisely what they could do to themselves if they did not possess the appropriate legal documentation.

"No, Mr. Stewart. We don't have one. But we'll have one

faxed in within the hour,'' Ray fibbed, ''if you don't open the door.''

There was a bump, something breaking—glass?—a curse, more noise: cardboard compacting, an object sliding across carpet, plastic being wadded up, wood meeting wood, labored breath. Finally the door creaked open a crack and two bleary eyes peered out from a haggard face. Stewart looked ill.

''Let's see some ID.''

Ray flashed his badge. Billy Bob held his up to the crack.

''What seems to be the problem, officers?'' He suddenly sounded like their best friend, accommodating, personable, but the door didn't budge.

''It's about the body,'' Billy Bob drawled.

Stewart sniffed, then cleared his sinuses. ''Body?''

''Yeah. The one in the pipe casing.''

''Mind if we come in?'' Ray asked, taking a step forward.

The man swallowed hard, his thin neck shooting forward like a chicken's. ''Well . . . I—I—'' He hesitated, snorted again, then swung back the door. ''I guess not.''

►► EIGHT ◄◄

ED STEWART WAS an emaciated shell of a man, dressed in baggy, wrinkled gym shorts and a stained Led Zeppelin T-shirt.

Sniffing, he gestured toward the only chair. It was a single room—one bunk, one desk, one chair. Stewart took up position in front of the closet, feet shoulder-width apart, arms crossed, as if guarding some prize.

"Well? . . ." A tongue reached out to lick at two dry, chapped lips. "What do you want to know?" The tone was semi-conciliatory, but the man seemed on edge, nervous to the point of being neurotic. He sniffed again, this time using a finger to hold one nostril closed. When a thin trail of blood leaked out, he swore and wiped it on his sleeve. "What do you want to know?"

Distracted by Stewart's living quarters, Ray missed the question. The room was a disaster area: soiled clothing scattered about the floor in piles, balled up on the desk, hung over the headboard of the bed, draped along the blinds . . . And the smell! Despite the dirty laundry, the place reeked of alcohol. Ray glanced at the closet behind Stewart. There were tiny shards of glass on the carpet and a dark, irregular stain, as if something were trying to escape under the door. Since every oil camp on the Slope was dry, that made Ed either a secret drunk or a dealer—or both. And the constant sniffing . . . Somehow Ray wasn't convinced that Stewart was suffering from a cold. Maybe he used the profits from the bootlegging operation to fund his cocaine habit.

"It's about the body you found," Billy Bob said.

"I didn't find no body," Stewart argued. His pupils were pinpricks at the center of two gray-green orbs, the whites of his eyes yellow, riddled with angry red veins.

"Okay, then," Ray tried. "The pipe that was clogged."

"What about it?"

"When did you notice the clog?"

"I don't know." Ed seemed unable to focus, his eyes flitting about like insects unwilling to light anywhere for longer than a few seconds. Stewart looked at Ray's legs, at the bunk, at Billy Bob's boots, picked at various spots on the floor.

"Just tell us what happened."

"What do you mean? Nothing happened." He was defensive now, breathing rapidly. He snorted, then shook his head. "I don't have to tell you nothin'."

"No," Ray agreed, stepping toward the closet. "You don't *have* to. We were sort of hoping you'd *want* to."

"Huh?" Stewart's eyes grew wide in terror. "What do you mean?" He backed toward the closet, protecting it. Billy Bob took the little man by the arm, nearly lifting him into the air. Ray knelt and tapped at the wet carpet with a finger. It was wet. He sampled it with his tongue. "Tequila."

Billy Bob pulled the closet door open. "Wow!"

Wow was right. The small storage area was packed, floor to ceiling, with cardboard boxes: a case of vodka, two cases of scotch, a half case of gin, three cases of Budweiser . . . In front of the boxes a saturated label floated in a shallow pool of pale brown liquid and broken glass. The deputy picked it up. "Yep. Tequila. Sauza Gold."

Ray slid past him and flipped open an unmarked box. It contained a dozen or so zip-lock bags, each bearing white powder, something akin to baking flour. He lifted one into the air and examined it.

"What's that?" Billy Bob asked in his most convincing hick voice.

"Coke." Ray tossed the baggy back into the box.

"You mean like cocaine?"

"Yeah. Like cocaine." Ray reached into another box and withdrew a small paper sack. Inside he found a selection of chemicals in pill form along with a litmus strip and a measuring cup.

"More drugs?" Billy Bob wondered, peering into the sack.

"No. This is more like a chemistry set." He replaced the sack, noting that there were probably fifty others in the box.

"What're they for?"

"To help *customers* beat random drug tests," Ray surmised. "Right, Ed?"

Behind them, Stewart broke down, weeping as if he had just lost his closest friend. Sinking to the bunk, he cradled his head in his hands, gasping repentant curses through the tears. "Don't . . . bust me . . . Please . . . I got—I got a wife and three—three kids back home . . . in Tulsa . . ." he sobbed. "Please . . ."

"We're not DEA, Ed," Ray comforted. "Tell us what we want to know and we'll be on our way."

"But I don't know anything!"

"When did you notice that the pipe was clogged?"

He sniffed and snorted. "About . . . midway through the shift, I guess."

"How'd you find the clog? Why didn't ya just set the pipe?" Billy Bob asked.

"It wasn't my fault," he blurted out. A trembling hand reached up to push back a stray lock of oily brown hair. "I didn't do anything."

"We didn't say that you did," Ray offered. He shot Billy Bob a puzzled look.

"I was up on the monkey board the whole time," Ed said, as if this explained everything. He was perspiring freely, his shirt dark with sweat.

"And you seen the clog as you was about to set the pipe?" Billy Bob tried.

Stewart's head rocked back and forth. "Yeah."

"You didn't check it out in the yard?" Ray asked.

"Huh-uh." Here his head shifted direction, shaking emphatically. "Prudhoe's supposed to do that, before the casing gets here."

"Nobody checks it here?" Ray clarified.

"No. Why should we?" The pendulum had returned from panic and was swinging back toward the realm of veiled paranoia. After snorting and wiping at the resulting blood, he blurted out, "I'm supposed to. Okay? I'm responsible for inspecting the casing before a job. Satisfied?" His arms were like hyperactive snakes—uncrossing, shooting hands into the pockets of his shorts, jabbing at his hair, recrossing. It made Ray anxious just watching the man fidget.

"Why didn't you check it this time?" Ray pushed.

"I . . . forgot.'"

"You forgot?"

"I got busy. With my . . . my business." Here he gave the goods in the closet a forlorn look. Then, "I told the *muktuk* twins to do it." He cursed the native workers until he noticed the expression on Ray's face. "Oh, uh . . . sorry, man. I didn't mean anything."

Muktuk twins? Ray glared at him. Ed was obviously one of the jerks Jim had eluded to. Ray had the sudden urge to send the boozed up hophead across the room with a high kick. Instead, he asked, "You told the roustabouts to check the pipe?"

"Yeah. Sam and Jim," Stewart explained, attempting to redeem himself. "Good men. But they must have forgot to do it."

"Uh-huh."

"Any way you look at it," Ed sighed, sniffing back the blood, "it's Prudhoe's fault. Those . . ."—he chose several expletives to express his disdain for the men at the main camp—"they're supposed to check every piece of equipment that shows up in Deadhorse. But half the time, they don't bother. They just stick it on a truck and send it up here. They're the ones who screwed up."

"That's assuming the body was placed there before the casing arrived here at the rig," Ray pointed out.

"Huh?"

"Maybe the body was stuffed into the pipe while it was sitting out there in the yard."

Apparently Ed hadn't considered this possibility. His sharp

features contorted. The idea seemed to be too much for his hazed, drug-confused mind to entertain.

Ray showed him the sketch. "Know this guy?"

Ed's head moved closer, tilted back, leaned in, his eyes attempting to focus on the image. "Nah. Never seen him in my life."

"Okay," Ray sighed. He frowned: another dead end. "Thanks Mr. Stewart."

"What about . . . what about . . . ?" Ed asked, gesturing to the closet.

"I'd advise you to close up shop before you get caught."

"You're not gonna . . . arrest me?"

Ray shook his head.

"Thanks. Thanks officer. I really appreciate that. Thanks . . ."

He was still gushing his appreciation at them as they started down the hall, toward the stairwell. When they were out of earshot, Billy Bob asked, "What now?" In the deputy's language, the word "now" was two syllables: nay-ow.

"First, we turn in Ed," Ray thought aloud as they descended the steps. "Then . . ."

"But you said—"

"I said I wasn't going to arrest him. I didn't lie. I'm not going to. For one thing, he's not in my jurisdiction, but I am going to tell Simpson about Ed's little enterprise."

Billy Bob's face screwed up at this. It was clearly beyond the cowboy's limited vocabulary.

"His drug and liquor business," Ray clarified. "If the oil companies are as fastidious . . ." Here he paused to choose a simpler word. "As *discriminating* as they're said to be, Davis will send old Ed packing. And in my opinion, that's what he deserves."

The deputy's headed bobbed at this.

"In my opinion," Ray continued, building steam, "that guy represents the lowest rung on the human ladder, just below insurance salesmen." He took a deep breath, forcing himself to end his tirade on the detrimental effects of bootleggers and drug dealers before he reached full stride, but it was difficult. These were the two most destructive forces the Inupiat had ever encountered. Together they had helped to defeat a once noble people, transforming them into prisoners, slaves to the new, highly addictive gods. Tequila had stolen Ray's father; cocaine had nearly taken a close friend captive in college. That Stewart was pedaling his wares to white men made no difference. In Ray's book, Ed was still a sorcerer: a wicked *anjatkut* who lulled men into bondage and robbed them of their paychecks in the process.

Back in the cafeteria, Ray poured a cup of coffee, handed it to Billy Bob, then poured another.

"This thing's giving me a headache," Ray muttered.

"Whattya mean?"

Ray chewed his lip, studying the floor. "We've got a body. But no time of death or motive. We can't even ID the guy." He blew air at the tangle of loose ends. "When was the body loaded into the pipe?"

Billy Bob shrugged, his expression made all the more ignorant by his bunny teeth.

"And why wasn't the pipe inspected?"

Another shrug. "Ya got me."

"Apparently it's standard procedure to inspect the pipe before setting. Yet nobody did. The body wasn't discovered until they were about to screw the thing into the ground. And then only by accident. If it hadn't been for Ed, the victim may never have been found."

"Naw. It'd a been found alright. They couldn't have drilled with the casin' clogged like that."

Ray sipped his coffee. "You mean the process of drilling wouldn't have cleared it?"

Billy Bob shook his head. "The mud's shot in under pressure. But the body . . . there's no place for it to go, even if it was busted up."

"Mud?"

"The slurry solution that irrigates the bit and washes out the debris. The body mighta been tore up a bit, but . . . It wouldn'ta made it out of the pipe."

Ray watched the steam rising from his cup, thinking.

"Who're our suspects?"

"We don't have any," Ray sighed.

"Member though, Mr. Simpson mentioned foul play. And that Sam, he seems suspicious to me. Meaner than a road lizard. And Stewart, that guy's a criminal. He's at the top of my list."

"Oh, yeah? And how's that?"

Billy Bob shrugged. "Say this guy in the pipe owed him money, say for drugs. So he pops him."

"Right," Ray scoffed. "Some corporate exec comes to the end of the earth to buy dope and a six pack of Bud, but forgets his wallet. So Stewart shoots him and slices him up, Native-style, and sticks him in a pipe. Then he's the one who realizes the pipe's clogged and calls it to everyone's attention."

"Makes him less suspicious, findin' the body."

"Yeah. A whole lot less suspicious."

"Guess it don't exactly fit."

"Doesn't fit at all," Ray noted.

"What if the dead man was Stewart's supplier? Maybe he was tied in with those cartels down in Co-lumbia."

Ray ignored this. Finishing off his coffee, he said, "As for Simpson, he's just concerned about staying on schedule—getting this thing cleaned up, keeping the bosses back in Houston happy. Sam and Jim . . . They're saving up for a dream. Why blow it by knocking off some guy?"

"That don't leave us with much," Billy Bob lamented.

"That leaves us with zip."

"Where do we go from here?"

"We have to identify our John Doe," Ray said. He surveyed the cafeteria. It was half full—fifteen or twenty men scattered among the tables, throwing down breakfast. Setting his coffee down, he climbed onto a chair.

"What're ya doin'?" Billy Bob asked, gawking.

"Excuse me!" Ray called. "Excuse me! Could I have your attention please!"

The room grew quiet, conversation falling off abruptly, forks hovering between mouths and plates.

"I'm Ray Attla, Barrow PD." He flashed his badge. "In case you haven't heard, there's been a . . . *death* here in camp. We're trying to determine who the man is and we would appreciate your help. I'm going to pass out these drawings. Take a look, see if you recognize the face."

With that, he hopped down and began handing out copies of his sketch. The papers filtered around the room, tired eyes taking cursory glances before sending the portraits on their way down the line. While they waited, Ray tore sections from a cinnamon roll.

"Maybe we'll get lucky," Billy Bob chirped.

"Maybe," Ray replied gloomily. It would be great if someone identified the body. It would be better still if one of the men stood up and confessed to the murder. Short of that, the case had the look of a long-term assignment. His chance of making the wedding shower back in Barrow was starting to fade.

When the papers had all migrated to the far end of the room, Ray mounted the chair again. "Anybody recognize the face?"

Heads shook, faces frowning up at him.

"There's another crew over at the rig."

Ray turned and saw Simpson approaching. "Is that right?"

He nodded. "And Gene Driscoll, the drilling foreman who was there when Stewart noticed the clogged pipe, he's still on."

Ray hopped off the chair. "About Stewart . . ." he started to say.

"He's out of here," Simpson declared gruffly. "Work's been suffering for weeks. Then he forgets to check the pipe. That was the last straw."

"You know about his little . . . business?"

Another nod. "Through the grapevine. He'll be shut down by noon and on the first plane out of Deadhorse. That's saying this blasted storm lifts, of course."

"Of course." Ray was satisfied with this. To Billy Bob he said, "Let's go over to the rig and show the picture around."

"Pick up a hard hat in the doghouse on your way in," Simpson advised. "And be careful in there. It's dangerous. Not sure we're insured for visiting policemen."

⇒ NINE ⇐

IT WAS STILL Saturday morning. The clock in the mudroom read: 8:17. But night reigned over the yard, over the camp, over the featureless arctic sky. Clad in parkas, masks, boots and mittens, Ray and Billy Bob crunched across the dark yard into the bitter, icy wind, hurrying from one silvery pool of halogen to the next, as if they offered some modicum of relief from the storm. As they approached the rig, a truck the size of a moving van materialized in the blowing snow. The red and gray monstrosity was roaring with the determination of a freight train, competing with the voice of the gale for their attention.

Mounting the slick steps of the rig enclosure, they entered one end of the doghouse, an 8 x 20 rectangle of metal. A built-in, hinge-top bench ran along one wall. Above it, a row of hooks suspended wet, heavy parkas. The other wall was occupied by a stand-up desk. Next to the only other door, a steaming coffeepot was perched on a wooden crate. A bulletin board at eye-level bore a collection of notices and charts, and the bold message: SAFETY FIRST.

"Nobody home," Ray observed.

"They're inside, cementin'," Billy Bob informed him, nodding at the door. A sticker on it warned: CAUTION—HARD HAT ZONE.

Ray reached down and took a pair of blue hard hats from a leaning stack. Handing one to the deputy, he asked, "How do you know so much about oil?"

"My Granddaddy was an oil man; my Pappy was an oil man," he explained. The "i" was missing from his version of the word oil. It became "ole." Slapping on the hat, he added, "I worked a rig a few summers ma-self."

"Is that right?" Ray tried on the hat. It was too small. He traded it for another.

"Yes sirree. And I'll tell you sompthin'. That there is hard work. Dang hard work. Sure don't have no trouble sleepin' after a day in the ole field."

"I bet not." When Ray pulled the door open a wave of warmer air rushed to greet them. It was accompanied by bright, glaring light and a strong industrial smell: a mix of greased steel and diesel fuel. Three men in blue coveralls were huddled along the far wall fifty feet away, applying white paint to the chipped and scarred metal. Closer to the door, another man was washing down the floor, spraying dirt from the non-skid bumps and hosing it toward a section of grating. At the center of the enclosure, beside some machinery, a figure in a red RefrigiWear suit was bent over a thick stub of pipe. A flexible hose hooked to the stub ran up and, Ray assumed, into the overwrought truck outside.

"Can I help you fellas?" The question came from a short, stout man in blue coveralls. The southern accent and the felt flaps dangling from the man's hard hat brought to mind visions of the cartoon character Huckleberry Hound.

"Gene Driscoll?"

"Me? Why, no sir." Huckleberry seemed to think this was funny. "Nah," he chuckled. "Fred Brannon, driller." A gloved hand shot out at them.

Billy Bob shook it first. "Deputy Cleaver, Deadhorse Police."

"Ray Attla, Barrow PD." He gave the glove a squeeze, then presented his badge.

Huckleberry squinted at the badge, then looked up at Ray. As he did, the expression on his face changed from one of open hospitality to one of unbridled curiosity. The wheels were turning beneath those fabric ears. Ray braced himself for *the question*. "Say . . . you're a—a . . ." Huckleberry's voice trailed off, as if the word Eskimo wasn't in his vocabulary. "Boy howdy. You're plenty tall for a—"

"A police officer?" Ray tried sarcastically.

"No. For a . . . you know."

A *you know*? Ray had been referred to by many names and labels in the course of his lifetime—both complimentary and derogatory—but, *you know*? That was a new one. "What's he doing?" He gestured to the man attending to the pipe stub, successfully diverting Huckleberry's attention from the topic of ethnic background and its effect on height.

"Cementin' the casing, below the permafrost." The puzzled look on Ray's face apparently inspired an explanation. "The cement holds the casing in place, so we can drill deeper. We use a special cement, with a low heat of hydration, that prevents the permafrost from melting."

Ray nodded at this, much of the jargon flying right by. "Know anything about the man they found in the pipe?"

The two-story V-doors creaked open midway through the question and the wind howled wickedly through the enclosure. A man in bright red RefrigiWear stepped in, pushing the doors shut behind him. After he had trotted to his partner's side at the pipe stub, Huckleberry turned to Ray. "What was that?"

"I wondered if you knew anything about the man in the pipe. Were you there when they found him?"

"Nah. That was before my shift. But I heard about it. Ain't that just the dinkdums?" He shook his head at the bizarre tragedy. "Poor fella."

Ray offered the sketch. "Seen this man before?"

Huckleberry studied it, then shook his head. "Nah. Cain't say as I have."

"Is Mr. Driscoll around?"

This seemed to puzzle him. "Not in the doghouse?"

Ray shook his head. Next to him Billy Bob mimicked the action.

"Probably over at the shop."

"The shop?"

"Across the yard. North, past the sheds."

"Okay." Ray turned to leave, then, "Say, would you mind if the deputy here showed this sketch to your crew?"

"No problem," Huckleberry grinned. Two gold front teeth blinked out at them. "We was just fixin' to go on break anyhow. Give us a good excuse to grab some coffee." He used his two index fingers to whistle at the men. "Break!"

"I'll check the shop and meet you back at the camp in a few minutes," Ray told Billy Bob.

"Sure thing."

Ray sloshed across the rig floor, bunny boots squeaking against the wet steel. The doghouse was still empty. No Driscoll. Outside the storm seemed to be building, horizontal snow and vengeful blasts of wind combining to create an impressive whiteout: nearly zero visibility. The weather had the effect of making the darkness even more complete, as if it were alive, intent upon crushing all hopes of spring, light, and life.

As he trotted north, blinded by flying ice, Ray was reminded of Grandfather's words. Indeed, the conditions were ripe for *piinjilak* and *tuungak*. Anyone else, anyone with any common sense, would stay indoors and wait it out. *Why was he here?* He reached a shed and began feeling his way along the wall, squinting into the darkness. Where was the shop? Beyond the feeble output of the shed's lamp the world was a black hole. He took ten tentative paces forward. It was like walking into an abyss. He was suddenly reminded that the rig was on an island. Somewhere out there in front of him was the Beaufort Sea: vast, bleak, horribly unforgiving.

He had begun to wonder if Huckleberry had been mistaken, if perhaps the shop was south rather than north, and was about to turn back when a gust of wind revealed the prize: faded, blue trim floating in a miniature pond of halogen. As he approached, Ray recognized the bays—three garage-style doors shut against the cold. A pickup was parked in the shadow of the building, a larger diesel truck hiding further back.

The bay doors were closed and refused Ray's attempt to raise them. They were either locked or frozen shut. He tried the metal door to the left of the bays. It was open.

Inside, two of the three stalls were occupied by ailing vehicles. The workshop area was cluttered with hydraulic tools and winches, and to the side, a door led to a small office. A fluorescent tube over a tool bench provided the only light. Hoists hung motionless over the stalls.

"Hello?"

Ray listened for a response. Wind. The electric ticking of a space heater. Metal creaking. He started for the office. As he opened the door there was a mechanical click. "Hello? Mr. Driscoll?" Between the gusts Ray could hear the blood pulsing through his ears. And . . . breathing? His own? Or . . .

"Hello?"

He found the light switch and flicked it. The office was tiny, an 8 x 8 space with a makeshift desk and chair. The desk was cluttered with automotive manuals, candy wrappers, screw drivers, an oil rag, empty pop cans. In the corner was a suitcase marked: FIRST AID. The center of the room was occupied by a wounded generator. The back had been pried off of the boxy unit and wires trailed out.

Ray was in the process of kneeling to inspect the generator when he heard something. A thud. The wind? Or was it a footstep? His hand instinctively reached for his revolver and found nothing but air. He swore at this. The pistol and its holster were back in Barrow. He selected a large wrench, turned, and took three careful steps back into the shop. His eyes scanned the shadows for movement.

"Hello?"

The wind assaulted the building again, causing the metal to groan in protest. Ray laughed at this. Spooked by the storm, the dark, the hellishly isolated camp. He set the wrench down on the bench and chided himself for letting his imagination affect his judgment. Grandfather's talk of ghouls and ghosties, and a lack of sleep, had obviously gotten to him. He was on edge. Ready to do battle against the wind. If he wasn't careful, he might whack some poor, unsuspecting oil worker in a vain attempt to ward off an unseen and nonexistent evil. He took a deep breath. "Get a grip," he muttered.

Facing toward the entrance, he heard a cracking sound and managed to take one step before something jumped out at him. It hummed out of the darkness with smooth efficiency, streaking toward his head. Ray was in good shape and had quick reflexes. As a youth, he had won several ribbons in the Eskimo Olympics and in the years since, had managed to maintain a regimen of physical training, but none of that helped. There simply wasn't time to react. The attack was too swift, wholly unexpected. In the instant before impact, his brain recognized what was happening but was impotent to direct his body to act. He couldn't duck or bob away, only bend slightly to accept the blow on the top of the head. Thankfully, the hard hat was still there, secure beneath his parka hood.

Ray felt the collision, noted the accompanying arrival of intense pain, and reeled, his legs wobbling. Before he collapsed, the room seemed to explode in light: stars and fireworks performing a shimmering dance. An electric mist descended. Purple, red, flaming orange and brilliant golden hues draped themselves over him like gentle wraiths attending a fallen spirit, as consciousness slipped away.

➤➤ TEN ◀◀

LIGHT . . .

He longed for it, thirsted for it, was searching desperately for it, an instinctive reaction to the endless night that had eclipsed all matter, threatening to consume him.

Alone in the *umiak*, he pulled at an oar, fighting the current. He could feel the boat surging forward, meeting resistance, falling back, drifting into oblivion. He was losing the battle.

Weary arms fought to maintain the rhythm, stroking, resting, stroking . . . eyes scanning the future for light. Had he been floating for minutes? Days? Years?

There was a splash, icy droplets tickling his cheek. He heard it surface, something large, something alive, breath escaping in a whoosh. Another splash. Fine crystals stinging his face. Reaching a trembling hand over the side, he felt it: wet skin, smooth and cold.

"Where is it?" he implored.

"What do you seek?" a deep voice responded.

"Day . . . the Light."

"Of the deep, I know much. Of the Day, I am ignorant."

With that, the docile leviathan slid back into the sea, taking hope with it as its fluke sank beneath the waves.

He was alone again. Alone and afraid of the night.

Hours passed. The darkness seemed to swallow him, engulfing the *umiak*, drawing him toward the edge of an interminable chasm. He had given up, despair sapping his resolve, stealing away his will to live, when the craft suddenly met solid ground. An island. It was as black as the sea, yet its stability encouraged him like a forgotten promise.

Climbing out of the boat, he stood facing east, waiting—for what, he knew not. Then it happened.

Light . . .

Ghostly at first. Dim, slender rays climbing the horizon. They multiplied magically, dividing, swelling, illuminating a dead, slumbering world.

When the orb appeared, a rounded sliver balanced on the taut line of frozen water, it seemed to sing, to call the world to life, golden shafts urging the universe to celebrate.

He smiled at it, squinting into the circle of fire as it rose, hovering upward, into the cloudless, passionately orange canopy. Loneliness and terror fled, chased away by laughter. His mission plain, his hope restored, he took his seat in the *umiak* and turned the bow east, toward the warmth, toward his destiny . . . toward the sun.

Light . . .

"Is he dead?"

The light became more intense with each confident stroke.

"No. He's breathing. Got a pulse."

The sun expanded, Day reaching to embrace him.

"Good thing he was wearing a hard hat."

Heat . . . Intense heat . . .

"Lucky as heck. Otherwise his skull'd be bashed clean in."

Fire . . . Throbbing . . . Pain!

"Officer Attla? Can you hear me?"

Ray blinked, squinted, his eyesight weak. He was still floating, the world weaving, images merging. Light glared at him. The fire returned, flames licking at his head. Pain! He clamped his eyes shut against it.

"His neck doesn't seem to be broken. Back looks okay."

"Let's get him up," a voice advised.

He felt himself rising, limp arms draped over phantom shoulders, shaky legs supported by invisible angels. He wondered if he were dead. The sharp stabs of electricity pulsing across his temples assured him that he was not. Maybe he had reached the sun. Maybe this was his reward.

"Here. Let's put him on the workbench."

"What happened?" He regretted the question even as it left his lips. Waves of harsh, pounding grief crashed over him, beating against his forehead, threatening to dislodge his eyes from their sockets.

"You went one on one with a winch," a southern voice drawled.

"And lost," another informed him.

"Where am I?"

"The shop."

He looked up at a blurry outline of Goofy: buck teeth; dull, stupid expression. Huckleberry Hound was next to him— silly, felt ears, slack jaw. Slowly, the faces took on definition, edges hardening until they became flesh. Billy Bob and the driller were hunched over him, thick heads highlighted by the hanging, fluorescent lamp above them.

Ray glanced around, half expecting to see the sun, the sea, the *umiak* . . . They were gone. But not the pain. It was still there, more real than ever.

A third man, someone Ray didn't recognize, entered the frame above him. He was older, with graying sideburns, and wore an expression of serious concern. Reaching a hand up, he pulled at Ray's eyelids, examining the pupils again under the beam of a flashlight. "Responsive," he grunted. "He'll survive."

The new face exited the frame. Glass clanked. The face returned and began applying something to Ray's brow. It stung.

"Am I cut?"

"Yeah. Not from the winch, though. From the fall after the fact." Paper rattled. The man produced a square bandage and taped it into place above Ray's right eye. "There. You're as good as new."

Ray raised himself to a sitting position. His skull punished him by beating out a new, more energetic cadence. The room dimmed, a flurry of sparkles encroaching upon the outer edges of his vision. He cringed, shaking them away.

"Man . . . my head . . ." he muttered.

"Yeah," the amateur doctor grunted, nodding. "It'll hurt pretty bad for a few hours, maybe even a day or so. Probably feel like you really tied one on. But you'll live." He handed Ray a small, plastic bottle. "These'll help," he promised, closing the first-aid kit. "But go easy. They're prescription strength. Knock you on your butt if you're not careful."

Ray fought with the top, cursed it. When he finally managed to pry off the lid, he shook out three tablets and tossed them into his mouth, gulping them down without water.

"Might want to see a doctor when you get back to Barrow. Just in case you've got a concussion or something." With that, the Slope's answer to Marcus Welby pulled the hood of his parka up and left the shop.

"What are you trying to do? Double our insurance rates?" Simpson, who had apparently just arrived, asked.

"Don't worry. I won't sue," Ray replied. He reached a tentative hand up and pressed his bandage gingerly.

After removing his hood and mask, Simpson glanced about the room, at the system of pulleys and hoists overhead, at Ray, at the dried blood on the gray, concrete floor, making a mental assessment of the event. "Beaned by the lift, huh? Those things can really crack your noggin."

Ray studied the chain and the mechanical components. They looked guilty but unrepentant, proud of the number they had done on his head.

"That's why we wear these blasted things," Simpson told him, rapping on his hard hat with a mitten-clad fist. "Not the first time something like that has happened, you know."

"These things try to kill people on a regular basis?" Ray asked. He could feel the pills working already, dulling the pain slightly and giving him the curious sensation of falling backward through space.

As Simpson continued blathering, spouting something about OSHA regulations and safety precautions, Ray recalled the dream. The plot elements returned to his mind in flashes of clarity. He realized that they were from another of Grandfather's old stories—a legend about how a brave young man had captured the sun for his people, bringing Day to the Eskimo. That he had dreamed about folklore was a little disturbing, but understandable. He had grown up on the stories. That he had been the main character, that was downright weird. At least Margaret hadn't made a cameo appearance this time. At least she hadn't risen from the sea in the form of an evil sea monster and chased him toward the sun, snapping at his boat.

". . . it's a wonder we can work at all." Simpson followed this with a curse. "Government agencies, they'll be the death of us."

"You say this has happened before?" Ray asked, attempting to stand. His knees buckled and he latched onto Billy Bob in an effort to avoid performing another face plant.

"Whoa, there, partner!"

"You sure you're okay?" Simpson wondered, eyeing him suspiciously.

"Yeah." He released his grip on Billy Bob and took two halting steps. "See?" The room seemed to twirl and bob around him. "About the hoists . . ."

"Right. When the mechanics finish a job," Simpson explained, "they pull the hoists back and hook them over here." He pointed to a row of metal prongs. "So they can get the vehicles out. They're supposed to lock them down. Sometimes, actually, usually, they get busy and forget. Problem is, in real cold weather, like we got this time of year, the metal gets brittle." He stepped to the prongs and reached up to finger the third prong. Unlike the others, it was sheered off. Crouching, he ran a mitten over the floor. "Here you go." He offered them the shard of metal. "Prong snapped. The winch came whizzing down. And you happened to be standing in exactly the wrong place when it did. Bad luck."

"Yeah. Guess so." Ray was satisfied with that. Sort of. The only other explanation involved purposeful violence— that someone had actually attempted to kill him. In the absence of motive, that seemed farfetched. Or at least, Ray hoped it was.

"Here." Billy Bob handed him the hard hat.

Ray examined the shell before putting it back on. It was made out of a tough plastic and fiberglass material. There was a black scuff, presumably where the hoist had collided with it, but otherwise it was undamaged, no crease, no dent, nothing. Ray silently thanked it, thanked the *tuungak,* even thanked Margaret's white God that the barrier had been in place as he remounted it on his head. The blue hat was his savior, the only reason Ray was still among the living.

Simpson led them out of the shop and across the darkened yard toward the camp building. The wind was gusting from the south now, pushing them back on their heels. It was just after nine a.m., but the sky above was an ebony mask. Snow assaulted them, pelting their parkas, playing at their hoods.

When they reached the office, Simpson lifted the phone. "I'll call Prudhoe. They got a nurse over there. She can check you."

"What about Driscoll?" Ray submitted. His own voice sounded distant, foreign.

"Huh?"

"I was looking for the drill foreman, Driscoll, when the winch snuck up on me. We still need to talk to him."

Simpson seemed puzzled by this. "Should be on the rig floor. Or in the doghouse. I'll have someone check." He looked to Billy Bob. "Can you run him to Prudhoe?"

"I'm fine," Ray argued. He wasn't fine. He was flying, a human plane spinning out of control. The pain had receded, replaced by a groggy, growing sense of euphoria. He felt like he was accelerating upward, out of his boots. The walls of the office seemed to be in on the joke. They were extending skyward, getting taller. "Find Driscoll."

"Okay," Simpson grunted.

When the supervisor had left to attend to the chore, Ray reached for the phone. As he dialed, Billy Bob asked, "Ya sure yer okay?" The cowboy stared into Ray's face. "Yer eyes look funny."

"I'm fine," Ray repeated. He sank into Simpson's chair, cradling the receiver to his ear as his stomach threatened to convulse. "Just kind of woozy. That's all."

The line rang twice before a woman answered. "Barrow Police Department."

"Betty?"

"Hey there, Ray. You still out on the ice with that popsicle murder?"

"Yeah," he sighed.

"How's it comin'?"

He blinked away another wave of nausea. "Oh . . . kinda slow."

"Nobody confessed, huh?"

"Not yet. The captain in?"

"Hang on a sec."

"I think Mr. Simpson's right, Ray," Billy Bob drawled. "I think you oughta let me run ya to Prudhoe. Let the doctor give ya the once over."

Ray considered this. It was probably the smart thing to do, if only to rule out a concussion. He was about to answer the deputy when he noticed the computer screen at the center of Simpson's desk. It was glowing, moving, drifting to the right. The desk was caught in the same invisible current. The entire room seemed intent upon slipping away from Ray.

There was a rattle on the line, then, "Attla?"

"Yes, sir."

"What do you have for me?"

"Not much, sir. We questioned the men who found the body. And we showed the sketch of the victim around."

"No ID?"

"No, sir. No one seems to know how he wound up in the pipe. No one recognizes him. The going bet is that he was already in the casing when it showed up in camp."

"You buy that?"

"I don't know. Without an autopsy, it's hard to . . ." His words trailed off, and with them, his concentration trickled away.

"Attla?" the Captain prodded. "What's the matter? You alright?"

"I had a little accident."

"What sort of accident?"

"A bonk on the head. But I'm fine."

"You need to come home? I could send Lewis. Be a real pain in the neck logistically, air traffic's still grounded, but we could arrange something. Cat train him over there maybe—''

''No,'' Ray protested. ''I'll stick it out.''

''You sure?''

''Yeah. I'm sure.'' In truth, he wasn't sure. His head was throbbing and spinning, the pain a dull, faraway threat. He was exhausted, hungry, and sick to his stomach at the same time, disoriented, void of ambition. Returning to Barrow, to his own bed, to Margaret . . . It was tempting. But the trip itself would be a bear. And more importantly, he still had a job to perform. Ray wasn't a workaholic. He wasn't obsessive with his vocation. Still, he was dedicated, determined to finish what he had started. Grandfather had instilled that in him: a strong sense of duty and honor. Margaret called it a stubborn streak. Whatever it was, it would not allow him to simply give up and quit.

''Okay, then, what next? Got any other leads?''

''Not really,'' Ray answered, ''but I was thinking about heading to Prudhoe. Maybe somebody over there could ID the victim for us.'' He purposefully left out the part about seeing a doctor.

''Good idea. I been on the horn to the Davis people all morning. They're in a swivet. Got some bigwig corporate execs coming in for an important meeting as soon as the weather clears. The locals are in a panic. Maybe you can settle them down a bit.''

''I'll try. Call you from Prudhoe.''

As he hung up the phone, Simpson reappeared. ''No luck. Nobody seems to know where Driscoll is.''

''Didya try his room?'' Billy Bob asked.

Simpson nodded. ''Not there. Not at the rig.'' He shrugged at them.

''Keep looking,'' Ray instructed. He gestured to the sketch. ''And keep showing that around.''

Simpson nodded. ''Will do.''

''What now?'' Billy Bob asked.

''Head to Prudhoe, I guess,'' Ray offered without enthusiasm.

The deputy's bunny teeth made an unscheduled appearance. "I'll go warm up the Explorer."

"I'll go with you," Ray said. "We can load the body."

Billy Bob made a face at this. "He'll melt with the heater going."

Ray shook his head. "We'll put him in my sled."

"But . . . I'm not sure I can hook it to my truck."

Ray could see the cowboy struggling to envision this. "I'll tow it," he added. "Behind my machine."

"Wait a minute. You ain't plannin' to . . ."

"I'll follow you." In response to the disapproving look he said, "I've been driving snow machines since I could walk. Prudhoe's only what? Forty-five minutes? I could drive it in my sleep."

Billy Bob's scowl only intensified. Simpson muttered something and rubbed his flattop.

"I'll need some fuel. Unleaded."

"Pump's in the third shed," Simpson told him with a sigh.

"Okay." Ray stood and zipped his parka. The room grew fuzzy, wavered, then came back into focus. "Let's go."

The deputy held his ground. "I don't know . . ."

"Don't worry about me," Ray said. He was wobbly but surprisingly alert, a fresh surge of energy engulfing him. He felt like he had just downed a half dozen cups of strong coffee. "I'm fine. Really! Come on. Let's load that corpse and get out of here."

⟫➤ ELEVEN ⫷⟪

IT WAS LIKE navigating through a sea of oil: thick, liquid curtains of black pushing in from above, from the sides. The only points of reference were the beam of the Polaris, a weak shaft of light illuminating a few short feet of ice and snow, and the ruby taillights of Billy Bob's Explorer twenty yards ahead.

Ray glanced at the speedometer: 30. They were plodding along, fighting a gale-force head wind, sliding blindly down the lumpy, slick haul road. At this rate they wouldn't reach the Davis main camp in Prudhoe before noon, which might not be all bad, he decided. Maybe he would feel better by then. The combination of movement, lack of a discernible horizon, and subzero temperature wasn't helping his situation. He had already thrown up once, and he was about ready to take another break. He could feel his stomach knotting up. At least his head had stopped pounding. It felt fat now, his thoughts dull.

He was certainly in no condition to evaluate his future or analyze his upcoming marriage. But in the absence of visual stimulation or mental distraction, his mind seemed obsessed with the subject. As he gazed through his goggles into the howling, vacuous gulf, he silently listed the negatives. First, and most importantly, was Margaret's personality. She was aggressive and strong-willed. She liked to be in control. These were traditionally masculine character traits. Was he getting himself into a situation where he would wind up in a sub-

missive role? Did marrying her mean sacrificing his manhood?

Ray followed the curving haul road, eyes transfixed on the
ghostly taillights of the Explorer. Second, she was a modern
woman, almost a feminist. She wanted her own identity. Her
own job. He admired her ambition, but in some ways, her
"career" was a slap in the face, proof that he could not support them, that his job wasn't good enough, that *he* wasn't
good enough.

None of that mattered, Ray knew. The list of nitpicky reasons not to marry Margaret could have filled a book and he
still would have disregarded them for one simple truth: he
loved her. That was the bottom line. In fact, the so-called
"negatives" were some of the things he loved most about
her. He loved that she was spirited, that she seldom backed
down, even when facing off against a man. He loved that she
was independent, that she was fiery, zealous, often unstop-
pable. He loved her, loved her with every fiber of his being,
and knew that he always would. And he was certain that life
apart from her would be empty, without purpose or joy. She
possessed his heart.

So the question wasn't whether or not to merge his soul
with Margaret's. The question was how to make the integra-
tion smooth and permanent. Beyond her penchant for a more
modern worldview, something Ray tended to embrace just as
readily, there was still the issue of religion. Margaret believed
in the white man's God. She had become interested in Jesus,
the Jewish savior, in college while attending a predominantly
native church. Ray had gone with her a couple of times and
been nonplussed. He failed to see the draw. But Margaret had
become a convert, a Christian, and was committed to raising
their children according to the tenants of that faith. Ray
wasn't sure how he felt about that. What about Inupiat cus-
toms and traditions? Would their children grow up without a
sense of who they were, who their elders were, what their
culture was?

Ray shook off the array of perplexing questions, consoling
himself with the conviction that everything would work out.
Satisfied for the moment, he shifted his hazy thoughts to

something more imminently troubling: the murder.

Ahead of him a furious gust drove the snow pellets into a frenzy. Glowing beads flew past horizontally, then whirled, consuming the Explorer and leaving Ray without direction. It was a fitting picture of the case, he decided as he let up on the throttle and squinted to find the edges of the road. He was without direction—no clues, no theories, no real strategy. His only recourse was to keep going, to follow standard procedures, to ask questions, seek answers, wait for a solution to present itself.

Despite the absence of light and warmth, his head seemed to be clearing slightly. Maybe thoughts of love had worked some miracle cure, he mused. Whatever the reason, he felt more able to consider the facts.

A man had been murdered: shot, cut like an animal, stuffed into a pipe. His body had been discovered at a remote ice rig as the crew was in the process of setting casing. The man was a suit, an executive. No one knew him. The obvious explanation was that the victim had been killed elsewhere, at the main camp perhaps, his corpse hidden in the pipe. In order to determine who had killed him, three questions had to be answered. First, who was he? That bit of information might help with motive. It was tough to figure out why a man had been murdered when his identity was a mystery. Second, why had the body been desecrated? Shooting someone was one thing. Slitting the worm and attempting to sever the head, that was something else altogether. Why treat a man as if he were a bear? Third, why had the body been hidden? If you were going to take the time and effort to slice and dice someone, why dump them in a pipe with the job only half finished? Because you were in a hurry? Because someone showed up unexpectedly while you were in the middle of it? Because you didn't want the man to be found anytime soon?

The mental problem-solving session served to bring back Ray's headache. His sight was clearer now, his thinking crisp, but the pounding was returning. Apparently the pills were wearing off. He considered taking another set, before the pain peaked, but decided against it. Better to remain alert and experience some hurt than sleepwalk through this case.

Ray suddenly realized that the Explorer had not reappeared. Twisting the throttle, he decided it was time to catch it. The needle on the frost-encrusted speedometer jerked to 36, 43, 47 . . . Nothing. No Ford. No Billy Bob. They were somewhere beyond the stubby headlight beam. The needle trembled up to 50. Ray's head swung from side to side, checking the drifts that comprised the shoulders of the road. He was still on it, still headed, presumably, toward Prudhoe.

Ray was about to goose the machine when he saw something. A blink of light. It was colorless but could have been the Explorer. Before he could find out, the Polaris coughed and sputtered, like a horse that had been ridden too hard and was giving up the race. Ray twisted the throttle in a vain attempt to maintain the machine's momentum. It was useless. The engine continued to sputter for another thirty seconds, barking in protest before dying completely. The skis slid to a halt and, as if to punctuate the extent of the snow mobile's problem, the headlight went out.

The darkness was absolute. Ray cursed at it, swore at the Polaris, and dismounted. Feeling his way back to the sled, he found his tool chest and switched on a flashlight. It was a joke. The tiny bulb barely lit up the end of the plastic tube. Holding it an inch from the chest, he fished for tools with which to resurrect the dead machine. The way it had sputtered made him think it might be something to do with the carburetor. Stuffing two screwdrivers and a socket set into his parka, he trudged back to the snow mobile. Even with a neoprene mask, his nose was cold.

Balancing the flashlight on the dash, he lifted the miniature hood and inspected the engine. It was already cool and if he didn't manage to get it running in the next hour or so, the oil would be reduced to the consistency of chilled molasses.

Poking a screwdriver into the nest of wires and hoses, he reflected on his plight. Stranded, alone, in one heck of a bad storm. If the machine was beyond repair, he could survive, thanks to the emergency supplies in the sled, but it wouldn't be fun.

Yep, carburetor. Ray removed it, fiddled with it, called it a derogatory name, tossed it into the darkness.

Where was Billy Bob? Had the idiot just gone off and left him? Probably too busy listening to country hits in that heated cab to look back or even give Ray another thought. The cowboy would tootle into Prudhoe and wait, drinking coffee at the Davis camp until Ray showed.

He went back to the sled and dug through the boxes. Twenty minutes later he had assembled a replacement carburetor from two Snow Cat relics. As he was in the process of attaching the transplant, he wondered why he was bothering. The oil was sludge by now. The chances of the Polaris even starting, much less running, were slim to none. With the carburetor in place, he tried anyway. The first turn of the key made the machine shimmy. A puff of smoke exploded from the tailpipe. That was something. But the successive turns were silent—not so much as a click. Dead in the water. Or more precisely, dead on the ice.

Slamming the hood, he gazed up and down the road, at black nothingness. It would be just his luck that a truck would come roaring along and squash his rig, turning the Polaris into a metal pancake. He bent and began pushing the machine toward the shoulder. Grunting at the effort, he managed to burrow it into the edge of the right-hand drift. Next he slumped to the sled and opened a black plastic crate. It contained a down sleeping bag, a one-man snow tent, a thermal pad, a compact white-gas stove, a steel pot, several cans of beans, a can opener, knife. He pulled a waterproof tarp from the nylon tent sack and struggled to wrap it around the front end of the sled. The wind made this almost impossible, kicking at the corners and threatening to lift the tarp up and away, into the invisible sky.

When the tarp was in place, forming a thin, makeshift barrier against the wind, Ray crawled into the bed of the sled, pressed out the insulating mat, and wriggled into the down bag. The bag was reportedly good to 70 below zero, the mat to 85 below, the parka even lower. Yet Ray could feel the icy wood against his back as if he were lying there in nothing but a flannel shirt. The corpse didn't seem to mind the accommodations. Lying close enough to touch, the plastic-enshrouded lump of deep-frozen flesh and bones was without complaint. Ray rapped it with a knuckle. The man, whoever he turned out to be, was more than just dead. He was rock hard. He could just as well have been made of marble. The perfect companion for a situation like this, Ray decided. An inanimate statue that didn't argue about who's fault this was.

Staring into the noisy black void of wind, snow, and angry nylon, he outlined a plan of action. He would be fine like this for another couple of hours. After that, if no one showed up, he would need to break out the tent and crank up the stove. That would hold him for the rest of the afternoon. If he wasn't found by evening, he might need to take more extreme measures, build an ice house, burn part of the sled, begin worrying about hypothermia and frostbite. Wouldn't that be a hoot for old Billy Bob: an honest to goodness Ezkeemo holed up in an honest to goodness igloo!

Ray could feel the cold stalking him, watching him, bending low, draping itself over him like a garment. The tips of his fingers were tingling. His nose was numb. So were his toes. Despite the layer of air in his bunny boots, his ankles were stiff. His other joints, elbows and knees, seemed to have run out of lubricant and were reluctant to swing. Maybe he wouldn't last an hour. Maybe he needed the tent now, before he too became an ice sculpture.

He was trying to decide how to set it up in the wind, where to set it up, what to anchor it to, when he heard it. The sound blended with the storm at first, but its rhythm soon distinguished itself. The volume rose. It was manmade. Mechanical. A vehicle. The tarp became visible, illuminated from behind.

Ray scooted out of the sled, tripped, and clumsily rolled, prostrating himself before a blinding light. He was still in the sleeping bag, a down-filled worm begging for mercy at the throne of a mysterious, unknown god. His cheek stung. He had skinned it in the fall and when it thawed it would smart. Lifting his head, he gazed up at the light.

Something clicked, steel sliding against steel. As Ray fought to extricate himself from the bag, he heard steps, boots on snow. The wind relaxed for an instant and a truck materialized. The grill was less than five yards from Ray, the word

Toyota written in brilliant chrome. The tires were enormous, pitted with studs to give it traction on the ice. It had two wings, open doors. They slammed shut simultaneously.

Another gust arrived, beating the snow with renewed fury. The pellets responded by performing a frantic dance. More crunching. Two shadows stepped into the headlight beams. Still on the ground, Ray examined their boots. Sorrels. One pair was big: size 11 or 12. The other was even bigger: 15+. All new. All expensive. Deluxe arctic attire.

"Having a problem?"

Hands gripped his shoulders, lifting him to his feet. He blinked at the hooded figures. "Yeah. Who are—?"

"Davis Oil Security," a deep voice responded.

"You Officer Attla?" another asked.

"Yeah."

"Got a call. Said you might be lost out here."

"Not lost. But stranded. My machine conked out."

"Get in the truck. Warm up. We'll figure out a way to tow your rig."

Ray started to object, to insist that he'd help. But the fire attacking his toes and fingers convinced him otherwise. "Okay." He hurried to the truck and climbed into the back. It was a five-seater with a small cargo bay. The heater was pumping enthusiastically, the air suffocatingly warm. Ray began pulling off layers: mittens, liners, goggles, mask.

Outside, the two men studied the snow mobile for a moment, gestured to each other, then began pushing it toward the truck. A few minutes later, they had the machine up in the sled and the sled hooked to the truck via a chain.

As they got into the Toyota, the driver cursed. "Nasty stuff," he exclaimed, slamming the door. He toggled the windshield wipers and they began scraping at frozen lumps on the glass.

"Heck of a storm," the other agreed. He patted his hands together, then reached for a thermos. "Coffee?"

Ray nodded. "Sure." His lips were still thick and useless.

"Good thing your partner gave us a jingle," the driver said. "Otherwise, you might have been a goner."

"An Eskimo pie," the passenger added somewhat glee-fully.

Ray studied the back of the man's hood, uncertain whether he was just making conversation or being intentionally offensive. Probably the former. These guys probably didn't even know he was a Native. Retracting his own hood, he gazed into the rearview mirror.

The driver glanced up, surprise registering in his eyes. He swore softly. "He didn't mean anything."

"Huh?" The passenger turned to hand Ray his coffee. "Oh . . . oops. No offense, man."

"No problem." He accepted the cup and cradled it between his legs, bathing his bare hands in the steam.

The driver took the radio mike and thumbed the button. "Pilgrim-two, this is Pilgrim-one. How do you copy?"

After a burst of static, a voice replied, "Four by four, Pilgrim-one. What's your ten-twenty?"

"On the haul road about thirty minutes out. We got the package and we're on our way home."

"Roger, that. See you back at camp. Pilgrim-two, out."

The man in the shotgun seat removed his hood revealing a severe, bleach-blond crewcut. Even with the parka on, it was clear that he was a bodybuilder, wide, impressive shoulders, almost no neck. He looked Scandinavian. A towheaded Arnold Schwarzenegger.

The driver had short, dark hair that accentuated an angular, weather-worn face. His eyes were narrow and intense. He reminded Ray of a military drill sergeant.

"Hear they had a murder up at seventeen," the driver said. He eyed Ray in the mirror.

"Yeah."

"Sounded kind of . . . grizzly."

"Yeah."

"Got any suspects?" Musclepig asked.

"No. Not yet."

"Figure out who it was that got killed?" the driver wanted to know.

Ray shook his head. "Nope." He ripped open a Velcro pocket on his parka and removed a folded copy of the sketch.

Handing it into the front seat, he asked, "Recognize this face?"

Musclepig squinted at it, grunted, "Huh-uh," gave it to the driver.

"Looks a little like that VP from Houston. What was his name?"

Taking the sketch back for another look, Musclepig muttered, "You mean . . . uh . . . Weinhart?"

"Yeah!"

"Mmm . . . I don't know." Musclepig frowned. "Maybe."

"You know him?" Ray asked, leaning across the seat.

The driver shrugged. "Could be a suit from Houston. Vice President of . . . Domestic Services, I think."

"Davis has got dozens of veeps," Musclepig grumbled. "Everything from accounting to toilet management."

"His name is Weinhart?" Ray asked.

"Yeah. Hal or . . . Harry . . ."

"Hank," Musclepig suggested.

"That doesn't sound right. Anyway, his last name's Weinhart." The driver shot another glance at the sketch. "There's a resemblance. Except . . ."

"Except what?"

"Except this is a picture of the stiff, right?"

"Right."

"So it can't be Weinhart."

"Why's that?"

"All the wheels left yesterday morning," Musclepig told him. "They took the company jet out of Deadhorse. Got out just before this storm hit. Lucky bums."

"And Weinhart was on the plane?"

"Yep." The driver downshifted to navigate through a section of deteriorated ice. "At least, he was supposed to be."

➤➤ TWELVE ◆◀

A TREMENDOUS BLAST of wind found the Forerunner and they were suddenly traveling sideways, studded tires grating angrily against the ice. The vehicle rocked wildly on groaning shocks and threatened to perform a 180.

The driver responded nonchalantly, twisting the wheel to counter the spin. When the Toyota was under control again, he said, "Didn't properly introduce myself. I'm Tom Reynolds. Head of security for Davis." Turning in his seat he offered a hand.

Ray shook it. The grip was firm, confident, a fitting complement to Reynolds's demeanor.

"Greg Leeland," Musclepig said. His hand was large, the thick, sausagelike fingers and fleshy palm threatening to crush Ray's hand. Leeland was not the kind of guy you wanted as an enemy. Ray wondered if a carbine would so much as slow this horse-of-a-man down.

"You're out of Barrow, huh?" Reynolds asked, eyes on the sheets of snow assailing the glistening haul road.

"Yeah."

"Is that where you're from?" Leeland asked. "I mean . . . I know you're a—a—a . . . But are you from Barrow?"

"No. I grew up in Nuiqsut."

"Huh. Never heard of it."

"West of here about seventy miles," Reynolds reported. "As the crow flies."

"Right." Ray was warm now, his cheek stinging, the

wound on his head throbbing. "What about you guys?"

"I'm from Fairbanks," Reynolds said. "Grew up there, served at Eielson Airforce Base. Greg here's from Washington."

"D.C.?"

"No. State. I was born in Ballard. Lived in Seattle until about two years ago."

Ray looked out the side window. The glass was wet inside the cab, frozen outside. "What brought you guys to the Slope?"

"Money," Leeland replied. He flashed Ray a Cheshire cat smile. "Big money. No other reason we'd come to this god-forsaken armpit."

Ray waited, wondering if either of them would catch the insult in the remark and realize that this "godforsaken armpit" was his home—the land of his people.

"I don't know how them Eskimos can . . ." Leeland's voice trailed off. Bing! "Oh . . . Uh . . . Hey, man, uh . . ."

"You'll have to forgive Greg, here," Reynolds advised in a fatherly tone. "He suffers from foot-in-mouth disease."

Obviously, Ray thought. He'd had enough chitchat and was ready to get back to the business at hand. "Deputy Cleaver called you guys?"

Reynolds nodded. "Yep. Said the two of you were headed down from seventeen and he lost you somewhere along the way."

"He say why he didn't come back for me?" Ray asked, trying to mask his anger.

"The deputy had car trouble too," Leeland reported. "Slid off the road about two miles from camp. A truck was pulling him out when we left to find you."

"I appreciate the lift," Ray told them. He began working his feet out of the bunny boots. "Mr. Simpson, the supervisor up on the rig, he said you guys were supposed to come up this morning, to check out the body, assess the situation . . ."

"We were," Reynolds grunted. "The response plan was to send the whole security crew up with the emergency medical team. Problem was, the EMTs high-centered about ten minutes out of Prudhoe. The idiots were in an all-wheel drive van." He shook his head at this. "If it ain't a four-by-four, it shouldn't be up here. That's my opinion."

"We spent three hours getting them out of the drift," Leeland lamented. "We're talking cold. Darn cold. Nearly frostbit my . . ."

"By then," Reynolds interrupted, "visibility was in the toilet. Zero, if that. And we got the report that the body at seventeen wasn't in need of medical assistance. The man was dead. So Red called us back to camp and told us to wait out the storm."

"Red?"

"Mr. Bauer, supervisor of Davis operations on the Slope," Leeland said. "Everybody calls him Red."

"You'll see why when you meet him," Reynolds said.

"Maybe he could tell us about Weinhart. Whether he was on that plane or not."

"I can find that out for you right now," Reynolds announced. "Or at least, get the ball rolling." He reached for the radio mike. "Home Sweet Home, this is Pilgrim-one. How do you copy?"

As the static surged, keeping time with the wind, Leeland told Ray, "Tom here is ex-Marine. Came up with all the code names himself. If you couldn't tell."

Reynolds ignored this. When there was no response on the radio, he tried again. "Home Sweet Home, this is Pilgrim-one. How do you copy?"

Five seconds later a tiny voice responded through the audio noise. "Pilgrim-one, this is Home Sweet Home. I read you, but just barely. Try another channel."

Reynolds reached for the radio. "Switching to channel twelve." He twisted a knob, then repeated his mantra. "Home Sweet Home, this is Pilgrim-one. How do you copy?"

"Better," a clearer voice said. "Not perfect, but I can actually hear you now, Tom."

"Grace?"

"Yeah. What's your location, Tom?"

"We're about . . ."—he let his thumb up and asked Leeland—"You see the cut off to ARCO yet?"

"No. But that doesn't mean we haven't been by it."

"We're maybe five miles out—give or take. It's hard to tell. But we're creeping our way home."

"Did you find the missing police officer?"

"Ten-four. Got him in the backseat. He's fine. Listen, Grace, I need you to get Houston on the horn. Have them fax a passenger list for the company jet—the one that left Prudhoe yesterday A.M. See who was on it."

"I can tell you that. Three VPs, the regional director, and Mr. Parker, the manager of California/Alaska operations. The only exec who hung around was Makintanz."

"*Chief* Makintanz?" Ray wondered aloud.

Reynolds nodded. "I know the whole gang was supposed to be on the plane, Grace. But we need to know who actually got on board in Deadhorse and who got off down south."

"Okay. Give me a few minutes. I'll try to have that for you by the time you get here."

"Oh, and Grace? You know Weinhart, the VP? What's his first name?"

"Hank," she replied without hesitation.

"Told you," Leeland said.

"Thanks. See you in fifteen. Pilgrim-one out."

"Home Sweet Home, out," Grace's distant voice replied.

Ray watched Reynolds replace the mike, then asked, "What's Chief Makintanz have to do with Davis Oil?"

Leeland blew air at this. "Everything."

When there was no further explanation, he prodded, "Everything?"

"Makintanz is on the board of directors," Reynolds said. He was gripping the steering wheel with both hands, concentrating on staying on the road.

"Since when?"

"Since about . . . oh, maybe a month ago."

"How'd Davis ever convince Makintanz to sit on their board?"

"Money," Reynolds replied.

Ray considered this. "Money? The chief may be greedy, but . . . He's been giving the oil companies a hard time for years. Isn't his son-in-law still the president of Arctic Slope Regional?"

Reynolds nodded.

The Arctic Slope Regional Corporation, or ASRC, was a Native corporation, one of thirteen that had been formed under the Alaska Native Claims Settlement Act of 1971. The purpose of the corporations was to manage the money and land bestowed on the Natives by the government. In Ray's mind, the Native corps were on one side of the fray; British Petroleum, Arco, Exxon, Davis and the rest of the oil interests on the other. The former acted as a landlord—protecting the environment while accepting a healthy "lease fee." The latter was relegated to the role of renter, paying handsomely for the privilege of sucking crude oil from beneath the permafrost.

"Guy's playing both sides of the deal," Leeland observed.

Still nodding, Reynolds added, "He's tight with a group that manages the Slope. You know he's gotta be raking in the bucks, especially since ASRC just raised its lease rates. They're making the oil companies pay big time to get their petroleum. And at the same time, he's getting a big fat paycheck from Davis, just for riding the jet down to Houston and promising to make the annual shareholder meetings."

"I can't decide if they hired him for his clout or his skin," Leeland grumbled. "Must look pretty good having an Eskimo at the conference table. A token *klooch,* if you know what I mean."

Ray did, and wasn't particularly fond of Leeland's choice of words. "Sounds like a conflict of interest to me."

"Exactly," Reynolds conceded. "That's what everybody thinks. Including the North Slope Borough, the FTC, the BLM, and the State of Alaska. Consequently, he's being sued by a dozen interested parties—breach of trade agreements, conflict of interest, breaking various and sundry laws."

"Why hasn't this been in the news?"

"The whole thing's been pretty hush-hush," Leeland pointed out. "Somehow they kept it out of the press mostly."

"The only reason we know is cause we work for Davis," Reynolds confessed. "The guys in camp got a pool going— how long Makintanz will be working for Davis, whether or not he'll get the shaft in court, that sort of thing. I'm betting he'll squeak through, get off clean and that much wealthier, as usual.''

"Especially with the Davis legal eagles fighting for him," Leeland added.

That Chief Roger Makintanz was experiencing legal difficulties was no surprise to Ray. The man was famous—or rather infamous—for his flamboyant, and often illegal, business ventures. Though he was Tlingit, born in Southeastern Alaska, the chief had adopted the far north as his home back in the 60s, presumably because the open, Wild West atmosphere was conducive to his wheeler-dealer lifestyle. It was a land ripe for exploitation. Head of his own tribe—a group composed solely of close relatives—Makintanz had bestowed upon himself the title of Chief and used it, along with his smooth, forked tongue to build an impressive empire of wealth and influence. In the past thirty years he had been accused of everything from real estate fraud to embezzlement to income tax evasion, yet never been convicted. Everyone in Alaska knew he was a crook, nothing more than a talented con man, a charlatan, but no one seemed able to slow his rise to power.

Makintanz had burrowed himself into the landscape like a tick, securing a place in the thick hide of the Last Frontier. He was unwelcome, yet inescapable—a pushy uncle with bad breath who had come for a visit and wouldn't leave. No one liked him. The whites were jealous of the way money seemed to flock to him. The People resented his attempts to play the Eskimo, dressing in wolf parkas and mukluks, pretending to be an elder, despite his heritage. Still, he was tolerated because he served a purpose. The money he made stayed in-state, most trickling its way into Native businesses. And in recent years he had proven to be a very effective lobbyist for various Native corporations, helping to bleed more and more economic benefits from the government and the oil companies. Though he was not altruistic in the least, what was good for Chief Makintanz turned out to be, in the long run, good for the Inupiat.

Why would Davis put the chief on their board? Ray wondered. It was tantamount to making the devil a cardinal and inviting him to take an office in the Vatican. Maybe Leeland, the bigot, was right. Maybe the chief was a *token klooch*, placed on the board to bolster public image—to make Davis seem empathetic toward the Natives. Even so, why would they provide him with legal assistance? Ray was about to submit these questions to his hosts when the main camp flickered into view: a scattering of halogen lamps winking at them through driven snow.

"Home Sweet Home," Reynolds announced.

"Depressing, ain't it?" Leeland grumbled.

Actually there *was* a depressing aspect to it, especially in this weather. The camp was bigger than the one at the ice rig, but just as bleak. Despite the lights, the collection of low buildings appeared lonely and deserted in the blowing snow—drab, gray structures that could have been abandoned days, even months ago.

Ray was used to it, however. To him, it was more a scene of seasonal inactivity than of hopelessness. Barrow was every bit as lifeless in the dead of winter. At this latitude, human beings were aliens, creatures out of their element. In order to survive, they had to build cocoons, to seek out warmth and shelter and remain protected.

Understanding the circular rhythms of the land made the harsh, often brutal environment more tolerable. Recognizing that each season was limited, inevitable, and served a distinct purpose was the key. Denial of these fundamental truths led to discontent, even insanity. The Inupiat had long accepted that their world fell under a frozen spell of darkness for eight months. This was a celebrated event, an integral part of their culture. Such was the case with spring, the thaw bringing great joy to the People. Summer above the Arctic Circle was fully appreciated, perhaps more than anywhere else on the globe. The month-long growing season was honored, even as the return of fall was embraced—and with it, the approach of death.

"Least we got good facilities," Leeland was saying. "You should see the weight room." He paused to punctuate this with a curse.

Ray imagined that Leeland spent his every off-hour there,

lifting slabs of calibrated lead. It had to take several hours a day to satisfy that hyper-buff physique.

"Nautilus, free-weights," Leeland continued, his voice laden with praise.

"Is that right?"

"Chow's tops too," Reynolds said. "Davis has the best cooks on the slope. You like pastries?"

Ray nodded politely. Actually, despite his occupation, he wasn't a big donut fan.

"You're in for a treat, then," Reynolds told him. "Sticky buns, apple fritters, bear claws, eclairs . . ." He licked his lips as if he had just sampled these.

"I'm starving," Leeland panted.

They passed a wooden sign half buried in snow. The trembling placard announced their arrival at Davis Oil—Prudhoe Bay. There was no formal entrance, no fence, but the buildings formed an uneven circle, like wagons circled against an Indian attack.

Reynolds navigated across the yard, past an array of diesel trucks and pickups, before pulling to a stop in front of a wide, two-story modular. It was almost identical to the camp back at the rig—the same stocky, trailerlike outershell but incorporated more windows and occupied perhaps three or four times more square feet. A thermometer next to the door read minus 48.

"At least it's warmer here," Ray offered, gathering his gear.

As Reynolds switched off the Forerunner, he shook his head at the thermometer. "That's wrong. Off by a good ten degrees."

"Yeah," Leeland said, frowning. "Probably more like minus fifty-eight. Crank in the chill factor and it's maybe a hundred below. Cold enough to freeze your . . ."

"Come on," Reynolds urged. "We'll introduce you to Red."

"Then get some grub!" Leeland insisted.

The doors popped open and they made a dash for the entrance. As they did, Ray realized that the security guards were right. The thermometer was way off. Having neglected to redon his mask and goggles, he could feel the skin of his face freezing. When they reached the door ten seconds later, his chest was already aching from sucking frigid air directly into his unprotected windpipe.

The men hurried through the entrance, escaping into a warm, bright womb. It was more luxurious than Ray had expected: attractive tile in the entryway, generous closets with hinged wooden doors along the side walls, two paintings of wintry oil rigs adorning the back wall, a couch and chairs that looked brand new.

After discarding his cold weather attire and boots, Reynolds offered Ray a pair of polar-fleece slippers with leather soles.

Ray stared at them, puzzled.

"Take 'em. Everybody wears 'em inside. Saves wear and tear on your socks."

Leeland had already pulled his on and was waiting at the door. Having shed the bulky parka, the man magically swelled in size, his shoulders broader, his neck even less apparent.

"Ready?" Reynolds asked. Though trim and clearly in good shape, he was dwarfed by his partner.

"Yeah." Ray followed them down a carpeted hallway into a spacious atrium. It was like something in a hotel lobby: glass skylights, ferns, several couches and overstuffed armchairs. A coffee table held a neat fan of oil-industry journals and two worn copies of last year's *Sports Illustrated* swimsuit edition.

"Meet you in the office," Leeland said. "I'm gonna get some chow." He peeled off to the right, striding like a man with a purpose

After traversing another corridor, this one lined with handsome art—mostly horse-mounted cowboys gazing at distant oil rigs—Ray and Reynolds reached an outer office area where a secretary was busy on a computer. She was in her early twenties with a trim figure, an attractive face and well-kept auburn hair.

"Say, Judy. The boss in?"

When the woman looked up, her expression changed from

one of concentration to one of amusement. "Yes, he is, Tom," she replied, eyelashes batting. "I suppose you'd like to see him."

"Yes, ma'am. If he's got a minute."

"He's always got a minute for you, Tom," she said, already reaching for the phone. "Sir, Tom Reynolds is here to see you." She gave Reynolds a coy smile as she listened to the response. "Yes, sir."

"Well . . . ?"

"Go right in."

Reynolds winked at her and started for the door. Ray trailed after him, feeling slightly uncomfortable, a tagalong who wasn't privy to some private joke.

The office they entered was impressive. Unlike Simpson's crowded hovel back out on the ice, this was a large room that had been decked out in oak: bookcases, chairs, and a huge, sturdy desk. The walls were papered with a subtle texture and graced with modern art. It effectively made you forget where you were, that this was part of a trailer at Prudhoe Bay. Ray suspected that it could have passed for an executive's quarters back in Texas.

Before he had time to fully inspect the office and appreciate the various sculptures and wall hangings, a small man sprung up from the desk and strode to the middle of the room to meet them.

"Franklin Bauer," he beamed, extending his hand.

Reynolds stepped to the side, allowing Ray to accept the greeting. Bauer shook his hand enthusiastically.

"You must be Officer Attla."

"Yes, sir, Mr. Bauer."

"Call me Red. Everybody does."

Of course they do, Ray thought, nodding. It would be virtually impossible to call him anything else.

THIRTEEN

RED BAUER WAS clownish in his appearance: red hair, red shirt, speckled red tie, even his skin was tinged red with orange-red freckles. It was as if a vandal had snuck up on him and sprayed him with a can of vermilion paint. He immediately brought to mind Red Buttons, except this Red was redder. And smaller. He was a tiny man with wiry limbs and thin hands like those of a miniature mannequin.

"Wow!" Red exclaimed, his face animated. "You're pretty big for an Eskimo."

Looking down at the doll-sized man, Ray nodded. "Yeah. I guess I am."

"Have a seat." Bauer gestured to the armchairs and couch arranged in a semicircle around his desk. When he had retaken his place beyond the wide, gleaming desk, he said, "So, any progress on our little problem?"

Ray stared at him, at the cherublike face, the energetic eyes, the placid expression. Little problem? Was he serious? A corpse that had been hacked up, nearly decapitated . . . A *little* problem? "We're still investigating," Ray told him.

"I'm confident in your abilities, Officer Attla," Red beamed. "I'm sure you can wrap this thing up as quickly and quietly as possible."

Ray was about to nod his head, to humor this guy with a few police clichés. Before he could, Bauer added, "Especially since it appears that the crime in question was committed by one of your own people."

"My people?"

"An Eskimo. A Native . . . whatever." Bauer was still exuding charm, but his eyes had changed somehow. Resting above the everything-is-fine cheer and rather dopey grin, his eyes conveyed a serious, almost threatening message.

"I'm not sure I follow," Ray tried, attempting to draw Bauer out.

"We got the fax," he said, still smiling. Opening a manila folder, he lifted a single sheet and shook his head at it. The grin disappeared. Suddenly he was mourning the deceased, acknowledging the cruel way in which the man had been dispatched. "Terrible. Just terrible. Cut up that way. Just like an Eskimo cuts up an animal." His head continued swiveling, a scowl testifying to his disapproval of the tragedy. "I hate to point fingers, but it sure looks like one of your people did this."

"That's one possibility," Ray acknowledged.

"Any suspects?"

"Discounting myself?"

Bauer's eyes flashed with contempt, then the smile returned. "You know what I mean, Officer."

Ray dug the sketch out of his parka. "Recognize this face?"

Bauer glanced at it, then fished through the folder. He lifted a slightly blurred replica. "Looks a little like our VP of domestic operations, Hank Weinhart. But it couldn't be him because—"

"He flew out on the company jet two days ago," Ray interjected.

"Right."

"We're checking the passenger list, to make sure he was on the plane," Reynolds said.

Bauer nodded at this, his enthusiasm waning. "Well, rest assured that we will cooperate fully with your investigation, Officer Attla." He rose, signaling the end of the meeting. Shaking Ray's hand again, he said, "I wish you luck. We want this thing cleared up, and the truth exposed, posthaste. We also want to make sure that the press doesn't exploit this tragedy. It has to be *handled*—swiftly and diplomatically, with kid gloves. And I know you're the man to do that.''

"I appreciate your confidence,'' Ray replied, somewhat sarcastically. At the moment he wasn't certain that he was the man for the job. So far, he hadn't done much of anything to warrant such lavish praise. Aside from that, he questioned Bauer's sincerity. Apparently "find the klooch fast and keep it quiet'' was the running corporate line.

After they had been ushered out of Bauer's office, Ray asked Reynolds, "What about the passenger list?''

Reynolds nodded at this. "Grace should have that by now.'' He led them past the cute, flirtatious secretary, down the hallway and into another cluster of offices. They were entering a door marked Security when Billy Bob appeared.

"Ray! You alright?''

"Fine,'' Ray responded coolly, still irritated at having been deserted by the deputy. Even if the cowboy had slid off the road, that was no excuse for ditching his partner. Not in this weather.

"Hey, buddy, ya had me scared,'' he drawled. "When I lost ya in the snow, I stopped for a while and waited. Then, when I tried to turn around, I went off the road. Listen, I'm real sorry. It was all my fault. I screwed up.''

Ray studied Billy Bob's sullen expression, the hound-dog eyes, lips turned down to hide the buck teeth. He seemed genuinely apologetic, even guilt-ridden. "Don't worry about it. I'm okay.'' He turned to Reynolds and started to make the introductions.

Reynolds cut him off. "We've met. How you doing, Billy Bob?''

"Not bad. Better, now that I'm not stuck in the snow.''

Inside the security office, they found Leeland behind a desk, phone to his ear.

"How's the list coming?'' Reynolds asked him, sliding into his own desk.

Leeland held up a hand. "Yeah . . . Yeah . . . How much longer? Okay.'' He hung up the phone and stuffed a quarter of a sandwich into his mouth before answering. "Ten or fifteen minutes,'' he slurred through the bread. "Grace has the list but she's trying to confirm the whereabouts of all the passengers."

"Where's the body?" Billy Bob asked.

"Out front, in the sled," Ray answered.

"Maybe we should put it some-wheres," Billy Bob suggested. "In a shed or somethin'."

"Good idea," Reynolds agreed. "Help them put it in barn two," he told Leeland. With that he picked up the phone, making it clear that he wasn't going to be assisting them.

Leeland cursed, gulped down the last of his sandwich, then rose. "Come on." When the trio reached the mudroom and Ray and Billy Bob were donning their gear, Leeland said, "I can *tell* you where barn two is. It's the second medium-sized shed past—"

"The body's heavy," Billy Bob lamented. "We'll need help."

Leeland swore again and pulled on his boots. "We can drive it over, I guess."

Three minutes later, mittens, masks, and goggles in place, they stepped into the wind. It was just past one in the afternoon and the sky was effectively hiding this fact: a gray haze reflecting the lamps, a deep pitch beyond their glow. It looked like midnight during the year's worst storm. Unfortunately, it was neither.

Leeland unplugged the electrical cord connecting the engine block to the exterior outlet with a yank and hopped into the driver's seat, triggering the ignition as Ray and Billy Bob climbed into the Toyota. He kicked at the clutch with his left leg and shifted the stick forcefully. Ray wondered at the Forerunner's ability to survive this brute's abuse.

They jerked away from the camp building, slid to a halt, then spun forward, studs fighting for traction. A half dozen pools of halogen raced past. The speedometer trembled up to 40 before diving for zero again as Leeland aimed the vehicle, sledlike, at a shed.

Ray eyed the shed, gripped the armrest, checked the sled. It was still in tow, swaying back and forth against the frosty chain guard. At the center of the sled the Polaris sat wounded, defeated. He would attend to that later. Hopefully the camp had parts.

Suddenly they were sideways, Leeland performing an impressive fishtail approach that parked them within two feet of the building. "Okay."

They hopped out and walked back to the sled, boots crunching on the brittle snow. Leeland unhitched the sled and toggled the winch. They watched as the chain disappeared into the back of the Toyota. "Let's just push the whole thing into the shed," he suggested.

Ray nodded. Why not? Then, when he did come out to repair his machine, he could do so in the relative comfort of the steel prefab.

The three of them nudged the sled, ushering it backward, away from the truck. It skated obediently. But when they tried to twist it for the final trip into the shed, it resisted. The weight of the snow machine was enough to dig the rails into the ice. Bending into the effort, they turned the trailer and lined it up for the shed door.

After Leeland had pulled back the double doors, they guided the sled inside, the rails grinding as they scraped across bare, dry concrete. It groaned to a stop between two identical blue pickups. The enclosure was more of a garage than anything else. Aside from the twin vehicles, it contained a pyramid of oil cans, a mostly dismantled snow mobile, and a simple wooden workbench. Car parts and tools were scattered on the grease-stained workbench in haphazard fashion, like discarded toys in a child's nursery.

The walls shook visibly with each new gust of the storm. There were gaps at the corners, light and snow pellets sneaking in from all directions. When Leeland slammed the steel doors shut, the squall dissipated but did not disappear. You could still feel a vigorous breeze. Ray decided that the temperature inside was nearly the same as the temperature outside. Working in this deep freeze would be nigh unto impossible, thus the forgotten tools. He scrutinized the Yamaha, wondering if it had a working carburetor.

"Nobody'll bother your stuff in here," the hulking security officer promised. "This old barn is just for storage." He stepped across the shed to the access door and shook the knob. When nothing happened he used both mittens. "Piece of junk is frozen."

"Can't we just go back out . . ." Ray started to suggest, already gesturing to the large, double doors. But Leeland was working the knob as if it had offended him. He seemed determined to teach it a lesson.

As the musclepig battled the door, Ray glanced into the sled. It was a shambles of loose parts, supplies and tarps. He wondered how much he had lost on the trip in. The Polaris had crushed some of his equipment boxes and the wind had probably robbed him of some of his gear. At least the corpse was too heavy to . . . Ray leaned in and flipped a tarp back. He lifted another. Climbing into the bed, he shoved at the boxes.

"What are you doing?" Billy Bob called above the wind.

The door finally gave, creaking open on repentant hinges, its face now bearing a size 15E bruise. Leeland returned triumphantly. After watching Ray for a moment, he asked Billy Bob, "What's his problem?"

The deputy shrugged.

Ray was frantic now. Grunting, he tilted the Polaris, kicked beneath it with his boot. He let the machine down with a thud, then knelt and reached under the tarps. Thirty seconds later he stood up. Breathing hard, he stared incredulously at the disheveled contents of the sled and cursed.

"Lose something?" Leeland asked.

Ray swore again, more emphatically.

"What is it, Ray?" Billy Bob wondered, wide eyes looking out from his goggles.

"The body," he panted. "It's gone."

➤ FOURTEEN ◀

"IT CAIN'T JUST be gone," Billy Bob protested.

Ray shook his head at the sled. "It's not in there."

The three men stared at the contents—at the Polaris, the boxes, the tarps, the tools—as if the non-animate objects were somehow responsible.

"Maybe it fell out when we towed it in," Leeland suggested. He stepped up into the sled and began rummaging. "You sure it's not in here?"

Ray's answer took the form of a dramatic sigh. This was just what he needed. Not only had he failed to ID the corpse, he had failed to keep track of the corpse. The captain would have a conniption fit. He suppressed a curse and started across the shed for the door.

"Where you goin'?" Billy Bob wanted to know.

Ray ignored him. Where did the hillbilly think he was going? To get a latte? The body was gone. It represented the only hard evidence that a murder had been committed. Ray's new mission was to recover the body.

A blast of air met him as he exited the building, pushing him back on his heels. It was symbolic, he decided, representative of this case. It had him on the defensive, reacting rather than taking the initiative. He felt like he was fighting an invisible, insurmountable foe, wasting energy and time in a fruitless search for answers that were swirling away from him like the drifting snow.

Resisting the urge to curse the weather, and the entire investigation, he steadied himself, adjusted his goggles, and set out for the camp building. The wind could be good or evil, Grandfather had always told him. It all depended upon your attitude. A fool fought against it, allowing it to become an enemy, something that taunted him on his journey. A wise man embraced the wind, welcoming it as a friend. Instead of battling it, he used it for his benefit, harnessing its power, and allowing it to become a companion in the lonely hours. As simplistic as it sounded, the advice was basically true. It was counterproductive to worry about what you couldn't change. The key was to turn the wind—obstacles, problems, challenges—into an opportunity and go with the flow.

How could he do that with this case? Ray wasn't sure, but he had to do something, to take a different tack. His current strategy of police work certainly wasn't reaping anything worthwhile.

As he walked into his "Friend," leaning against each new gust, Ray studied the ground. If the body wasn't in the sled, someone had taken it. And if someone had taken it, they would have left tracks. The problem was, footprints had about a two second life span in this weather, blowing clean almost as quickly as they were made. He looked anyway: part of a tire imprint here, lumps of snow there, an oil stain encased in ice . . .

Ray had never been a brilliant tracker. Not like Grandfather. The man was a master, able to follow a fox or a herd of caribou or a wolf for miles. He could read the most subtle signs, interpret them, anticipate the animal's next move. Ray had been reasonably good as a teen. Hunting had been something of a religious rite, something he had practiced diligently. But now . . . years later . . . Though he still hunted on occasion, whatever skill he had once possessed had atrophied. He remembered a little, how to discern the direction of an animal's travel, how to estimate the time since it had passed by, but his principal means of bagging a caribou these days was to set up camp in a known migration path and wait. When they showed up, he knew what to do.

Ray reached the spot in front of the camp where the Toyota had first been parked. The ground was a dirty white, mud and compact snow forming a slick, shiny surface for the blowing pellets to dance across. Tire marks were in abundance, all weeks old. He bent and studied the area where the sled would have been. Rubbing a mitten over it, he contemplated the question of the hour: why? Why would someone rip off a dead body?

When no answer presented itself, his mind moved to the next step in the mysterious progression: who? Without knowing why, determining who was tricky. Motive would give rise to suspects. He stood up and mentally stepped back from the dilemma. First, who could have physically managed it, given the circumstances? The body was heavy. It probably would have taken two individuals. And they would have needed a place to stash it. Those prerequisites narrowed it down to every worker in camp.

Unless . . . What if the body had been missing back at the rig? No. Ray had spent a short time bunking with it in the sled. So it was there when Reynolds and Leeland showed up. Maybe it had simply rolled out of the sled on the way in. The ride was bumpy. No. The two-foot high sideboards would have prevented that. Either the body pole vaulted out or someone helped it.

Ray moved to the space where the Toyota had been and crouched. He reached a mitten down and tapped the snow. It was dark. Oil. The Forerunner had a leak.

Rising again, he frowned beneath his mask and pondered the second question again. Who?

Leeland and Billy Bob crunched past.

"We'll be in the office," the deputy told him.

Ray watched them enter the building. No. It was a crazy notion. Ridiculous. Still, he couldn't seem to avoid it. Billy Bob? Mr. Buck Teeth? The good old boy from Texas?

According to Billy Bob, he had been stuck in a snowdrift when Ray's Polaris died. Okay. But where had he been when the sled was sitting there in camp, unattended? Where had the deputy been when Reynolds and Ray were meeting with Red Bauer? For that matter, where had bunny teeth been when Ray went one on one with the hoist back at the rig?

It was more than just a leap to get to that conclusion. It

was a commuter flight. But . . . what if . . . Okay, say Billy Bob had been involved—heck, why not go all the way and make Billy Bob the murderer? There was still the big puzzler: why? Why would a police officer assigned to Prudhoe Bay assault a fellow law enforcement representative? Why would he steal a corpse? Well, if he'd killed the guy, he would want to hide the evidence. In fact, he might even sabotage a snow machine, in hopes that a nosy policeman would freeze to death.

Ray shook off the preposterous line of thinking. Lack of sleep, a possible concussion, and hunger were wreaking havoc with his logic. Why would Billy Bob kill a man and cut him up, Eskimo-style? Answer: he wouldn't. And even if he did, which he *didn't*, how could he manage to coordinate a cover-up like this? Answer: he couldn't. He probably wasn't smart enough. And moving the body . . . That would require assistance—a partner. Sure. Why not a gang? Why not a host of conspirators? All of Davis Oil was probably caught up in this. The government too, even the CIA. It was no doubt a huge conspiracy, a plot against Ray personally. An attempt to drive him crazy.

The last sentiment was at least feasible. This whole mess was starting to make him crazy.

In the absence of bloody footprints leading to the murderer or arrows in the snow pointing toward the missing body, Ray returned to the camp. He found Billy Bob in the security office with Reynolds and Leeland. Reynolds was on the phone.

Billy Bob looked up at him expectantly. "Any-thang?"

Ray shook his head. "What about Weinhart?"

"He was on the plane," Reynolds answered glumly. He seemed disappointed.

Leeland handed Ray a list of the passengers, pointing out Weinhart's name helpfully.

"You talk to him?"

"No," Reynolds grunted. "He's on vacation. Skiing in Colorado."

Before Ray could ask his next question, Reynolds answered

it. "Condo. No phone. We're trying to get a message to him."

"Is he married?"

Reynolds shook his head at this. "Divorced. His ex didn't know where he was—didn't care. I'm guessing they're not friends."

"What about the pilot?"

"What about him?"

"He see Weinhart get on?"

Reynolds shrugged. "I haven't talked to him."

"Why not?"

"I didn't think about it. Besides, Houston has about a half dozen or so pilots. They rotate. I'm not even sure who was flying the jet on this trip."

"Can you find out?"

"I guess. But whoever it was, they aren't going to remember who was on board."

"Why not?"

"Because they're pilots. Not stewardesses. They don't greet the passengers personally."

"Can you just check?"

"Yeah . . ." Reynolds nodded to Leeland, silently delegating the chore. Leeland picked up the phone and started dialing.

"What else can we do for you?" Reynolds asked rather sarcastically.

"Now that you ask . . ." Ray fell into a chair next to Reynolds's desk. He was exhausted, his head pounding again. It took effort just to think. "Send someone out to look for the corpse."

Reynolds stared at him. "You serious?" He chuckled, revealing a mouthful of gleaming teeth—a jolly barracuda.

"Maybe it fell out on our way in," Ray suggested half-heartedly.

"Fell out?" Reynolds's thin features contorted.

"The only other alternative is that someone here in camp took it."

This had a sobering effect on Reynolds.

"Can you send a truck out to check the road?"

"You're asking me to deploy my people . . . in this?" Here he aimed a thumb at the window. "To scan snowdrifts for a wayward corpse?"

"Right."

He rolled his eyes, muttered something under his breath, then picked up the phone. "Okay. But chances of finding it are—"

"Slim. I know. But I'd hate to start accusing Davis Oil workers of stealing it, if the thing just bounced out of the sled."

Reynolds began making the arrangements, barking orders to Pilgrim II. As Ray waited, he glanced over at Billy Bob. The deputy was leaning against the wall, eyes drooping. He looked as tired as Ray felt. He was also a little pale. Probably from hunger. Ray tried to find guilt or duplicity in the young man's face. It either wasn't there, or Billy Bob was one heck of a poker player. Was the country hick coldhearted enough to snuff out a human life and then implement a calculated strategy for avoiding detection? Was it all an act—the drawl, the naiveté, the stupidity? Was Bugs Bunny actually an unconscionable sociopath? Ray didn't think so. Maybe Yosemite Sam. But not Bugs.

"There." Reynolds replaced the phone and looked at Ray. He seemed resigned to the role of support person. "Now what?"

"I could use some parts for my machine," Ray said. "If you don't mind, I could cannibalize one of the Yamahas out in that shed."

"Don't worry about it," Reynolds mumbled. Phone in hand again, he punched buttons. "Al? There a snow machine in Barn two. It's a . . . What kind?"

"Polaris."

"Polaris. See if you can get it running. Priority. Thanks."

"Anything else on your wish list, Officer Attla?"

Ray smiled at him. "A phone and a meal."

"Probably want a room too, huh? Bet you two are beat." He pointed across the office. "There's your phone. Hit nine to get out of camp. Cafeteria's that way," he gestured. "Turn right at the end of the hall. Go past the gym and the theater.

Can't miss it. I'll arrange a place for you to bunk down."

"Thanks." Ray stood and faced Billy Bob. "I'll meet you in the cafeteria. I have a couple of calls to make."

The deputy nodded slowly, sleepily, and staggered for the door—a member of the walking dead.

Ray took up the phone and tried to decide who to call first: the captain or Margaret. Neither one would be fun. The captain would chew him out for losing the body. Margaret would be concerned that he wasn't en route to Barrow yet. If he told her about the incident with the winch she would be worried, and might even start crying. He weighed the choice: get chewed, or be cried at.

He decided on the latter and placed the call. As it beeped through, he checked his watch. 1:52. The line rang once, twice, three times . . . On the fourth ring, Ray breathed a sigh of relief. He heard the click, then Margaret's recorded voice telling him to leave a message.

"Hi, honey. I'm still in Prudhoe. Everything's fine. I'm trying to get this thing flanged up soon and get back home. I love you and I miss you."

Hanging up, he reflected on the truthfulness of his words. Yes, indeed he loved and missed her. Yes, he honestly hoped to get the case closed soon. He hadn't lied. Not exactly. But everything wasn't fine and making the party was looking more and more like a long shot.

He dialed again and was gloomily considering the repercussions of missing the shower, when Betty answered.

"Barrow Police."

"Betty? Ray."

"Hey there. What's shaking?"

"Not much. The captain around?"

"No. He's still at lunch." Her voice shifted, taking on a regal tone. "Dining with the mayor."

Another bullet dodged. "Tell him I'm in Prudhoe. And . . ." Ray considered the missing corpse. Not the sort of thing you told someone via phone message: I lost the dead man. "That's it. I'll call him later."

"Okay. Say, the weather report says that this storm is gonna get worse. So you take care of yourself, all right?"

"Yes, Ma'am. I will."

Ray replaced the receiver, nodded to Reynolds and Lee-land, both of whom were involved in their own phone con-versations, and set out for the cafeteria. He was feeling good, better at least, buoyed by two near misses. There was some-thing slightly sick about that, about getting a rush out of avoiding conflict and confrontation. But at the moment, he didn't really care. He was merely relieved. A good meal, a few hours rest, and he might feel almost human again.

Ray took a right at the end of the corridor, as instructed. He passed an Olympic-sized pool and watched as two human fish gasped, gulped, and splashed their way from one end to the other. One was overweight by a good fifty pounds, the other rail-thin: a beluga whale and a sea snake with goggles.

Just past the pool was the gymnasium. A dozen men were playing basketball, grunting and sweating as if they were en-gaged in an NBA Championship Final. The skins scored a backdoor layup and the shirts were regrouping, when Ray spotted the racquetball courts. Beyond these was the weight room. Separated from the hall by clear plexiglass, it displayed bodybuilders like animals in a zoo exhibit. Aside from a few skinny runts that seemed determined to become the next Charles Atlas, there were some who rivaled Leeland in size and sculpture. The scene reminded Ray of something out of a prison movie: men intent upon inflating their bodies to al-most cartoonish proportions.

The clatter of silverware signaled his arrival at the cafeteria. It was twice the size of the modest one at the rig, three times as elegant. For starters, the floor was covered in low-pile gray carpet. A score of men were in various stages of eating, moc-casins and polar fleece slippers padding from the meal line to the polished wood tables. The plates were ceramic, the glasses real, not plastic. Inset studio lights and a forest of potted ferns in gleaming brass pots gave the room a warm, comfortable feel. It was almost like a bona fide restaurant.

A gangly arm waved at Ray. He followed it to a table on the farside of the room.

"Have a seat," Billy Bob offered, smiling. His face had color now. In front of him was a half-empty plate and an empty mug. "Talk about hittin' the spot . . ." He whistled at the food. "I'm gonna live."

"Where's the line start?"

The deputy grinned and pushed a nearby plate at Ray. "Already took care of that."

Ray gazed hungrily down at the selection: club sandwich, pickle, steak fries, potato salad, coleslaw, roll, baked beans . . . It looked delicious.

Billy Bob hopped up just as Ray sat down, hurrying toward the serving line. Ray ignored him, turning his attention to lunch. By the time the deputy returned, two minutes later, Ray had confirmed that it did, in fact, hit the spot. The sandwich was one of the best he had ever tasted, the surrounding side dishes worthy of a gourmet feast.

"Here." Billy Bob set a steaming mug in front of Ray. "Wait till you sample that. We're talkin' some decent joe."

Ray set his fork aside and took up the mug. He sniffed it critically, then sipped. It was hot. It was strong. It was heaven. "Man, these people know how to do lunch."

"I'll say." Billy Bob dove back into his meal.

"Once we eat ourselves into a new pant size, let's hit the sack. I think we'll both perform better after . . ."

Billy Bob was shaking his head. "Cain't."

"Huh?"

"The two men responsible for checkin' the pipes? They're goin' back on shift at three—headin' to a rig about fifteen miles out. If we're gonna talk to 'em, we gotta do it now."

Ray sighed at this, frowned, took another long draw of coffee.

"Maybe they can help us figure out who it was that got himself kilt," Billy Bob added.

"Maybe." He spooned in a mound of beans and washed it down with more coffee. "Who are they?"

"Frank McMillian and Eric Ford. Roustabouts. They're in their rooms right now. Leeland said he'd let 'em know we was comin'."

Ray glanced at his watch and sighed again. "All right. But after we talk to them, murder or no murder, missing corpse or no missing corpse, I've got to lie down . . . before I fall down.''

''I'm with you, partner,'' Billy Bob replied between bites. ''I'm with you.''

➤➤ FIFTEEN ◀◀

"LEELAND SAID BOTH of 'em was on the second floor," Billy Bob reported, starting up the steps. "Room 232. Supposed to be down at the end of the hallway." The cowboy aimed a thumb in the air like a disinterested hitchhiker.

Ray followed him up the stairs, silently hoping this wouldn't take long. Despite the meal, or perhaps because of it, he was about ready to collapse. The coffee had served only to make his head pound with greater vigor. He felt heavy, his legs aching. The latter happened whenever he allowed himself to become totally depleted. It was a signal warning him that he needed to seek out a dark, quiet place and assume a horizontal position for an extended period of time before he keeled over—or made some grievous error of judgment.

When they reached the top of the stairwell, they found themselves in a lounge area. It was comfortable, overstuffed couches and chairs forming a semicircle around a big-screen television. Ten or so men were present, eyes glued to the 4 x 4 square of electric light as uniformed warriors streaked down the ice.

Ray glanced left, then right. The hall stretched in both directions, the closest door marked MAINTENANCE.

"Which way to room 232?" Billy Bob asked.

It was bad timing. His words fell on deaf ears, the men leaning forward in their seats, shouting their encouragement as one team, apparently the team of choice, launched a fast break. A slap shot made it past the defensemen and struck the post, sending the goalie into a frenzy of arm and leg flailing maneuvers. Curses arose from the audience.

The puck was ringing the boards, a half dozen players converging on it like angry bees, assaulting each other with punishing checks when Ray repeated the question. "Which way to room 232?"

Only two men even bothered to look away from the game. One of them nodded to the left before returning his attention to the screen. The other gave them a suspicious glance, as if he wasn't sure they were worthy of the information. Finally he grunted, "Down at the end."

As they walked along the hall, inspecting door numbers, the noise of the game fell away, replaced by another sound. It was random, irritating, like static issuing from a demon-possessed radio, one with no hope of ever finding a station. It was only when they were nearing the final foursome of doors that the noise took on a semblance of order: individual screeches forming an electric, distorted whole. It reminded Ray of tomcats fighting in a chimney.

Billy Bob stopped in front of room 232, stared at the door thoughtfully. "Stevie Ray Vaughn," he announced, eyebrows raised.

"Huh?"

"Stevie Ray Vaughn."

Ray blinked at him, then tapped the number on the door. "232. It should be Ford and McMillian."

"No. The music. It's 'Pride and Joy.' "

"Music?" He listened, his ears straining to make music out of the discordant shrieks. A single note hummed into a feedback squeal. Silence reigned for a second or two. Without warning the song began again, from the top.

"Wow."

"Wow, what?" Ray asked.

"Listen. No drums. No bass. No backup."

"So?"

"So that's not a CD. Somebody's playin'. And whoever it is, they're darn good."

Why would anyone intentionally play that? Ray felt like asking. Instead, he rapped on the door.

The cats continued their frantic battle.

He knocked again, harder.

There was an abrupt ceasefire, and after one final clunk of fuzz the door swung open.

"Yeah?" The voice was annoyed, the face that went with it clearly offended by the interruption. Both belonged to a man in his mid-thirties. He was average height and build with neatly cut hair, a well kept beard and round, wire-rimmed glasses. He looked almost scholarly, not the wild rocker Ray had envisioned to be responsible for the cacophony.

"We're looking for Eric Ford and Frank McMillian."

"Well, you found 'em." The door opened wider and the man deserted them, returning to a gleaming brown guitar perched on a stand. Picking it up, he strapped it to his chest and began fiddling with the knobs of a suitcase-sized amplifier. Satisfied, he toggled a control board on the floor with a shoeless foot. The man plucked a string, twisted a machine head, tuning his instrument as if Ray and Billy didn't even exist.

Without warning he struck out on another barn burner. Ray could actually feel the notes impacting his chest, shaking his heart. He watched as the man's fingers performed a manic dance on the fingerboard, bending the strings and notes out of shape.

" 'Voodoo Chile,' " Billy Bob shouted into Ray's ear.

Ray shrugged. Whatever. He reached a hand up, attempting to pacify the cats.

The man looked at him, played another roller coaster rift and silenced the guitar with a tap of his foot.

"Are you Ford or McMillian?" Ray asked.

"Ford," he said, eyes on his instrument. His foot pressed a new button and a pair of harmonic notes rang out. Another tap and they faded away. He nodded toward a lump in one of the bunks. "That's Frank over there."

Ray stared incredulously, amazed that anyone could sleep through Ford's six-stringed barrage. "Don't you get complaints about the noise?"

Ford looked at him like he was insane. "Noise?"

"How can people sleep?"

"I play through my amp from two to three. Everyone knows that. The rest of the time, I use headphones."

"What about your buddy here?"

"Earplugs," Ford told him. "The kind they use on airport tarmacs. I bought them for him for Christmas."

"You're good," Billy Bob blurted out. "Real good." He was obviously in awe of this guy, his expression one of admiration. "Where'd you ever learn to play like that?"

"Austin," Ford replied. "I'm not that good, though. My chops are okay. I can do some machine-gun blues, mimic a few of ol' Stevie's tunes." He lifted a book of tablature toward them. "But I'm not original. Don't have my own sound. Haven't written any music. I just like to play. It's the way I get through these long tours."

"How long you up for?"

"This time it's twelve weeks." He paused, then added, "I need the money. Got alimony payments, child support. And this gear isn't cheap." He patted the guitar affectionately. "Plus I'm saving to go to music school. Maybe. Just an idea. Figure I might study music theory and jazz for while. See if I have any real talent."

Ray dug the sketch out of his pocket. "This face familiar?"

Ford leaned on his guitar and studied it. "Don't think so. Should it be?"

"This man was found dead in a piece of casing up at rig seventeen."

"Hmph." The mustache turned down. His left hand began to tap the strings.

"We're trying to figure out who he is, when he died, how he got in the pipe, that sort of thing."

Ford nodded, fingers ripping licks a half inch above the strings.

"Are you and your partner responsible for checking pipe when it comes into camp?"

Another nod. "Us or the other roustabouts. There's probably . . . a dozen in camp this winter." His right hand was busy now, pick plucking at the deactivated instrument. The resulting notes were weak and thin, like something from a child's toy ukulele.

"Did you check the pipes that were trucked up to seventeen yesterday?"

"Yep." His fingers froze on the fingerboard and he squinted at them. "Who are you guys?"

"Officer Attla, Barrow PD," Ray told him.

"Barrow?"

"And Deputy Cleaver, Deadhorse Sheriff's Office."

This seemed to placate him. "Yeah. We inspected that load of casing yesterday afternoon."

"What time? Do you remember?"

Ford shrugged. "Oh . . . maybe four or so."

"Do you know how long it was after that, before the casing was trucked up?"

"Not exactly. Probably about an hour or two."

"Between five and six?"

"Yeah. About then. They wanted it up there early, I know that much."

"Any idea why?"

He shrugged again. "There were gonna start setting around midnight. Guess they were running low on casing and didn't want to chance running out in the middle of the job. That can really screw up a hole."

"So I've heard," Ray said. He tried to think of another question to ask but couldn't. "We need to speak to your partner too," he finally submitted, rather apologetically. Actually, he wasn't sorry so much as reluctant. He remembered what it had been like to wake up Sam back at the rig.

Ford glanced at his watch. "Time for him to get up anyway. He sleeps till the last possible second, gets up right before shift, doesn't even take a shower, just pulls on his coveralls, grabs a half dozen donuts, and heads for the yard. The bum." He returned to his practice, jamming enthusiastically without the benefit of electronic amplification.

Ray waited, expecting Ford to assume the role of human alarm clock. After a few stanzas, Ford noticed this and said, "Go ahead, wake him up."

Ray looked at the lump, then at Billy Bob. The deputy stared back with wide eyes. "You heard 'em. Wake him up, Ray."

After shooting fire at the cowboy with his eyes, Ray begrudgingly approached the lump. "Frank?" When that didn't so much as disturb the snore pattern, he tried again. "Frank?"

"He can't hear you with those earplugs," Ford offered, still jamming. He was rocking now, his entire body involved in the process of making music.

Great. Placing a hand on what he assumed was a shoulder, he rocked the lump gently. It began to move, limbs repositioning themselves beneath the blanket. Another easy shake produced a head. It twisted until bleary eyes looked up at him.

"Frank?"

The response took the form of a coughing fit. "What time is it?" he whispered. Before Ray could answer, McMillian lifted his arm and brought his watch to his face. He squinted at it. "Go away. I got another ten minutes."

"Frank?" Ray shook him again.

McMillian coughed again, his entire body shaking, and slowly sat up in bed. After removing his earplugs, he looked at them with a pathetic expression. "What is it?" he wheezed.

"These guys are cops, Frank," Ford told him, attention still focused on his instrument. "They found a dead body in a piece of casing. One of the pieces that got sent up to seventeen."

"Yeah? So?"

"So they want to know if we saw anything—when we did the walk-through inspection."

McMillian snorted, attempting to unclog his sinuses. "I didn't see nuthin'." The words came out raspy, a smoker's voice.

"Nothing out of the ordinary?" Ray tried.

"Nuthin'." He yawned, revealing a mouth of yellow teeth. After scratching at his long, matted blond hair, he added, "Just empty pipe."

"Could someone have put a body inside one of the pipes after you inspected it?"

"Suppose so. If they wanted to." McMillian didn't seem interested, much less surprised at the suggestion of murder.

"Could someone have managed that, hidin' a body, I

mean, without being seen?" Billy Bob drawled.

"Probably." McMillian began coughing again, serious convulsions this time. When it finally passed, he swore and reached for a pack of cigarettes. Lighting up, he leaned back against the wall, sucking in the antidote to his worries. His face grew calm. He looked relieved, content.

"If the body was placed there after you inspected the casing," Ray clarified, "but before it was trucked out, when would that have been?"

McMillian inhaled nicotine, held it, exhaled bluish smoke. "Six?"

Across the room, Ford was nodding, plinking madly.

"What about the truck driver?" Billy Bob asked.

It was a good question, something Ray should have thought of. "Yeah. Is he around? Can we talk to him?"

McMillian wheezed, as if his lungs were about to be expelled from his chest, then answered through a fresh plume of smoke. "No idea."

"Do you know who it was?"

He considered this, sucking slowly, blowing out thoughtfully, like the stack on an idling train engine. "Think it might have been . . . either Burt or Mike."

"Burt," Ford confirmed. He ran a blues scale, bent a note into another time zone, before adding, "Burt Singletary. He drove the seventeen load."

"Is he here? Could we talk to him?"

Ford shook his head. "You'll have to check. But I think he went to twelve after seventeen. That was about the time that Red, Mr. Bauer, shut everything down. It was iffy taking the pipe up last night. Coming home, without a load . . . Burt's a good driver, but I doubt even he could keep his rig on the road in this storm."

"We'll ask Reynolds," Ray told Billy Bob.

McMillian took a final suck on his cancer stick, then lit another from the waning butt. "If that's all, fellas, I need to get up and get going." He pushed back the covers and stood up. Ray unconsciously took a step backward. McMillian was wearing only a tank top and a pair of briefs. The skin of his legs was pale, almost powder white, between and around an impressive array of tattoos: snakes, dragons, a demon with a sword . . .

"Like 'em?" he asked with a grin.

"Nice," Ray answered. The man looked diseased, over-grown, as if a jungle fungus had attacked him in his sleep. "Thanks for your help."

As they started for the door, McMillian pulled a wrinkled sweatshirt over his oily hair. Ford thumbed a button on his amp and it erupted in a fuzzy, sustained power chord. They could hear him doing a number on the traditional blues, the notes a flurry of grinding and hissing, most of the way down the hall.

" 'Travis Walk'," Billy Bob noted appreciatively.

"Uh-huh," Ray grunted.

"Ready to find them beds?"

"More than ready. Why don't you ask Reynolds where we're bunking. And have him check on the truck driver."

"What are you gonna do?"

"See about my snow machine."

They parted ways at the bottom of the stairwell, Billy Bob turning toward the office suites, Ray heading for the mud-room. When he had encased himself in Gor-tex, down, neo-prene and rubber, Ray exited the camp building and reentered the arctic winter: perpetual night, cruel cold, relentless wind.

The womb of the ancients, Grandfather called it. Ray could hear the old man repeating the phrase in Inupiat, his hoarse voice laden with awe and reverence. Grandfather, like the elders before him, held a deep respect for this seemingly ad-versarial, merciless environment. To him it was not a wicked foe but a life giver, the sustainer and nurturer of the People. The Land and its harsh, stormy moods was their caring Mother.

As Ray made his way toward the shed, his tired mind tried to make sense of that sentiment. He had always found it dif-ficult to maintain a favorable attitude about a place so unfor-giving. He couldn't help but wonder why the Inupiat had willingly remained here, why they had remained faithful to such an angry "Mother." Why had the Tareumiut, the Inupiat tribes of the northern seacoast, made the upper reaches of the

Arctic Circle their home? Were they fools? Did they have a death wish? Or were they, as the legend claimed, blessed with wisdom that others failed to grasp? Had they somehow learned to live in harmony with one of the harshest, most brutal ecosystems on the globe?

Over the years, Grandfather had related countless stories about their connection to the Land, their adaptation to its whims and desires. He had taught Ray to honor and accept the Arctic rhythms, to appease the fickle gods, to accept and endure the love-hate relationship that forever bound them to the territory that now bore the label Alaska. It made sense, in an odd sort of way. No matter the climate or the severity of the seasons, the Land did provide for those willing to seek out its peculiar forms of sustenance.

Ray understood that. Yet at the age of 28, he was still struggling with one question: Why was he here? Why had he decided to remain in this godforsaken place, where winter was a lifestyle rather than a season, survival the chief occupation of daily routine? He could have left—still could. With his education and experience, he could land a job in Anchorage or Seattle. Why stay? Why put up with this abuse year after year?

He stared past the halogen lanterns, into the looming darkness beyond, half-expecting an answer to materialize, like a spirit riding the storm.

Completing the journey to the shed, he reached for the door handle and froze. He knew the reason he was there and had known it all along. Somehow, he simply couldn't admit it to himself. The answer was part of him. As much as he sometimes resented it or wanted to change it, Ray was one of the People. Despite his sophisticated ways, his adoption of modern devices and technology, even his disbelief of and impatience with the backward traditions of the elders, he was nevertheless an Eskimo and always would be. That sense of identity would not allow him to depart. He felt inexplicably tied to his home, to his people's home. Whether that umbilical cord was emotional, spiritual, wholly imaginary, he didn't know. But of one thing he was certain. Abandoning the Land would mean disowning himself. To leave it would be to die.

Pulling open the door, he hurried inside, away from the moaning night, away from the terrible reality that his destiny had been preordained, his future foretold long before his life had ever begun.

➤➤ SIXTEEN ◀◀

"TRY IT AGAIN."

The man straddling the Polaris nodded and jiggled the ignition. The machine roared to life and the rider twisted the throttle, causing the engine to rev enthusiastically.

When it shuddered, issuing a cloud of blue smoke, the first man peered under the miniature hood, reached in and made an adjustment with a socket wrench. The Polaris purred smoothly in response. He listened for another moment, then gestured across his throat with a finger. A second later the machine was silent again.

"Sounds good," Ray offered.

The two men glanced up at him warily, as if he had intruded upon an intimate moment. They were both wearing blue RefrigiWear suits, both rather small in stature. Hunched over the snow machine, they reminded Ray of elves repairing a toy.

"This your machine?" the man with the wrench asked.

Ray nodded. "Is she gonna live?"

"Oh, yeah." He stood up and stretched, setting the wrench on a red tool cart that had been wheeled into the shed.

"Nice machine," the other man said, still astride the seat. He gripped the handlebars and pretended to drive it. "Bet this baby can move."

"Yeah." Ray pushed back his hood and began removing his goggles and mask.

"I got two Suzukis back in Anchorage." He made a face.

"Pieces of junk. Took one of 'em up the Susitna last winter. Thing croaked before I got to Kashwitna. Had to totally rebuild the engine. Cost almost as much as I paid for the thing." He swore at this. "I'm saving up for a new one. Either an Arctic Cat or a Polaris. Heavy on the horses."

"Was it the carburetor?" Ray asked.

"Huh-uh," the other man grunted, shaking his head. He started to say something else, then gawked at Ray. The guy was probably 5 foot 7 or so, a good half a foot shorter than Ray.

"You a Native?" he finally asked, as if that couldn't possibly be the case.

Ray nodded. "Inupiat."

"Man!" the mechanic on the Polaris exclaimed. "I ain't never seen one so big."

"Me either!"

Ray tried to think of a polite or at least humorous comeback but couldn't. He was tired, his creativity and wit having forsaken him, and he had to fight the urge to shoot back with bullets: *And I've never seen a naluaqmiu so stupid*. Instead, he said, "So the carburetor I put on was okay?"

With that, then the two men returned their attention to the snow machine. "Yeah," the one standing said. "Ran a little rough till we adjusted it, but the part was fine."

"Hmm ... It wouldn't turn for me," Ray told them. "Didn't get anything."

Both mechanics shrugged at this. "Probably a fluke," Shorty offered.

"Yeah, a fluke," the man on the Polaris agreed.

"We charged your engine warmer too."

"Did it hold it?" Ray asked.

"Uh-huh. Got to watch those lithium batteries, though."

"Yeah. They're supposed to be ultra cold-weather, but ..." Rising from the seat, he cursed the manufacturer.

"It's brand new," Ray explained. "Guaranteed for five seasons."

"I don't trust 'em, no matter what they say," Shorty grumbled.

"Me either. My motto is always carry a backup everything.

Especially batteries. 'Cause when they die, they do it in a heartbeat.''

Shorty took a step back and invited Ray to inspect the machine. "She's ready for you."

Ray gave it a cursory once over. The mechanics had not only repaired the engine, but cleaned it as well. The pieces gleamed at him in the fluorescent light.

"Thanks guys. I appreciate it."

"And we gassed her up," Shorty added.

"I went ahead and put in Supreme," the other said, pulling up his hood. "My Snow Cats have seizures on plain old unleaded."

"Thanks."

When their mittens were in place, the two men rolled the tool cart to the door, swung it open, and lifted the cart through.

Closing the door behind them, Ray returned to the sled and began rummaging through the contents. He still had his shovels, and his tools were safely stowed in their plastic chest. The tent was there, and the sleeping bag, their cardboard box split and ailing. As he tossed it aside, he realized that the insulated pad was missing. It had apparently blown out. So had one of the extra tarps. The survival kit was intact: propane stove, matches, white gas. Two stubby snowshoes protruded from beneath one of the crates, and most of the spare snow machine parts seemed to be present.

Removing the black box that held the radio, he set it by the door. It was battery driven and more than a few hours at this temperature would effectively kill it. He had slipped on his gear and was about to leave when he remembered the engine warmer. Toggling the power knob, he watched as the needle on the meter jumped to 100 percent. Fully charged. He plugged the device into the engine block, covered the sled, and flipped off the overhead light. Lifting the radio, he started for the camp.

Billy Bob was waiting for him in the mudroom.

"How's your machine?"

"A couple of mechanics got it up and running," Ray replied. He set the radio down and slipped off his parka. After stuffing his mittens, goggles and mask into the pockets, he hung it in the closet.

"Oh, they got ahold of the pilot."

"And? . . ."

"He don't 'member if Weinhart was on the plane or not."

"Great." Ray tossed his boots in and slammed the closet door in frustration. He sank to the bench and began putting the polar-fleece slippers on.

"But he checked the passenger role and had the flight attendant make a count. It matched. There were twelve people on board, just like the list said."

"Flight attendant?"

Billy Bob nodded at this.

"Anybody talk to her?"

The deputy shrugged. "I don't know. Want me to go find out?" The look on his face made it plain that he was hoping the answer would be negative.

Ray eyed his watch. 3:07. "No. Let's get some sleep. At least a couple of hours. Then we'll get some dinner, talk strategy, decide where to go from here."

"Okay." Billy Bob was visibly relieved.

"Did you get us a room?"

"Yep. We're right down the hall here." He led Ray away from the offices, cafeteria, and fitness complex, into a short cul-de-sac of doors.

"These here are for VIPs," Billy Bob announced, bunny teeth gleaming. He was obviously pleased with the accommodations he had procured. Producing a key, he unlocked a door marked C.

"Gosh!" Billy Bob exclaimed.

"Gosh is right," Ray muttered. The room was less like a dorm, more like a hotel suite. There were two queen-sized beds, a small efficiency kitchen, a bathroom, and a sitting area with an attractive table bearing a beautiful arrangement of artificial flowers. The walls were adorned with attractive paintings, all oil field related, and the entire room, bedspreads, wallpaper, carpet, was color coordinated in subdued earth tones.

Billy Bob yanked on the handle of the miniature refrigerator. It was stocked with tiny bottles of booze, long-neck beer, fruit, chocolate. "Wall, I dee-clare!"

Ray glanced at it, nodded, then turned his attention to the big-screen TV system. It was state-of-the-art: flat panel screen, the control unit equipped with a built-in VCR. Four small Bose speakers were poised near the ceiling at the four corners of the bedroom, creating surround sound.

"Wanna beer?" Billy Bob asked.

"No, thanks."

There was a hiss as the deputy twisted the top off a bottle, a crackle as he broke open a package of cashews. "Ya sure?"

"Yeah." Ray tapped a button on a CD stereo built into the shelf between the two beds. Country music blared. Another jab of his finger silenced the components. He flipped through the CD cases stacked neatly next to the player. All country, except for one classical release.

"Are we livin' er what?" Billy Bob drawled, mouth burdened with nuts.

Ray deposited the radio unit on one of the chairs. "*Er what*. Too bad we won't have a chance to enjoy this."

"Yeah." Billy Bob frowned, took a long swig of Budweiser.

"I'm gonna jump in the shower," Ray informed him. He was already peeling off layers—neck warmer, flannel shirt, cotton shirt, polypropylene long underwear top . . .

Billy Bob picked up a miniature alarm clock and began fiddling with it. "What should I set this for?"

Barechested, Ray looked at his partner and shrugged. "Three hours? How's that sound?"

"Sounds great." The cowboy began shedding clothes. Slipping off his pants, he pulled back the spread on one of the beds and got in. "First one to sleep gets a prize."

"Right."

In the shower Ray fought a wave of guilt. Here they were, engaged in a murder investigation, and he was about to crash in a luxury suite. What would the captain say? Considering the fact that Ray had slept maybe two hours in three days, been cracked in the head by a malevolent hoist, stranded on an ice haul road . . . The captain would probably order him to catch a few Z's, if only to clear his head.

The hot water had a reviving effect on his weary muscles. Breathing in the steam, he realized that the pounding in his head was subsiding. Distant drums kept a steady but subtle beat.

He could feel himself relaxing, drooping like an over-cooked noodle. Sleep would come easily, before he managed to towel off if he didn't hurry.

Dry and wearing only his long johns, he slid into the empty bed. The sheets were smooth, the blankets soft. He wondered if he had ever been on a more comfortable mattress. It was like resting on a cloud.

"So now we got ourselves a window," Billy Bob announced.

"Huh?"

"The pipe was checked at around four, right?"

"Yeah." Ray felt heavy, listless.

"And it was shipped around five or six."

"Uh-huh." His breathing slowed, lungs inhaling gently but deeply.

"So that means the murder was committed between four and six."

"Maybe."

"Now if we kin just pin down this Weinhart fella."

Ray considered responding, but decided it required too much energy.

"Be nice if we could talk to that rig foreman too. What was his name? Briscoe?"

Resisting the urge to tell Billy Bob to shut up, he grunted, "Driscoll."

"Right. Wonder where he disappeared to?"

Eyes closed, Ray imagined various locations that might answer Billy Bob's question: the toilet, his bed, the Bahamas—steel drum music, warm, humid air, ocean waves crashing, palms swaying in the trade winds. If Ray was a foreman on an ice rig located less than 1400 miles from the North Pole, he would disappear to somewhere tropical, someplace where it never snowed and they put little umbrellas in the drinks. A scene materialized: Margaret in a patio chair. Her eyes were masked by dark glasses, a minuscule string bikini accentuating bare skin that glowed bronze from the intense equatorial sun. He had never seen her look so sexy.

Ray was in the process of joining her in the fantasy, watching objectively as his own body approached her, clad only in flowery jams and flip-flops, when a voice asked, "You think we met him yet?"

"Uh?" The vision disappeared, taking Margaret with it. Ray swore softly. "What?"

"You think we met him yet?"

"Who?" Ray asked with a sigh.

"The murderer. You think we talked to him?"

Ray struggled to consider this, his enervated mind projecting a montage of caricatures against a screen of hazy gray: Simpson, phones glued to both ears, Jim the roustabout, staring with suspicious eyes, his buddy Sam's angry glare, Stewart the drug dealer, Huckleberry and his goofy felt ears, Drill Sergeant Reynolds, his partner Mr. Universe, Mr. Bauer, glowing like Rudolph the Red Nosed Reindeer, the two mechanics, Shorty and the snow machine fanatic, Ford the bluesman, his slob of a roommate, McMillian, and a cowboy with a grin that put Goofy to shame. Ray wasn't sure if that was the entire cast of suspects. And didn't much care. The faces wavered, rearranged themselves, merged, slipped away.

"You got me," he finally groaned.

"Hard to imagine one a those fellas killin' somebody, like that."

"Yeah . . ."

"Hard to think *anybody* could do somethin' so sick."

"Uh . . . huh . . ."

Billy Bob said something else, but Ray missed it. He was floating, rising to an airy, almost magical dreamscape. He realized that he had won the contest. The prize the deputy had offered was Ray's for the taking. He punctuated the victory with a nasal snort.

➤ SEVENTEEN ◄

THE CRACKLING HISS sounded half-human, half-electronic like an alien attempting to communicate from deep space. The erratic popping and clicking came in pulses, surging, then fading. Each wave seemed loud and offensive in the quiet room. Ray was oblivious, caught in a heavy, dreamless sleep. It was only when a shrill tone mixed its voice with the audio show, nudging him with the subtlety of a cattle prod, that he flinched and sat up. Squinting into the darkness, he strained his ears to determine the source of the disturbance.

The first instant of consciousness was like stumbling out of a drunken stupor. His mind was having trouble forming and classifying the simplest of thoughts. The popping had stopped. If there had been any to start with. Maybe he had imagined it.

Static shot at him from across the room. He rubbed his eyes and glared at the tiny blinking red light. *The radio.* Rising, he staggered over, switched off the squelch, and returned to bed. Hiding beneath the blankets, he silently cursed the device, the timing of its intrusion, then, begrudgingly, considered checking the time. His limbs were dead, his brain fuzzy. Instead of being groggy from too much sleep, he was probably still semi-comatose from sleep deprivation.

Ray swore at the radio again, wordlessly willing it to a hot, fiery resting place in which it could burn long and hard, before glancing at it. The red light was still blinking. Whomever had been calling was still at it. Did he care? No. Should he care? Probably. Should he get up and answer the blasted thing? Unfortunately . . .

Sitting up on the edge of the bed, he depressed the Indiglo button on his Timex. He sighed at the numbers when they finally came into focus: 3:48. He had managed a whopping thirty minutes. Wow.

After rubbing his stinging eyes, he examined his forehead with a timid finger. The bump had swelled. It was tender, angry. A gentle touch sent a bolt of pain down his temple and behind his eye. He felt like he was suffering from a severe hangover, his body pleading with him to lie back down and sleep it off. Across the room, the radio beckoned.

Driven by the steady snoring of his partner, Ray approached the black box and lifted the mike. Twisting the knob, he thumbed the button and sighed, "Attla here."

The response was a surge of empty static.

"Attla here," he repeated with obvious irritation.

More static. A distant voice. Snatches of words.

"Attla here. I'm not reading you." He fiddled with the controls. "Say again."

The speaker popped, crackled. ". . . bout . . . . . . ders . . . . . . Raymond . . . . . . ngak . . . king . . ."

"You're breaking up," he said. "Adjust the squelch."

There was a brief pause, static howling like the wind. Finally, "I call about murders, Raymond. *Tuungak* speaking."

"Grandfather?"

"Ayy."

"Where are you?"

"Nuiqsut. Emily Foxglove got radio."

Closing his eyes, Ray shook his head. Being rudely awakened to attend to official police business was bad enough. But being jarred from a well-deserved sleep by an old, quite possibly senile, relative was more than he could bear. "Why are you calling me?"

"Important. Much important."

"What is it?" Ray sank to the floor and propped himself against the wall, waiting for an explanation.

"Spirits. They talk Maniilaq."

Ray resisted the urge to curse. Maniilaq was the shaman

of Nuiqsut. His given name was George Johnson, but he had changed it some years back, adopting the name and mantle of a famous, almost godlike Inupiat shaman who had lived in the 1800s. Among other things, the original Maniilaq had predicted the future of the People, foreseeing the arrival of the *naluaqmiut*. In Ray's opinion, old George, the new and improved Maniilaq, was a big fake who had entered the shaman business simply because it offered easy money. By promising to keep the spirits at bay, George managed to bilk poor, ignorant Eskimos out of their welfare checks.

"Tuungak much worried," Grandfather continued.

"Good. The spirits are worried. Wonderful. Listen, I—"

"Ayy. Not wonderful. Bad. Very evil. They tell Maniilaq of killings."

"Huh?" Ray blinked at the mike. Was it his imagination or was Grandfather making even less sense than usual. "I don't follow you."

"Killings."

"Yeah. I caught that part."

"*Tuungak* angry. Killings not please them."

"What killings?"

"Killings you track."

"You mean the murder up at the rig? How did you know about that? Was it on the news or something?"

"*Tuungak* tell Maniilaq."

"Oh, yeah," Ray groaned.

"Danger, Raymond. Many danger."

"Is that right?" He allowed his head to tilt back and rest against the wall. "You're calling me because the spirits told George Johnson about the murder I'm investigating? Is that it?"

"Ayyy. Many danger. *Anjatkut* do killings. Want do more."

"Uh-huh. If that's all, Grandfather, I really need to get some—"

"No. Not all. Must come."

"What? Who must come?"

"Raymond must come. You come, talk Maniilaq."

"No."

"No?"

"No. I'm not coming to talk with Maniilaq. If he has information for me—which I seriously doubt—tell him to radio it in."

"Tuungak know killings."

Ray suppressed a curse. This was really starting to get laborious. "Listen, first of all, I can't come. I'm in the middle of a case. You know, work. Doing my job. Second of all, the spirits got their wires crossed. It's not killings, plural. It's killing, singular. One. There has been one murder. I'm not sure how Maniilaq found out about it. Maybe the gossip grapevine. However he managed it, I'm not about to make the trek back to Nuiqsut just so I can watch him do some ridiculous ceremony and tell me there's 'much danger.'"

When Ray let up on the button, Grandfather was already grumbling back in Inupiat. The old man finally switched back to village English and said, "Tuungak say two killing. Much if you not come. Many blood. Many death."

Ray rolled his eyes at the scare tactic. That sort of thing might work on simpleminded Natives in the Bush, but . . .

"Maniilaq say you barely killed already. Steel and ice look for you. They no get you. But *anjatkut* still try."

Steel and ice . . . ? No. That couldn't be referring to . . . A knock at the door brought an end to the outrageous speculation. "Just a second Grandfather."

"Two killing," Grandfather's voice continued as Ray rose stiffly and walked to the door. "Two killing. Much soon. You come . . ."

Leeland was waiting behind the door, wearing a Nike T-shirt that seemed ready to rip if the guy so much as took a deep breath, along with a bored expression.

"What is it?" Ray wondered. "You find Weinhart?"

The brute shook his head. "Not yet. We located the flight attendant, faxed a picture of Weinhart to her."

"And?"

"She doesn't remember him being on board."

Ray nodded thoughtfully at this.

"That's not why I'm here, though. We just got word about Driscoll, the foreman up at seventeen."

"Yeah? Did he recognize the sketch?"

"No," Leeland replied, frowning.

Ray frowned with him, mourning the passing of yet another possible lead. "Where did he turn up?"

"About a quarter mile north of the shop."

"A quarter mile north? Wouldn't that be . . . ?"

"Yep. Outside camp."

"Is he . . . ?" Ray's hazy brain struggled toward the logical conclusion. "Is he dead?"

Leeland's square head rocked up and down on his wide shoulders. "Frozen solid. They haven't thawed him out yet, but there's blood. Looks like somebody cut on him."

"Great," Ray muttered. He took a deep breath, let it out, stared at Leeland. "I'll wake up the deputy and we'll meet you in the security office in ten minutes."

Leeland grunted and turned to leave. As he watched the musclepig depart down the hallway, Ray's tired mind posed a question: where had Leeland been when Driscoll was being murdered and dumped on the ice? It was a lame idea, wholly without merit, the result of too much work, not nearly enough rest. Still, what if Leeland had somehow managed to make the trek to the rig, kill Driscoll, and get back to the main camp without being noticed. Reynolds said that Bauer had grounded most of the operation, suspending travel until the storm passed. Maybe Leeland had used the down time to sneak up and kill Driscoll. For that matter, maybe he had killed both men—the pipe casualty and the rig foreman.

Ray closed the door and began punching holes in the accusations. There were several problems with them, most notably the lack of motive. Why would Leeland murder two men? Aside from the fact that he was big, physically capable of ending any life he so desired, why suspect him more than the rest of the four thousand or so workers on the Slope? And why limit the list of possible perps to workers? What about visitors, even roaming Natives? The first body bore marks of Eskimo ritual, and the second sounded like it might also. Maybe some demented tribal elder had gone off his rocker and launched a killing spree, cutting up men as if they were grizzlies.

The bottom line was that, in the absence of clear motive, obvious opportunity, and clues and evidence of any sort, almost everyone within a fifty mile radius was a suspect in these violent crimes. And that was precisely the problem Ray and Billy Bob were facing. They were hunting for a raven at midnight, without the benefit of a flashlight.

The crackle of the radio jarred him from the disjointed, frustrating brainstorming session. Lifting the mike, he told Grandfather, "I can't come. Something's happened."

"Must come. If no, maybe three. Soon much. Much dead if no come. Two killing just beginning."

Two killings! Ray was suddenly impressed by the coincidence. Maniilaq claimed that the spirits had told him of two killings, not just one. How could he have known? Was it possible that . . . No. It couldn't be. But what if . . . Spirits? *Spirits?* Still, suppose George, aka Maniilaq, really was communicating with the *tuungak,* which Ray seriously doubted, and say the spirits had an inside track on these crimes. So what? What possible benefit could that offer Ray? He was a law enforcement officer, not a witch doctor. What were the spirits going to do for him? Point out the killer in a lineup? Catch the perp red-handed, cuff him, and put him in jail? Turning to the spirits for assistance was loopy. Besides, making the trip to Grandfather's in this weather would be arduous at best. It was a bad idea all the way around. A stupid idea. Only a fool would—

"No be fool, Raymond," Grandfather continued. "You come. You come before evil find you. Learn about *anjatkut.* See face. Understand ways so can catch. You come."

"I'll think about it," Ray finally told him in a patronizing tone.

"You come."

"I said I'll think about it, Grandfather," Ray barked back. From across the room, Billy Bob snorted. Rolling over, the cowboy mumbled, "What's goin' on?"

"You come," the old man repeated. "*Tuungak* call. You come. Must come."

"I'll think about it," Ray responded laboriously.

"I wait for you. You come."

"Attla over and out." He switched off the radio before Grandfather could argue further.

"What are you doin'?" Billy Bob wanted to know. "What time is it? Is somethin' wrong? How long we been asleep?"

Ray picked through the questions, chose the last. "Long enough."

"Huh?"

"They found Driscoll."

The deputy sat up in bed. "Yeah?"

"Dead."

Billy Bob drawled a curse.

"He was frozen, and someone sliced him up."

"Just like the other one?"

"Sounds like it. Another assisted popsicle."

"So what are we gonna do? Go back up to the rig?"

"I don't know." Ray put on the first in a series of shirts. Despite his initial reluctance, he could feel himself wavering, beginning to seriously consider Grandfather's summons. "Let's talk to Reynolds first. Get the details, then . . ." They had no leads. No direction. The old man and his witch doctor friend probably had nothing to offer either, nothing of value at any rate. But, well, suppose they could help somehow. Ray had read about city cops in New York and LA using psychics to catch serial murderers. The CIA had even employed mind readers and ESP experts in counterintelligence operations during the Cold War. Was seeking the advice of a shaman any crazier?

"Then what?" Billy Bob prodded. He climbed out of bed, stretched, and climbed into his shirt in slow motion.

"I don't know."

Seven minutes later, coffee in hand, hair uncombed, looking like a couple of street beggars who had slept in their clothes, Ray and Billy Bob entered the security office. Reynolds was behind his desk, legs propped on a chair, talking on the phone. Leeland's work cubicle was vacant.

Reynolds removed his feet when he saw them and invited them to sit with a wave of his arm. "Yeah . . . No . . . I don't know . . ." he said into the phone. "Well, the police are here so . . . Right . . . Okay . . . Yeah . . . I'll call you back . . .

Right." Snapping the cordless unit shut, he closed his eyes and began massaging his temples. His lips drooped into an exaggerated frown.

"What time did they find him?" Ray asked.

The scowl took on a pained aspect. " 'Bout half an hour ago," he answered without opening his eyes. "Couple guys were driving out of camp to check the ice depth, saw something in the snow. Turned out to be Driscoll."

"Leeland mentioned blood. They have a cause of death yet?"

Reynolds shook his head. "He was curled up in a ball, stiff as a board. There was frozen blood, but they couldn't tell where it came from. They're gonna thaw him out and have Jorge look him over." He ran a hand across his short, dark hair, then leaned forward and filled his mug from a coffee maker perched on a shelf next to his desk. "I've been working Slope security for almost ten years, eight with Arco, the last two with Davis." He paused to curse. "I never seen anything like this. Men get killed once in a while. Working on a rig is pretty dangerous, especially up here. My people, they cart a corpse to Deadhorse and put it on a plane maybe once a year. And of course, we get brawls on a regular basis. Guys with attitudes, pulling two or four months on, they decide they don't like each other and wind up settling their differences with a fist fight. We break 'em up and keep an eye on them. One time an office geek tried to sneak out confidential papers, you know, industrial espionage, but on a real small scale. And there's always the drugs and alcohol the men smuggle in. But this . . . Murder just doesn't happen. I don't know if it ever has. And multiples . . ." He swore again, angrily this time.

"What's the weather ree-port?" Billy Bob asked. "This thang lettin' up anytime soon?"

Reynolds blew air at this. "I wish. The storm's supposed to move on by tomorrow. But there are two or three lined up behind it as always. We'll probably have a day or so of calm, then the wind'll start in again, from the other direction, of course, bringing all the snow back with it."

"You sound like you need a vacation," Ray observed.

"Or maybe a job change," Reynolds reflected. "A decade in Purgatory takes it's toll on a man. I don't know how much longer I can last." He looked at Ray. "How do you people stand it?"

Ray shrugged. "Home is home."

"I guess. Me? I get paid real good and I do my off time in Kauai. Got a condo on Poipu Beach. If it wasn't for that, I couldn't bring myself to come back." He muttered something, then added, "And now we got ourselves two murders." This was followed by a curse.

"It looks that way," Ray observed. "How would you and the deputy here like to go up and get the full story on Driscoll?"

Reynolds replied with a dry chuckle. "I'd love to. A hundred below, darker than pitch, blowing snow, zero visibility . . . There's nothing I'd rather do than drive to an isolated rig out on the ice and check on a human Klondike bar."

"We need a time of death," Ray said, ignoring the sarcasm. "Who saw him last, where they saw him, talk to the two men who found him, that sort of thing."

"What're *you* gonna do?" Billy Bob asked.

Ray sighed heavily. "I have an errand to run."

" 'N errand?"

"Something that may or may not have a bearing on this case. But, I don't know. I guess I just feel like I need to do it. It's hard to explain."

"Mind if I ask what it is?" Reynolds prodded.

"You wouldn't understand," Ray promised.

"Try me," Reynolds dared, brown eyes scrutinizing him.

Ray shrugged. "I'm going to visit a shaman."

⪢ EIGHTEEN ⪡

A HALF MILE out of camp, Ray veered left, aiming the Polaris west down a trackless, single lane road. Reynolds had been wrong. Visibility wasn't zero. It was more like twenty yards. The storm seemed as vehement as ever, with no intention of subsiding.

As he navigated, squinting through the clear goggles to ensure that he stayed on the road, Ray mentally calculated the time it would take to make the trip to Nuiqsut and back. He had left the Davis facility after four. Add a round trip travel time of 3 hours, 30 minutes to humor the old man and glean anything of value from the shaman, that would put him in camp between eight and eight-thirty. Billy Bob and Reynolds would be back from the rig by then. They could trade information, go over the case, grab some dinner, and head for bed, for some actual sleep this time.

Going to see a shaman. Ray shook his head at the idea. Was he nuts? The captain would have a stroke when he found out. *If* he found out. Ray wasn't planning to mention it. He was too embarrassed, still aghast that he was answering Grandfather's strange request. This trip had about a one in a million chance of being even remotely beneficial. It was a goose chase, an act of complete folly. Yet here he was, plowing away into the night.

There was a bright side, he decided. At least he had managed to avoid returning to rig seventeen to examine another cadaver. That was something. Poor Billy Bob, or rather poor

Reynolds, for having to ride with the talkative cowboy.

Ten minutes later he met another Y. A sign noted that the left branch led to the Deadhorse Airport. An arrow pointed in that direction, but no distance was provided. The right branch apparently went nowhere. At least, according to the sign. It certainly looked forsaken: a flat, drifted surface that was virtually indistinguishable from the open spaces on either side. As Ray set off into the pristine powder, breaking trail on a road less traveled, lights materialized to the north. Arco, he decided. BP would be next. After that, he would be on his own, alone in the dark.

The Polaris purred beneath him, its skis making neat parallel grooves in the light, airy snow. Thoughts of Margaret swept through his mind as he watched wind-driven crystals twirl and spin beautifully through the beam of the headlamp. He probably should have called her again, just to check in. She would be concerned if she didn't hear from him soon. The shower was important to her, but the idea of her fiancé blundering around the Slope in a blizzard looking for a murderer would cause her to worry. Being a worrier wasn't a good quality for a police officer's wife. *Wife* . . . Ray swallowed hard. Marriage, commitment, children, responsibilities . . . These seemingly positive ideals were haunting him with increasing regularity. They were like two-faced gods: angels that promised to fulfill his dreams one moment, demons threatening to rob him of his manhood and enslave him the next. Either way, he felt certain that the relational journey he was about to embark upon, whatever its true nature, would irreparably change him and shape, if not dictate, his ultimate destiny.

With that sobering thought rattling through his brain, Ray noticed the lights of the BP facility shimmering through the shifting veil of white. The dim, miniature galaxy twinkled, hid behind the storm, then fell away as the road twisted and traversed a low ridge. Ray encouraged the snow machine forward with a twist of the throttle.

It wasn't Margaret that bothered him, he decided, eyeing the speedometer. It wasn't even the potential for suffocation in long-term monogamy. What concerned him most was himself. What if he couldn't handle being a husband? Though he didn't want to admit it, Ray was frightened. Despite his age and occupation, he was scared stiff. Instead of a brave policeman, he felt like a scared little boy, like a kid facing a tough exam and wishing he could simply run away from it.

Cold feet, he told himself as he powered along the ice, arms fighting to keep the machine from sliding out of control. It was the sense of helplessness and fear men always experienced as they contemplated marriage. It was to be expected.

This positive self-talk seemed to slow the rising tide of emotions, and Ray made a concerted effort to build on it, to focus on the reality of the situation. He loved Margaret. Margaret loved him. They would endure good times and bad, like all couples. Their union would be a celebration, if they chose to make it that, full of joys, sorrows, victories, defeats, and most importantly, shared experiences. Instead of facing life alone, Ray would know the deep satisfaction, and the price, of walking alongside another human being.

No matter his current misgivings, Ray was as certain as a bachelor could be that he would never regret investing himself in another, pouring his energy and self into a woman who had captured his heart and now held it with gentle, tender hands close to her own. With her, he would know happiness, struggle, confrontation, delight. Without her, only emptiness.

Gazing ahead, into the vacant darkness, Ray decided that he would choose the former and never look back. He was sure, determined, suddenly and inexplicably confident that his next steps would be into the path of wisdom and light.

Nearly ninety minutes later, still buoyed by the intoxication of Margaret's love and the expanding hope of their future together, he reached Nuiqsut. It looked like a ghost town: a deserted, unmanicured street, wind-ravaged shanty shacks in various states of disrepair, the skeletons of old cars, pickups, and snow machines peeking out from beneath snowdrifts. The only evidence of occupation came from the windows: sour, yellow light that seemed void of warmth or life in the raging storm.

Ray left his mark on the village, thin rails in the soft-pack, straddled by a wide-stanced skier, and motored another quarter mile, then turned south, toward Grandfather's *ivrulik*. Here the drifts were deep, snow seeking refuge in the dips and gullies. It was work steering the Polaris, avoiding crevasses that were poised to swallow up the trailing sled, yet Ray found it stimulating. The physical activity and concentration this required had an energizing effect on him. With the wind at his back, visibility seemed to stretch. For an instant, he almost thought he saw the stars overhead.

He spotted Grandfather's house from a hundred yards away. Dull light blinked at him through the blowing snow. Abandoning the trail, he set off across a lumpy ice field.

Pulling the Polaris close to the building, he killed the engine and activated the battery. As he made his way toward the door, slipping and plodding, he heard something: a wolf call. It came from close range, too close. He was considering going back to the sled for his rifle when the wolf signaled its presence again, a mournful cry affirmed by an entire chorus of howls. Great. A whole pack. And they sounded like they were nearly upon him, probably circling in preparation for an assault. Usually wolves were skittish, afraid of humans. But if they were hungry enough . . .

Heart pumping rapidly, he stared into the surrounding darkness, eyes straining to make out shapes and movement. Behind him, the glow from the *ivrulik* created a dim rectangular shadow, the door. It was about twenty feet away. Run for it?

He had already taken two hurried steps toward refuge when another howl arose. Close. A matter of yards. It was followed by a round of frenzied yelping. Ray froze. Those weren't wolves. He listened. Dogs! Trudging to the back of the house he poked his head around the corner of the building. Six dogs were lying on their haunches in the snow, all tethered to a wooden sled. The team hopped up in unison when they saw him, tails wagging enthusiastically. They yipped a greeting, pulling at their harnesses. The sled, anchored firmly in the ice, groaned as the dogs struggled to greet Ray. He shook his head at them, reaching to pet the lead. He was scraggly, with radiant blue eyes. *Dogs!* Ray chided himself for being so paranoid, for mistaking malamutes for wolves. Fatigue and the nature of this case were obviously effecting his powers of observation.

"Raymond?" a gruff voice called.

Turning, Ray saw someone approaching with a flashlight. It was a short figure clad in a thick, hooded fur parka.

"Grandfather."

"You meet dogs. Good dogs."

"Yeah. Great dogs," Ray muttered. "They scared me to death."

The old man laughed at this, his gray, weathered face stressed by a smart-alecky grin. "Maniilaq's team."

"I figured that out."

"He inside. Much happy you come."

"Uh-huh. I'm overjoyed, myself."

The two of them left the dogs and returned to the front of the house. As they passed Ray's rig Grandfather gave it a cursory pass with the flashlight, then pronounced, "Sled. What mess. Tarp loose. I no teach you better?"

Ray tried to ignore the dig as he followed the old man inside. He was having second thoughts, wishing he had gone popsicle hunting with Bugs Bunny.

It was warmer in the *ivrulik,* a balmy 40 degrees. Grandfather was playing the *tukkuq,* the host, running the generator to support a trio of ancient space heaters. They were more fire hazards than anything else, their exposed coils glowed a threatening orange.

A kerosene lantern on a rod iron post provided illumination for the main living area. A man was seated in the decrepit armchair that Grandfather had salvaged from the dump, along with the rest of the furniture. The visitor was about Grandfather's age, deep wisdom lines riddling his high, sloping forehead, running away into a mat of steel-gray hair. A worn caribou parka was draped over his shoulders, his feet covered by knee-high mukluks. Gloves hid his hands and arms to the elbows, both adorned with elaborate bone beads. A labret decorated his lower lip, the ornamental plug giving his face an unbalanced appearance. A drum sat next to the chair: seal intestines stretched across a thin wooden frame. Leaning against the wall was a gruesome mask with an exaggerated, frowning lower lip, to symbolize the presence and activity of bad spirits. The old man's eyes were closed, as if he were basking in the heat and light of the lantern.

Ray wanted to go right back out the door and start up the Polaris. This was ludicrous. Consulting a shaman. A dog-team-driving, labret-wearing shaman. If the guys back in Barrow ever found out, he would be a laughing stock.

"Sit." The word came quietly, but with authority, and was accompanied by a brief wisp of vaporized breath.

Ray glanced at Grandfather and sighed, reminding himself of his job and mission. He was there to gather information. If that meant playing this ridiculous game, well, then he would play along with at least a pretense of respect.

Taking a seat on the couch, he removed his gear and examined Maniilaq. The man seemed to be thinking, or sleeping. His breathing was deep and regular, his head slightly bowed. Ray checked his watch and tried to be patient. He allowed the silence to stretch, listened as the wind shook the *ivrulik,* looked to Grandfather. The old man had his eyes closed too. Praying? To whom?

The Inupiat didn't have a central God, like the Christians. Their religion consisted of a network of taboos intended to appease a menagerie of animistic powers, all related to sustenance and season: the spirit of the hunt, the spirit of the fish, the spirit of the sky, the spirit of the whale, of the caribou, of the walrus, various weather gods. It was built on the idea that if you said the right things, to the right deities, at the right times, they might have pity on you and not let you starve or freeze to death. The key word was *might*. No matter how you attempted to humor them, there was still a good chance that they would allow you to perish. There was no rhyme or reason to their actions. They were fickle and uncaring, unmoved by human anguish. In the absence of a true religion, the People had set up a vague system of supernatural causes and effects that all hinged on one emotion: dread. That they had suffered under this sick delusion for so long amazed and angered Ray.

At least the white man's religion was less arbitrary. It too seemed to be fear based, revolving around the threat of going to Hell. From what little Ray had absorbed from Margaret, the Jesus church was concerned with behavior, with doing good deeds and not doing evil ones. But at least Christianity involved only one idol. It seemed more logical to tremble before a single angry God than many malevolent, unpredictable ones. Actually, in Ray's opinion, there was little logic in religion of any variety. Whatever the label, it all came down to superstition.

Maniilaq's head tilted back and he moaned pitifully. It reminded Ray of a caribou that had been downed by a bullet and was in the process of dying. The cry soon assumed a more regular form, developed a beat, then took on a melancholy melody. Inupiat lyrics followed. Ray struggled to translate, his mind recognizing the tune, but fighting to place it. He had heard it before . . . at . . . a funeral! It was a dirge for the dead! The words said something about . . . the spirits descending . . . in the form of ravens . . . and whisking the deceased away to . . . Ray missed the punchline. Heaven or the next world. Something like that.

As he glared at the shaman, already growing weary of the theatrics, he wondered if going to church with Margaret could be any worse than this. Church seemed relatively painless. Boring but painless. But this . . . As if listening to Grandfather drone on about the old ways wasn't bad enough, here he was suffering through an ancient rite: observing an Eskimo funeral, minus the deceased, conducted by a known fake. What a waste of time.

When the shaman's lament subsided, Ray made the most of the opportunity. "Grandfather said you might know something about . . ." That was as far as he got. Both Maniilaq and Grandfather cut him off with stern looks. They appeared to be offended, insulted, their eyes raging against Ray's insolence.

"Adiii!" Grandfather ordered. "No talk!"

Ray raised a palm toward them in a gesture of goodwill. The men scowled at him, then closed their eyes again. The shaman took up a new chant. It had to do with an evil hunter. That was all Ray could make out.

He checked his watch again, sighed, leaned back and stared

at the rugged ceiling. An aroma caught his attention. It was bitter, strong . . . coffee! Grandfather was brewing coffee. Straining, he heard the soft hiss of the propane stove. This really was a special occasion. Grandfather didn't waste propane on just any guest.

Leaning forward, Ray rose and took a careful step toward the kitchen. He was almost at the doorway when the old men jerked alert, scanned the room, and caught Ray red-handed. He smiled at them thinly. "Coffee?"

Grandfather glared at him and pointed to the couch with a bony finger. "Coffee later. First, sit!"

Ray obeyed, while Maniilaq launched out on another depressing chant, this time singing about the dangers of dark *anjatkuts*.

Fifteen minutes later, the shaman's hoarse, off-key voice finally found the end of the song. He exhaled loudly, blowing out air as if a sharp instrument had just punctured him. Opening his eyes, he looked directly at Ray. The man seemed dazed, sedated. Ray stared back, wondering if old George was high on something.

It was another two minutes before Maniilaq whispered, "*Tuungak.*"

"What about them?" Ray asked, his voice edged with irritation. This was taking too long.

"*Tuungak* speak."

"And what do they say?" he prodded.

Still staring at Ray, Maniilaq offered an impassioned reply, in Inupiaq.

"Tuungak afraid," Grandfather translated.

"Afraid? Of what?"

Maniilaq supplied a paragraph of garbled, nearly indecipherable words. When he had finished, Grandfather nodded, his expression grave.

"*Tuungak* afraid evil *anjatkut*. Afraid he make do . . . Do bad. Do evil."

Ray almost rolled his eyes at this. "Could you be a little more specific?"

Maniilaq responded with a raised voice. It echoed from the sod walls.

"Afraid much killing. Much killing," Grandfather began translating. "Afraid . . ." He paused, the blood draining from his face.

"What?"

"Afraid *anjatkut* kill three. This night . . . three . . ."

"Three? Three more?"

Grandfather shook his head. "You. You three. Afraid *anjatkut* kill you . . . this night."

➤➤ NINETEEN ➤➤

"How much?" Ray asked with a sigh.

Maniilaq seemed genuinely puzzled. The old man turned to Grandfather and shrugged, muttering an Inupiaq phrase.

"I'm in danger. He can protect me," Ray deadpanned. "Ask him how much he wants."

Grandfather conferred with the shaman in hushed tones, then replied, "He no understand."

Ray scoffed at this. Maniilaq was nothing if not clever. The man could speak patois—village English—as well as anybody else. Strange how he was suddenly unable to comprehend a simple statement when money was at issue.

"It's a shakedown, Grandfather," Ray grumbled. "Maniilaq has information that I need. How much does he want?"

"Adii!" Grandfather bellowed. "Raymond, no respect. No respect Maniilaq. No respect *tuungak*." He paused, his face falling in an expression of utter disappointment. "No respect me. No respect People."

Ray was in no mood for this. "I'm just trying to move things along. If there's a powerful *anjatkut* after me, I need help," he said, making an attempt to sound halfway sincere. "Maniilaq here is my only hope," he lied. "How much would be appropriate to procure his services."

The two men discussed this at length. When they were finished, Maniilaq grunted, "Twenty dollar."

As reasonable as any other informant, Ray thought. Fishing

at his wallet, he laid a twenty on the floor in front of the shaman.

"You no got change—smaller bills," Maniilaq complained.

Ray almost laughed. Instead, he forced himself to keep a straight face as he traded the twenty for two five's and a ten. "How's that?"

The shaman nodded appreciatively.

"Now, what can you tell me about this . . . *anjatkut*?"

"Much powerful," Maniilaq replied, still nodding. "Much powerful."

"I don't suppose you've got a name . . . a description, maybe?"

The shaman's nose wrinkled up—the nonverbal cue for no.

"Is it a man?"

The eyebrows rose, the eyes widening: *yes*.

"Does he work for an oil company?"

Again the eyebrows jumped toward the ceiling.

"So he's not a Native?" Ray clarified.

Maniilaq's lips formed a pronounced frown.

"Is he a Native?"

His eyes grew wide.

"Okay. Male, Native, works for an oil company."

Maniilaq groaned, then uttered an explanation in Inupiat. Ray caught a few words: responsible, many, powerful, evil, many . . .

When he was finished, Ray turned to Grandfather. "What'd he say?"

"If you study ways of People, you know."

"Grandfather!" Ray insisted. This wasn't the time for a lecture on keeping the old ways and language alive.

Grandfather blew air at him. "Aiyyaa . . . He say *anjatkut* make killing. Many help."

"Many help? What's that supposed to mean? How many *anjatkuts* are there?"

The old man raised a thin finger toward him. "One just. But many evil. Army. Much killing. Maybe."

"Army? Are you telling me this guy is military?" Ray immediately thought of Reynolds.

Grandfather shook his head, clearly annoyed by the question. "*Anjatkut* kill. Others help. Much powerful."

Ray's head was beginning to ache—from lack of sleep, from this convoluted, veiled description of the murderer, from sitting in an *ivrulik* with two senile old men. Rubbing his temples, he clarified, "So one man did the killing, others helped him. Did he force them to help? Did he threaten them? Or did they want to help? Is this some sort of conspiracy?"

Maniilaq mumbled something to Grandfather. The old man listened, then said, "You make ... twisted. But no. Not twisted. Simple."

"Simple, right." Ray shook his head at them.

The shaman cleared his throat and leaned forward. "*Anjatkut* end life. Much evil. Naluaqmiut serve. Honor *anjatkut* power."

Ray closed his eyes and tried to think through the gibberish. A Native oil worker had murdered a man—Hank Weinhart by the looks of it. Possibly two men, if Driscoll fit the MO. Then white men had helped cover the killings up. Why? Because of the Native's power? That ruled out the roustabouts. They had no power whatsoever. They were the low men on the totem pole. Who was in a position of authority? Simpson? Bauer? Wrong race. Finally, a face materialized in his mind: chubby brown cheeks, cheerful olive eyes, thick lips and a smile that revealed a mouth full of sharp yellow teeth. Chief Makintanz?

It was a good guess. The only problem was, as usual, motive. Why would Makintanz kill a Davis Oil VP? Makintanz was now on the Davis board. Killing Weinhart would be like shooting himself in the foot. And if he had committed murder, or double murder, why in the world would Davis people help cover it up? Answer: they wouldn't. Especially if he had murdered two of their own. No. It made absolutely no sense, except that it fulfilled Maniilaq's vague portrait of the perpetrator.

Ray stood, disappointed, more weary than ever, suddenly aware that he had actually been expecting this little conference to provide him with some sort of practical direction in the investigation. For some reason, he had allowed his exectations to rise, in the face of common sense, and had actually been hoping that Maniilaq would magically solve the ase. That obviously wasn't going to happen. He chided himself for being such a sap.

"I need some coffee," he announced on his way to the itchen. "Then I need to get back over to Prudhoe."

A dented steel pot was quivering frantically on the propane tove, the hissing blue flame causing the liquid inside to bub*le* and gurgle. Removing it from the heat, Ray wondered ow Grandfather kept from burning the *ivrulik* to the ground. *He* was growing more and more forgetful, more and more eglectful, more and more dangerous. Two months earlier the *ld* man had left one of the space heaters on for three days *while* he went seal hunting. By the time he returned, the eater was nothing but a shell of melted coils and wires. That hadn't exploded or erupted in flames was something of a niracle.

Ray poured himself a mug of coffee and sipped it carefully. : was too hot, too strong, too bitter, slightly burned. Just the ay Grandfather liked it.

He was in the process of filling two more mugs when rrandfather appeared at his side. The old man watched him losely, as if he were performing some delicate task that re*uired* precision and skill. Finally, he whispered, "No go."

Ray handed him a mug. "I have to. I have work to do."

Grandfather rested a hand on Ray's shoulder. "I worry for aymond."

"I'm a big boy now. I can take care of myself."

The old man shook his head, a grave look on his face. This no bully. This evil. No go. Let Maniilaq talk *tuungak*. *lelp* you."

"Grandfather . . ." Ray groaned. "You asked me to come, came. Okay? Now I have to get back." Taking the remainIg cup, he returned to the front room and handed it to the naman. "*Taiku*. I appreciate your help," he told him, only alf seriously. Maniilaq frowned at this. The three men spent *le* next five minutes drinking their coffee, attending to the ind, watching wisps of steam rise from their mugs and curl layfully toward the ceiling.

When Ray's coffee was nearly gone, he began climbing back into his cold-weather gear. The two old men sat glaring at him, scowls creating deep furrows in their leathery faces: the brothers glum.

Ray was pulling on his boots when Maniilaq muttered, "Doubt."

Grandfather nodded thoughtfully, as if this one word pronouncement answered every dilemma that had ever faced mankind.

"Doubt cloud eyes. No can see."

"No can see," Grandfather repeated, still nodding.

Zipping his RefrigiWear suit, Ray pretended not to hear them.

"*Tuungak* say ground move. No steady, Raymond."

"Is that right?" He pulled on his parka.

"No trust anyone."

"Uh-huh."

"But you . . ." Maniilaq tossed his head back and issued a screech, something akin to a bird in pain. Ray stared at him. The guy was nuts, probably doing drugs.

"*Tuungak* afraid *anjatkut*."

"So you said."

"But they more afraid you."

"Me? Listen, if you're looking for another twenty, forget it."

"They afraid you . . ." Maniilaq moaned. His eyes were closed again, his face toward the sod roof. "Great of Tuungak follow you."

Fastening his hood, Ray pulled his mittens out of a pocket.

"Great of Tuungak . . ." The shaman's voice cracked and he slid from his chair. He donned the grotesque mask with trembling hands before grunting, "Great of Tuungak."

Ray sighed at this. Either the guy was going all out for an extra tip, or he was having a stroke. Whichever, Ray didn't have the time or the energy for it.

Kneeling on the earthen floor, Maniilaq lifted two quaking arms into the air. His breath was coming in gasps, amplified by the mask. He was almost sobbing.

Okay, so the joker was convincing. Ray pulled out his wal-

et, removed the twenty, placed it on the floor. "There. And
o, I don't have change."

Maniilaq never even gave the bill a glance. Hidden beneath
ne brittle face of twisted stone, he groaned, "Great of Tuun-
ak . . . Great of Tuungak . . . He mark you."

"Huh?"

"Mark you his own." He mumbled something in Inupiaq,
nen added, "I see boy . . . full of dark . . . Listen doubt long
me . . . Light come. He run away. Light chase. Hungry Light
. . Only Light . . . Light swallow him. He make like moon—
eflect only Light in dark. No more doubt."

Ray finished his coffee in a gulp. Whatever.

"Danger look you," he continued. "Evil look you. But
ireat of Tuungak . . . Light . . . Only Light . . . He cover you
. . like blanket. You no die. But almost."

"Hopefully I can flange this thing up in the next day or
o," Ray whispered to Grandfather.

The old man grimaced at him, as if in pain. "You stiff-
ecked. No listen to wise man."

"I listened. But I'm responsible for investigating a mur-
er," Ray said, growing angry. "Two murders now. I appre-
iate your help but I really need to . . ."

Grandfather silenced him with a finger. "You listen!"

"Boy has foot in sea, foot in river," Maniilaq continued.
'Sea is old, never change. River always new. Boy must walk
rooked—part old, part new." From beneath the mask, he
vhispered, "You crooked boy."

The word picture, hokey as it sounded, struck a chord in
.ay. Maniilaq might have been misguided, but he had hit the
nark with that description. Ray was, after all, attempting to
nd a balance between the old ways and the new, between
is Inupiat roots and the ever-changing world of white cul-
ire. Being an Eskimo at the dawn of the twenty-first century
vas both a blessing and a curse. *Crooked* . . .

Maniilaq removed the mask and rose awkwardly, like a
nan stumbling out of bed after a long sleep. Taking Ray's
ands in his own, he said, "*Anjatkut* mad. Crazy. Part him
iding. Salome . . . Salome betray him . . . dishonor him . . . in
eauty. Make much angry. He hide in place of kings. You

find. Go where all man go. To beauty. Salome in beauty. You find." He paused, then, "You path uneven. Ground move. No trust—except Great of Tuungak. He guide. He protect. You no doubt, you no die."

"That's good to hear." As Ray turned to leave, the shaman refused to let go of his hands. The grip was surprisingly firm. "You take," he said. Reaching inside his coat, he removed a leather satchel. He spun Ray around and attached something to the ponytail hidden in the layers of his clothing. An amulet, Ray decided, unable to see it.

"You trust sign of Kila. Mighty Kila. You trust."

"Okay. I will." He shook Maniilaq's hand, gave Grandfather a hug, and adjusted his goggles. "I'll do that. *Taiku.*"

"Mighty Kila go with you," Maniilaq said, his right arm outstretched. "Protect."

Opening the door, Ray made his escape. Outside, it was bitter, intensely cold, yet to Ray it was almost refreshing. He would much rather brave the elements, hostile as they might be at present, than be badgered by a witch doctor, verbally berated for his lack of "faith," treated like an ignorant, disobedient child who was not capable of comprehending the higher ways of the elders. The experience had left him frustrated, annoyed at having allowed himself to be swept up in such a silly charade.

Fruitless. That was the word that came to mind as he started the Polaris and urged it away from the *ivrulik.* Totally and utterly fruitless. Other than a confusing, nonsensical prophecy from a fake shaman, he had gained nothing from the venture. Nothing except a pounding headache—and a lighter wallet. Despite the coffee, he felt depleted. If only he could go home, go to bed, take that time off he had coming.

Unfortunately, that wasn't possible. Not unless one of two events occurred. He would either have to close this case, or the weather would have to break, allowing the authorities from Anchorage to make it into Deadhorse. Staring into the frenzied snow and the vacant sky behind it, he decided that the *tuungak* in control of this storm had no intention of providing relief anytime in the near future. So that left him with the first alternative: close the case. In order to do that, he would need to solve a puzzle that was missing a number of pieces, and which he was being forced to work on blind-folded.

He reevaluated the case as the Polaris plowed along the trail: the murder, the earmarkings of *nigiluq*, the disappearance of the John Doe corpse, the discovery of another body, this one the rig foreman . . . What did it all mean?

Motoring through the loneliness of Nuiqsut, Ray reflected on Maniilaq's rantings. *Great Tuungak . . . Great Kila . . . Going toward the light . . .* Gibberish that didn't offer so much as a shred of useful information. And the *anjatkut . . .* According to the shaman, the murderer was a powerful *anatkut*, a Native with great influence. That still brought Makintanz to mind.

As he left the flickering mercury lamps of Nuiqsut behind, Ray tried to imagine Chief Makintanz "hunting" humans as if they were animals. The guy was a quack, a charlatan who liked to practice the old ways while living in white-man comfort and wealth. A pretend Eskimo. Still, was he clinically insane? Wouldn't you have to be to slice a man up like that? And was the chief bodily capable of such an act? The last time Ray had seen a picture of Makintanz in the news, the guy was about the size of a house: folds of flabby skin, thick, stubby limbs, grotesquely expanding waist . . . a four hundred pound advertisement for the horrors of gluttony. A heart attack waiting to happen. Motivation aside, Makintanz seemed an unlikely candidate for the suspect list.

Ray shook off the case and its impressive array of dangling loose ends as the Polaris continued skating east. The wind was changing, whipping the snow south, then reversing itself to blow the same pellets northward. Each gust rocked the Polaris on its skis, threatening to dislodge the sled from its hitch and send it cartwheeling into a drift.

For the hour and a half that followed, Ray ordered himself to think of something else, to give himself a respite from the frustrating mystery. He occupied himself with images of Margaret, their upcoming wedding, the shower he was probably going to miss.

The lights of the BP camp were shimmering on the horizon,

when a phrase floated into his mind: *Hiding in beauty* . . .
That was what Maniilaq had said about the *anjatkut*. What
was that supposed to mean? Probably nothing, just more animistic mumbo jumbo. It was nonspecific enough to bear almost any application—the trait of a good prophecy. It could
never be proved, but then, it could never be disproved either.
Hiding among beauty . . . *Hiding in a place of kings* . . .
Maybe the murderer had fled the country and was hiding out
in the Bahamas. No. Maniilaq had further explained that it
was a place *where all men go*. Where did all men go? To
work? To breakfast? To bed? To the can? And what was that
business about *Salome*? Was that a name? Of whom? Maybe
it was patois for an unfaithful person, a traitor. According to
Maniilaq this Salome had betrayed the *anjatkut*. What did that
mean? Did it mean anything? What a bunch of . . .

Ray felt more than heard the initial hiccup. The Polaris
hesitated for an instant, as if momentarily unsure about its
course, then continued on, confident and determined. Ten seconds later, the machine coughed, losing speed. Ray instinctively gave the throttle a squeeze. The Polaris responded by
roaring forward. He eyed the gauges: the gas tank was three
quarters full, the oil pressure and temperature needles perfectly centered. It was another mile or two before the next
stutter. Ray urged the vehicle on with a twist of his wrist.
This time, instead of accelerating, the machine began to hack.
Soon it was having a seizure, bleeding speed, the engine fighting to remain alive.

As the Polaris ground to a halt, smoke belching from the
tailpipe, Ray cursed his luck, or lack thereof. He cursed the
malfunctioning beast, cursed the fact that if it had only waited
another twenty minutes, he would have been back at the Davis camp, or at least within walking distance of it, cursed
Grandfather for convincing him to make the trip, cursed himself for agreeing to it. Still swearing angrily, he squinted in
the direction of the BP camp, or where the lights of the camp
had been. They were gone now. The storm was playing
games, snow lifting to reveal great expanses one moment,
settling in to smother him the next. It had to be at least a
couple of miles to BP. Maybe more.

He tried the ignition. The Polaris sputtered once, then died beneath him, leaving only the wind to keep him company. It was louder than ever, seemingly ecstatic that he was stuck, alone and helpless within its domain.

Check the engine, he told himself as he dismounted. Find the problem. Fix it. If it can't be repaired, radio for assistance. Stay warm, wait for help to arrive. If help doesn't arrive . . . well . . . It might be necessary to take a little walk and find out exactly how far it is to that BP camp.

⋙ TWENTY ⋘

RAY FISHED A penlight out of his parka, unlatched the hood on the snow machine and glared at the engine. What an ordeal this was turning out to be. As if being subjected to Grandfather, Maniilaq, and their spooky psychic forecasts wasn't bad enough. Now his machine seemed to be giving up the ghost. Just over a year old, the Polaris had performed almost flawlessly the previous winter. The dealer in Fairbanks had promised that it wouldn't need so much as a tune up for the first eighteen months. It was still under warranty. A lot of good that did him out here.

After a few moments of examination, Ray determined that the malfunction might have something to do with the carburetor, maybe the one the Davis mechanics had installed was a rebuilt one. Poorly rebuilt, apparently. He flicked on the battery-powered engine warmer and checked the gauge. The needle was frozen to 0. Either the gauge was broken or the battery had been totally drained. Great.

As he trudged back to the sled, fighting the urge to give the Polaris a swift kick, Ray rethought his strategy. He would radio in first. Then, while the cavalry was inbound, he would work on resurrecting the carburetor.

When he pulled back the tarp on the sled, he realized that there was a serious problem with his plan. Most of the crates and boxes were intact, but they were empty. There was a shadowy hole where the survival kit was supposed to be. His sleeping bag was gone. So were the tent and stove. And the extra fuel. And his shovels. And his flashlight. And his compass. And his rifle. No wonder the sled hadn't gotten stuck in any drifts along the way. It was too light to dig in. The steel toolbox, which was still there, contained a pair of pliers and a plastic jar of miscellaneous bolts and nuts. Lifting a crate, he found his snowshoes. The radio sat at the back of the sled, outside the tarp, where he had placed it at the start of his trip.

A radio, snowshoes, a pair of pliers, and a tarp. Things could have been worse, he decided. A gust of wind wrenched the tarp from his hands. It peeled away, rippled violently, and then, before Ray could grasp one of the ties, lifted into the air like a majestic bird and disappeared into the darkness. He trotted a few steps in pursuit, shining the tiny beam of the penlight in the direction of the prodigal tarp. It was gone. The night and the storm had swallowed it whole.

A radio, snowshoes, and a pair of pliers . . . Things could have been worse. A little anyway. Taking up the radio mike, he flipped the power switch.

"This is Officer Raymond Attla of the Barrow Police Department. I'm stranded approximately three miles west of the BP camp at Prudhoe Bay. Request assistance be dispatched immediately. Repeat, immediately. I am without shelter or emergency survival equipment."

He let up on the button and waited. When there was no response, he tried again. Bending, he placed a hood-covered ear to the speaker and strained to hear through the angry elements.

"This is Officer Raymond Attla of the Barrow . . ." That's when he noticed the power light. It was dark. The radio wasn't even on. He toggled the switches, twisted the knobs, banged the device with his fist. Nothing. It was as dead as the snow machine.

That left him with snowshoes and a pair of pliers. Things could have been worse, but Ray couldn't imagine how. Time for a new plan. The primary objective was to remain calm.

Snowshoes and a pair of pliers . . . He pulled back the sleeve of his parka and examined his watch under the pale glow of the penlight. If he didn't show up back at Davis in the next couple of hours, someone would come looking for him. Wouldn't they?

Ray kicked at the snow with a bunny boot. It had the consistency of fine sand: individual grains of brilliant white powder. He knelt, took a handful in his mitten and gave it a squeeze. Opening his hand, he was rewarded with a palm-sized mound of albino flour. It had resisted his attempt to compact it and exploded into dust with the next blast of wind. He wouldn't be building any ice houses this evening. At this temperature, without the aid of water and a decent shovel, it would be virtually impossible to sculpt any sort of shelter. That left only one alternative. He would have to hoof it to the BP camp. The odds of successfully hiking three miles in this weather were slim. But it was a chance, possibly his only chance, to avoid becoming a popsicle.

Ray sat on the edge of the sled and strapped on his snowshoes. Unlike the bulky, ungainly wooden and gut shoes Ray had grown up clomping around in, the same four-foot monsters Grandfather still used, these were compact models, a combination of titanium, rubber, and webbing.

As he abandoned his rig, he wondered who had done this. A thief? Was someone back at Davis so hard up for tools, a propane camping stove, a sleeping bag, that they would rip off a cop? He aimed the penlight toward the horizon, wishing it was a spotlight and could show him the way to BP. When had the equipment been removed? It was there after the mechanics worked on the carburetor. It was there when he set off for Grandfather's. Wasn't it?

He had taken a dozen or so steps beyond the relative stability of the icy road, into a vast sea of glistening white waves, when he was struck by a sobering thought: I could die out here. Fall, get buried in a drift, become a popsicle, not to be found until July. And even then the wolves would probably be the first ones on the scene. It wasn't an inspiring mental picture.

Ray plodded on, wind pulling at his RefrigiWear pant legs, tugging against his hood as if it was determined to invade his cocoonlike suit. He had covered what he estimated to be a quarter of a mile before an idea occurred to him. What if his rig had been sabotaged? What if someone had purposefully ransacked the sled, taking out his equipment so that . . .

Maybe the cold was taking its toll on his mind. Maybe it was fatigue. Whatever the reason, Ray's thought processes seemed to be moving at the speed of molasses. Why hadn't he figured it out earlier? Someone was trying to kill him—or at least, to ensure that the land and this hellish storm killed him.

Striding with a steady rhythm, he studied the theory with as much objectivity as he could muster. His nose was numb now, but he could still feel his toes, his kneecaps, elbows, and fingers. The key was to keep moving.

The first breakdown, on the way in from the rig, that could have been the luck of the draw. The Polaris simply had a problem. But the second one . . . It seemed highly unlikely that an engine that had just been repaired by two qualified mechanics would give out again. Both times he had been alone and the possibility of freezing to death had been real—and still was.

If he were closing in on solving the case, Ray could have understood why the killer would do something drastic to silence him, but he was light years away from finding the murderer. He had yet to make sense of the crimes or line up any suspects. So why get rid of a police officer? Maybe the bad guy, whomever it turned out to be, had an attitude about Natives. Nah. Not even a bona fide white supremacist would go to the trouble of disabling a snow machine and stranding him without survival gear. Would they? Prejudice and hatred were venomous emotions, but . . .

Right now, it didn't really matter who was responsible. What mattered was that he keep walking. His arms were stiff and cold, his calves threatening to cramp. He wanted to stop, to rest, to sleep. That was the beginning of the end, he knew. Hypothermia and frostbite teamed up to cloud your thinking and sap your strength. When your head was foggy, your body unfeeling, uncomplaining, you sat down for a little break, and never got back up again.

Keep going! Ray demanded. He began repeating the words as if they were part of a life-sustaining mantra.

He had walked for nearly seventy minutes and was on the verge of collapse, buoyed only by the hope that he would ascend a pingo rise and see the BP camp at any moment, when something materialized on the horizon. Flickering lights. The vision crushed him. It was the camp, alright, but it was off in the distance, far to his left. Still miles away. He could have been there by now if only he had known what direction to walk. It would take another hour to reach those lights. An hour he wasn't sure he had.

Reorienting himself, he did his best to pretend that it was no big deal. It would merely be a little longer before he was rewarded with a hot meal and a warm bed, but the miscalculation had taken its toll.

Ray had no sensation in his legs from the thighs down. They were dead weights that swung forward awkwardly, begrudgingly. His fingers burned. His forearms and shoulders were numb. He was slightly dizzy.

Hypothermia. Ray recognized the early stages. His feet and hands were probably already frostbitten. He wondered what Margaret would say if they had to be amputated. Would she marry a man who couldn't walk without assistance, who didn't have any fingers to run through her hair? Suddenly overcome with emotion, tears streamed down his cheeks beneath the neoprene mask. The penlight fell, burrowing deep into the snow. He knelt to retrieve it, trying to remember why he was crying.

The darkness seemed to swirl in around him. The wind had stopped. The snow was gone. The cold had retreated, replaced by a comforting warmth.

Stretching out on the soft, overstuffed mattress, he gave himself permission to think of something happy, something that would carry him to the morning.

Margaret . . . He could see her, a seductive apparition in a daring, purple dress. She flew toward him, arms extended. Embracing him, she gave him a long, mischievous look. Finally she kissed him, delicately at first, then with the passion of a banshee just loosed from a centuries-long imprisonment. Her lips were like honey, her perfume a narcotic. Ray ran his hand down her neck, tracing a line along the smooth curve of her shoulder. Margaret moaned her appreciation, her breath hot and rapid. She kissed him again, almost violently, as if a fire had been ignited in her soul, a raging inferno that sought to consume him.

Ray was in heaven.

⇛ TWENTY-ONE ⇚

YOU'RE DYING.

The diagnosis was conveyed in a calm, almost contemplative tone. Ray heard it, tried to dismiss it, but couldn't. Somehow he knew that it was true. He *was* dying. His life was being stolen from him, drained moment by moment. And he was content to simply sit by and let it happen.

He watched himself with Margaret, studying the scene passively, a tangle of determined limbs, throaty sighs and grunts, smooth olive skin glistening with the heat of passion. The decision seemed remarkably clear: continue to embrace the fantasy and die a contented man, or fight to wake up, maybe live a little longer, and then face a brutal death. It was not an easy choice. The pleasure of Margaret or the pain of deep winter? The first was easy, immensely satisfying. The second horribly difficult. He knew what he wanted to do, but the survival instinct was powerful—even more powerful than his overactive libido.

Shaking off the delusion, he saw Margaret waver and disappear, abandoning him like a wounded lover. Consciousness returned slowly, as if reality were the dream. The world became black again. He opened his eyes. More black. Maybe he was already dead.

The wind assured him that he wasn't. It roared over his hood, peppering his goggles with snow. The cold was still beyond him, his body paralyzed, an unfeeling lump of frozen flesh. He tried to rise, his brain issuing the order to stand, but his muscles refused to obey.

Lying there, impotent to alter the situation, he was reminded of something Grandfather used to tell him. When a man starts to freeze to death, the old man had explained, it's like putting on a rabbit parka. There is a sense that you're getting warm, when, in fact, you are really at your end.

Death . . . It was greatly feared by the Inupiat. Sick people were left alone to die, their friends and family not wanting to be near when the spirit made its exit. The ailing themselves tried not to linger. Spirits of the dead were considered powerful and extremely dangerous. Not even a shaman could tend to a dying person. Traditionally, the Eskimos of the far north had chosen not to bury their dead. Instead, they placed the deceased in old animal skins and dragged them into the wilderness for the wolves, foxes, and ravens to consume. In that way, the bodies would return to the Land, continuing their journey through the circle of life.

He could feel himself sliding again, moving effortlessly toward unconsciousness, like a sled gliding across a lake of ice. The wind was still howling, but it was faraway now, an unobtrusive soundtrack accompanying his mental reflections.

Suddenly there was light. It was everywhere, surrounding him, engulfing him in a brilliant, comforting glow. He was no longer cold. He could move his arms and legs. Renewed energy actually pulsed through him. Ray laughed, giddy with a sense of overwhelming relief. It was like nothing he had ever experienced. Light, life, existence seemed to merge into a singular emotion: joy.

In the next instant, the light retreated, soaring away toward the horizon. Ray stood, determined to chase after it. That's when he realized that the snow was gone. So was his parka, his boots, his mask, and goggles. He was naked, but warm. It was summer. He was in a boat, a single-seat kayak resting on a body of water that seemed limitless. The light was beckoning, calling to him. Ray took up a double-ended paddle and set out for it.

He was excited, almost ecstatic with anticipation. He didn't understand this, and didn't try to. Instead he made each stroke count, pulling at the water with renewed strength, with the fresh, tireless muscles of a zealous youth.

The light was growing, golden tongues reaching skyward, lapping up the remnants of dawn. A mist materialized out of nowhere. It stretched to touch the kayak, then quickly enveloped it in a thick veil of dull gray. No longer able to see the light, Ray was nevertheless confident in his direction, a heavy, inexplicable peace hovering over him.

Without warning, the cloud departed. It rolled away, leaving only a wall of deepest black. The light was gone. The joy, the peace, the unexplained ecstasy forgotten. Ray could feel the kayak bouncing under him. The wind had begun to blow, churning the sea and urging waves to break over the edge of the boat. He was wet, chilled, afraid.

A terrible noise rose above the howling gale and echoed over the water. It was ghoulish, dreadful . . . alive. Ray twisted his head, trying to discern the source. Before he could so much as lift the paddle, two long arms reached up from the sea. They were like giant, faceless snakes, scaled and slimy. Wrapping themselves around him, they began to squeeze. In the next instant, Ray realized that they weren't snakes. Rather they were horns or antennae anchored to a hideous green head that shot out of the water. It was a . . . a creature . . . a sea monster! Two luminescent eyes glared at him hungrily. Ray tried to move, but the grip only tightened. The thing opened its mouth slowly, revealing hundreds of enormous teeth. It slid toward him, smiling.

As it climbed into the kayak, he realized that it had feet—scores of them. They were small, stunted like a caterpillar's. The thing roared again, the resulting vibration shaking Ray's chest, shaking his very soul. It was at that moment, with the creature poised to consume him, that Ray remembered the story. Grandfather had told it to him many times. A Giant Sea Serpent had plagued the People for centuries, until a brave shaman had frightened it away with a drum and a song.

Ray didn't have a drum. The tentacles were squeezing him, his lungs nearly empty. Singing was impossible. This was it. Death had finally come for him.

The mouth opened, the green teeth approached, the two

snakes continued their quest to suffocate him. A pair of fiery, piercing eyes gazed at him, peering into his spirit, searching for fear.

"Great Kila . . ." Ray gasped. "Great Kila . . .

"Is he dead?"

"Nope. Least, not yet."

"Good. Let's get him into the truck. Take off his snow-shoes."

Ray squinted as the glare from the monster's eyes became intense, painful. "Great Kila . . ."

"What's he saying?"

"Got me. Probably hallucinating. That happens when you're suffering from exposure."

"Will he make it?"

"I don't know. Depends on how frozen he is. If we can warm him up fast enough, he'll probably be okay. Might lose a couple toes or something. Grab his legs."

Ray could feel himself being swallowed by the creature. The snakes released him and he was suddenly in a free fall, diving into a deep, black well.

"Here . . . Lay him down in the back here. I've got some blankets."

"Geez, I hope he's alright."

"Crazy Eskimo, wandering around in this weather."

"His snow machine musta broke down again."

"I guess so. But I thought he was smart enough to pack emergency supplies. Most Eskimos do that, you know. They're good about that sort of thing."

"Hey, looky here. A crucifix."

"Must be Catholic."

"Must be."

"Crank up the heater."

"It's cranked."

"Okay, let's get him back to camp."

"Right."

Ray heard the thing moan, a strange sound when experienced from within the beast.

There was no pain, yet. No more squeezing on his chest,

just an ominous hum. He was obviously in the monster's stomach. Still alive, he would be digested slowly, torturously. Ray begged death to take him.

Instead, the light returned. Opening his eyes, Ray found himself in bed somewhere. It wasn't home. Wasn't Grandfather's place. It was . . . a hospital? A curtain attached to a curving metal channel in the roof surrounded his bed; between that, the chrome arms on the twin-mattress, and the smell, it was a dead giveaway. At the bedside were a bank of monitors. A tiny screen displayed a green light that blinked in time with an electronic beep. There were wires attached to him, tubes stuck to his arm.

He tried to remember what had happened, why he required medical care, but couldn't. He recalled the sea creature, the journey in the kayak, both vividly, as if they were actual memories. Yet before that . . . what?

A simple wiggle of his toes brought everything back. Electric pain ran up his calves, racing all the way to his buttocks. His toes felt like they had been severed, crushed, burned . . . *frostbitten.*

Ray was entertaining thoughts of tragedy, the idea that even amputated limbs offered ghost pain for a while, when he heard the door open, close, then the curtain was ripped back. A woman stood there, her face to a clipboard as she wrote something. She was young, with short brown hair and a stern, businesslike expression.

When she finally looked up, she flinched, obviously startled. "You're awake!"

Ray nodded at her.

"How do you feel?"

"Like I was mauled by a polar bear."

"How are your fingers?" she asked, examining them. "Can you bend them for me?"

Ray made a fist with one hand, then the other. The skin stung as it tightened around his knuckles.

"Good." The woman sounded like a kindergarten teacher praising a five-year-old. She scribbled something on the clipboard, then, "Let's have a look at your feet." The sheet was whisked back.

"So they're still there?" Ray raised up and stared down the bed. His feet were tinted gray near the toes with ragged, blistering skin. They were ugly, but at least they were still connected to his legs.

"You're lucky," the woman announced, leaning to examine them. "You only froze the epidermis. The subcutaneous tissue was still in good shape."

"Meaning? . . ."

"The skin will peel. Your toes will be painful for a couple of weeks. They might bother you a little, you know, burn some the next time you're out in the cold. But otherwise—"

"I can walk?"

"Sure. It'll sting, but you can walk." She paused to check the monitors. "You're doing fine. You were dehydrated. We pumped you full of fluids. Gave you a few mild pain meds. A good night's rest and you won't be much worse for the wear." She looked at him, smiling for the first time.

"Thanks, doctor."

"Nurse," she corrected. "We don't have a doc in camp. When somebody needs serious medical attention, we send them to Anchorage. I'm just here to take care of the scratches and sniffles."

"Well, thanks for your help."

She nodded, absentmindedly, her attention on the clipboard. "Since you're awake, let me go ahead and get some information for your chart. We have to file everything with our insurance provider. Let's see . . . You're name is Raymond Attla. Uh . . . age?"

"Twenty-eight."

"Employer?"

"North Slope Borough, Barrow Police Department."

The nurse recorded this dutifully. "Are you contracting with Davis?"

"No."

"Social security number?"

Ray recited it, wondering why that was necessary.

"Religious preference . . . Catholic." She checked it off with her pencil.

"Catholic?"

"You are Catholic, aren't you?"

Ray shook his head. "No."

She took a step toward him, a hand reaching for his ponytail. "Then what's this?"

"What's what?" Ray craned his neck to see. Just below the elastic keeper was a silver icon: a thin, two-inch vertical shaft, a thin one-inch horizontal piece, a shrunken sculpture of a human body attached to the bars. Its tiny arms were outstretched, legs bent at the knees, feet stuck to the vertical piece with a miniature nail. Upon the head was a crown of sharp prongs. The expression on the face, though drawn in silver and almost too small to appreciate, was one of agony.

"Maniilaq . . ." he muttered.

"Excuse me?"

"Someone gave it to me."

The nurse released it and returned her attention to the clipboard. "Okay, then . . . Religious preference?"

"What are the choices?"

"Catholic, Protestant, Buddhist, Moslem—"

"How about none of the above?"

"Fine."

"Name of a relative or friend to be notified in the event of an emergency?"

"My grandfather, Charles Attla."

The nurse noted this. "Phone number?"

"He doesn't have a phone. You'd have to contact him through the Foxglove family in Nuiqsut, by radio."

The nurse nodded at this, writing. "What's your insurance?"

"Group Care."

"OK, I can get the rest of the details from you tomorrow."

"I might not be here tomorrow. I'm on a case and I'll be—"

"You'll be in this bed for the next twelve hours."

"But you said I was okay."

"Right now you are. But if there are any problems, they'll probably occur in the next twelve hours."

"Listen, you don't understand. I have to . . ."

She shook her head at him. "It's not open to debate, Officer Attla. I may not be a doc, but this is my infirmary. I call the shots. And sleep is what I'm prescribing for you. We'll see how you're doing in the morning."

"Can you at least get me a phone. I need to make some calls."

"In the morning." She raised her eyebrows at him. "Okay?"

"Okay . . ." Ray groaned.

The nurse grinned victoriously, then turned to leave. "Push the call button on the bed control if you need me." The door swung open, swung shut, and Ray was alone.

He glanced at the closet. His clothes were probably in there. The tubes in his arm could be easily detached. Escape would be simple enough. His toes and fingertips were victims of a dull, smoldering fire, but it was nothing he couldn't endure.

On the other hand, he *was* tired. Not just tired. Depleted. Exhausted. Even if he hadn't been bashed in the head by an automotive winch and nearly turned into a popsicle, his body would still have been begging for rest.

Would the investigation fall apart, as if it hadn't already, if he crashed for a few hours? He could call the captain in the morning, call Margaret, talk to Billy Bob and Reynolds, examine the case with a fresh mind, from a *sane* perspective.

Turning a control dial, he watched the lights dim. After repositioning himself in bed, he took a deep breath and closed his eyes. Maybe the nurse was right. Maybe sleep was the best medicine.

A pleasant sense of contentment washed over him as his muscles relaxed. He felt himself sinking into the soft warm mattress, his mind rapidly descending toward slumber. Just before the world evaporated, he was struck by a thought. Why did it take a near-death experience and a hard-nosed nurse to convince him to take time out?

The questions hovered and drifted like wistful clouds before fading into a heavy, dark horizon. Oblivion. Relief.

➤➤ TWENTY-TWO ➤

"THE HOLY MOTHER musta been lookin' out fer 'em."

Ray opened his eyes and gazed up at a face. It was long, cartoonish, with two enormous buck teeth. For an instant he wondered if he were dreaming: a nightmarish vision of what it would be like to be trapped in a Warner Brothers short.

"And all the angels," another voice added. Ray swung his head to the right. It was Reynolds.

"Holy who?" Ray whispered. His mouth was dry, his throat sore. He licked at chapped, cracked lips with a thick tongue.

"Musta said a whole heap a Hail Marys," the cowboy surmised.

Ray found a cup of water on the table by the bed, downed it, then asked, "What are you talking about?"

"I'm not much for religion," Reynolds confessed, "but this is, I don't know . . . weird."

"What's weird?"

"The fact that you aren't dead," Reynolds replied. "The fact that we found you." He shook his head at Ray. "I've never been sure about God and all that. But either this is a miracle or it's the darnedest coincidence I ever did see."

"Coincidence?" Ray shut his eyes and gave them a rub. He felt rested, sort of, but his headache was back and he was somewhat disoriented, as if he had just woken up from a decades-long nap.

"Yeah. The deputy knowing that you were in trouble."

Here Reynolds actually cursed to punctuate his amazement. "And knowing where to look . . . Weird."

Ray squinted at Billy Bob.

"We were driving back from the rig—" Billy Bob started to say.

"Driscoll," Ray remembered. "Did you get a look at the body? What happened to him?"

Reynolds stopped him with a raised palm. "We'll get to that. First, you gotta listen to this."

"We were driving back from the rig," Billy Bob repeated, "and I fell asleep."

"Just nodded off," Reynolds threw in, shaking his head.

"I was beat. Couldn't stay awake to save my life. Anyway, I had a dream that—"

"Listen to this part," Reynolds emphasized. "It's weird."

"I dreamed that you was out in this boat."

"Me?"

"Yeah. Kind of a . . . I don't know. Like a can-oo. One of them one-man jobs that're covered on the top, 'cept for a hole ya climb in."

"A kayak?" Ray asked.

"Right! That was eatin' at me all night. I couldn't remember what it was called. So you're in this here kayak, out on the water someplace. Maybe on the ocean. I'm not sure. It's night. Real dark, 'cept fer a light way over on the—"

"Horizon?"

"Yeah."

A shiver ran up and down Ray's spine as his own dream came back to him in flashes.

"You were paddlin' toward the light when this . . . this *thang* comes up to yer boat."

"Some kind of monster," Reynolds said with a shrug.

"Real ugly. Green with lots a teeth, lots a legs, and these . . . antennae thangs."

Ray stared at them, dumbfounded. "What happened next?"

"The monster thang attacked you," Billy Bob reported. "It grabbed ya and started to eat ya, boat and all."

"And? . . ."

"And then I woke up."

"Weird," Reynolds muttered. "Tell him the rest."

"Well, after I woke up, I had this picture in ma mind. It was a map of the Slope and there was this flashing dot on it. Somehow I knew that was where you were and that you needed help."

"I thought he was nuts," Reynolds confessed. "Certifiable. Goofy as they come. He kept on insisting that we go looking for this dot that was flashing in his head."

"As it turned out, you was right where I thought you'd be," Billy Bob submitted. "In a drift, a couple a miles from BP." His eyes grew wide. "I cain't explain it."

"Weird," Reynolds repeated.

"You bein' a Catholic an all, maybe it was the Holy Mother watchin' out for ya."

"I'm not Catholic," Ray corrected.

"What about . . . ?"

Ray reached up and grabbed his ponytail. "This?" He flashed the crucifix at them. "It was a gift. From the shaman."

"Weirder still," Reynolds announced.

The three of them stared at each other for several seconds. Reynolds was right, Ray decided. It *was* weird. Apparently, some Great Kila really was looking after him. Either that, or he was one lucky guy.

"What time is it?"

Reynolds and Billy Bob performed identical maneuvers with their left arms, heads drooping toward their watches.

"Almost nine A.M.," Reynolds got off first.

"Six till," the deputy specified.

"What *day* is it?"

"Sunday," Reynolds told him with a smirk.

"I need to get up." Ray raised himself to a sitting position. He felt okay, though he was making a conscious effort not to move his toes or fingers. "My clothes in there?" He nodded at the closet.

Billy Bob opened the door. "Uh-huh."

"Help me up." He looked to Reynolds, who offered an arm. Ray slid his legs over the edge of the bed. So far so good. It was as his feet made contact with the floor that he realized he wouldn't be running any marathons in the near future. The pain was harsh, intense . . . unbearable?

He was weighing the punishment, considering climbing back into bed when the nurse came through the door.

"What do you think you're doing?" Reynolds and Billy Bob instinctively stepped backwards, away from the confrontation.

"I'm . . . uh . . ." Ray could feel his cheeks blushing. "I'm getting up."

"Who said you could get up?" The nurse's hands were on her hips, feet shoulder width apart, a deep scowl pasted on her face.

"You told me to stay in bed," Ray argued. "I did, and I feel better for it. Now, I've got work to do." He stood up, shrugged, held out his hands. "See, I'm fine."

"You're either a quick healer or you've got one heck of a high threshold for pain."

Both, Ray thought.

The nurse nudged him back to the bed with a bony finger. "Let me check your vitals."

Ray waited as she looked at the monitors, stuck a digital thermometer in his ear, took his pulse . . .

"Healthy as a horse," she announced begrudgingly. "And lucky as they come."

"So I can go?"

"I suppose. But stay off your feet. Walking will be painful for a week or so and could build up extra scar tissue. Trust me, you don't want that. When you get back to Barrow, see a doctor. You may need some rehab therapy."

"Okay."

"That's a prescription-strength painkiller," she said, gesturing to a plastic bottle on the table. "I'd encourage you to take some right away." She offered something approaching a smile before leaving. When she was gone, Ray tried standing again. Blood rushed to his injured feet, bringing tears to his eyes. Hopefully the meds would reduce the discomfort to an acceptable level. He reached for the bottle and fought with the lid, doing his best to avoid using his fingertips. Pouring out three tablets, he swallowed them without water.

"Maybe ya should rest," Billy Bob suggested.

Ray ignored him. After struggling awkwardly into his long johns, he said, "Tell me about Driscoll."

"Not much to tell," Reynolds replied. "Bullet through the heart. Dead before he knew what hit him."

"And he was missin' that thang under his tongue," Billy Bob added.

"The worm?"

"Yeah. Just like the first body."

Ray thought about this as he pulled on another layer of clothing. Two men dead. Both treated with a reverence normally reserved for animals.

"Where's the body?" he asked.

"Out in a shed," Reynolds reported.

"Is someone watching it?" Ray carefully began threading his swollen toes into a sock.

"Yep. We've got a man posted around the clock to make sure he doesn't go anywhere."

"Good." Ray grimaced, amazed that socks could sting with such authority. "Anybody see anything?"

"Nope," Billy Bob grunted. "Driscoll was at the rig. He left fer the shop. Nobody seen 'em again till two fellas went to do an ice sample and nearly ran over him with a pickup."

Ray sighed at this. Another dead end. He was tempted to ask, out of sheer frustration, how someone could kill two men without so much as a whisper, but he knew the answer. Up here on the Slope in this weather, a battalion of Russian troops could have landed and set up a command post without being noticed. It was the perfect place, the perfect season for murder. A terrible, nearly impossible setting to attempt to track and apprehend the perpetrator.

"What about my machine?"

"I sent Leeland out to look for it a little while ago."

"No. I mean, any idea who might have ripped off my gear and tampered with the engine?"

"Ripped off your gear?"

"What did you think I was doing out there, stretching my legs?"

"You sayin' somebody . . . that you was stranded on purpose?" Billy Bob stuttered.

"Yeah. The Polaris is new. It's fitted out with the whole array of cold-weather adaptations. The carburetor wouldn't go out twice, in one day."

"Stranger things have happened," Reynolds submitted.

"And I suppose my survival kit and tools just jumped out of the sled of their own accord."

"Maybe they blew out?"

"Yeah, right. More like someone wants me dead."

Billy Bob and Reynolds stared at him soberly.

"Dead?" Reynolds finally said. His face contorted, as if this was beyond the realm of possibility. "Why? Why would someone want you dead?"

Ray flung his hands into the air. "No idea. Maybe the murderer thinks we're closing in on him. Although that's pretty far-fetched, since we're stuck at square one. Or maybe someone just has a problem with Natives in general. Who knows?"

"Trying to kill a police officer . . ." Reynolds muttered. "That's crazy."

"I agree," Ray nodded. He slid a foot into one of the bunny boots. Stars closed in on his field of vision. He sank to the bed and put his head between his knees, waiting for the fainting spell to pass, for the room to reappear.

"You okay?" the deputy asked, his drawl laced with concern.

"Yeah." The sparkles slowly dissipated. Ray put the other boot on while still sitting on the bed. It hurt but didn't make him dizzy.

"You sent Leeland after my machine?"

Reynolds nodded.

"Where was he last night?"

"What do you mean? When?"

"When I was out for my little stroll in the snow."

"Here. In bed, I guess." Reynolds's eyes suddenly flashed with recognition. "You're not implying that . . ."

Ray waved him off. "I'm not implying anything. Just asking. The only way to find the perp is to figure out who had the opportunity, and then work on motive.''

"He didn't have either," Reynolds assured him.

"As a security guard, he has access to a vehicle and—''

"So does the deputy here," Reynolds shot back. "That doesn't make him a killer."

"And he can move freely around Prudhoe, in and out of camp . . .''

Reynolds cursed the theory. "That's the stupidest thing I've ever heard."

"Okay, so it's stupid. Call me paranoid. Coming within a few short minutes of popsiclehood can have that effect on a person. You start to question everything and everyone."

"Screws with your logic too, apparently," Reynolds said.

"Fellas," Billy Bob called in a calm voice, "come on now. Let's not fight.''

"Step outside and I'll show you a fight," Reynolds grumbled. "Start asking questions about my partner and you'll find out—''

"Hey! Cool off!''

"Okay," Ray sighed. "I apologize. You're right. I'm not thinking clearly. I didn't mean anything by it."

This seemed to placate Reynolds. He leaned back against the wall, arms crossed.

"What about Makintanz?" Ray asked.

"The chief? What about him? You think he's trying to kill you too?''

"Is he still here?''

Reynolds nodded. "Waiting for the meeting."

"Meeting?''

"As soon as the storm lifts, the president of Davis and the players from Arctic Slope Regional are flying in to sign an agreement to open a field east of Prudhoe for exploration."

"East of Prudhoe?" Ray said. "Wouldn't that be the National Wildlife Reserve?''

"There's a patch of land between the Petroleum Reserve and the Wildlife Reserve. Davis apparently has first dibs on it. Thanks to Makintanz. He's the middle man who's making the deal happen."

"Don't they have to get approval from the Department of Natural Resources to extend the drilling boundary?"

"And Congress," Reynolds confirmed. "Makintanz already took care of that."

Ray looked to Billy Bob. "We need to have a talk with this guy."

"What fer?"

"To see if he knows anything."

Reynolds swore at this. "First you accuse my partner, now you're accusing Chief Makintanz?" He cursed again. "I've heard of grasping at straws but—"

"Sometimes an investigation is like that," Ray told him. "You just blunder around, asking dumb questions and offending people, until something lines up or a piece of the puzzle falls into place."

"Well, you're succeeding with the first part," Reynolds said. "Blundering around . . . That's not how we did things in the military."

"Yeah? Well, this isn't the military. It's small-town police work in Alaska."

"Obviously."

"How 'bout we get us some coffee?" Billy Bob suggested in a bright tone.

Reynolds frowned at Ray. Ray smiled back. "I'm stumbling around in the dark, Mr. Reynolds. Trying to solve a double murder: two seemingly related crimes that no one witnessed, that were committed for no discernible reason. I'm beat up, tired, and out of my league here. Forgive my clumsiness." He extended his hand.

Reynolds examined it suspiciously, hesitated, shook it.

"The bottom line is that I need your help. This has to be a group effort."

The statement was met with a sigh of resignation. "What do you want me to do?"

"Tell us where to find Chief Makintanz."

►► TWENTY-THREE ◄◄

"WHY ARE WE doing this?"

"I told you, to see if he knows anything."

Billy Bob examined Ray from the driver's seat. "Nah. I mean really. Why talk to this Chief fella, as opposed to a hundred or so other Davis Oil employees?"

It was a fair question, one to which Ray didn't have a sensible answer. His motivation for seeking out Makintanz involved nothing even remotely tangible: a mystical prophecy about a powerful *anjatkut,* a "miraculous" rescue that served to make the shaman's words somewhat more credible, and a sizable dose of old-fashioned intuition. Makintanz was a crook. If something illegal was afoot and he happened to be in the vicinity, it was only logical to look for a connection. It was a standard operating procedure in law enforcement: start with the most obvious suspects, those with a history of crime, and work out from there.

"Just a hunch," Ray finally answered, gazing out the window. A dull glow rested on the frozen tundra to the south: the slightest inkling of daylight, with it the promise that one day, perhaps six weeks in the future, the sun would return to the Arctic.

"Storm's blowing itself out," Ray observed.

"Yeah," Billy Bob grunted. He braced himself, gripping the steering wheel tightly as a gust rocked the Explorer on its shocks. "You can almost see the road now."

"This is the last hurrah," Ray assured him. "We'll be able

to see the stars tonight. Tomorrow will be calm. Probably get hit with another storm by Monday.''

"Is that right? How can you tell?"

Ray shrugged. "You live up here long enough and you start to notice the patterns."

"Patterns?" Billy Bob frowned at the windshield. "All I see is dark . . . and snow."

Ray swore.

"What? What did I say?"

"Nothing. I forgot to call in."

The deputy pointed at the glove compartment. "There's a phone in there."

Ray popped the box open and began rummaging through the debris: maps, candy wrappers, a lighter, several pens . . . a Magnavox cellular unit. Flipping it open, he punched in the number for Barrow PD. The phone beeped rudely, then began to ring.

On the third ring a deep, female voice answered, "Barrow Police."

"Hi, Betty. This is—"

"Ray! Where have you been?" It was more of an accusation than a question.

"I . . . uh . . ."

"The Captain was about ready to send out a search party."

"Really?"

"He was worried. And angry that you hadn't checked in. He's been trying to reach you on the radio since yesterday. Just a minute. I'll patch you through."

Great, Ray thought. Nothing like getting chewed out—long distance.

"Raymond Attla!" a voice barked. It had the ring of a father preparing to read his son the riot act.

"Yes, sir."

"Where in the blazes have you been? What's going on over there? Why didn't you call me? Is there something wrong with the radio?"

"Uh . . ." Ray wondered which question to answer first, which one was the least likely to dig the hole deeper. "There's been another murder, Captain," he announced, hoping this would provide a distraction. The trick worked.

"A what?"

"Another murder, sir. Same MO. Some workers up at seventeen, the rig where the first body was found, recovered another."

"Stuffed in a pipe?"

"No, sir. This one was out in the open, a few hundred yards north of the yard. Shot through the heart. Worm cut out."

The Captain swore at this. "Any witnesses?"

"No, sir. No one saw or heard anything."

"You ID either of them yet?"

Ray waited as a blast of wind hammered the Explorer, static surging on the line.

"Attla? You there?"

"Yes, sir."

"I can barely . . . now. Where are . . . ?"

"We're headed for Deadhorse."

The wind effectively stole the entire sentence.

"Where?"

"Deadhorse!"

The captain said something unintelligible. When the gust suddenly subsided, Ray quickly said, "The second body was a man named Driscoll. He was the rig foreman."

"What about the first?"

"We think it's an executive."

"You think what? Speak up, Attla!"

Billy Bob swore. "I cain't see squat!" He was leaning toward the dashboard, squinting.

"We think it's an executive, a VP named Weinhart," Ray repeated. "Worked for Davis."

"I can't . . . breaking up . . . on the radio?"

"The radio's dead."

"What?"

The Explorer was shaking, icy breath streaming in from around its supposedly air-tight windows.

"The storm's blowin' itself out, huh?" the deputy scoffed.

"It does this before it leaves," Ray told him. Into the phone he shouted, "I'll call you back later."

There was a blast of static, but no voice in it. Ray flipped the Magnavox shut. "So much for that." Ray silently thanked Mother Nature for cutting the conversation short. The weather was a great excuse for avoiding the more embarrassing details of the case: the missing corpse, their inability to get a positive ID on it, visiting a witch doctor, nearly becoming a popsicle, going to Deadhorse to speak with Makintanz.

Ray was putting the phone back into the glove box when the deputy said, "What about yer sweetie?"

He sighed at this, retrieving the phone. "Maybe I won't be able to get through."

"What's the matter?" Billy Bob asked. "Don't ya miss her?"

"Of course I miss her. It's just . . . I don't know. If I tell her about the case, she'll worry. If I gloss over it, make it seem routine, she'll expect me to make it back for the shower this evening."

"Who knows," the deputy drawled. "We might just catch the killer in time fer you to . . ." He cursed as the right front tire left the hard pack and dove into a drift. The Explorer stopped abruptly, throwing them forward against the seat belts. Shifting, the deputy backed up, turned the wheel and started forward again. "Maybe this Mackenzie fella—"

"Makintanz," Ray corrected. He watched as the tires slid toward the edge of the road again. "Stay left!"

"I'm doin' the best I can. You wanna drive?"

The line rang. Ray began to pray that Margaret wasn't home.

"Maybe this Makintanz fella did it. Maybe when we talk to him, he'll confess and this whole thing will be over with. Then you can head home to be with your sweetie."

"Yeah. And maybe malamutes will sprout antlers."

"Hello," a voice answered. It wasn't Margaret.

Ray took a deep breath. "I'm calling for Margaret."

"Is this Raymond?"

"Yes, ma'am."

"This is Edna Wood, Margaret's aunt."

"Oh, hello, Aunt Edna."

"Are you getting excited about the shower? We're putting

up decorations, making all sorts of dishes. It's really going to be something."

"It certainly is. Can I speak with Margaret?"

"I'm sorry, Raymond. She isn't here right now."

Ray leaned back in the seat, relieved.

"She and . . . to the store . . . putting together . . . recipe . . . not enough . . ."

The display on the phone was blinking "no service."

"I'm on a cellular, Aunt Edna and we're moving into a dead spot."

". . . leave a message?"

"No. Just tell Margaret I called."

". . . tell her . . ."

Static reclaimed the device and Ray hit the end button.

"Dodge another bullet?" the cowboy asked with a grin.

"Yeah."

"Course, yer gonna have to face the music sometime, partner," he said, as if he was an expert in these matters. "Specially with your sweetie. Once ya get married . . ." Billy Bob whistled a warning. "She's gonna wanna know where you are and what yer up to night and day." Here he chuckled, clearly amused at Ray's predicament.

"I'm here to tell ya that once they get their hooks into ya, it's over and done with. I'm not saying marriage ain't a good thang. It is."

"Are you married?"

"Well, no. And I ain't never been. But I've seen many a couple march down the aisle together, let me tell you. And once, I came right close myself. Why back . . . oh . . . it's been 'bout three years now, I met this woman . . ."

"Is that right?" Ray grunted and nodded on cue, doing his best to ignore the story and the unsolicited sermon on the pitfalls and rewards of matrimony that followed. Billy Bob was still dispensing pearls of wisdom, when Deadhorse materialized. Low-frame buildings huddled in the harsh glow of halogen spotlights. There was a grainy surrealistic quality about the town, as if it had arisen out of an old black-and-white photograph.

To call it a town was something of an overstatement in Ray's opinion.

"Deadhorse looks pretty darn dead," Billy Bob observed. "Don't it?"

Ray surveyed the empty streets, the silent houses, a seemingly deserted mini-mart grocery. It didn't look dead, exactly. More like it was hibernating. There were people inside the buildings, he knew, people who had chosen to live in a region where waiting out the weather was part of a seasonal routine.

"There's my office," Billy Bob noted proudly. He pointed out the driver's window at a short row of storefronts connected by a raised, wood-plank sidewalk. Wedged between a Laundromat and a barber shop, the narrow unit bore a large gold star. Bold letters on the door told the world that this was the Office of the Sheriff of Deadhorse. Except for the telephone and fax numbers listed below, it could have been something out of a spaghetti western, the kind of place you expected Clint Eastwood to frequent.

Having cruised all three blocks of downtown Deadhorse, they passed a sign that pointed toward the airfield. A quarter mile farther, they came upon the old hotel that had been converted into a roadhouse. Orange neon letters in the blowing snow announced that Harry's was open, had Bud on tap, and featured pool and darts. A pickup and two sport utility vehicles were sitting outside, black extension cords connecting their engines to a row of exterior outlets. They reminded Ray of horses tied to posts.

"So this is where everyone is," he said.

"Always are," Billy Bob said knowingly. " 'Bout the only action I ever see around here is at Harry's—breaking up a fight or somethin'. 'Tween the booze, the gamblin' and the prostitutes, things can get a little dicey."

"Prostitutes?"

"Yeah. They got a whole string of 'em. Fer the oil workers."

"That's illegal."

Billy Bob nodded. "Yep. Shore is."

"Why don't you shut it down?"

He shrugged. "It's against the law, but the oil companies

call the shots around here. First thing the Sheriff told me when I got to town was don't mess with Harry's. Just look the other way. And unless somebody kills somebody else, don't arrest nobody.''

"Interesting philosophy of law enforcement," Ray mumbled.

Harry's disappeared in the wind and for the next three minutes, they drove into an abyss. To the uninitiated, it seemed as though they had left civilization behind and were sliding toward some hellish underworld where light and life had been banished for eons.

"Ever been in the Bradbury?" Billy Bob asked.

"No, but I've seen pictures."

"It ain't the same. You got to see it to believe it."

Without warning, a monolith rose up out of the ice, its shape outlined by a host of twinkling stars. The monstrosity reminded Ray of a Mayan temple he had seen in an anthropology text back in college: steep stone sides forming a triangle with a spire that seemed to reach halfway to heaven. The structure had been forged out of glass, enormous windows hung on a silver metal frame. It would have fit neatly into the Seattle skyline. But up here . . . in Deadhorse? How it withstood the wind was beyond Ray. And how they kept it from freezing into an oversized block of ice was downright baffling.

Billy Bob steered the Explorer up the curving driveway. Miraculously, it was bare black pavement looking up at them through horizontal snow pellets.

"Heated," the deputy said, anticipating Ray's question. "Just like the ones in Colorado, at Vail and Aspen. Them fancy ski resorts all got 'em."

Ray shook his head at the idea. Considering the location, the architecture, and this "heated" road, a night's lodging at the Bradbury had to be equivalent to a down payment on a house. Actually a mortgage might be more economical.

Billy Bob pulled down a short concrete ramp into a covered parking area. The Ford was still rolling when a pair of men adorned in knee-length purple parkas, shiny black bunny boots, and golden polar fleece top hats with earflaps descended upon them. Trotting toward the vehicle, they split up, one hurrying to the driver's side, the other attending to the passenger's side.

When the Explorer came to a halt, gloved hands reached for the handles, popping the doors open before Ray and Billy Bob could even unfasten their seat belts.

"Welcome to the Bradbury," the valets chimed in unison.

⇥ TWENTY-FOUR ⇤

"POLICE." RAY FLASHED his badge at them. "Where should we park?"

"We'll take care of that for you, sir," the man at his door informed him. He then extended his hand, as if Ray were an invalid and required special assistance.

Refusing the offer, he climbed out and hobbled around to join Billy Bob on the sidewalk, his feet reminding him that they had been sorely mistreated. One of the valets leapt into the Explorer and drove off. The other gestured with a gloved hand. "Right this way, gentlemen." He led them to a set of nine-foot double doors. Pulling on one of the enormous brass handles, he bowed again. "Enjoy your stay."

"Welcome to the Bradbury." The greeting came from a man, wearing a purple coat and top hat, standing at attention just inside the door. His sole purpose seemed to be welcoming guests. "May I be of service?"

Ray displayed his badge. "Looking for the manager."

The man turned stiffly and directed them forward with an arm. "Through the lobby. At the end of the reservations desk, just before you reach the concierge's station."

"Thanks."

"May I take your things? Your coats, hats . . . ?"

Ray and Billy Bob slipped off their gear. The man opened a door hidden in the wall behind him and began hanging the apparel on a rack.

"Boots?" he asked, offering them each a pair of polar-fleece moccasins with leather soles.

"We can't keep our boots on?" Ray asked. He wasn't sure he could manage without the thick, insulated cushion.

"Well . . . you can . . . but—"

"Great. Then we will."

"Enjoy your stay." The man resumed his position. Ray decided that the guy would have made a great guard at Buckingham Palace.

The hallway leading to the lobby was impressive. The floor and walls were emerald green. Marble. Probably the real thing, Ray surmised. Pieces of art were displayed on marble pedestals, each illuminated by studio lights inset in the ceiling. Ray admired an original Birdsall that portrayed the northern lights shimmering in the night sky above a field of snow-encrusted tundra. The next work was an elaborate six foot totem: ovoids, lines, and interlocking images skillfully etched in red cedar. The plaque beneath it described the role of the totem in Native culture. Ray didn't bother to read it. Chances were the explanation was bogus. For some unknown reason, whites had long ago gotten it in their minds that totem poles were objects of worship. In actuality, the poles were works of art intended to memorialize various events in the history of a clan or individual. Something like an historic marker, or a tombstone. And while totems had become the unofficial mascot of the Eskimo, they were only found among the southeastern peoples, the Tlingit and Haida. The Inupiat and Aleut had never carved any such posts. That didn't seem to phase the souvenir vendors or their patrons. Tourists weren't exactly sticklers for accuracy.

"Perty nice, huh?" Billy Bob was grinning.

"Yeah," Ray grunted. Somehow, *nice* didn't do this place justice. Palatial was more like it: a residence fit for royalty. At the entrance to the lobby the roof fell away revealing a seven-story glass atrium full of trees, tall ferns, fountains, pools, and artificial streams. In Ray's experience, a lobby was a place where you checked in, picked up a key, bought a Mars bar from a vending machine, and used the telephone. But this: gleaming marble floor . . . rustic tree-trunk benches scattered throughout an indoor jungle . . . chairs and couches clustered in alcoves along the outer wall . . . It was like a taste of Eden served up at the North Pole. Yet all Ray could think of were the logistical challenges of running and maintaining this miniature paradise. How did they keep the plants alive? How did they keep the water from freezing? He glanced down at his bunny boots, then back at the trail of muddy water behind them. How did they keep it so clean?

"Over there," the deputy said, aiming a thumb at a door marked Manager.

They squeaked their way across the expanse, toward the door. Before they reached it, a woman behind the counter chimed, "Welcome to the Bradbury. How may I be of service?" She was about twenty, with blond hair, blue eyes, and a winning smile.

"We're looking for the manager," Ray told her, extending his badge.

"You must be Officer Attla and Deputy Cleaver," she said, still smiling. "I'll let Mr. Henderson know you're here." With that she lifted a phone and began punching buttons. A moment later she added, "He'll be right with you. If you'd like to have a seat . . ." She waved at a couch hidden at the foot of the closest row of ferns.

When they were seated, a door opened at the end of the counter. A young man in a khaki uniform pushed out a mop and bucket on wheels and started toward them. Stopping directly in front of the couch, he began sloshing the mop back and forth, erasing their boot tracks.

"How'd ya like to get stuck in a place like this?" Billy Bob asked.

"Pretty tough, alright." Ray watched as a group of suits emerged from the forest half a football field away and gravitated toward a stand nestled under a grove of what appeared to be dwarf palm trees. One by one the men placed their orders, the attendant scurrying to fill them. Two minutes later they retreated into the foliage, caffeine jolts and sugary snacks in hand.

Ray eyed the espresso stand. Though he couldn't smell the coffee, the mere sight of it had ignited a craving. He was considering making the trek into the woods when the woman from the counter appeared in front of the couch.

"Mr. Henderson will see you now," she said, beaming. "If you'll follow me."

"I'd folla you anywhere," Billy Bob said stupidly, gawking at the woman's legs.

She either didn't hear him or was disciplined enough to ignore the comment. "Right this way." She opened the door and ushered them into the manager's office. "Mr. Henderson will be right with you."

Left alone, Ray and Billy Bob stood there, waiting. It was a surprisingly small room, considering the size and scope of the lobby: modest desk, waist-high bookshelf, two filing cabinets, a pair of chairs. A nondescript painting of a bowl of fruit was the only wall decoration. Framed photographs littered the desk.

The side door opened and a short, balding man in a brown suit entered. His chubby cheeks were buoyed by a sanguine expression. "Gentlemen, welcome to the Bradbury." He shook their hands enthusiastically, as if they were long lost friends. "Please have a seat." Slipping behind the desk, he asked, "Now, what can I do for you?"

"I'm Officer Attla and this is . . ." Ray started to explain.

Henderson was nodding. "I've been expecting you. How can I be of service?"

"We're looking for someone."

The manager leaned forward in his chair, expectantly. "Yes?"

"Roger Makintanz."

Suddenly his features soured. "The chief?"

Ray nodded.

"Might I ask why?"

"Police business," Ray told him.

This seemed to bother Henderson.

"Could you tell us what room he's in, please?"

Now Henderson seemed pained. "I'm not at liberty to give out information about our guests."

"Even to the police?"

He shrugged and lifted his palms, as if the entire matter

were out of his hands. "Company policy, gentlemen. I'd really like to help, but—".

"We just need to know what room he's stayin' in," Billy Bob said.

"I understand, but I'm not at liberty to provide you with that information." The grin returned. It was more of a defensive look than a willingness to please.

Ray studied him. "Do we need a court order just to get a room number?"

"Possibly," he answered. "And even then I would need authorization from Anchorage."

"Can you just ring the chief and let him know we're here?"

Henderson thought this over, sighed, examined the ceiling, pressed the tips of his fingers together. Shaking his head, he muttered, "The chief has asked not to be disturbed—"

"This is important," Ray assured him. He paused, caught Henderson's eyes, then said, "We can get that court order, if you'd like us to, but I'll bet Anchorage won't be too happy about that. You know, the publicity and all."

"Publicity?" The manager's face fell. Apparently he hadn't thought of this.

"Court orders are public record. If the press got ahold of it . . . Well, you know the media. There's no telling what slant they might put on it."

"What do you mean? What could they possibly . . .?"

Ray shrugged, careful not to push the threat any further.

"Be a shame if this place went under," Billy Bob added innocently.

Henderson took a breath, stared at them, and caved. "Okay. I'll call him, but it's up to him whether or not he wants to see you."

"Fair enough," Ray said.

Henderson picked up the phone and dialed. "Chief Makintanz?" He swallowed hard. "Yes . . . Uh, sir . . . This is Mr. Henderson, the manager of the Bradbury . . . No, sir. There's no problem. I apologize for disturbing you, sir, but . . . There are two law enforcement officers here to see you . . . Yes, sir. No. No, not that I'm aware of." He covered the phone with a hand. "You don't have a warrant, do you?"

Ray shook his head. "Not yet."

"No, sir . . . Very good, sir . . . Yes. All right. I'll send them up." When he hung up, Henderson was out of breath, his brow glistening with perspiration. "Listen officers, the Chief is one of our biggest clients. We can't afford to lose him."

"Who said anything about losing him?" Ray asked, rising.

"Please try not to, you know, offend him or anything."

"We'll try not to."

Henderson led them through the side door and down the corridor. "The chief is in the Penthouse. It's only accessible through the express elevator."

"How often does the chief stay here?" Ray asked.

"Once every six weeks or so. Always takes the Penthouse. His room-service bill alone is enough to keep us in business," Henderson chuckled wryly.

Henderson stopped at a set of chrome doors and pushed a button. The elevator opened with a whoosh. "You'll have to pass through security outside the chief's suite."

Ray and Billy Bob got on. Still in the hall, Henderson pushed another button. "Go easy," he begged as the doors began to shut. "I need this job."

The elevator bounced slightly, then rushed upward. "So this chief fella is loaded, huh?"

"Yeah," Ray replied. "You could say that. Worth around two billion dollars, last I heard. And he's got an in with everybody: Davis Oil, several Native corporations, the teamsters . . . He's buddies with the governor, liaison to the NorthWest Indians Association, even does consulting for Boeing. He's a slimeball, but an extremely well connected one. Arguably the most powerful man in Alaska."

Billy Bob's dopey face adopted an expression bordering on deep thought. "So why would this fella murder two people?"

"Who said he did?"

"Why else are we talkin' to 'im?"

"Just to—"

"To see what he knows," the deputy mumbled, frowning. "If you don't wanna tell me, just say so."

"Okay. I don't want to tell you."

"Fine. See if I care. You want to keep secrets . . ."

A tone sounded and the doors slid open. As they stepped off, a pair of gargantuan men in three-piece suits rose from their seats in the hallway and trotted to meet them, like half the defensive line of the Seahawks rushing the quarterback.

Ray was in the process of reaching for his badge when an enormous paw stopped him. The grip was robotic, unmerciful. Before he could react the paw spun him around and he found himself performing an up-close inspection of the wallpaper. Another paw patted down his back, legs, and waist. Beside him, Billy Bob was wide-eyed, his cheek flat against the wall, an arm twisted behind him. The brutes swiftly relieved the deputy of his sidearm and badge, Ray of his ID.

"Driver's license says Raymond Attla," one of them declared, still pressing him against the flower-covered plasterboard. "From Barrow."

"At least you can read," Ray observed. "Some gorillas can't."

"Funny guy, huh?"

Ray's arm jerked up between his shoulder blades, his hand scraping against the crucifix on his ponytail. Something in his shoulder cracked. A knee hit him in the kidney sending pain down his leg and up his right side. He felt himself lean backward, then rush at the wall, impacting with a sick thud.

"How's that for funny, funny guy?"

"*Police officer* guy," he offered through a grimace, nose folded in half. "I'm a cop."

"A cop?" the man grunted disapprovingly. "No kidding." He held Ray at bay with an elbow as he rifled the wallet. "Oh . . . here we go. *Officer* Attla."

"This one's *Deputy* Cleaver," the other beast read. "Cleaver? As in Beaver?"

Laughing, the security guards backed away, releasing their charges.

Ray turned around, massaging his shoulder. His nose felt crooked. Before he could check to see if it was broken, a hand dove into his shirt. "No wires, right guys?"

"No."

Another hand checked Billy Bob in the same fashion, fingers feeling around the collar, under the arms, along the sternum.

"Clean."

"What's your business with the chief?"

"It's private. He's expecting us."

"Is that right?" The man glared at Ray, wide shoulders squared, as if daring him to move past.

"Yeah. That's right."

The Neanderthal toggled a tiny device in his ear. "Sir, we've got an *Officer* Attla and a *Deputy* Beaver Cleaver out here. They claim you're expecting them." There was a pause. The brute's face grew even dumber then, "Yes, sir." He frowned at them. "Go ahead."

Both men seemed disappointed. Tossing the ID badges back, they returned to their chairs and newspapers.

"What about my thirty-eight?" Billy Bob wondered.

"Antique," the second strong-arm declared. "Cops are always behind the times." He pulled back his suit coat and displayed a semi-automatic pistol. "You wouldn't stand a chance against one of these babies. I pull this, you better start digging your grave."

"Thanks for the tip. Can you just give him back his gun?" Ray tried. Though dangerous, no doubt lethal, these clowns were getting on his nerves.

"On your way out."

Ray considered arguing, asserting his authority as a law enforcement officer, but somehow he got the feeling that Jughead and Archie here had little respect for authority, much less the police. He glanced at Billy Bob, shrugged, and started down the hall.

At a set of double doors, Ray reached for the knob but the doors clunked mechanically and retreated on their own, swinging back to reveal a spacious suite: plush, champagne carpet, striking Native wall hanging, leather couches and chairs, two primitive tables decorated with jade trinkets and fresh flowers, a wet bar framed by racks of glasses, wine, and liquor.

"Hello?" Ray called, sticking a tentative foot across the threshold. "Anybody home?"

"Gentlemen," a voice replied, the speaker hidden. "Come right in. I've been expecting you."

➤➤ TWENTY-FIVE ◀◀

THEY FOUND CHIEF Makintanz in the dining room, seated at the far end of an ornate oak table, utensils in hand. The china platter in front of him was heaped with food: roast beef, eggs Benedict, strawberries, cinnamon roll, shrimp, baked salmon. An array of chrome serving boats littered the table, their contents steaming.

"You're just in time," Makintanz announced with a smile. The expression caused his beefy cheeks to rise, nearly erasing his eyes. He was wearing a black silk shirt and a shiny black cloak with an elaborate Haida whale pattern on the lapels. Together with his girth, balding head, and ring of dyed, artificially black hair, the man looked like a middle-aged bowhead that had conveniently beached itself at an all-you-can-eat buffet brunch.

Instead of rising to greet them, the chief stuffed a forkful of salmon into his mouth. "Have a seat. I'll have the maid bring you some plates."

"No, sir. We really can't," Ray argued.

"Oh, I insist. You boys do a fine job of protecting our communities. The least I can do is feed you. You are hungry, aren't you?"

Ray instinctively licked his lips, drinking in the rich aromas. Actually, he was starving and the dishes were so inviting. "Really, sir, we—"

"Rosemary!" Makintanz bellowed. "Two more plates! And some silverware!" After swallowing a forkload of scalloped potatoes, he asked, "What would you like to drink? Coffee? OJ? Dom Perignon?" He lifted a crystal goblet bearing a bubbly, golden liquid, gazed at it longingly, and gulped it down. "Not the best year, but it'll do."

An African-American woman came through the swinging door behind Makintanz carrying a stack of china and a collection of utensils. Without speaking, she set a place for Ray, one for Billy Bob, then left the room.

Ray eyed the plate, surveyed the food.

"Go ahead. Dig in," Makintanz urged.

Shrugging at Billy Bob, Ray slid the chair back and sat down. The deputy did the same, immediately reaching for the shrimp.

"Inupiat?" Makintanz asked Ray.

He nodded, stabbing a slice of roast beef. It was tender, rare in the middle, the edges dark brown.

"Good people," the chief grunted, stuffing a wad of eggs in his mouth.

"The Real People," Ray answered from rote. He poured coffee from a chrome decanter and sampled it: hot, earthy, full-bodied, with a pungent aroma. Not Folgers by any means. It was exotic, some of the best coffee Ray had ever tasted.

"Sumatra," Makintanz said, answering the unvoiced question. "Harvested in Indonesia. Roasted to perfection in Seattle. The Bradbury has it shipped up weekly."

Ray took another sip, savoring the flavor. If it was imported, that meant it was expensive. No doubt too expensive to afford on a cop's salary.

"What group?" Makintanz wanted to know. "Nunamiut?"

"Tareumiut."

"Ah . . . People of the Sea," the chief said in an approving tone. He lingered on this for a moment before downing a golf ball-sized strawberry.

The maid returned with a pair of champagne glasses and efficiently filled them.

"Mr. Makintanz," Ray began.

"Please. Call me Chief. Everyone does."

"Okay, Chief. The reason we're here . . ."

"How much you make a year, Ray?"

The question caught Ray off guard. The size of his paycheck was none of Makintanz's business. And how did this clown know his first name? "Excuse me?"

"What do you bring home in a year? You work in Barrow, right? Must net about what, a hundred grand a year?"

Ray stared at him, wondering what the point of this was.

"I could use a solid man like you, a good strong Tareumiut. You wouldn't believe how hard it is to find qualified Natives. For my security team, I mean." He paused to guzzle another glass of champagne. After wiping his mouth he said, "Most Eskimos are either too small or don't have the experience. You . . . you'd be perfect."

"Thank you, sir, but—"

"I'll beat your present salary by . . . fifty thousand."

"Really, I couldn't—"

"Okay, I'll double it. Whatever you're making now, times two. I know talent when I see it, Ray."

Ray squinted at him. What a salesman. He was smooth, polished, able to sidetrack you in the blink of an eye. No wonder he was rich. No wonder he was always in trouble with the law. The man was a snake, in whale's clothing.

"How do you know my name?" Ray asked.

"I know things," Makintanz assured him with a mischievous smile. "Your friend here, Billy Bob, he's too small. No offense. I just have standards. Requirements. And I'm predisposed to hire Natives. Those bozos in the hall are Italian. Bricks for brains, cloth ears, but they're good with their hands—and their guns. So . . ." Here he sighed melodramatically. "But I could use you, Ray. Kind of a personal assistant and bodyguard. I'll bet a quarter mill a year would have Margaret doing cartwheels."

"How did you know—"

"I told you, I know things," Makintanz chuckled. He tossed down two jumbo prawns. "I know about your grandfather too. One of the last great *umialiks*. A fine man."

Ray suddenly had the feeling that he was being threatened. Subtly, almost imperceptibly. But intentional or not, the vague implication was there.

"One thing I don't know," the chief admitted. "How in blazes did you get that way?"

"What way?"

"So big."

Ray shrugged at this.

"What are you, six foot?"

"Something like that."

"Amazing. A six foot full breed . . ." He shook his head at this as though it represented one of the great wonders of the world. "You are full Inupiat, aren't you?"

"As far as I know. Listen, Mr. Makintanz, we're here to discuss a murder."

"You mean two murders," he said playfully. "Don't you?"

"So you've heard?"

The chief nodded. "Bad timing."

"Excuse me?"

"The murders. We don't need that sort of thing right now. Not with Davis and Arctic Slope Regional about to jump into bed together."

"You're talking about the deal to extend the exploration field."

"Right. It's a touchy situation. The Corporation doesn't want to get robbed. They're paranoid. They think all oil companies are out to rip them off. Still hung up on tradition. You know, the old kinship thing. Never trust a stranger unless he forges a bond with a member of the clan."

"Isn't that what you are: a liaison?"

Makintanz smiled thinly at this. "Basically. Yes." Tossing in another prawn, he said, "On the other side, you've got Davis. They want to accept the lease Arctic Slope's offering, but don't want to get taken to the cleaners on the mineral rights. So they're being cautious. Then there's Hiro Hiroshuto." The chief went on to describe the man as an illegitimate son of a canine. "His conglomerate is waiting in the wings, drooling over the possibility of horning their way onto the Slope. If Davis so much as blinks, Hiroshuto will come rushing in like a bore tide, gobbling up that contract. That's all we need, the Japs getting their grubby little paws on the

Prudhoe reserve. They already own half of America. Why not give 'em Alaska." He swore, obviously disgusted by the idea. "It's a delicate situation. Everyone's on edge. Wouldn't take much to spoil things for Davis. Precisely the wrong time to have a madman running around killing folks. Especially if that madman turns out to be a Davis employee."

"You think it might be?"

"No idea. But if Arctic Slope even thinks that's a possibility, who knows. They might walk away from the table and hand the lease to the slant eyes."

Ray sipped his coffee, trying to size up his opponent. Makintanz was a strange one. Descended from Asians himself, it was odd that he could be prejudiced against the Japanese. He reminded Ray of one of those lizards that had the unique ability to change colors depending on their circumstances and surroundings. Getting straightforward, honest answers out of him would be like trying to wrestle a walrus: cumbersome, energy-intensive, potentially hazardous.

"You know a man by the name of Weinhart?"

"Hank? Sure. I did."

"Did?"

"He's dead. That was his body you found in the pipe up at seventeen. Wasn't it?" He gazed at them, puzzled. "I hope that's not news. You boys are supposed to be in charge of the investigation."

Ray produced the sketch. "Recognize this face?"

"Looks a little like Hank."

"A little?"

"Hard to say for sure."

As he refolded the sketch, Ray asked, "Was Weinhart up here because of this deal with Arctic Slope?"

Makintanz nodded, then grumbled, "Hank was Davis's closer. He was supposed to put the icing on the cake." The chief cursed at this. "The incompetent boob."

"You weren't impressed with his abilities?" Ray asked. He had given up on his roast beef and was working on a slab of salmon.

"Hank was about as agile as a lame moose when it came to negotiating. I still can't figure out how he got where he was. The guy was a lawyer. Went to Harvard. Good credentials, but no business savvy. No instincts. You have to have good instincts to anticipate your opponent's next move and get there before he does.''

"How'd you two get along?" Billy Bob asked over a sticky bun.

"We didn't. From the day I got elected to the board of Davis to the day Hank was murdered we butted heads like a couple of Dall sheep.'' He lifted the bottle from its ice tub, shook it, then hollered, "Rosemary! More DP!''

"What do you mean by 'butted heads'?" Ray asked.

"Just what it sounds like. We disagreed on everything. Especially this deal. Old Hank just wouldn't get on board.''

"And why was that?"

"He thought Arctic Slope was charging too much for too little. He failed to see the big picture, as usual. Sure, it's a relatively small plot, but the potential for production is out of this world. Well worth the price they're giving us. And if it was any bigger, the BLM and the Department of the Interior would get all hot and bothered. As it is, we've got a dozen environmental groups breathing down our necks, promising to bring suit if the deal goes through." The chief sighed, then shouted, "Rosemary! Where's that champagne?!''

The maid hurried through the door, bottle in hand. Makintanz scrutinized the label, pursed his lips, ultimately pronouncing it worthy to drink. Rosemary popped the cork. After filling the chief's glass, she stood waiting for him to hand down a verdict.

"Fine," Makintanz grunted after a cursory sip. He waved her away with his hand and began loading his plate with another helping of beef, a half dozen more shrimp, more eggs Benedict. "Believe me, Hank's death is no great loss. He was a liability, a blight on Davis. The putz. When he wasn't fouling up contracts, he was fooling around, with the ladies. Real tomcat. Couldn't keep his pants up. And if there's anything Davis doesn't need, it's a sophomoric Don Juan. That behavior just leads to scandal. And scandals kill deals. You ask me, those Casanova types get what they deserve in the end. One way or another, they wind up paying for their sins.''

"Is that right?" Ray wondered how Makintanz had the audacity to pass judgment on Weinhart when he was himself a repeat offender. Condemning adultery? It was public knowledge that the chief was a shameless womanizer. Word had it that he had fathered enough children to field a small army.

"Any idea who mighta wanted 'im dead?" Billy Bob asked.

"What are you doing out of your room?" Makintanz demanded in an angry tone.

"Daddy . . ." a voice complained from behind them. Ray and Billy Bob turned to find a woman in her early twenties standing in the doorway, fists on hips. She had long, dark hair and the face of a movie starlet. Her vibrant red blouse was stressed to its limit, buttons threatening to give way. A black belt was wrapped around her pencil thin waist. Below it, hips curved dangerously toward supple thighs, all accentuated by a pair of jeans that looked as though they had been spray painted on. Ray was amazed that she could breathe. And when she smiled, he forgot to: perfect teeth surrounded by full, red lips, long lashes fluttering over alluring, bedroom eyes.

"Wow . . ." Billy Bob sighed, mouth agape.

Ray was staring too, hypnotized by the combination of shapes, makeup, and smooth, bronze skin. The woman looked as though she had leapt off the page of one of Margaret's *Cosmopolitan* magazines. He decided that she was a blend of Tlingit and something . . . possibly Hispanic. And it was an eye-pleasing mix.

"Daddy . . ." she purred, the smile growing. "I'm going to go—"

"Back to your room!" he insisted in something approaching a shout.

"But Daddy—" she whined. Fingers began playing with an errant strand of hair. "I just want to—"

"Go back to your room. I'll tell you when you can come out."

The ruby lips formed a pronounced pout. She hissed something, turned, and flounced out. Ray and Billy Bob watched, entranced.

"Daughters . . ." Makintanz lamented. "You have to watch them every second. That one's goal in life is to cause me deep and lasting grief."

Ray dabbed at his brow. It was wet with perspiration. Miss Native America had elicited a hot flash. After a deep breath, he said, "Back to the question of who might have killed Weinhart, if that is, in fact, who the body turns out to be."

The chief chewed his beef, thinking. "Could have been someone from Arctic Slope. Someone who didn't want Hank to screw up the deal. Or it could have been someone from Davis. For the same reason."

"Someone like you," Ray suggested.

"Yeah. Like me. But I don't believe in violence. I've never been a fighter. Except when it comes to my family. You want to punch me in the nose, I'll probably turn the other cheek. Even in business. I'm pretty forgiving. But mess with my family and you better find a deep hole to hide in." His expression was suddenly serious, angry, almost evil. He chased a slice of pineapple, stabbed it with a fork. As he chewed it, his countenance magically changed, the jovial, relaxed look returning.

He glanced at Ray, then at Billy Bob. "I'm confident that you two will succeed in bringing this unthinkable atrocity to a quick and conclusive end."

It sounded to Ray like a rehearsed speech. And there was something familiar about the words, as if he had heard them before.

Makintanz was gazing out one of the darkened windows overlooking the Beaufort Sea. "Weather can be your friend or your enemy. Right now, it's our friend. Until it breaks, the groups can't get in here to hammer out the agreement and sign the papers. That gives you time to clean up this nasty business. I trust you'll do your best."

"Yes, sir."

Though Makintanz didn't rise, it was plain that the meeting was now over. Ray stood and waited as Billy Bob took a last bite of beef, a final gulp of coffee.

"I appreciate the time you've given us, Chief," Ray said,

only half sincere. He turned to leave, but a thought stopped him. "Does Salome mean anything to you?"

"Salome?" Makintanz popped a prawn into his mouth, his expression pensive. "No. Give me a hint. Is it mineral, vegetable, or animal?"

"Never mind."

"There's a dish called *salmi,* a wonderful blend of seasoned game that's roasted, then stewed in wine." He kissed the pointer finger and thumb of his right hand and flourished them in the air. "Prepared correctly, it is excellent."

"Thanks for your help."

They left the chief to his feast, retracing their steps through the suite, into the hall, back to the elevator. This time the security patrol barely offered them a glance. One was napping, the other engrossed in the sports page. Billy Bob found his gun on the floor.

Inside the elevator, he asked, "Salome?" His tongue gave it an acutely southern slant, as if it were the name of a flower found only in Texas.

"Don't ask," Ray grumbled.

The cowboy shrugged and stared stupidly at the spot above the door where the floor numbers should have been but weren't. "What now? Back to Davis?"

"Huh-uh. Not yet. First let's do a little fishing."

"*Fishing?*" The deputy made a face, buck teeth fully exposed. "Fer what? Icebergs?"

"No. For clues."

⇒ TWENTY-SIX ⇐

"THIS IS IT."

The manager pulled a plastic card from his jacket and zipped it down the slot next to the door. The device beeped at them. A green light blinked on and the lock mechanism clicked.

"But I'm afraid you're out of luck." He swung the door back. "The maids did a full-service cleaning after Mr. Weinhart checked out."

"So you said."

Henderson flipped a switch on his way in and two rows of inset studio lights came alive. The trio performed a quick walk-through. It was a large suite, with a main living area, connected dining room, kitchen, two bedrooms, each with its own bath. The walls bore contemporary Alaskan art. The furnishings were handsome and comfortable. Still, it seemed modest, almost primitive in comparison with Makintanz's penthouse.

"What is it you're looking for?" the manager wanted to know.

Ray shrugged.

"We're fishin'," Billy Bob chimed proudly.

"Fishing?"

"Thanks for your help," Ray muttered. He was inspecting the coffee table. An oversized hardcover titled *Inside Alaska* sat at the center. Ray leafed through it: vivid color photos of moose, dog sleds, float planes, *Ezkeemos* in fur parkas . . . On the side of the coffee table, facing the couch, was a shallow drawer. He pulled it out and found two decks of Bradbury playing cards. He looked up and saw Henderson hovering over him like a protective mother. "We'll lock up when we're finished."

"You won't have to," the manager explained. "The door is self-locking. When you leave, just be sure you're finished. You won't be able to get back in."

When he was gone, Ray told Billy Bob, "Check the kitchen."

"Fer what?"

"You'll know when you find it." *I hope*, Ray almost added. Despite the deputy's dopey facial structure, and Looney Tunes teeth, he seemed competent enough. Not brilliant, but he wasn't brain-dead either. He was simply young and rather naive. Actually the kid would probably make a good apprentice, if some older cop wanted to take him under his wing. Ray wasn't sure he was up to that task.

He ran a hand under, then behind, the cushions of the sofa. Nothing. Not even lint. Henderson hadn't been exaggerating when he said the maids had totally serviced the place. Kneeling, he peered under the couch, looked beneath the adjacent chair. Spick-and-span. Not so much as a crumb or a fleck of dirt.

A bookcase, with gold-lettered hardcovers set in neat rows, was pushed against the opposite wall. Ray surveyed the titles: *Moby Dick, Great Expectations, The Brothers Karamazov, Hamlet, Pride and Prejudice, War and Peace*. He had heard of most of these classics, but never aspired to read them. And from the condition of the volumes, it appeared that none of the guests had either. Lifting *The Scarlet Letter,* he examined the spine. It was perfect, nary a wrinkle or a bump. When he opened the cover, it crackled in protest, the thin, tissuelike pages inside still stuck together at the edges. Part of the illusion, he decided. The Bradbury was a high-brow establishment, the sort of hotel that oozed sophistication and culture. Staying here was supposed to make you feel smarter, wealthier, better than you actually were.

Ray selected books at random, pulling them out, peeking

behind them. Still nothing. Not even dust bunnies. The wood of the bookcase smelled of lemon oil, the books of crisp new paper.

Giving up on that "fishing hole," he moved toward one of the bedrooms. "Find anything?" he called to Billy Bob.

"Oh, I done found lotsa thangs," the deputy drawled back. "Wine, cheese, smoked oysters, choc-a-lut, even some ca-vee-ar. But nothin' I'd call a clue."

"Keep looking." The first bedroom was decorated in a subdued flower pattern, where bedspread, wallpaper, even art-work all complemented this theme with pastel pinks and blues. It looked like something a woman would appreciate.

Pulling back the spread, he checked the sheets. They were fresh. No need to ruin the maid's work further. He replaced the spread and glanced under the frame. Zip. Just air, carpet, the faint scent of flowers. There was a phone on the night stand, two phone books in the drawer: Anchorage and Seattle. The wall directly in front of the bed was paneled in light wooden squares. Ray found a handhold and slid one of the squares sideways. As he did, three other squares magically retreated to reveal a big screen television, a CD stereo, and a mini-bar, complete with a tiny sink and a miniature refriger-ator. Nice. He rifled the cable guide, glanced at the pay-per-view movies, then closed the panels again.

The bathroom was dressed in terra cotta tile and pale green terry cloth. There were two toilet stalls with doors to allow for privacy, four sinks, and an oversized whirlpool bath. A thin shower stall fashioned from crystal bricks stood next to the tub. The ceramic surfaces gleamed under the track light-ing. The towels looked as though they had been hand pressed. Paper-encased soap and a line of hair products were lined up along the counter, as if this were a beauty parlor. Ray found it hard to imagine anyone ever using the room for waste elim-ination or dirt removal. He opened drawers, examined the linen closet, considered taking a sample of the soap for Mar-garet.

"Anything?" he asked on his way to the other bedroom.

"Nah," came the reply.

Ray stuck his head in the kitchen. Billy Bob was perched

on the cabinet, one leg outstretched awkwardly as he strained to look behind the refrigerator.

"Find a body back there?"

The deputy flinched, lost his balance and toppled to the floor. Swearing, he got up and glared at Ray. "You scared me."

"Sorry."

"This place is amazin'," he announced, massaging a sore elbow. "You could eat off the floor, it's so dang clean. Not even any fuzzies in the coils in back of the fridge. They musta spit polished the whole darn place."

"Looks that way. You do the dining room or the hall bath yet?"

"Huh-uh. But what's to do? Look for crumbs under the table? Try to find hairs in the shower?"

"Good idea." Ray smiled at him and started down the hall. Maybe having an understudy wouldn't be all that bad. There was always the "gofer" factor. You could order a subordinate to do just about any job, no matter how pointless or demeaning.

The remaining bedroom was larger than the first, decked out in Native patterns: stylized versions of Haida images forming a thin border along one wall, the bedspread featuring Tlingit drawings made to look even more primitive than they really were. The room was dressed in teak. More of a man's decor. Ray decided that this was where Weinhart would have slept. With that in mind, he began a careful examination.

Fifteen minutes later, he arrived at the same conclusion: the maids at the Bradbury were exemplary, able to remove all evidence of human occupation. The entertainment center in this room was hidden along the north wall, behind an Athabaskan mural of a dogsled team traversing an ice field. Ray discovered this by toggling the remote on the night stand. There was a hum, and an instant later the mural split in two—something he was certain the original artist would not appreciate. There was the big screen set, the stereo, the bar. The latter had been restocked, beer, undersized bottles of whiskey, gin, tequila . . . lined up in uniform rows. Even determining

Weinhart's taste in booze was impossible, thanks to the exacting cleaning staff.

Ray punched the power button on the stereo, then ordered the CD player to open with his thumb. The device whirred and complied, offering four empty caddies and one disc. Ray rotated the caddie and removed it. Garth Brooks. So Weinhart liked country. Weinhart or some other previous guest. The maids obviously hadn't been instructed to scrutinize the stereo for forgotten discs. Either way, it didn't matter. That Weinhart, or any other oil exec from Houston or Dallas or Denver had a penchant for country music was less than a revelation.

Replacing the disc, Ray closed the caddie and turned off the power. Picking up the cable guide, he paged through. It was the same guide, the same pay-per-view movies. He was already putting the guide down when he realized that something had caught his eye. Leafing through it again, he found a page of adult features. Color pictures displayed naked bodies of varying sexes engaged in heated wrestling matches. Next to the list of titles and times someone had stuck a small, yellow Post-it note. There were no words on it, just a telephone number.

Ray lifted the note from the page. It was probably nothing. Most likely, some oil baron had jotted down a note while talking on the phone and left it behind. Besides, there was no area code. Who could tell what part of the country, what part of the world for that matter, the number corresponded to?

Sinking to the bed, he picked up the phone.

"Bradbury switchboard," a friendly female voice said immediately. "How may I direct your call?"

"I'd like an outside line, please."

"May I dial the number for you, sir?"

"No. I can do it if you get me out."

"Yes, sir. When you hear the tone, the line will be ready for you. In the future, if you would like an outside line, merely press seven."

"Okay." Two seconds later the tone sounded. Ray hesitated. What was the area code for Houston? He yanked open the drawer of the nightstand, pushed aside a copy of the Bible and removed the phone book. He was paging through the front when the spry operator asked, "Is there a problem, sir?"

"No. I'm fine, thanks." He found the code and punched it in, along with the number from the note. The line clicked and beeped. Then a mechanical voice announced, "Your call cannot be completed as dialed. Please redial or wait for an operator to assist you."

Ray hung up, pressed seven, waited for the tone. He tried Anchorage. Dallas. Denver. Fairbanks. Tulsa. Los Angeles. Each time the computerized voice instructed him to try again. The public transit authority answered in New York City. The man had never heard of Weinhart or Davis oil. He was a clerk, underpaid, he claimed.

More out of frustration than anything else, Ray dialed the number without any area code. Maybe it was for Barrow. Why, he couldn't imagine.

"Fanny's," a voice answered. It was a woman. She sounded tired, almost irritated at having to answer the phone.

"*Fanny's?*"

"Is there an echo or are you deaf?" she asked sarcastically. The question was followed by a curse. "What do you want?"

"Is this a business?"

"The oldest."

"Where are you located?"

"Who is this?"

"I got the number from a friend and I just don't . . ."

Billy Bob appeared in the doorway. "I done checked everwhere and there's nothin' that . . ."

Ray waved him off. "I don't know where you're located."

There was a cracking noise, gum smacking. "You know Deadhorse?"

"Yeah."

"You know the old hotel, Harry's roadhouse?"

"Yeah."

"I'm in the back."

"Okay."

"I don't take reservations. First come, first serve. You want a particular girl, you wait for her if she's busy."

"Girl?"

She swore at him. "I got blondes, brunettes, redheads, all

shapes and sizes. I aim to please. But I ain't got no men. If that's your thing, go out to one of the camps. They got plenty of action.''

"So you specialize in—in female companionship?"

"That's right, honey. Come on over. I got ladies just waitin' to party with you.'' She cackled like a witch before hanging up.

"Who was that?" Billy Bob asked.

"Fanny."

"Fanny? You mean from the . . . ?"

Ray nodded. "The madam herself."

Billy Bob looked at him suspiciously. "I tell ya, Ray, I'm as open-minded as the next feller, but, I gotta say, this ain't the time to be foolin' around, buddy. Not in the middle of a murder investigation. Besides, ya got ya a sweetie back home that . . ."

Ray frowned, holding the Post-it up to him.

"What is it?"

"Fanny's number. It was in the cable guide. Somebody left it in there."

"So?"

"So maybe it was Weinhart."

"So?" The deputy was clearly confused.

"So maybe Weinhart patronized Fanny's establishment while he was here. I'll show them the sketch. Maybe we can place Weinhart at the bordello. That would give us a time reference. We might even get lucky and turn up a witness to the murder.''

The deputy squinted at the Post-it. "All that from that little thang?"

"Come on."

Ten minutes later the Explorer rolled to a stop in front of Harry's. Three lumps of snow were parked at odd angles near the door. Judging from the shapes, they were pickups, their specific colors and makes obscured by a layer of powder.

"Storm's almost over," Ray noted as they got out. Crystallized pellets were still dancing in the air, but the wind had lost its fury. Above, stars could be seen in and through a misty veil of clouds.

" 'Bout time," the deputy lamented. He slammed the driver's door and bent to plug the engine into an outlet. "Feels every bit as cold, though."

"I didn't say it was spring."

"Maybe them boys from Anchorage can get themselves up here before the next one sets in," Billy Bob said wistfully. "Shore would make our lives a whole lot easier."

"Don't count on it." He opened the door and held it for the deputy. Warm air rushed out to greet them. After passing through a narrow mudroom, they entered the bar. It was surprisingly quiet: a long counter bearing dirty glasses, vacant stools, a trio of tables covered with empty beer pitchers and steins, four pool tables, balls akimbo, cues leaning against the walls, left on the floor, bare fluorescent bulbs humming . . .

"Looks like it was some party," Billy Bob noted. "Where is ever-body?"

"Maybe the bar's closed on Sunday morning."

There were no patrons in evidence. Just a short figure hunched behind the counter, its back to them. It was a man, from the looks of the build, possibly a Native: stooped shoulders, dark hair, small hands. His attention was focused on a sink stacked high with dishes, wiping, washing and rinsing in slow motion, as if the chore required a great effort. A radio offered static-laced accompaniment, turning his actions into a stilted ballet.

Ray was about to call to the man when he noticed a door behind the pool tables. A handwritten sign above it read "Fanny's—Full Service Bordello." They crossed the room toward it, the dishwasher never taking his eyes from his work. Ray reached for the knob.

"Where you think you're goin'?" a deep voice asked.

They turned and watched as something crawled out from under one of the pool tables—a thick, square of faded denim, long greasy hair, green tattoos, and bulging muscles. The man stood, wavered, braced himself on the table, then spit on the floor.

"How's it going?" Ray offered respectfully. This guy put the brutes back at Makintanz's place to shame. Not quite as tall as Archie and Jughead, he carried as much weight as both of them put together, and looked twice as mean, a Hell's Angel on steroids.

"I asked you where you thought you was goin'?" he repeated, bloodshot eyes struggling to focus.

"Fanny's," Ray replied, twisting the knob. "Want to come along?" He smiled innocently. Might as well humor this jerk.

A thick finger thumped Ray's chest. "Cain't you read?" The biker spun Ray around, squeezing his chin as he aimed Ray's head at another handwritten sign. This one declared: "NO KLOOCHES ALLOWED!"

"You see that? You understand what it says?"

"Yeah." Ray tried to swallow but couldn't. The man's elbow was across his Adam's apple.

"Now is you or is you not, a klooch?"

"Hey, buddy . . ." Billy Bob started to intervene. A forearm to the chest lifted the cowboy from his feet and sent him skidding across the floor.

"Is you?"

"Yes, sir. I'm an Inupiat."

The malodorous, puke-speckled beard jiggled as the man laughed. "Inupy-what?"

"Inupiat. Those are my people."

"Muktuk kissing, blubber-breathed . . ." He kneed Ray in the gut. Ray staggered, fighting for breath. "Stinky, dumb, dog-ugly . . . Only thing you people is good for is to beat the daylights out of. I'm gonna air mail you back to yer igloo with a lumpy head."

"Wait," Ray puffed. He fished out his badge.

The man swore at it. "A klooch cop . . ." He grinned at Ray with smoke-stained teeth as if pummeling a Native law enforcement officer would be a special treat.

"I was afraid of that." Ray sank his boot into the man's groin with as much force as he could muster. Goliath leaned, grunted, swore, but didn't go down. A high kick to the head felled him. He sprawled to the floor, blood gushing from his nose.

Ray helped Billy Bob up. "You okay?"

"I thank so," he answered, rubbing his chest. "Where'd ya learn to do that?"

"Eskimo Olympics. I was champ of the high-kick competition, four years running. Never thought it would come in handy."

Ray opened the door and glanced back. The dishwasher was working on a platter, diligently scraping at dried food. If he was concerned about the incident with the bouncer, he certainly was hiding it well.

➤➤ TWENTY-SEVEN ◆◆

"CAN I HELP you?"

The question came from a woman sitting at a rickety wooden desk, the only item in the tiny, dimly lit room at the top of the steps. A cigarette poised in her fingers, a tumbler of translucent copper-colored liquid at close reach, she was scrutinizing a newspaper with a deep scowl.

Ray offered his badge. The woman glared up at it, obviously unimpressed, and sucked on her cigarette. "So?" she puffed. "You want to see one of my ladies or what?"

"I talked to you on the phone, I think," Ray said. "You're Fanny, right?" He waited for some sort of recognition, but there was none. The woman turned the page of the paper, lifted her glass, took a swig. Her hair was disheveled, a brownish gray mat, thinning severely on the top of her skull. It was difficult to judge her age. Her face was sickly thin, cheek bones protruding through the wrinkled, parchmentlike skin. Ray decided that she could have been in her late seventies, enjoying moderately good health or in her early forties, weathered prematurely by a very difficult life. Either way, she looked bitter, hard.

"We'd like to ask you and your *ladies* a few questions," Ray tried. "If you don't mind."

She sucked the cigarette down to a butt, pulled a pack out from the pocket of her shirt, and lit a fresh smoke. "Why should I mind? Long as you pay for the time."

"Pay?"

She cackled loudly. "You can spend just as much time with my ladies as you wants to. Long as you pay. They don't work for free."

"We don't want to . . . to—you know . . ." Ray argued. "We just want to ask a few—"

"Questions," she said, nodding. She spit a piece of tobacco at their feet. "Fine. Whatever turns ya'll on. Still be $50."

"$50?"

"Per quarter hour. Per person."

"You've got to be kidding."

"I kid about a lot of things, honey, but money ain't one of 'em."

"We could get a warrant and shut this place down," Ray threatened.

Fanny found this hysterical, nearly spilling her booze. "You do that, honey. You do that. Closest white judge is Fairbanks. That's four hundred miles. And I guarantee he won't care none about what we're doing up here in Deadhorse. So you just go on, try to get you that warrant. Have a nice trip." She returned her attention to the paper.

Ray glanced down at it: *The Anchorage Daily News*. According to the date in the corner, it was the Sunday paper, Sunday of last week. He turned to Billy Bob. "How much money do you have?"

The deputy began digging in his pockets. A moment later he replied, " 'Bout twenty two dollars."

Ray inspected the contents of his wallet. "I've got . . . twenty eight."

The woman smiled up at them. There was a gap where her two top front teeth should have been. " 'Cordin' to my math, that makes fifty dollars. Pay up and one a ya'll can go back and 'sperience fifteen minutes of heaven."

"This is robbery," Ray lamented as he handed over the money. "You know that don't you?"

"Call a cop," Fanny told him, giggling through her missing incisors.

Ray displayed the sketch. "Ever see this man?"

Fanny gave it a cursory glance. "Maybe . . . maybe not."

"He was probably wearing a suit."

"I don't pay much notice to what our clients *wear*." She was already engrossed in the newspaper again.

"It would have been a couple of days ago," Ray pressed. He pushed the sketch in front of her again.

Fanny sighed at it, picked it up, frowned. "Maybe."

"Yes or no?"

This drew a curse. "I told you, I don't pay much notice. I don't memorize faces or nothin'. It's best not to. A man pays for his playtime, I don't care if he's the governor, a jock like Michael Jordan, pretty as Mel Gibson, or gosh awful ugly as sin." After finishing off her drink, she belched, then said, "The clock's runnin'. Ya'll are wasting your time. Them ladies are waitin'."

Ray turned to Billy Bob. "You want to go? Or do you want me to go?"

The deputy shrugged back, blushing.

"Don't be shy now," Fanny encouraged without looking up. "Two and Four are occupado. But other 'n that, you got your pick of the litter."

"I'll go," Ray groaned.

Billy Bob punched him on the shoulder and shot him a crooked smile. "Now 'member, you keep thinkin' about your sweetie while you're in there."

"Right." He opened the door and left Billy Bob to the grumpy madam. It swung shut behind him and he found himself in a narrow hallway. Lit by a single, naked bulb, it offered a series of doors before dead-ending into a fire-hose box and humidifier unit. The first door on his left was marked with a large red 2. He had already rapped on it when he remembered Fanny's admonition. Someone inside, a man, swore at him, encouraging him to go directly to a fiery eternal home. He performed a 180 and addressed door 3. When he knocked, the same deep voice cursed him from room 2. He knocked again, waited, then twisted the knob. The door creaked open.

"Hello?" The room was dark and quiet. "Hello?" Ray took a tentative step forward, a hand feeling blindly for a light switch. When his fingers found it an overhead fluorescent light panel began to flicker, before blinking on. The room was the size of a small storage closet; no chairs, no sink or toilet, just a twin mattress and box springs sat on the tile floor. The mattress was covered in worn gray sheets twisted into knots. Next to the door was a boombox and a short stack of cassette tapes: The Rolling Stones, AC/DC, Bon Jovi . . . The music of love.

Under the harsh glow of the fluorescent light, the scene reminded Ray of a prison cell. A man had to be pretty desperate to pay $50, per quarter hour, for this, he decided. Of course, if you were pulling a suicide shift, working seven twelve-hour days a week for half a year or so . . .

Ray shut the door and continued down the hall. He eyed room 4. Fanny was right, he realized as he passed it, ears straining to make sense of the frantic shrieks and animalistic grunts. The room was in use. Either that or someone was watching a *National Geographic* documentary about the mating practices of baboons. Pausing at number 5, he tapped on the door. Nothing.

Sighing, he turned the knob and pushed the door open. Room number 5 looked more like a cheap motel: stained carpet, Formica nightstand, lamp with a red bulb, double bed with a chipped and rusted brass frame, mirror on the ceiling . . . There was a lump beneath the flowered spread, snakelike locks of dark hair on the pillow.

"Excuse me?" Ray called.

The lump didn't move. A bottle next to the lamp stand told him why. A fifth of gin, nearly empty. Ray gently pulled the spread back and found a woman. She was in her twenties, probably quite pretty once but now appeared grim, wrinkled, used. Her eyes were ringed by dark circles, her breath coming out in toxic puffs. She mumbled something, kicked, as if fending off some unseen attacker, then began to snore.

This was turning out to be a waste of time and money, Ray thought as he left the room. With only two doors left, he began to wonder if Fanny would see fit to refund his money. No. Not Fanny. She'd laugh and tell him about her policy of no guarantees, no refunds.

He knocked on room 6 and was already turning to try 7 when a voice in the former responded.

"Come in." It was female, pleasant, inviting.

Ray opened the door and was met by a blonde. She was young—eighteen, sixteen?—with a toned but skinny figure. Behind her was a waterbed decked in black silk sheets. The soft strains of Mozart rose from a miniature CD player. An array of candles, a bouquet of fake flowers, and the aroma of incense completed the fantasy. Wearing only a black negligee, she approached Ray with a wicked smile. "I've been waiting for you," she purred.

"Is that right? What's your name?"

"Honey," she replied sensuously. Draping her arms around his neck, she pressed her chest against him and giggled. "But you can call me whatever you want to, Lover."

"How about *witness*?"

She blinked at him, then, "If that's what turns you on, Baby."

Ray peeled out of her embrace and submitted his ID.

Honey's countenance fell. "What do you want?" she sighed, sinking onto the bed. She suddenly seemed exhausted, her face heavy with clownish makeup. "You gonna bust me?" She paused to swear, then lifted both wrists to him, ready for handcuffs.

"I just want to talk to you."

This drew another curse. "Either bust me or hop in and let's do it," she said patting the bed. "Otherwise, leave me alone. I had a long night, mister. You wanna talk, you go see a shrink. I ain't in the mood."

"Know this guy?" Ray asked, offering the sketch.

Honey glanced at the picture, frowning. "Should I?"

"He might have been in here a couple of days back."

She took the sketch and studied it. "I don't know, maybe."

"Maybe?"

"He wasn't one of my johns, but . . ." She lifted the sketch to eye level and squinted at it. "I don't know, I might have seen him in the hall."

"Whose *john* was he?"

"Don't know."

"He was probably wearing a suit. About six foot, brown hair . . ."

"I said I don't know. Maybe I saw him. That's the best I can do."

Ray folded the sketch and put it into his pocket. "Thanks."

"What'd he do?"

"Who?"

"That man? He rob somebody or something?"

Ray shook his head. "No." He turned to leave, then stopped. "How old are you?"

Honey told him where to go.

"I'm serious."

"Thought you said you weren't gonna bust me."

"I'm not."

"Then it's none of your business. Now if you'll excuse me, I need to get some sleep before rush hour."

"Rush hour?"

"That's what we call Sunday afternoon. Saturday night we're booked solid. Then there's a lull on Sunday morning. The *clients* are all sleeping off their hangovers, some of them are going to chapel service to confess their sins. Then just after noon, when the headaches and the praying are past, things pick up again." She shrugged, as if the mystery of the pattern eluded her.

"Humor me," Ray prodded, watching her eyes. Thanks to the eyeliner, lipstick, and rouge, Honey could have passed for a college kid. But her eyes . . . they betrayed her youth.

"What do you mean?"

"How old are you? I promise I won't arrest you. I'm just interested."

She glared at him. "Eighteen."

"No. Really."

"Seventeen?"

"The truth."

"Okay, fifteen and three months. Satisfied?"

Ray shook his head at her. "What are you doing up here?"

The question drew laughter. "What's it look like I'm doing?" She stood, swayed her hips back and forth provocatively, then fell back onto the bed. "Lotta men, not many women."

"You know what I mean. Where's home?"

Her face grew stern, jaw clenched, eyes flashing with either anger or fear. "This is home." As she said this, her lower lip quivered.

"What about your parents?"

She got up and threw on a robe. "I need some sleep before rush hour."

Ray considered pushing the issue, finding out where Honey belonged, why she had run away, encouraging her to contact her parents—doing the concerned public servant bit. And it wouldn't have been without genuine concern. But this wasn't the time. Honey didn't seem to be comfortable discussing the subject. He dug a card out of his parka. "Listen, I work in Barrow. It's long distance, but if you ever need to talk . . ." He offered it to her, but she was studying the floor. Placing it on the nightstand, he added, "Call collect. I'll accept the charges."

With that, he returned to the hall and knocked on door 7. "Don't bother," Honey said from behind him. She was peering out a four-inch opening in the door like a frightened child who wanted help but couldn't bring herself to trust a stranger. "She's not there."

"Okay. Thanks."

Ray could feel Honey watching him as he went back to the reception area. Fanny glanced at him as he passed through. "Have a good time?"

He ignored this, still wondering if there was something he could do to help Honey out of what had to be a bleak, hopeless existence. He found Billy Bob in the bar, playing pool. The bouncer was slumped across three chairs along the wall, asleep, his beard and hair caked with dried blood. His nose was already purple.

"Ready?"

Billy Bob set the cue down. "How'd it go?" he asked with a wiggle of his eyebrows.

Ray frowned and shrugged back at him. "One girl might have seen Weinhart . . . maybe. Nothing firm."

"So where does that leave us?"

"Same place as always," Ray lamented. "Square one."

"What now?"

"Back to Davis, I guess. I still need to take a look at Driscoll. Not that it will help."

They donned their gear and were at the door when Ray thought of something.

"You go ahead."

"Huh?"

"Go start your truck. I'll be there in a minute."

"Okay." The cowboy reluctantly set off to attend to the chore.

Ray trotted back up the stairs to face Fanny. "I need to ask Honey one more thing."

"Fine," Fanny grunted. "That'll be fifty dollars."

"Come on, just one question. It'll only take a minute."

Fanny looked up at him thoughtfully. After sucking her cigarette, she grunted, "Twenty-five dollars."

"One question," Ray implored. "And I don't have any more cash."

Fanny's lower lip hung down forming a pouty expression. "Poor baby."

"Fanny!"

"Gotta credit card?"

"A what?"

She pulled a credit card device out of the desk. "We take VISA, MasterCard and Discover. No American Express."

Ray dug out his wallet, handed over a MasterCard. "This is highway robbery."

"Ain't it though," Fanny grinned as she ran the card. "There you go. Seven minutes, thirty seconds."

"Thanks . . ." Ray grumbled. He hurried down the hall to Honey's door. "Honey?" He knocked hard.

In a moment the door creaked open. When Honey saw him, she groaned. "You're not gonna badger me are you? I'm not going back there. I won't. I'd rather die than go back there."

"Back where?"

"Juneau." It sounded like a derogatory term.

"No. I just thought of something else I needed to ask you. Have you ever heard the name Salome?"

"Sure. I know her."

"*Her?* Who is she?"

"That's her room," Honey replied, pointing at number 7. "But she's not there right now. She only shows up a few times a month. Sometimes not that often."

"Was she here two days ago?"

"Uh . . . I think so."

"Could she have seen the man I was asking about?"

Honey thought this over. "Maybe. She's not here much, but when she is, she serves a lot of customers."

"Why's that?"

" 'Cause she looks like a beauty queen. She's older than me. Got more . . . you know. And she's Native."

"So?"

"So the guys up here really dig that. When she's here, her card's full."

"She was here a couple of days ago, when this man," Ray patted his pocket, "would have been in?"

Honey nodded. "Yeah."

"Any idea where I can find her?"

"Huh-uh. Fanny doesn't even know where Salome lives. She just shows up when she pleases, disappears the same way. I don't think she does it for the money."

"Why would she do it then?"

Honey shrugged. "Kicks, I guess. Can I get some sleep now?"

"Sure. Thanks for your help." When the door was shut, Ray tried the knob on room 7. It was locked. He wondered if Fanny could open it. Probably. But there was no telling what it would cost him. Returning to the entry room, he found her on the phone.

"You bet. Okay. Right . . ."

When she hung up, he said, "Room seven is locked. Do you think you could—"

Fanny looked at him without seeing him and swore. "He's coming!"

"Who? Who's coming?"

She ignored him, disappearing down the hall. Ray considered going after her, but decided it wasn't worth the effort. The chances of finding anything of value in Salome's room were scant. Although, what were the odds of finding a woman on the Slope named Salome in the first place?

On the way to the Explorer, he chewed over the coincidence and the remote possibility that Maniilaq wasn't all hot air. When he climbed inside the Ford, Billy Bob was on the phone. The deputy sat listening for a full minute before exclaiming, "Hot diggety dog!"

After he hung up, Ray looked at him expectantly. "Well, what is it?"

Bunny teeth protruded from a big down-home smile. "That was Mr. Reynolds. They caught him."

"Caught who?"

"The killer. They caught the killer!"

➤➤ TWENTY-EIGHT ◄◄

THE WIND WAS still gusting, but intermittently now. Low clouds were rolling in from the north. A ghostly band of hazy colors reached up from the dark gray horizon: green, purple, dull red. The Northern Lights.

In the penetrating glare of the Explorer's high beams, the landscape looked pristine, virginal, a fair maiden sleeping breathlessly beneath a fleecy blanket of whitest white.

Ray failed to notice any of it, his mind distracted by the revelation that the case had reportedly been closed.

"Are they sure it's him?"

Billy Bob shrugged at this, as he had done in response to most of Ray's questions. "I told you all I know. They caught the guy tryin' to make off with yer snow mo-bile. And when they brought 'em back to camp, he confessed."

"He confessed . . . just like that?"

"I guess. How's a killer supposed to confess?"

"If I had just shot and slashed a couple of people, and sabotaged a police officer's vehicle, I wouldn't hang around waiting to be caught. And I wouldn't spill my guts just because somebody saw me messing with a snow machine. It doesn't make sense."

"'Course it don't. Killin' never makes good sense. Sometimes killers is crazy. Sometimes they're angry. Sometimes they're greedy. Sometimes they're clever as they come. Sometimes they're dumb as a post. But what they done don't hardly never make no sense."

"Don't . . . hardly . . . never . . . ?" Ray repeated, trying to untangle the sentence.

"That's right."

"And you're an expert on the inner workings of the violent criminal mind because . . . ? You took psych in college? You conducted exhaustive research on the subject? You worked homicide somewhere?"

Billy Bob shook his head. "TV," he replied matter-of-factly.

"TV?"

"I watch a lot of them detective show reruns: 'NYPD Blue,' 'Murder One,' 'Homicide: Life on the Street' "

Ray laughed at this. "Oh, no wonder then."

"Don't laugh. Some of 'em are very realistic."

"I'm sure."

"Most of the killers are too big-headed to think they'll ever get caught. They hang around, kinda thumbin' their nose at the law. Till they make a mistake and wind up behind bars." He shifted gears, turning into the Davis facility, then added, "Ain't no such thing as the perfect murder."

"Is that right?" Ray rolled his eyes at this. Investigation by cliché police drama techniques.

"And the bad guys almost always return to the scene of the crime."

"Uh-huh."

Billy Bob parked the Explorer in front of the main building and killed the engine. "You don't sound convinced."

"I'm not."

"You should be happy," the deputy told him with a smile. "The case is closed and now ya can go back to yer sweetie."

"We'll see about that."

They climbed out and Ray waited as Billy Bob plugged in the Ford. It was still cold, maybe 50 below zero, but with the wind starting to relent, it seemed almost pleasant.

After discarding their gear in the mudroom, they squeaked their way to the security office, a trail of dirty puddles accompanying them. Reynolds was on the phone. He smiled and waved them to a seat. Leeland was at his desk, cellular glued to his ear.

"Yes, sir. About forty-five minutes ago," Reynolds was saying. "Yes, sir. Yes, I'll be sure to tell him."

"He was hunched over the snow machine when I got there," Leeland was telling someone. "Trying to steal parts, I think. Anyway, I yelled at him, told him to get away from it, and he started running. I pursued on foot and tackled him about, oh, maybe fifty feet from the machine. He confessed on the ride back in."

Ray tried to imagine the scene. The killer is stripping the snow machine. A security guard shows up, spooks him, and the guy runs. Runs? Why run? Why not put a bullet through the security guard's heart too? Make a hat trick out of it. But the underlying question was why a murderer who had already killed two men in a unique, stylized fashion would be out in foul weather ravaging a dead Polaris? And then, without any coercion, he decides to admit to a double murder? Yeah, right. And what did Leeland consider coercion? Ray decided that he would probably find it within himself to confess all manner of imaginary sins if properly motivated by Mr. Musclepig.

Reynolds hung up his phone first. "That was Houston," he declared with a grin. "They're so happy we caught our man—so relieved it wasn't a Davis employee—they're doing somersaults. We cleared this up just in the nick of time. With the weather starting to clear, the VIPs can fly in tomorrow morning, minus one gosh awful mess."

"What about the authorities from Anchorage?"

"They're hoping to make it up by this evening, but it doesn't matter. We caught the guy." He stood and pumped his fist in the air.

"Where is he?" Ray asked.

A whoop from Leeland, who had just hung up the phone, drew their attention. "That was the *Anchorage Daily News*. Right before that, I did an interview with the *Seattle Times*."

"Next thing you know," Reynolds said, " 'Hard Copy' will be up here doing a feature."

"How did the media find out?" Ray asked.

"Houston put out a flash press release," Reynolds informed him. "The phones have been ringing off the hooks ever since."

Leeland's cellular buzzed, as if on cue. He answered it and began relaying the details of the capture to yet another reporter.

"All this in forty-five minutes?" Ray wondered.

"Good news travels fast," Reynolds replied.

"Where is he?"

"Who?"

"The alleged murderer."

"Alleged? . . ." Reynolds chuckled at this. "I like that . . . alleged . . . Sounds fair and just, but we got this guy dead-bang."

"Is that right?"

"We told you he confessed."

"I'd like to see him."

"He's in the storage closet."

Ray squinted at him. "The storage closet?"

"We don't have a jail. When we turn him over to you and the deputy, you can escort him back to the sheriff's office in Deadhorse and lock him up."

Reynolds set off down the hall, never looking back to see if they were following.

"You read him his rights?"

"Of course. It was a citizen's arrest, but still . . ."

"And you informed him of the right to have a lawyer present?"

"He didn't want one."

"How'd you take the confession? Written, recorded . . . ? Did he sign anything?"

Reynolds swore at this. "Leeland asked the scumbag if he did it. The scumbag said yes. I asked the scumbag if he did it. The scumbag said yes. That's confession times two."

After fishing a key ring from his pocket, Reynolds unlocked a door marked JANITORIAL. The small room was lined with shelves bearing various cleaning supplies and chemicals. In front of the shelves was an office chair into which a Native man had been bound with ropes. A rectangle of gray duct tape had been fastened over his mouth. Wide, almond-shaped eyes stared at them. The man was obviously terrified. His right cheek was swollen with broken blood vessels. A ragged gash ran crookedly down his forehead.

"What happened to him?" Ray asked.

Reynolds shrugged. "He fell down."

"What's the tape for?" he asked, struggling to remain calm. The guy looked more like a kidnap victim than a killer.

"He was yelling and carrying on," Reynolds explained gruffly. "I told him if he didn't shut up I'd have to tape his mouth shut. He kept on, so . . ."

Ray peeled the tape off as gingerly as possible, but the man flinched anyway. "What's your name?"

The eyes were sad now, sorrow overshadowing fear.

"What's his name?"

"No idea," Reynolds grunted.

"What's your name?" Ray repeated.

There was no response, just heavy, panicked breathing, the man's chest pushing at the ropes.

"Was he violent?"

"Huh?"

"Did he resist Leeland? Or did Leeland just smack him for the fun of it?"

"He ran. And I guess he put up a fight."

"I'd run too if that monster was chasing me. Let's take his ropes off."

Reynolds shook his head. "I'm not sure that's a good idea."

Ray ignored this, pulling at the knots until they unraveled. The man's hands bore red burn marks from rubbing on the jute.

"There. Better?" Ray asked.

The man glanced at Ray, then at the open door. Suddenly he was on his feet, making a break for it. Confusion reigned as Ray fought to grab an arm, while Billy Bob and Reynolds struggled to grasp other limbs. The man seemed possessed now, evidencing the strength of Hercules. He shouted something and Ray saw Billy Bob fly into the shelves. Reynolds had a foot and was holding on for dear life, his entire body flailing as the man kicked at him. Ray twisted the arm he was attached to, then kicked the man's planted leg with a foot.

All three of them fell to the floor. One of the shelves wobbled and threatened to topple onto them. Instead, it began raining cleaning supplies: rolls of paper towels, rubber gloves, bottles of dishwashing detergent, toilet paper . . .

Reynolds ended the scuffle with a forearm to the prisoner's face. The man groaned as his head bounced against the concrete floor and, though he remained conscious, all resistance evaporated. They put him back into the chair and refastened the ropes.

"Told you," Reynolds puffed.

Billy Bob was staring blankly at the captive, more clueless than ever.

"Got yer bell rung, didn't ya kid?" Reynolds laughed.

The deputy blinked and began massaging a lump on the back of his skull.

Reynolds swore at the man in the chair. "Gotta watch these klooches every second. No offense, officer."

"Let me talk to him alone," Ray said. He was developing a healthy dislike for Reynolds.

"Whatever you say. Just don't let him loose. You're gonna have to wheel him to Deadhorse in that chair, you know." He laughed at this and led Billy Bob back toward the office.

When they were gone, Ray sank to the floor next to the man. "What's your name?"

The man stared at him. He had the look of a caged animal: dangerous, unpredictable, desperate.

"You're being accused of murder, you know that, right?"

Nothing.

"Did you kill those men?"

Silence.

"Did you kill them? Yes or no?"

"Yes." His eyes grew wide.

"Why?"

No response. The man was glaring at the floor now.

"You're Inupiat," Ray surmised.

The man continued his examination of the concrete. The gash on his forehead had been reopened by Reynolds' blow and blood was trickling down his brow. Ray felt like a Nazi interrogator.

After wiping the blood with his sleeve, Ray asked, "Do you speak English?" When this failed to elicit so much as a glance, he translated the question into Inupiaq.

The man looked at him with a forlorn expression. "No."

In Inupiaq, Ray asked his name.

"Mike."

"Mike . . ." Continuing in their native tongue, Ray explained the problem, summing it up with, "You're being accused of murder."

The eyes flashed with terror, the man's breathing becoming labored again. "Adiii!"

"Exactly." Ray studied him for a moment, then asked in the People's language, "Did you kill anyone?"

"No!" It took the form of a plea.

Ray tried English again, an experiment. "Did you kill two men in cold blood?"

"Yes?" It was more of a question than an answer. The man was simply aiming to please, to get himself out of a situation he didn't understand.

"Hang on." Ray left and returned two minutes later with Reynolds and Leeland. Billy Bob trailed after them, still looking dazed.

In the storage room, with all four of them gathered around the accused, Ray asked, "Did you kill two men on the North Slope?"

The man's eyes glanced at his interrogators. "Yes?"

"See?" Reynolds said victoriously. "Listen, before you take him to Deadhorse, can we get a few pictures, of us with him, for the press?"

Ray silenced him with a hand. "Did you kill JFK?"

The eyes darted around, then, "Yes?"

"Have you ever worked for Sadaam Hussein?"

"Yes?"

"He's out of his mind," Reynolds surmised angrily.

"No. He just doesn't speak English," Ray announced.

Reynolds and Leeland took turns muttering profane phrases.

"But he ran," Leeland argued. "He was doing something to your snow machine."

"Probably after spare parts," Ray said. He submitted the question to the man in Inupiaq. A long explanation followed. When he was done, Ray said, "Yep. He needed parts for his Snow Cat. Couldn't afford to buy them. Saw my machine and . . ."

"He's a thief!" Leeland asserted.

Ray nodded. "Guilty of stealing, or at least attempted robbery. But not murder. And since I don't plan to press charges . . ."

"You're not thinking of letting him go?" Reynolds bellowed incredulously.

Ray nodded, already untying him. He told the man not to worry, that everything would be okay and he would not be hurt if he would simply cooperate. The man seemed to accept this. Once unbound, he darted through the door and disappeared down the hall.

"Stupid *muktuk* . . ." Leeland muttered. "What are we supposed to do now?"

"Call Houston back," Reynolds said. "Tell them . . . tell them it was a mistake."

"Right. I'll tell them it was a mistake, that all the press stuff was premature, and they'll tell me I'm out of a job. Sounds easy enough." He began rubbing his temples. "How were we supposed to know the idiot didn't understand us?"

"Yeah, imagine a person from another culture not speaking English," Ray said. "If you had something other than a lump of muscle attached to your shoulders . . ."

Leeland told Ray where to go. Ray considered trying his new high-kick maneuver out on Leeland's face.

Reynolds pushed them apart gruffly. "Come on. Call Houston," he said to Leeland. "I'll go see Red." He cursed. "He'll have a fit. A stack-blowing, through-the-roof, conniption fit."

"I'll go with you," Ray said. "I need to talk with him anyway. And it's been a while since I witnessed a good conniption fit."

⇒ TWENTY-NINE ⇐

BAUER WAS GRINNING into a telephone receiver when they
reached his office. He waved them in, beaming.

"No, sir. He had absolutely no connection to Davis whatsoever." The small ruddy man paused, listening, the smile
expanding. "As far as we know . . . Yes, sir. Just a solitary
Native, a lunatic that went nuts and killed a couple of our
guys." Bauer laughed heartily. "Who knows, with the right
spin, we might even use it to our advantage . . . Exactly.
'Crazed Eskimo slays oil workers in murderous crime spree.'
If nothing else, it'll give the Corporation something to think
about. Bad PR is bad PR. Might even strengthen our position.
Public opinion will naturally swing toward the innocent victims, in this case, Davis oil employees." He chuckled again,
almost gleefully, as if the murders were somehow fortuitous,
the best of luck.

Ray, Reynolds and Billy Bob stood waiting, all reluctant
to accept the two seats Bauer had offered.

"Anything on Weinhart?" Ray whispered.

Reynolds's face was suddenly animated. "Yeah. The guy
never checked into his ski condo down in Colorado."

Ray considered this. No one could confirm Weinhart's
presence on the company jet. No one back in Houston knew
where he was. And he hadn't made the vacation he was supposed to be taking. Short of finding the missing corpse and
getting a positive ID, this was about as close as they were
going to get to confirmation. Hank Weinhart was either pur-

posefully out of touch, or he was dead, his life ended by a bullet, his body desecrated by an *ulu*. Both hypotheses were plausible, but Ray tended to believe the latter. It made more sense, given the facts they had to work with. Why would an executive whose company was involved in a big deal choose this particular time to drop off the face of the earth? Go skiing? Sure. Especially if he wasn't invited to the negotiations in Deadhorse. But disappear? It was difficult to imagine a grown man, a vice president, off sulking somewhere over a disagreement in business strategy.

"No, sir," Bauer was saying. The smile had lost intensity, like a moon waning. "No, I hadn't thought of that, but . . . No. I'll have to check that out, but . . . I doubt it, sir. I really do. But even so, I don't see why that would . . . Yes, sir. Oh, I understand. Certainly . . ."

Bauer hung up the phone and swore. "When it rains it pours," he muttered. After staring intently at his desktop he said, "That was Dale Shawshank, CEO and chairman of the board. He and Parker, our president, are stuck in Anchorage, waiting out the weather."

Bauer began to pace back and forth behind his desk. After a half dozen passes, he asked, "Any chance our murderer could be connected with Arctic Slope Regional?"

"That's . . . uh . . . actually that's why we're here, sir," Reynolds said in an apologetic tone.

"Because if he is . . ."—Bauer continued without hearing him—"that could be advantageous, or it could be disastrous . . ."

"Sir, the, uh, suspect . . ." Reynolds tried.

But Bauer was pacing again, studying the carpet. "If he was linked to Arctic Slope, we might use that as leverage. You know, play on our victimhood. Force their hand. On the other hand, they might back off, maybe even refuse to deal with us because of the embarrassment of the whole thing. You know, losing face. Of course, that's more of an Asian thing, the Japanese especially." He stopped and looked to Ray. "What about Eskimos?"

"What about them?"

"They worry about losing face?" He started pacing again.

"Mr. Bauer," Reynolds interjected. "The, uh, the suspect, he . . . uh, he didn't do it."

Bauer didn't seem to hear this. "Didn't do what?" he asked, distracted.

"He didn't murder anyone."

"Huh?" Bauer froze, an expression of shock on his face. "What did you say?"

"He didn't murder anyone."

"But he confessed."

Reynolds nodded. "Yes, sir, but the problem was that he didn't understand English. He didn't know what he was confessing to."

"Are you telling me we don't have the killer in custody?"

"No, sir. We don't."

Bauer shouted a curse that echoed from wall to wall. "We've got VIPs who will be inbound in less than twenty four hours. Arctic Slope is ready to sit down at the table. And there's still someone running loose out there, slicing and dicing our people?" He swore angrily.

Reynolds shrugged at this, head drooping.

"What about the press?" Bauer wondered. He slumped into his chair and ran off a string of profanities. "Houston is already playing this thing. What are we supposed to do? Tell the media, 'Oops, we didn't actually catch the killer'?" He answered his own question with a curse, then pounded the desk with a fist. "You idiots!"

"Leeland is calling Houston to update them on the situation," Reynolds relayed in a professional tone. "I'm sure the PR department can figure a way to put the fire out."

"That's not the point," Bauer mumbled. He looked at Reynolds, swore, then asked, "What do we pay you for anyway?" His eyes darted to Ray. "What are you doing here? Why aren't you out trying to track down this loon? Incompetents!"

"Actually I had a few questions for you, Mr. Bauer," Ray said calmly, trying not to respond in kind. It was tempting to tell old Red what he could do with his attitude and downdressing. "Regarding Hank Weinhart and Chief Makintanz."

Bauer fished a bottle of Advil out of a drawer and popped

a trio of tablets into his mouth. "What about them?" he mumbled, trying to swallow the tablets without the benefit of water.

"I got the impression from talking to the chief that the two of them didn't get along."

"That's an understatement." He swore, quietly this time. "Why does this have to be happening right now? Why not a month ago? Why not day after tomorrow, after the papers are signed?"

"There was animosity between them?" Ray asked, trolling for answers.

"You could say that. Weinhart opposed the decision to add Makintanz to the board. Hank actually called the chief a crook at one point. He said that despite the 'in' it would give us with Arctic Slope, having him at Davis was like inviting a boa constrictor to share a crib with a newborn baby. That's a direct quote."

"And after Makintanz was elected to the board . . . ?"

"More of the same. Name calling, arguments . . . Hank was a lawyer, always concerned with appearances. Having Makintanz around looked bad. Hank thought it would scare off investors. And as this deal with the Corporation took shape, he actually accused Makintanz of playing both sides of the game, taking, well, bribes from Arctic Slope Regional while he pocketed a salary from Davis. Who knows if that was actually the case."

"So the deal with Arctic Slope brought a head to their mutual dislike," Ray asserted.

"Sure. Hank was a tough negotiator. He wasn't about to let the Corporation get the best of us in this thing. I guess he thought the price was too high, the benefits too small. Anyway, Makintanz thought differently. And I think he put pressure on Shawshank and Parker to pull Hank from the negotiations."

Ray tried to make sense of this. The situation sounded volatile, but was the relationship between Makintanz and Weinhart vicious enough to elicit murder? It didn't sound like it. And Weinhart seemed to be the one who would have been out for revenge. Makintanz had succeeded in pushing him out. Why would he kill Weinhart?

From a business level, no one seemed to have a motive for killing Weinhart. The man might have been a nuisance, constantly playing devil's advocate and bemoaning the possible problems in the deal with Arctic Slope, but his bid to scuttle it had failed.

"Did Weinhart know Driscoll?" Ray asked.

Bauer squinted at this. "I don't know. I doubt it. VPs don't usually fraternize with the crews, and Hank wasn't exactly a people person."

"You can't think of any reason they would have met? Anything they might have had in common?"

This drew a wry chuckle. "Aside from being members of the human race, no. Weinhart was upper management, vice president of domestic operations. Despite the problems with Makintanz, Hank was being groomed to take over the company. The rumor is that Mr. Parker might be retiring next year. Hank was one of maybe three guys who stood a good chance of getting the promotion.

"Driscoll . . . He was just a blue collar from Oklahoma. Worked for our competition down in . . . Arkansas, I think. I hired him about two years ago. He was a good man: on time, worked hard, relatively intelligent, didn't get in fights or anything."

"Was he married?"

"Huh-uh. Lived in Ok City. I called his parents and gave them the bad news a little while ago." He frowned. "He was supposed to go on furlough next week."

Ray sighed at this. He hadn't really expected Bauer to supply case-breaking information, to magically tie Driscoll to Weinhart, or to solidify his suspicions about the feud between Weinhart and Makintanz. Yet the absence of anything even resembling a lead was disconcerting. From the start of the investigation he had entertained a latent hope that things would click into place with the right encouragement and nudging from Ray. Instead, he had spent two days spinning his wheels, asking stupid questions, getting absolutely nowhere. There were still two unsolved murders, still no suspects, still no evidence or clues.

Bauer swore, reverting to the role of peeved boss. "All I can say is that you had better get this thing tucked away before that meeting. It is absolutely imperative that the negotiations take place in a safe, nonthreatening, neutral environment. We can't afford to have the participants distracted."

"Murder can be distracting," Ray confessed, somewhat resentful of Bauer's demand.

"Guess I'd better call Shawshank back," he lamented, lifting the phone. He dismissed them with another crude pronouncement. "Get to work!"

In the hallway, Ray said, "A little disappointing."

"What's that?" Reynolds asked.

"You promised us a conniption fit. That was more of a mild tantrum, really. I'd only give it a six on a scale of one to ten."

"Maybe even a five," Billy Bob drawled. "You should see the sheriff chew my heinie when I screw up."

"We didn't screw up," Ray noted. "We just haven't figured this thing out yet."

"Same difference," the deputy said.

When they reached Reynolds's office, they found Leeland on the phone, backpedaling as if the person on the other end of the line had a sword to his throat.

"No, sir. No . . . Well, sir, there was really no way that we could have . . . No . . . No, sir. But we didn't think . . . Yes, sir. I know. But—but . . . Yes, sir. That's why we brought in an expert and he confirmed that the suspect didn't speak English . . . No, sir . . ."

Ray smiled at this. Apparently *he* was the expert. "I need to use a phone," he told Reynolds.

Reynolds offered him the desk. "Make yourself at home. I'm going for some fresh coffee."

"I can get it," Billy Bob offered.

"No. I need to walk off that butt kickin' we just got." He rubbed at his rear end as if it were sore.

After he left, Ray picked up the phone and dialed. As he waited for the call to go through, he told Billy Bob, "See if you can scrounge up a pencil and some notepaper.''

"What fer?''

"To make a sketch of . . .'' The line only rang once.

"Barrow PD.''

"Betty, Ray.''

"Our wayward patrolman,'' she announced in a husky voice. "The captain was starting to think that you ran away from home.''

"Is he in?''

"Yep. Hold on a second.''

Ray braced himself, mentally preparing for another verbal berating. He checked his watch: 2:20. Somehow it felt much later. This day seemed to be made of elastic, the way it kept stretching and stretching.

"What in blazes have you been doing, Attla?''

"Captain. Good afternoon to you too.''

"Where are you?''

"The Davis camp.''

"What in the heck is going on over there? CNN is broadcasting a story about how some lughead security man caught a multiple murderer in Prudhoe. We've been getting calls from every news bureau west of Missouri. And guess what I have for them. Squat. I don't know a thing. I gotta tell 'em that I can't comment because the investigation is still open. What the heck's going on?''

Ray sighed, wondering where to start. "I told you that we have two dead now?''

"Yeah. What about this man that was apprehended? Were you in on that?''

"Not exactly.''

The captain swore at him.

"They found one of our people looting my snow machine.''

"*They?* They who?''

"Well, the security guards here at Davis. Or, at least one of them.''

"So this killer just waltzed into camp and started in on your machine?''

"No. It was stalled west of here. Died on the way back

from Nuiqsut.'' Ray immediately regretted this disclosure.

"What in blazes were you doing in Nuiqsut?"

"It's a long story, sir."

"I've got plenty of time. Start talking."

Ray gave the captain a quick overview, touching but re-fusing to linger on Maniilaq, the prophecy, the breakdown ... He omitted Billy Bob's dream completely, crediting the rescue to dumb luck. Then he related their trip to Deadhorse, careful to describe it as a fact-finding mission. The story climaxed with "Mike's" bogus confession. Ray purposely left out the part about the infirmary, the brothel, the bouncer ...

When he was finished the Captain grumbled, "Are you trying to say that you've got nothing? What about the bodies? Are they wrapped and ready to ship to the morgue? The weather service says flights from Anchorage should get the green light by morning. Maybe sooner. Things are already starting to quiet down here in Barrow."

Ray tried to think of a way to avoid the question. "I'm going out to examine one of them in a few minutes. I'll sketch it, show it around . . ."

"It sure would be nice to close this before the city cops and the Feds show up."

"Yeah," Ray agreed.

"Well, you've got a little time. Do what you can. When Anchorage PD makes it in, turn it over. Work with them as long as they'll let you. Then come on home." The anger was rapidly receding, replaced by an almost paternal resignation.

"Yes, sir." Ray hung up and dialed again. Nothing like disappointing a superior to make a bad day worse. Now for the piece de resistance: telling Margaret that he definitely wouldn't make it to Barrow by this evening for the shower.

No one answered. They were probably too busy with party preparations to bother with the phone. Ray felt terrible. He left a short message on her machine: still stuck in Prudhoe. He purposefully left out the part about the frostbitten limbs and the murderer running loose. Margaret would be upset. She would mourn his absence, and, most of all, start to worry in earnest. He would probably be in the doghouse for a while, but he was a cop. Breaking personal promises and causing significant others grief was part of the job description. Margaret would either forgive him and get used to it, or dump him and find someone with a more acceptable, 9-to-5 job to spend the rest of her life with. Ray prayed for the former, unwilling to entertain the idea of losing her.

Replacing the phone, he glanced up at Billy Bob. The cowboy was waiting, pencil and paper in hand, like an eager, dumb-faced hound: Deputy Dog.

"Let's go have a look at that corpse."

➤➤ THIRTY ◄◄

THE STORM MAY have loosened its grip on Barrow, but it was reluctant to leave the Slope. The temperature was up slightly, to a balmy minus 46, and the snow had subsided. The wind, however, was once again possessed.

The short trek from the main building to the shed where Driscoll's body had been stored proved difficult. Billy Bob fell twice; Ray, once. With just a few yards to go, they were nearly taken out by a sheet of corrugated metal that had been ripped from the side of a building somewhere in the distance and flung with the fury of an angry god. It collided with an equipment hanger a quarter mile behind them, the resulting crash muted by the roar of air rushing past their hoods.

Inside the shed they found boxes of auto parts, a pickup that had been mostly dismantled, and a man sitting on a crate. Propped against the wall, he was bundled up—mask, goggles, wool scarf wound around his head like a turban.

"How's it going?" Ray asked politely. The man, fast asleep, snorted in response. "So much for posting a guard."

Ten feet from Rip Van Winkle was a six-foot bundle. Billy Bob leaned over the long, plastic-shrouded package and began unwrapping it. With a royal blue parka, matching hood and mask exposed, he asked, "What do ya think?"

Ray knelt over the body. "I think he's dead."

"Same MO though, huh?"

"Possibly." Ray poked the frozen block of flesh. It was hard to tell much of anything. The corpse was rock solid, encapsulated in a thick layer of ice, more like an elongated glazed ham than a human body. There were dark stains on the upper left chest, around a tiny, crusted hole in the parka where, presumably, a bullet had entered. Matching stains ringed the bottom of the mask. Ray tried to pry the head back to examine the neck but it wouldn't budge. Something chipped off in the process. He dug a three-inch long chunk out of the hood—a gray stone shaped like an ear.

"The worm was cut out, right?" Ray asked, stuffing the ear into one of Driscoll's pockets.

"Yep. Just like the other one. Wanna thaw 'em out so you can see?"

"I'll take your word for it."

"You gonna draw 'em?"

"If we can get the mask off, I guess."

They bent and began working it away from the skin, peeling neoprene and polar fleece like paper from a freezer-burned fudgesicle. "Careful," Ray cautioned. "Bad enough shipping him home in a body bag. It would be a shame for Mr. Driscoll to arrive earless."

When the mask finally came off, it did so suddenly, taking swatches of grayish purple skin with it.

Ray removed his mittens, took the paper and pencil, and began working to reproduce Driscoll's face. Thirty seconds into the task, his fingers had been stiffened by the cold, and what little talent he had was rendered moot. The pencil lines became primitive, reduced to chicken scratches. Making the job even more challenging was the fact that Driscoll now bore little resemblance to anything living. Recreating his features with any accuracy under these circumstances seemed impossible.

Five minutes later, the sketch as complete as it was going to get, Ray offered it to Billy Bob. "What do you think?"

"Hey, that's perty good."

"Does it look like him . . . at all?"

"Sort of . . . maybe . . . a little . . . around the eyes."

Ray had filled the closed, darkened voids of the corpse with wide, kind eyes. "I'm not sure his mother would recognize this. Looks like the work of a kindergartner, in a hurry, with a dull pencil." He jotted down an estimate of Driscoll's height, weight, guessed at his hair and eye color.

"What got him killed?" Ray wondered aloud as they covered the body back up.

Billy Bob shrugged.

"Did he do something? Say something? Why would someone hunt a vice president and a rig foreman as if they were animals?"

Bunny Teeth grimaced at this, as if it were an unfathomable mystery.

"For that matter, why try to take out one of the cops assigned to the case?" Ray gazed at the deputy. "If we assume that whoever wants me dead is also responsible for the two murders, then all we have to figure out is who had the motive and opportunity to steal my gear and rig the Polaris."

"Yeah . . . ?" Billy Bob replied, jaw slack. He seemed to be having trouble keeping step with these mental gymnastics.

"Somebody from seventeen? Simpson? Ed the dealer? One of the roustabouts? If any of them had a motive, I can't imagine what it could have been. And it would have been a real feat for them to rip off my sled. They would have had to come down from the rig, do the job and get back without being seen. Even in good weather that would be tough."

Ray sighed, still looking at Billy Bob. "And taking Weinhart's body, that had to be someone around here. Someone at the Davis main camp."

The deputy's eyes grew wide. "You mean the killer is one of the fellers we talked to already?"

"We've got the men responsible for checking the pipes," Ray continued, ignoring him. "They had the opportunity: access to the yard, to the pipes . . . But no motive that I can see. We've got Bauer. He's pretty anxious about the big meeting with Arctic Slope Regional. Does that give him motive? Maybe. Not really, though. And no opportunity. He sticks around the office. I can't see him trudging around in the snow, sabotaging Polaris carburetors."

"What about that chief feller?"

Ray nodded at this. "What about that chief *feller* . . ." he mumbled, frowning. "There again, he's all hot and heavy about the deal with Arctic Slope. Didn't get along with Weinhart. Possible motive, I guess. Fits Maniilaq's warning... sort of.''

"Who?"

"But there's no motive for killing Driscoll. Besides, Makintanz would have had to get up to the rig to do that. It's hard to visualize the chief setting foot outside of the Bradbury without a darn good reason. A reason I can't figure out.''

"Maybe he just likes to hunt,'' Billy Bob submitted.

"Actually he does. At least according to what I've read. But hunting humans for sport? Randomly nailing a couple of Davis employees? Not even the chief would do that. Kill someone, maybe. He's pretty ruthless. But he's not insane, at least not that I'm aware of. He'd need a motive.'' Ray swore softly at the tangle of events and their nonexistent explanations, and the confusion of it all was giving him a headache.

"And how the heck does Salome figure into this?''

"Sala-who?'' the deputy declared.

"I need some coffee,'' Ray announced, fastening his mask.

"And some lunch,'' Billy Bob agreed, following suit.

They left the dozing attendant to his duty and set out across the yard, this time hurried and pushed across the ice by a furious tailwind.

After discarding their parkas and gear in the mudroom, they trudged to the cafeteria. Men were gathered in clusters along the tables closest to the food line, talking, laughing, horsing down chow. Ray and Billy Bob had just filled Styrofoam cups with coffee and were in the process of loading their plates when Reynolds and Leeland came marching through the door.

"We just got a call,'' Reynolds announced with a somber expression. "There's been another murder.''

Ray cursed under his breath. "Where?''

"Deadhorse.''

"Was it Makintanz?''

Reynolds's brow furrowed. "Huh? No. Some girl. Worked at the roadhouse.''

"How was she killed?'' Ray asked, silently praying that the answer would involve a drunken brawl or a jealous rage.

"Same story: bullet in the heart, neck slit, part of the tongue chopped out."

Ray inhaled slowly at this disclosure. He glanced at Leeland, who was grinning, raring to go, as if a woman being brutally murdered was the ideal form of entertainment.

"I'm warming up the Toyota," Leeland said, on the verge of celebration.

"Don't bother," Ray told him.

"Huh?"

"What happens in Deadhorse isn't your concern."

"But . . ."

Ray waved him off. "You guys are assigned to this camp. You work for Davis. Crimes committed in Deadhorse are the deputy's jurisdiction." He aimed a thumb at Billy Bob. "Right Deputy Cleaver?"

The cowboy swallowed hard. "Uh . . . uh-huh."

"But we could help . . ." Leeland pled, his chance at playing policeman disappearing.

"We'll keep you informed and give you a call if we need your help," Ray assured him with a thin smile. This was almost fun.

"Here," Reynolds grunted. He handed Ray a slip of paper. "Her name was Honey. She was a call girl at Fanny's."

"Honey?!"

"Yeah. You know her?"

"Yeah. No. Well, I talked to her . . . today."

"I met her once," Leeland said, one eyebrow raised. "Quite a little lady. Trust me, what happened to her is a real shame."

"Your grief is overwhelming," Ray deadpanned.

"Course, you work that trade, you got to accept the dangers."

"Like being murdered at the age of fifteen?"

"She was only fifteen?"

Ray wrapped his sandwich in a napkin, then fastened a plastic lid on his coffee. "Back to Deadhorse," he told Billy Bob.

Ten minutes later they were rolling down main street. The town looked exactly as it had earlier—deserted, forsaken, abandoned. The only difference was that it contained one less living resident.

There were a dozen vehicles at Harry's now, several pick-ups, a gray sedan, and three snow machines. Business was picking up just as Honey had predicted. As they got out of the Explorer, Ray's mind presented a mental photograph of Honey: thin, pretty, heavy makeup—a mere child acting the part of a mature, sexually active woman. With the picture came an accusation: you should have done something!

"Yeah, I should have."

"Huh?" Billy Bob asked. He had just plugged the Explorer in and was waiting to go inside.

"Nothing," Ray muttered. He wasn't superman. He was just a cop. A cop who cared about people, maybe too much. Honey's fate hadn't been his fault. Still, he couldn't help wondering: What if . . .

Apparently the patrons of the roadhouse weren't aware of what had taken place in the back. Inside twenty or so men were busy drinking beer, shooting pool, throwing darts, swearing and laughing too loudly. The radio that had accompanied the lone dishwasher had been replaced by a jukebox that thundered country music.

The enormous bouncer had recovered from their earlier conflict and was standing, statuesque, feet shoulder width apart, in front of the door to Fanny's. If Harley Davidson had commissioned a gargoyle, this brute would be it: 380 pounds of muscle, attitude, and tattoos. His left arm was folded behind him, military style. In his right he held a pool cue. Somehow Ray got the feeling it wasn't for playing billiards.

As they approached, Ray noticed that the man's nose had swelled to twice its usual size. A ring of purple decorated the flesh of his left cheek. Ray's kick had actually damaged the clown.

When he saw them coming, the man smiled, twirling the cue through his fingers like a cheerleader's baton.

"How's it going?" Ray stopped at a point he hoped was out of cue range.

"Hard mornin'. But things is startin' to look up." The grin widened, offering a view of yellow, crooked teeth, a silver cap, a gap where a bicuspid had once been. "I'm just fixin' to have a *muktuk* for lunch. Care to join me?"

"Actually, we've already eaten."

"I insist, blubber breath."

Ray considered flashing his badge but decided the gesture would be wasted. "We got a call."

The man's eyebrows rose. "That right? I didn't call anyone. Far as I know, there ain't been no problems here . . . yet." The cue was moving like a buzz saw now.

Ray took a slow step backward. He looked to Billy Bob and found him retreating to the other side of the nearest pool table. "Fanny called."

"Huh . . ." the beast grunted, clearly uninterested. He started forward on two tree-trunk legs: a redwood scorned.

The roadhouse grew quiet. Someone pulled the plug on the jukebox. Conversation fell away. Instead of hunching over the billiard tables, the men were upright, leaning against their cues.

"That klooch givin' you trouble, Elvin?" a voice asked from across the bar.

"Nothin' I cain't handle." Taking the cue by the end, Elvin began swinging it like a baseball bat. "Ain't that right, officer?"

Ray backed up, bumped into a pool table, then felt someone push him forward, into the fray. Elvin lunged and sliced the air with the cue. Ray stumbled, ducking sideways. The cue found a table leg and cracked in two.

Elvin frowned at his broken weapon. "Good thing we got plenty a these things." He lifted his hand and another cue flew to it, as if by magic. "Thanks, Nick."

"Anytime," a deep voice responded. "Bust the klooch's head up, will ya?"

"Deputy," Ray said without taking his eye off of his stalker. "You have your gun?"

"Nope," Billy Bob replied. "It's in the truck."

"In the truck . . ." Ray repeated. "Good place for it."

Elvin took another swing. Ray bobbed. The cue sang as it whizzed through the air. Ray weaved. Hands pushed him back toward the arena.

"Stand still, seal bait!"

"Look out, Elvin!" someone warned.

Goliath let his cue droop and turned just in time to catch the 8 ball with his cheek. Stunned, he glared in Billy Bob's direction until the 12 caught him square on the forehead. In Biblical fashion, the giant wavered, then keeled over. Ray was tempted to yell timber.

The crowd of rednecks converged, yelling ugly sentiments about police, Eskimos, and the officers' mothers. Armed with three more balls, Billy Bob shouted, "Ya'll want your heads cracked open, you just keep on a-comin'." This had a slowing effect. In the moment of hesitation, Ray grabbed a pair of cue sticks.

"See this?" Billy Bob said, uncharacteristically forceful. He waved his badge at them. "This here says I'm the deputy sheriff. It gives me the power and authority to take yer sorry butts into custody, toss each an' ever-one of ya into the Deadhorse jail, and bring ya up on charges. So ya'll either back off, nice 'n' slow, or yer gonna have yourselves an all-expense-paid vacation to the pokey."

The threat caused the rowdies to pause and consider, giving Ray and Billy Bob time to slip through the door and up the stairs. They found Fanny at her desk, fondling a glass of bourbon, sucking a cancer stick, the paper spread out before her.

Ray stared at her expectantly. "We're here about Honey."

She looked at them sleepily. "Room six. Body's on the floor."

"Your compassion is mind-boggling," Ray told her.

"Hey, I'm as tore up as the next person. Honey was my second biggest money-maker. Being with a minor drove the men wild."

Ray took a step toward the hall.

"Hang on, now," Fanny called.

"Don't even try to weasel money out of us," Ray said angrily. "We're police. And there's been a murder."

"Hey now . . ." she said, rising. "Don't get all bent out of shape. I locked the door soon as we found her." Cigarette between her lips, tumbler of booze in hand, she led them into the hallway. "Ya'll might want me to open the room up for you, huh? Or is ya gonna break the door down, like they's always doin' on TV?"

➤ THIRTY-ONE ◄

IT WAS A horrific scene: arms and legs splayed in odd directions, robe twisted back to reveal smooth naked skin, face locked in an expression of terror and disbelief—eyes wide, mouth open, as if breathlessly pleading for mercy—and blood . . . what seemed like gallons of it. On her neck, her chest, running down her arms, pooling beneath her lifeless body, a ragged, vermilion pond soaking into the carpet.

"*The way of beauty . . .*" Ray sighed.

"Huh?"

He gazed at the spectacle, amazed that someone so pretty could be made to look utterly grotesque. Alive with adolescent rebellion one moment. Dead, resigned to the grave the next. It made him nauseous. Not just the blood, or the desecration of the body. The idea that a young life could be snuffed out so quickly, so totally, so brutally.

After a deep breath, he knelt and studied the girl's neck. It had been neatly sliced, the jugular severed. That accounted for the abundance of blood. He touched the carpet with a fingertip. Still warm. Turning his attention to the girl's midsection, he found a familiar mark: a circle the size of a pencil eraser just below the left breast. A trickle had escaped from the hole and snaked down her torso, pausing at the belly button before flowing into the crimson sea.

He gently tilted her head back and pried the mouth open. Her full, pouty lips were the color of steel. Ray extracted a pen from the inner pocket of his parka and moved the tongue to one side. It was soft, rigor mortis having yet to set in. Beneath the tongue he found more blood, and an empty space where the worm should have been.

Ray swore, then muttered, "He did it again."

"Who? Who did what again?" Fanny asked.

"Give Reynolds a call. Tell him what we got." When there was no response, Ray looked over his shoulder. Fanny was there, but no Billy Bob.

"If you was talkin' to yer partner," she grinned, "you'll have to wait a sec."

"Where'd he go?"

She aimed a thumb at the hall. "Pukin' his guts out in the toilet." Moving in for a closer look, she asked, "What the heck happened to her?" Apparently the sight of a corpse lying in a lake of blood didn't bother Fanny.

"Who came up after we were here?" Ray asked, standing up.

"Nobody." Fanny squinted at Honey's still, empty form. "Really is a shame," she lamented.

"Somebody was here," Ray asserted.

"We only had a couple a fellas in since you stopped by. Honey was sleepin' so I sent 'em back to Sherry and Vicki."

"What did the men look like?"

Fanny shrugged. "Couldn't tell ya. Didn't pay no attention to their looks, just their money."

Billy Bob's head poked in the door. His eyes were red, his face alarmingly pale.

"Call Reynolds," Ray told him. "Tell him we got another one."

The deputy took a gasping breath and hurried away.

"Another one?" Fanny asked. "What's that supposed to mean?"

"I'd like to talk with Sherry and Vicki."

Fanny didn't hear this. She was bending over Honey. "This stain's gonna be dang hard to get up from the carpet."

"You see a lot of dead bodies around here?" Ray asked. Fanny wasn't exactly broken up over this. Neither did she seem sufficiently shocked.

"Not a lot. A few."

"You sound like you're used to having murder victims around."

"Used to it? Huh-uh. But it happens. All sorts a things happen up here. Deadhorse is the jumpin' off place. Ain't hardly nothin' outside the realm of possibility. I had some of my girls kilt before. Don't like it none. But they ain't kin or nothin'. Just work for me. I don't get close with 'em. Don't want to start likin' them or nothin'. Only leads to heartache." She left the room and paused in the hall, expecting Ray to follow. Two doors away, she knocked forcefully. "Vicki!?"

A petite peroxide blonde answered. She was in her late teens, wearing a thick terry cloth robe, her legs wrapped in black sweatpants. Despite heavy makeup, a perm, and dangly silver earrings, she looked cold and frightened, more like a lost child than a prostitute.

"Vicki here found the body," Fanny announced unemotionally, as if the disclosure ranked right up there with small talk about the weather.

"Officer Attla," Ray said, flashing his badge. "Barrow PD."

Vicki's eyes darted from Ray to the badge and back again. She seemed to be on the verge of tears.

"You found Honey?" Ray prodded.

She nodded, her breath becoming irregular. Suddenly she was bawling, mascara running down her cheeks.

"I'll be up front if ya need me," Fanny offered, unmoved by the outburst.

Ray helped the girl to a chair sitting in front of a vanity table. He patted her shoulder, unable to think of anything to say. Vicki's room was nicer than Honey's he noticed as he waited for her tears to subside. The bedspread was black velvet, the mattress and box springs surrounded by an attractive brass frame. An antique dresser stood against one wall, a primitive armoire against the other. There was another door, presumably leading to a bathroom. No mirrors on the ceiling or walls. Instead of a traditional fixture, the room was lit by a row of inset studio lights.

Two minutes later, when Vicki had begun wiping her

cheeks with a tissue, Ray tried, "How well did you know Honey?"

"Not very well," she sniffed, "but she was nice." This statement was followed by something akin to a wail.

Ray patted her again, waited, then, "What time did you find her?"

"About—about . . . I don't know." She was trembling now, her entire body quaking.

"Listen, I know this is difficult, but if you can pull it together for a minute, you might be able to help us catch the killer."

This had little if any effect. A minute later, Ray asked, "Did you hear anything?"

Vicki shook her head.

"Why did you go to her room?"

She pointed at the array of cosmetics on the table in front of her.

"Makeup?"

She picked up a compact of blush and opened it, showing Ray that it was empty.

"You wanted to borrow some of that stuff?"

Her head bobbed up and down.

"So you went over and knocked on the door?"

Another nod.

"And no one answered, so you opened it."

Three enthusiastic nods.

"And you found her?"

"Yes . . ." the answer was more of a gasp than anything else and was punctuated by a mournful whimper.

"Did you see anyone? In the hall? In her room?"

Vicki shook her head, wiping a runny nose on her sleeve.

"What did you do next?"

"I—I told . . . I told . . . F . . . ann . . . yyy," she managed between convulsive gasps.

Ray gave her shoulder what he hoped was a consoling squeeze. "You had a—a *client* right before you found her."

"Yes." She took a deep breath, finally starting to compose herself.

"Can you describe him for me?"

She shrugged at this. "Just a regular guy."

"Was he tall, short . . . ?"

"Medium."

"What color was his hair?"

"Sort of . . . brown."

"How long?"

"Regular."

"Was he heavy, skinny . . . ?"

"Average."

"Any distinguishing marks? Tattoos?"

"Not that I saw."

"Did he leave before you found Honey?"

She nodded at this.

"How long before?"

"A couple of minutes."

Ray dug out the sketches and showed them to her. "Recognize either of these men?"

"No."

"How about the name Salome?" he asked, refolding the sketches.

"Salome?" She nodded.

"Know where she is or where I could reach her?"

Vicki frowned. "No. Ask Fanny."

Ray studied her face in the mirror, wondering what had driven this young girl to, as Fanny called it, the jumping off place.

"Do you have family?"

"A stepfather."

"Where?"

"Minnesota."

"Maybe you should consider going back there."

"I can't," she protested. "I just . . . I can't."

"I don't mean to scare you, Vicki," Ray lied, "but maybe you should think about getting into a different line of work. Something less . . . dangerous."

The tears were gone now, replaced by a hard, defiant look. "I would if I could," she answered. "But this is the only thing I know how to do."

Ray found one of his cards and fished a pen out of his

jacket. "My fiancée is a social worker—sort of," he told her, scribbling on the card. "Barrow's not exactly a boom town, but . . . I don't know, she might be able to help you find something. If not up here, maybe in Anchorage or even Seattle." He set the card on the vanity table and stepped to the door. "I'm sorry about Honey."

"Me too."

Ray found Fanny in the entry area, refilling her glass from a liter bottle of José Cuervo. When she saw him, she lifted the bottle in his direction. "Wanna snort?"

"No thanks. Could I speak with Sherry now?"

"Yeah." After stashing the tequila in her desk, she led him back down the hall, to room 2 and pounded on the door. "Sherry!" she yelled before returning to her desk.

Thirty seconds later the door creaked open and two bloodshot eyes looked out.

"Sherry?"

"Yeah . . ."

Ray displayed his badge.

Sherry glared at it before inviting him in. Wearing only an oversized T-shirt, the tall, slightly underweight brunette shut the door behind Ray, then slipped off her shirt. Naked except for a bright red G-string, she glumly sighed, "Ready to party?"

"I'm a police officer," Ray clarified. He could feel his cheeks blushing.

"I know. Otherwise you wouldn't be here. Fanny don't let in Eskimos." She sat on the bed, a bored expression on her tired face. "Want the lights on or off?"

Ray held his hands up. "On. I'm not here to—"

"Music or no music. I got rock, country—"

"No music. I'm here because . . ."

She shrugged at him. "It's your party." With that she slumped back on the mattress, apparently ready for him.

"I'm Officer Attla. Barrow PD."

"Good for you, lover. You gonna handcuff me?" She had her head back on the pillow, eyes closed.

"I'm here about Honey."

"Honey?" Her head popped up. An expletive escaped

from her shiny red lips. "Don't tell me you want me to pretend to be—"

"Honey's dead."

The brows fell, the eyes squinting.

"You didn't know that?"

She frowned at him. "Huh-uh." Sitting up on the bed she muttered, "Dead?"

Ray retrieved the T-shirt from the floor and tossed it to her. After pulling it on, she asked, "What happened?"

"Someone murdered her."

Sherry swore again, then reached for a pair of jeans. As she slid them on, Ray wondered at her age. She was older than Honey and Vicki. Much older. Thirty-five? Forty? The lines on her face made forty-five a possibility.

"Did you hear anything in the last hour or so?"

"You mean, besides heavy breathing?" she deadpanned.

"Gunshot . . . scream . . . ?"

She shook her head.

"Fanny said you were with someone."

"Yeah."

"Could you describe him for me?"

Sherry reached under the bed and pulled out a bottle: dark rum. Twisting off the top, she took a long sip, then offered it to Ray.

"No, thanks."

After another sip, she said, "Big guy. Say two hundred fifty pounds. Not in very good shape. You know, flabby. Smelled bad. You'd think these jerks would have the common courtesy to take a shower before coming over."

"Any distinguishing marks?"

"Had a tattoo of a snake on his shoulder. Ugly thing." She stood, unzipped her pants, and mooned Ray. "Now that's a tattoo," she told him, pointing to a small rose on her right cheek.

"It certainly is."

When her pants were up again, Sherry lit a cigarette. "Long, greasy hair. Beard. Went by the name of Bud. Probably wasn't his real name, though."

"What time did Bud leave?"

"I didn't clock him. But let's just say he didn't overstay his welcome. It was a quickie. He was pretty drunk."

"Drunk?"

"Could hardly walk much less . . ."

"I get the idea."

She cleared her throat and spit into a plastic cup sitting next to the bed. "How'd they do it?"

"Do what?"

"Kill her?"

"Honey?" Ray paused, trying to decide whether or not to relate the sordid details. Somehow Sherry seemed tough enough to hear them. "She was shot. Then . . . cut up."

"Cut up?"

"It was a . . . ritual thing."

"You mean like devil worshippers? I saw a thing on TV about how they cut up animals, even babies sometimes."

"No. It was a . . . a Native thing."

"Native? But Natives aren't allowed in here—'cept for cops."

"I know." Ray left his card. "If you remember anything that you think might help, call this number. They know how to get ahold of me. Thanks."

"Anytime," Sherry grunted, guzzling rum.

"Oh . . ." He pulled out the sketches. "Recognize either of these men?"

Sherry hiccuped, shook her head.

"How about Salome?"

She cursed at the name. "What about her?"

"You know her?"

"Sure. She's cost me plenty over the past year or so."

"How's that?"

"Stealin' my johns. Now my thinking is that if no Eskimos are allowed in, why let Eskimos work here, huh?" She took another shot of Bacardi. "Between her and Honey and Vicki . . ." Sherry stood and performed a slow 360. "How am I supposed to compete with that? I mean this body of mine has seen better days. Them? They're just kids. And Salome . . ." She swore again. "The jerks up here can't get enough of her." She plopped back onto the bed with a belch.

"Thanks," Ray told her.

When he reached the entry area, Fanny was bent over an old newspaper, leaning into an article about the wolf population as if she were going to be tested on the material.

"No one came up except the two johns?"

She looked up at him. "Nope," she responded, sucking on the stub of a cigarette.

"When I was here, you got a telephone call."

She frowned at him and exhaled smoke.

"You said, 'He's coming.' "

Fanny shook her head at this, the frown expanding into a grimace.

"Who was *he*?"

"Don't know what yer talkin' about." With that she returned her attention to the paper.

➤ THIRTY-TWO ◀

"TELL ME ABOUT Salome."

"What about 'er?"

Ray leaned against the edge of Fanny's desk. "Who is she?"

"Whattya mean?" Fanny responded without looking up. She worked her cigarette, turned a page of the newspaper.

"What's her real name? Where's she from?"

Fanny sucked, exhaled, lifted the corner of the paper toward her face. Finally, she grunted, "No idea."

"You must know something about her."

"I know she's my most profitable girl. If she worked full-time, I'd be rich enough to retire and move someplace warm."

"Why doesn't she work full-time?" Ray asked. He was getting irritated. Fanny was either totally disinterested or reluctant to cooperate. Whichever, trying to elicit answers was like fishing for grayling with a heavy spinner.

"No idea."

"Does she live in Deadhorse?"

"Not sure."

"You don't know where she lives?"

"Nope."

"Does she drive? Does she fly in here? Does she get around by snow machine, by dogsled?"

"No idea." Fanny turned another page, took a long sip from her tumbler.

Ray resisted the urge to curse at her. "How can you hire someone and not know anything about them?"

Fanny looked up at him, smoke shooting from the corner of her mouth. "Easy. Just don't ask no questions. I'm not nosy by nature. Not like you."

Billy Bob came trotting up the stairs. His cheeks had color again, the recovery probably spurred by his retreat into the cold.

"I called Reynolds," he informed Ray. "He said he'd contact Anchorage and notify yer captain in Barrow."

"Good," Ray muttered, only half meaning it. He tried to imagine the captain's reaction to the news that yet another murder had been committed on the Slope. There weren't that many people up here in the first place. That three were now dead and that Ray, the cop in residence, had been present while two of the slayings had been carried out was something of a disgrace. Or at least, the captain would probably see it that way. Instead of closing the case before the city police and FBI showed up, Ray was acting as a chronicler, watching impotently as a killing spree ran its course, succeeding only at keeping an accurate death toll.

Returning his attention to Fanny, he asked, "What can you tell me about Honey?"

"Whattya mean?"

Ray took a deep breath, determined not to lose his patience. "How long did she work here?"

Fanny's face wrinkled, contorted, ultimately settling on a pensive expression. " 'Bout . . . three months."

"Her next of kin will have to be contacted. Do you happen to know who that would . . ."

"No idea." Fanny lit a fresh smoke from the waning butt and began scrutinizing the classified ads as if they held the secrets of the universe.

"Any idea who might want her dead?"

This drew a shrug. "A john she ticked off. Maybe her past caught up with her."

"What past?"

"Don't know. But most a my girls is runnin' from somethin'."

Ray pulled the sketches out and set them on the newspaper, directly in Fanny's view.

Leaning back from them, she said, "You already shown me that one." A thin, chapped finger tapped at Weinhart's face.

"You've never seen him?"

"Maybe I have. Maybe I haven't."

"What about the other one?"

"Don't ring no bells."

"You think he might have been in here before?"

"Possible."

"Could he have seen Salome?"

"Possible."

"But you can't say for sure?"

"Nope." She pushed the pictures away and began scanning the garage sale listings.

Important stuff, Ray thought, miscellaneous junk being hocked in Anchorage a full week earlier.

A trio of men came stumbling up the stairs behind them, laughing, making crude comments about what they planned to do with Fanny's girls.

"If you'll excuse me," Fanny said, finishing off her tequila. "I got me some customers."

The men weaved forward, eyeing Ray and Billy Bob before presenting Fanny with a wad of bills.

"How're you boys doing this fine day?" Fanny asked them, counting the money.

"Good," one grunted.

"Yeah," another answered stupidly.

"Fixin' to be doin' a whole lot better," the third slurred. They all busted out laughing.

"Come on," Ray said, nodding toward the stairs. Billy Bob fell into step with him.

"What about Honey?" Fanny called.

"Don't touch anything. Lock the door," Ray instructed, already descending the steps.

"What about the stain?" Fanny asked, her voice finally evidencing concern.

"A girl, a teenager, was just murdered," Ray mumbled.

"And all that woman can think about is the carpet."

The blood began draining from Billy Bob's face. After swallowing hard, he asked, "Think she done it?"

"Fanny? I doubt it."

The deputy swore softly, bunny teeth hidden beneath his upper lip. "We ain't never gonna figure this out, are we?"

"Why do you say that?" Ray asked sarcastically. "Just because we don't have any suspects, no evidence, no clues . . ."

"We got bodies," he pointed out.

"And we've got a possible link."

"A what?"

They reached the bottom of the stairwell and Ray paused to explain. "Honey said Weinhart *might* have been in to visit Salome the day he was killed."

"Salome?"

"One of Fanny's . . . employees."

"So?"

"So, if that was the case, two of our three victims, Honey and Weinhart, were at Fanny's."

"So?"

"If we can place Driscoll here, that'll mean—"

"What? What'll it mean?"

Ray shrugged. "It'll mean . . . I don't know. But it'll be a link, something to tie the three together. Which is more than we've managed so far." He pushed the roll bar on the door and stepped into the tavern. Ten feet away, the bouncer was leaning back in a chair, holding a bottle of Coors to his bruised face like an ice pack. He eyed them, said something under his breath, but didn't rise. Apparently two less than positive encounters had taught the dimwit a lesson.

Moving across the room, Ray addressed the bartender. "How's it goin'?"

"We don't serve klooches."

"Yeah. I know." He offered his badge.

The man swore at it, scowling. He was big. Not quite as large as the bouncer, but impressively muscular. A weightlifter. A long, jagged scar had been etched into his jaw line. A tattoo of a cobra decorated his forearm, completing the tough-guy image. Given the choice, Ray wanted to be the man's friend, not his enemy.

"We're investigating a murder," Ray tried.

The man sniffed at this, his focus aimed at the tumblers he was drying and stacking.

"Murder?" a voice asked from down the bar. It came from a rail-thin man encased in a filthy down parka. He had a beard that reached almost to his waist. Squinting at them, his head wavering back and forth as if he were aboard a ship in rough seas, he repeated, "Murder?"

Ray turned away from the drunk and presented the sketches to the bartender. "Ever see these two faces?"

Two sleepy eyes glanced dispassionately at the portraits. "You ain't the sheriff, are you?"

"No. I'm with the Barrow PD."

"Then I don't have to talk to you." With that, he walked down the bar to refill a patron's glass with Wild Turkey.

When he returned, Billy Bob said, "I'm with the sheriff's department here in Deadhorse." He lifted his ID, but the bartender had his back to them.

Ray retrieved his sketches and started for the kitchen. The bartender was occupied with customers, the bouncer offering his advice to a couple of pool players.

Behind a set of double swinging doors, they found a tiny galley: single stove, microwave, a stainless steel sink piled high with dirty glasses and saucers, consumer-sized dishwasher unit, a stack of overflowing garbage sacks near a windowless door.

A man was standing at the sink. Hunched over the steaming faucet, he was attending to the dishes with gloved hands and a scrubber pad. Each movement was deliberate, either lethargic or careful, Ray couldn't decide. But even from the back, it was obviously the Native they had seen earlier, wearing the same apron, same shirt, sporting the same long, oily hair, with the same short, stocky frame.

"Excuse me?" Ray said. When this drew no response, he tried an Inupiaq greeting.

The man turned slowly and looked at them with innocent, almost childlike eyes.

"What the . . . He ain't no Ezkeemo," Billy Bob exclaimed. "What is he?"

"Down's," Ray answered.

"Huh?"

"Down's Syndrome." Ray smiled at the man. "How's it going?"

The large, mongoloid eyes grew wide and the man grinned at them lopsidedly.

"What's your name?"

"Randy." The word came out in a deep baritone grunt, without inflection.

"Hi, Randy. I'm Officer Attla."

"Policeman?" Randy asked, excitedly.

Ray nodded, still smiling. He showed Randy his identification.

"This a real badge?" he chuckled.

"It sure is."

"Where's your gun?"

"I don't have it with me today, Randy."

His face sunk, lips forming an exaggerated frown. "I like guns."

"Do you?"

"Yes," he answered, jaw extended unnaturally. "Cowboys all got guns."

"You a cowboy, Randy?" Billy Bob asked.

Randy began to breath rapidly. Discarding his rubber gloves, he hurried over to a storage shelf and produced a mock-Stetson. It was stained, the brim creased as if it had been stepped on repeatedly. Randy put it on and turned a slow circle, proudly modeling his hat. It was too small for his large head, held on by a draw string.

"Nice," Ray said politely.

"But I don't got a gun," Randy explained.

"Or a horse," Billy Bob said. "Good cowboy needs a horse."

Randy began to hyperventilate again. Twirling around, he reached for a mop, straddled it and announced, "Gotta horse."

"So you do," Ray observed. "Listen, Randy, we're conducting an investigation. Do you know what that is?''

His face drooped, lower lip quivering, as if he were about to cry. ''No.''

''It's okay,'' Ray consoled. ''It just means that someone did something wrong and we're trying to find him.''

''Randy do something wrong?'' he asked, clearly frightened.

''No, no,'' Ray said, patting his shoulder. ''But maybe you can help us. Would you like to help the police?''

Randy was panting, head nodding. Then he looked at the sink. ''What about the dishes?''

''This will only take a second,'' Ray assured him. He pulled out the sketches. ''Have you ever seen either of these men, Randy?''

His eyes darted from one picture to the other, to Ray, to Billy Bob, back to the pictures. ''Are they bad men?''

No, just dead men, Ray thought. ''No, Randy. Someone did something bad to them.''

This seemed to confuse him. ''I seen him,'' he said, patting one of the sketches with the palm of his hand.

''Where did you see him?'' Ray prodded. ''Can you remember?''

''I seen him going to Miss Fanny's.''

Ray glanced at Billy Bob, eyebrows raised. ''What about this other guy?''

''I didn't see him. But . . .''

''But what?''

''He looks mean. I don't want him to hurt me.''

''Nobody's going to hurt you, Randy,'' Ray said. On the heels of that statement he was struck by the fact that Driscoll had been killed around the time they were seeking to question him. Honey had been killed just minutes after her conversation with Ray. Were they placing Randy in danger merely by speaking with him?

''Thanks, Randy,'' Ray told him, offering his hand. ''You've been a big help.''

''I'm a police helper?''

''You betcha, partner,'' Billy Bob drawled.

''Now I get back to work, before I get in trouble.'' He

leaned his "horse" against the wall, returned the hat to its place on the shelf, and waddled to the sink. After pulling on the gloves, he took up where he had left off, wiping the plates and glasses with slow, meticulous motions.

Back in the bar, Billy Bob asked, "Was that the link you was lookin' fer?"

Ray shrugged. "Maybe. Honey said she thought Weinhart had been here. The key word being *thought*. She wasn't positive. Now we've got Randy placing Driscoll here. Question is, can we trust Randy? Is he reliable?"

It was the deputy's turn to shrug.

The roadhouse was filling up, workers from the surrounding camps congregating, like moths to a flame, at the only legal outlet of alcoholic beverages and female companionship within several hundred miles. It was something of an oasis, Ray decided as he surveyed the faces.

They walked to the bar and Ray ordered two Cokes. He had to repeat the order twice to be heard above the rising din. The bartender responded with a scowl and seemed poised to remind them that he wasn't required to serve klooches. Instead, he stepped to the fountain and began to fill two glasses with carbonated cola.

A new song erupted from the juke box, a country rock tune that seemed to shake the walls.

After the bartender brought their drinks and shot them a parting glare of disapproval, Ray told Billy Bob, "See if you can get their attention."

"Get whose attention?" he asked, guzzling his pop.

Ray motioned to the room. There were a dozen or so men huddled around the dart board, and the pool tables on the other side of the room were crowded now. "Maybe someone here can help us. Get their attention, we'll pass the sketches around."

Billy Bob looked at him as if he were out of his mind. "Huh?"

"Get their attention."

"How?"

"I don't know. Can you whistle?"

"Yeah. But . . . Are you sure we want ever-body lookin'

at us? There's enough guys here to kick our rear ends all the way to Austin.''

''I think we proved ourselves in that last encounter with the bouncer.''

''You *think*? What if all we did was make 'em mad?''

''We're cops,'' Ray reminded him. ''We have an investigation to conduct. We can't be put off by the possibility of personal injury.'' It was a hokey line and Ray failed to deliver it with a straight face.

''Why not?''

''Why not what?''

''Why cain't we be put off by the possibility of personal injury? I don't like pain.''

''Just get their attention.''

Billy Bob sighed. Finally, he stood and put his index fingers up to his bunny teeth. After a deep breath, and another look of protestation, he blew.

Despite the thundering music and the rising cacophony of laughter and loud, drunken conversation, the whistle produced immediate results. Heads turned, bodies swiveled, faces looked up from the billiard tables. Someone silenced the juke box and the bar became ominously quiet. All eyes were on Ray and Billy Bob.

➤ THIRTY-THREE ◄

"HI," RAY TRIED in a friendly tone. "Officer Attla, Barrow PD." He waved his badge at the sea of beards and leathery cheeks. From across the room, the bouncer gave him the finger and muttered something profane, Ray was sure.

"One of Fanny's girls was murdered today," he explained. The faces softened slightly, a few evidencing an expression that bordered on genuine concern. *And why not?* Ray thought. Losing one of your playthings was serious business.

"Who was it?" someone asked.

"Honey."

A gruff voice cursed. It was joined by a chorus of swearing. Apparently Honey had been well liked.

"What do you want from us?" one of the pool players asked.

"We need you to take a look at these pictures," Ray answered, lifting the sketches. "Tell us if you recognize either of these men." He handed them to a guy at the bar.

"You think one of 'em killed her?" a dart thrower asked with a sneer.

"Actually they're . . ." Billy Bob started.

Ray stopped him with an elbow to the ribs. "We don't know who killed her," he said, hoping to skirt the issue. To the deputy, he whispered, "Maybe if these guys *think* the faces represent possible suspects, they'll be more interested in IDing them."

"Gotcha."

"Take a look," Ray said, projecting his voice. "See if the faces are familiar. Okay?"

Heads nodded, and the sketches began to circulate. Five minutes later, the pictures had filtered through the room and been placed back on the bar. No one was able—or willing?—to ID either Weinhart or Driscoll. No one remembered seeing them at the roadhouse. One man thought he had seen Weinhart walking down main street with a rifle and a bottle of Jim Beam two weeks earlier. The same man also mistook Ray for Nanook of the North, Billy Bob for Barney Fife, and was unable to stand due to serious intoxication. Another guy remarked that Driscoll looked a little like his brother-in-law and that given the chance, he would beat his brother-in-law senseless for being such a jerk to his sister.

"So much for that idea," Ray sighed at the sketches.

"What about him?"

Ray followed Billy Bob's gaze across the room. "The bouncer?"

"Yeah. He didn't look at them pictures yet. And he'd know sure as anybody whether 'er not these two fellers been in here."

"Why don't you go ask him?"

"Huh-uh. Elvin's *yer* buddy."

"Yeah . . . we're buddies all right," Ray grumbled. He studied the man with a sense of trepidation: legs the size of Ray's waist, arms as thick as tree branches, grotesquely wide shoulders, a face bearing ragged battle scars from countless brawls, including Ray's boot to the nose, and eyes that seemed to emit fire. "That guy is the personification of the word mean."

"Meaner than a road lizard," Billy Bob agreed. "But we're cops. We can't let the risk of personal injury stand in the way of an investigation."

Ray swore at this. "You're coming too," he demanded. Taking the sketches, he started across the room, his mind racing to form a plan of attack—or at least a plan of retreat, a strategy for survival. Old Elvin wouldn't fall for the sucker kick routine or the 8-ball ambush twice. This time, if they came to blows, Ray and his sidekick Poncho would be reduced to whale fodder.

They were still ten yards away when Elvin made eye contact. Rising, he grinned and began stretching, as if he were about to engage in an Olympic event: Eskimo pummeling.

Ray held up his palm in an attempt to calm the giant, then shot him a peace sign. "We don't want trouble."

Elvin chucked at this. "Then you're in the wrong place, Mr. Muktuk."

"We need to ask you a few questions . . . about the murder."

"Ask all the questions you want." He lifted a pool cue, examined it to make sure it was true, and without further warning, swung it, grazing Ray's thigh.

"Hey!" Ray leapt backward. "Elvin, we're police. We could arrest you for assaulting an officer."

"Oh, yeah? Go ahead and try, klooch."

"What exactly do you have against my people?"

"Let's see . . . you're dirty, ugly, smelly, stupid . . ."

"Other than that, I mean."

Elvin laughed crudely.

"Me, I'm just a cop. Trying to do a job. One of Fanny's ladies was murdered. We're trying to find out who did it. You can understand that, right?"

"I understand that you slant-eyed savages should go back to your igloos."

"They don't live in igloos," Billy Bob argued.

Elvin frowned at him. "Who asked you?" He took a swing, but the deputy leaned out of range.

"I'll make you a deal, Elvin," Ray tried. "You answer our questions, take a look at the pictures we brought, then we'll leave you alone. How's that?"

"I'll make *you* a deal," the bouncer replied. "I beat you to a pulp, then throw your carcass out in the snow. How's that?"

Ray looked at the pool cue, then estimated the distance to the entrance. Though the giant had to be relatively slow, they probably couldn't make it to the Explorer and get it started before he caught up with them.

"What's your thing, Elvin?"

"Huh?"

"What's your thing? You like booze, women, money . . . What do you like?"

"I like 'em all." He swung; Ray dodged. "Stand still!" he demanded.

"No hobbies? Special interests?"

"Hogs," he announced, stalking forward.

"Hogs?" Billy Bob wondered. "You grow up on a farm too?"

"Motorcycles," Ray clarified. "What kind? Harleys?"

"Got two back home . . . *on the farm*." He jabbed the cue at Billy Bob, just to keep him honest. The crowd had lost interest, their attention back on darts, pool, and drinking themselves into stupors.

"What models?"

"'84 Softail and a '59 Sportster." The beast stood his ground, distracted.

"Nice bikes."

"Yeah. Except the Sportster needs a new tank. Been lookin' for one for months. Originals are tough to find nowadays."

"I know a guy back in Barrow who's got a '58 Sportster—Comp Hot. Mint condition."

"You're kiddin'? '58 CH?" The cue did a slow rotation to the vertical position and Elvin leaned against it as he reflected on this disclosure. "Those babies are hot."

"And he's got a '59 chassis."

Goliath's mouth fell open. "No way . . ."

"Yeah. He's been trying to sell it. But . . . well, in Barrow, there's not much of a market for vintage hogs."

Elvin swore, the anger gone. "I'd give my eyeteeth to get my hands on that chassis."

"Tell you what," Ray offered, "I'll put you in touch with him if . . ."

"If . . . ? If what?" he asked, licking his lips like a starving man who had just been allowed to glimpse a gourmet meal.

"If you help us out here."

"And ya don't kill us," Billy Bob added.

"Deal?" Ray extended his hand cautiously.

Elvin discarded the cue and smothered his hand in a vice grip. "Deal."

Ray showed him the sketches. "We need to know if these men were in here recently."

"What's the '58 got?" Elvin asked. " '74 OHV?"

"You'll have to ask. Now about these men . . ."

"I remember him," he said, poking Weinhart's picture. "Mr. Moneybags. Guy slipped me a hundred dollars just to get his scrawny, suit-wearing butt into Fanny's."

"When was that?"

"Oh, either yesterday or the day before. I think the day before. Yeah."

"Don't guess you know who he went to see?"

Elvin shook his head. "Nah. Could have been any of the girls."

"What about this guy?" Ray offered Driscoll's picture.

"Him . . . I'm not sure about. But I think he was here too. Pretty sure I saw him drinking and playin' pool. Might of gone up to Fanny's . . . maybe."

Ray began folding the sketches.

"You think one of 'em killed Honey?"

"No," Ray answered. "They're both dead."

Elvin's eyebrows fell, causing his forehead to grow. He looked Cro-Magnon now, like a caveman attending to a primitive puzzle.

"We think the same person may have killed all three of them."

He cursed at this, frowned, then said, "About that Softail . . ."

Ray fished out a card and scribbled a name and number on it. "Ask for Jack. Tell him Ray Attla mentioned the hog he's selling. He'll give you a fair price."

Elvin's face lit up as he stared at the number. The fierce, tough-guy aura quickly faded, replaced by a look of pure joy: a little kid who had just gotten everything he wanted for Christmas.

"Thanks, man," he sighed, seemingly overwhelmed. Suddenly the brute was hugging Ray, arms squeezing his breath away.

"One more thing," Ray panted, struggling out of the embrace. "What do you know about Salome?"

The name seemed to have a magical effect on him. "Not enough."

"You know who she is, right?"

"Oh, yeah."

"What can you tell us about her?"

"Not much."

"Do you know if that's her real name? Where she's from?"

"Nope."

"What *do* you know?"

"Just that she is one beautiful thing, man."

"She's a Native?"

He acted offended by this. "No. I mean . . . not like . . ." Then he grinned at Ray. "No offense, man, but most of your women . . . I mean . . ."

"You don't find them attractive?"

"Dogs," he confirmed. This was followed by a long coyote howl. "Bow-wows." He giggled, then grew serious. "But Salome, she ain't like that. She's special." He was almost panting. "There ain't many of Fanny's girls I'd want to get close to. Got diseases and stuff. But Salome . . ." He emitted a wolf whistle. "She's something else."

"You don't know where we can find her?"

"Huh-uh."

"Is there any chance the men I showed you were here to see Salome?"

"Sure. If they was smart." He paused, a thoughtful expression on his face. "You know what size tank that '69 had?"

"No. One last question, Elvin. When we stopped by earlier, Fanny got a phone call. After she hung up she said, 'He's coming.' Any idea who 'he' might have been?"

"Huh-uh."

"You didn't see anyone come in just after we left?"

Elvin shook his head. "I was still on the floor, bleeding."

"Oh, yeah. Sorry about the nose."

The bearded giant snorted at this, gently rubbing his wounded beak. "No problem, man. That was a nice move. Where'd you learn to kick like that? Kung Fu?"

"Klooch Olympics," Ray answered with a straight face.

The bouncer burst out laughing. "I'm starting to like you, man."

"Does this place have a back entrance?"

"Through the kitchen."

Ray looked in that direction, then asked, "Any other way out?"

"There's a fire exit in the stairs. But I ain't never seen nobody use it."

"Okay." He caught Billy Bob's eyes and nodded toward the door to Fanny's. "Thanks for your help, Elvin."

"Anytime. Thanks for the line on the Softail. Man, that's sweet."

In the stairwell, Billy Bob asked, "What are we lookin' fer?"

"Someone was coming up. Maybe it was the murderer. Or maybe whoever it was saw something. Either way, there's a chance they used this door."

"What door?"

They both stood looking up the stairs. Even in the semi-darkness, there didn't seem to be a door, or a sign, or any evidence of a fire exit. "It's gotta be here somewhere," Ray grumbled, starting up the steps. When he reached the landing he felt along the paneled wall. "Maybe it's hidden."

"A hidden fire exit?" Billy Bob wondered. "Don't make much sense."

"Check up on the next landing," Ray told him.

After ascending the stairs, the deputy gave the walls a quick rap, then reported, "Nothin' up here." He sat on the top step and watched as Ray patted the second of three walls on the landing. "Boy, howdy! I thought for certain that Elvin fella was gonna beat us black and blue. Shore is a good thing you know a guy with the right motorcycle."

"I don't," Ray grunted, starting on the last wall. This one bore a thin curtain.

"What do ya mean, you don't?!"

"I mean, I don't know anybody with a '59 Harley." He pulled the curtain back and found a concrete slab. "Those are rare bikes. No one in Barrow owns one."

"But—But you told Elvin—"

"I know what I told him." There was a gap in the concrete. He followed it with his fingertips. "I was betting he wasn't smart enough to realize there aren't many decent Harleys north of the Arctic Circle. And I was right."

Billy Bob swore loudly. "When he finds out . . . !"

"We'll be long gone." The gap was rectangular.

"No, *you'll* be gone. I work right down the block. He's gonna come after me."

"Bingo!"

"What? You want me to get myself tore down by a guy who makes Leon Lett look like a cream puff?"

"Who's Leon Lett?"

"All-pro tackle for the World Champion Dallas Cowboys," Billy Bob explained with obvious pride. "Listed at three hundred forty pounds. Actual weight, three hundred eighty. He's one mean mama."

"Sounds like a lot of man." He waved Billy Bob down. "I found it."

"Found what? My death certificate?" The deputy trotted down and squinted at a steel door. Ray extracted his penlight. Wide red letters declared: Fire Door. On the frame above a burned-out electric sign repeated the same words.

After nodding at it, Billy Bob muttered, "I'm dead meat."

"Relax," Ray consoled. "I *do* know a guy in Anchorage who's into Harleys. Maybe he can track down a Sportster somewhere in the lower forty-eight."

"Call him!" Billy Bob demanded.

"I will . . . later. Right now, let's find out where this goes." He gave the door a push. It clunked, but wouldn't open. With the aid of the penlight, he found the latch and depressed it. This time the door swung back, hinges singing. Frigid air rushed to greet them and they found themselves staring into the night.

➤➤ THIRTY-FOUR ◀◀

"Spooky," Billy Bob observed with a frown of disapproval.

Ray agreed, but refused to voice it. The howling wind, the near total darkness . . . It was like looking into a void, a black hole in space where only cold and evil existed.

"Bet Freddy Krueger's out there somewheres."

"Who?"

"Ain't you never seen *Nightmare on Elm Street*?"

Ray shook his head. "TV show?"

"Nah," Billy Bob replied, still transfixed by the vision. "Series of movies. Real scary. There's this feller named Freddy. He's got these long, killer fingernails and a dog-ugly face. He goes around slicin' and dicin' teenagers."

"I'm sorry I missed it. Sounds like Oscar material."

"Anyway, sometimes, he sneaks into their dreams, leaps out from nowhere."

They studied the scene for another ten seconds. When the deputy's beeper went off they both flinched. Billy Bob swore as he fought to deactivate it.

"It's Reynolds," Billy Bob said after examining the readout. "Should I call him?"

Ray nodded.

"You're not goin' out there, are ya?"

He shrugged at this. "We could use a break. Maybe I can scrounge up some evidence, bloody footprints . . . a murder weapon . . . a psychopath who wants to confess . . ."

"Well, I'll make this call and wait for you up front. Unless you want me to . . ."

"Go find out what Reynolds wants," Ray grumbled. "I'll be scouring the Styx for fingerprints if you need me."

The deputy offered a sideways grin before trotting down the steps toward safety. Ray pulled on his mask, hood, and his mittens, then used the penlight to check the outside door handle. The latch was locked. Once the door shut, he wouldn't be coming back in that way without a key. He found a clump of ice the size of a pineapple on the grated landing and wedged it between the door and the facing.

Armed only with the penlight, he began a slow inspection of the outer door. It was unmarked, covered with a sheen of ice. In the mini-pool of light, he noticed that the snow on the grating and on the steel steps leading away from it had been trampled recently, a waffle pattern repeated at opposing angles, as if the same individual had come and gone several times, or at least the same type of boots. Wide, tick-tack-toe design with snowflakelike diamonds: Sorrels. Since Sorrels were the most popular boots on the Slope, that narrowed the owner down to one of several thousand men.

At the bottom of the steps was a drift, bordered by a low wall. A garagelike roll door was hidden behind another drift. A loading dock, Ray decided. An old, obviously neglected dock, from the days when the roadhouse had been a hotel.

Boot prints left the stairs and, ten feet later, a trail of snowshoe marks set off into the darkness. North. Toward . . . nothing. The rest of Deadhorse was south. The airport was due west. The only thing north was the Arctic Ocean, the polar ice cap . . . And some three to five miles away, the Bradbury.

Ray knelt and felt the boot tracks with his mitten. They were deep. Whoever was in the boots was large, heavy. Without snowshoes, he wouldn't have made it out of the shadow of Harry's. The snowshoe tracks were shallower, and asymmetrical. Either Tubbs or Yuba. The mark left by the heel cleat and the fact that the Tubbs Ray was familiar with were ultralites, preferred by athletes, led him to choose the latter. Somebody, murderer, delivery man, shy john, or maybe even a disoriented drunk, had left by the back door in Sorrels, donned a pair of Yubas, and gone . . . where? For a walk? In the dark? At 50 below zero? In the middle of a storm?

Ray shined the weak beam at the trail of prints. Not a drunk. They were too even, the gait too smooth. Whoever left them was pretty good with snowshoes. A delivery person would have come to the front door, especially in light of the loading dock's condition. That left a john who feared exposure or the murderer. It was probably just a john, Ray decided. Although, why would anyone care about being spotted entering a roadhouse in Deadhorse? The townspeople probably wouldn't give it a second thought if the president showed up and stopped off at the bar for a quick belt. And just because you went in the tavern didn't mean you were patronizing Fanny's.

A gust of wind rushed across the snow, hitting Ray like an invisible ocean breaker. He dropped the penlight. The snow was deep and soft under his hands. It was only after he had dug a hole nearly a yard wide and a foot deep that he found the light. Gripping it tightly with his mitten, he set off in the direction of the tracks, intent upon locating the man who had forged the trail. The chances of a killer leaving such an obvious trail were remote, but in the absence of any other ideas . . .

Ray managed four unbalanced steps before sinking to his waist. A minute later, when he had climbed out, he took a single step and was buried to the chest. No wonder the mystery traveler had brought along the Yubas. The snow was virtually bottomless, Ray realized, the result of a swirling effect caused by the angle of the roadhouse. The drifts were probably three or four yards deep in spots. There was no way to follow the tracks, short of growing wings or going back to the Davis camp for his Northern Lites.

As he waded toward the loading dock, Ray heard a wail behind him, a low, angry voice warning that another unseen tsunami of vaporized ice was on its way. Hunching, he adjusted his goggles and braced for the attack. He floated forward with the blast, digging a path through the drift, until the wind was gone, the penlight disappearing with it.

If the light was still on, it was buried, its glow rendered

powerless. He brushed a layer of snow aside, felt, tapped, brushed another layer, felt, tapped . . . Ray cursed the thing, then swore at himself for losing his grip on it, twice. He considered giving up and going on without it. That would require locating a wall, in what seemed to him, absolute darkness, and using the wall to lead him to the stairs, then the door. And all of that hinged on maintaining a sense of direction. If he had gotten turned slightly, he might spend the next hour or so blundering around in the snow in back of Harry's. He suddenly had a humorously morbid vision of Billy Bob finding his body frozen solid just a few feet from the door, a popsicle that had succumbed to vertigo and died within reach of salvation.

After another minute of fishing through the powder, he felt something. It was hard. The light? Wrong shape. Wrong weight. This was flat, heavy. Taking it in his right mitten, he waded forward, toward the wall he hoped was still directly ahead of him. A dozen concerted steps later, he located the roadhouse, with his face. Falling against it with the grace of a drunken musk ox, his cheek slid along the cold, rock hard surface. The mask took the brunt of the scrape, but his skin stung, and his nose cracked audibly when it serendipitously discovered the ledge of the loading dock.

Righting himself, he followed the wall with a hand. In a matter of a few feet, he emerged from the snow, his boots meeting a hard-packed surface. He found the rail, the steps. He leapt up the grating, pulled back the door, and entered the warmth and dim light of the stairwell. Panting from the effort, he ripped away his goggles, mask, and hood, then started to take off his mittens. That's when he realized he was holding a prize: wide, fan-shaped blade, thick bone handle, razor-sharp edge stained dark red. An *ulu*.

Ray sniffed the knife. It smelled cold. He considered touching the blade with the tip of his tongue, then laughed at his foolishness. Not enough sleep. Too much caffeine. Only an idiot would lick a piece of steel that had been out in subzero weather. It was a sure fire way to lose taste buds.

Even without testing it, he was sure about the stain. Crusty, almost black, uneven . . . Blood. The *ulu* had been used recently. Possibly on Honey.

He shook his head at his luck. Had he really found the murder weapon? Ray sank to the stair and sat, thinking this over. It didn't make sense. Why would a killer go to the trouble of entering by the back door to avoid detection, slipping in and out without being seen, then discard the weapon casually and leave behind a set of snowshoe tracks?

Unzipping his parka, Ray tried to reconcile these observations with the long list of potential suspects, struggling to find a match. Simpson, the supervisor at the ice rig? . . . No motive. Stewart the drug and alcohol dealer? . . . Sufficiently psychotic, but lacking the drive and the brains. The roustabouts? . . . They would know Native superstitions, but otherwise . . . no motive, especially in the Weinhart murder. It wouldn't exactly further your career to kill a VP. Bauer? Why? Ray couldn't think of a reason, unless it had something to do with the upcoming deal with Arctic Slope Regional. Maybe Bauer had gotten upset with the way Weinhart was dragging his feet. You'd have to be more than just upset to shoot someone though. And why kill a rig foreman? Or a prostitute?

Ray rubbed his temple and took a deep breath. Leeland was mean enough. Smart enough? Doubtful. He would have to be working for someone.

That left only three names: Reynolds, Billy Bob, and Makintanz. Not Reynolds. He was too by the book. Given the proper motivation, he might shoot someone for you, but not cut them up. He didn't seem that cruel. Billy Bob . . . well . . . He could have killed Weinhart. Might have had time to ditch the body at Davis. Might have even sabotaged Ray's Polaris. He could have killed Driscoll while Ray was busy being assaulted by a winch. But Honey? No opportunity. Beyond that, Billy Bob was turning out to be an all right guy. As much as Ray hated to admit it, he was starting to like him, bunny teeth, southern drawl and all. The kid couldn't stomach a dead body, much less kill someone.

In the absence of any other ideas, Makintanz was the odds-on favorite. And even he didn't fit the bill perfectly. He was a weird blend of Native and white culture, probably screwy enough upstairs to end the life of another human being, if it suited his purpose. The problem was, these murders didn't seem to. Why would he kill Weinhart? Had an argument escalated out of control? No. These murders were calculated, premeditated. Anyway, say he did shoot Weinhart, then decided to "free his spirit" by slicing his neck. What about Driscoll and Honey? Ray couldn't imagine why the chief would kill them.

The prints out back could have been Makintanz's. They were deep enough. But could the corpulent quasi-Eskimo waddle back to the Bradbury after murdering Honey?

Ray swore softly, repeatedly at the brick wall. Maybe the best thing to do, he decided, was simply to back off and let the city cops handle the mess. Let them get headaches and go sleepless over the incongruities of these bizarre and seemingly unrelated events. It would be tempting to chalk the deaths up to coincidence. Different acts committed by different people, for different reasons. But with the same methodology?

Staring down at the *ulu,* Ray wondered if the city cops could do a DNA workup. They didn't have that in Barrow. They didn't need it. Things were never this complicated.

There were more than four thousand men and women on the Slope. Any one of them might have done this. Or maybe Reynolds was right. Maybe there was some Native out there just tagging people.

Ray began working on the other temple. His head was pounding. His tangle with the hoist seemed like ancient history. So did the jaunt in the snow after his machine died. It all seemed unreal, distant, like remnants of a disturbingly bad dream, but his body knew better. It was reminding him that he hadn't slept, hadn't refueled, hadn't recovered sufficiently. It was time to either hit the sack or start sucking down more coffee. He had little doubt which it would be.

Rising, he stuffed the *ulu* in his pocket, fastened the Velcro clasp, and started down the stairs. As he did, he recalled Maniilaq's promise: much killing. In Ray's mind, three corpses qualified as "much." The part about a "place of beauty" seemed to refer to the brothel. It was, after all, "where all men go." "Salome," who was, according to the shaman, the key to the whole exasperating puzzle, was nowhere to be found. That she even existed was something of a shock. Maniilaq had somehow tapped into a spirit, a ghost, or, more likely, a gossip pipeline, and knew about the woman. Yet she had vanished, and those who were acquainted with her were either unable or unwilling to provide additional information. Fanny had to know something. Maybe a warrant would help jog her memory, Ray thought, stepping into the bar area.

Harry's was actually crowded now, the chairs occupied, the standing room taken up by bodies, all male, all with beers and drinks in hand. Ray decided that the owner must be rich. The prices were more than double those of bars in Barrow, and the clientele were made up of men with plenty of money and nothing to do in their off-time.

Elvin was absent from his post, but Ray spotted Billy Bob at the bar, on the phone.

"Are you sure?" he was saying when Ray reached him. "Yeah . . ." He grunted, obviously displeased. "I understand, all right. I just don't like it." He rolled his eyes as he listened, then cursed. "Okay, okay . . . Hey! I know what my duty is . . . Nah . . . I can handle it . . . I said, I can handle it!"

When he hung up, Ray asked, "What's going on?"

The deputy took a deep breath and swore.

"What?"

"That was Reynolds."

"And?"

"And they found your stuff, from your sled."

"Really? Great."

"Well . . ." He sighed heavily, cheeks puffing out before falling into a severe frown. "Turn around for a sec," he said without enthusiasm.

"Huh?"

"Turn around."

Ray looked at him. "Why?"

"Trust me, Ray, just do it."

He shrugged and complied, turning away from the bar. Suddenly his arms were jerked back, his wrists snapped into a pair of handcuffs. Stunned, he demanded, ''What are you doing?!''

''Yer under arrest, Ray.''

''What?!''

''You heard me.''

''You've got to be kidding!''

Heads turned in their direction, eyes growing wide, men snickering at the sight. ''About time you rousted the klooch,'' a voice observed. This was followed by a chorus of laughter.

''Is this some kind of joke?'' Ray asked.

''No, sir.''

''I'm *under arrest*?''

Billy Bob took him by one arm and led him toward the front door. ''You have the right to remain silent, if you give up the right to remain silent . . .''

They met Elvin near the entrance. The truck-sized man was emerging from a short hall, zipping his fly as he ambled forward. When he noticed the cuffs, his jaw went slack. Swearing, he asked, ''What's goin' on?''

''I'm being arrested,'' Ray told him as the deputy continued to recite the Miranda.

''Arrested?'' Elvin shook his head. ''Bummer, man. That's a real bummer.''

➤➤ THIRTY-FIVE ◄◄

"AT LEAST TELL me what I did."

Billy Bob ignored this. Unlocking the door, he nudged Ray into the sheriff's office. It was cold, their breath issuing like smoke.

"Darned heater," the deputy said. He assisted Ray into a chair, then began tinkering with the thermostat. Down the hall behind them, the furnace ticked, then lit.

"Why am I under arrest?"

"Stand up."

Ray did. Billy Bob patted him down, removing from his person a pen, a small pad, wallet and ID, keys to the 4x4 that was waiting back in Nuiqsut. He removed Ray's parka and began checking the pockets. "What the . . ."

"Oh . . . I was going to tell you about that," Ray said.

"Really . . ." For the first time, the deputy sounded suspicious. "What is this? Blood?"

"I think so. I found that in back of the roadhouse."

"Is that right?" He pushed Ray roughly, forcing him back into the seat. "Just happened to find it, huh?"

"Yeah."

Billy Bob swore at him. "I trusted you."

Ray met his accusatory gaze. "What's that supposed to mean?"

"I trusted you and the whole time, I bet you was thinkin' what a stupid hick I was, laughing at me behind my back."

"What are you talking about?"

"In with the stuff from yer sled, they found a rifle and a knife." He lifted the *ulu*. "One a these here."

"In my stuff?"

"Leeland found it stashed in a snow bank 'bout two miles from Davis. According to Reynolds, the rifle was a 243, just the caliber to make the holes we found in Weinhart and Driscoll."

"You think *I* murdered them?"

"Reynolds does." Billy Bob sank into his chair and began pulling forms out of a drawer. "I'm not sure we got the right paperwork for three counts of murder one."

It was Ray's turn to curse. "You can't be serious."

"I didn't want to believe him. But he said if I didn't arrest you, he and Leeland'd come over and make a citizen's arrest on ya. And now, with this little goodie in yer pocket . . ." He waved the *ulu* at Ray, frowning. "I'm startin' to think they may be right."

"I didn't kill anybody," Ray offered with a meager chuckle. "I carry a 30.06, not a 243. As for the *ulu* . . . I found it along with some tracks in back of . . ."

"Shut up fer a minute and let me figure out this form." He began fighting with an old Corona, feeding in duplicates and carbon paper. "I told the sheriff we needed a computer when I first got here. Sure would come in handy right about now."

Ray stared at him, struggling to comprehend what was happening. Maybe he had nodded off and this was part of a nightmare. It had all the right components: an unthinkable situation, being wrongly accused, sitting in a Deadhorse jail in handcuffs . . . If it were a dream, he decided, it was time to wake up.

Billy Bob finally managed to get the paper straight against the roller and began asking Ray questions: date of birth, place of birth, social security number, mother's maiden name, closest living relative, place of residence, occupation . . . Ray went along, supplying answers and waiting as the deputy chicken-pecked the information, until they reached the subject of prior offenses.

"You think they'd let me on the force if I had priors?"

"I'm just doin' ma job."

"No. You're doing the job Reynolds wants you to do," Ray shot back. "You can't really think I'm a murderer. Do I look like a murderer to you?"

The deputy's head tilted up from the Corona and he scrutinized Ray. "Hard to say, I guess. Don't really know what one looks like. Ain't never seen one before."

"And you still haven't," Ray muttered.

When he'd completed the form, Billy Bob ushered Ray to the only cell in the building. It was spacious, even luxurious compared to most city facilities: a 10 x 10 square of carpet with a twin bed, miniature boom box, sink, and mirror. The walls were plaster, painted a light adobe tone. Aside from the fact that one wall was comprised of steel bars, it could have been a studio birth on an ocean liner.

"Where's the TV?" Ray joked as he sat on the bed.

"It's broke," Billy Bob replied. He unfastened Ray's cuffs. "Now the toilet's down this hall." He pointed. "So if you need to go—"

"I tell you and you let me out of my cage," Ray said gruffly.

"Nah. I was thinkin' you could just go do your business whenever you need to. I'm gonna leave this door open. This other door will be closed." He snapped a second wall of bars shut. "Long as you promise me you ain't plannin' on tryin' to bust out or nothin'."

"I'm not going anywhere."

"Better not. 'Cause I'm gonna be sittin' in there with my sidearm. Now, we're friends, Ray. And I hope like heck things ain't as bad as they look. But if you try to go wanderin' off, I'll shoot ya. It'd hurt my feelin's somethin' awful. But I'd sure as heck do it. Understand?"

Ray nodded. The deputy returned to the office area and began pecking at the Corona. It sounded to Ray like roughly five words a minute, slow even for a chicken. Stretching out on the bed he asked, "Got any coffee?"

"I'll make some soon as I finish up ma paperwork," Billy Bob called back.

"I'm having trouble with this charge," Ray said.

"I just bet you are," the deputy chuckled.

"Think about it, Billy Bob. How could I be the murderer? You've been with me since the investigation started. And I wasn't even here when Weinhart was killed."

"You weren't?"

"Of course not. I was at my Grandfather's."

"So you say."

"You don't believe me?"

"Tell you the truth, I don't know who to believe." He continued hunting and pecking, a letter every few seconds. A minute later, the deputy said, "You don't have an alibi for Weinhart."

"My Grandfather," Ray argued.

"He can place you at his house Friday evening?"

"No. But from midnight on."

"We both know Weinhart was killed earlier. Between four and six."

"I was at work until four."

"Coulda flown over to Prudhoe just in time to kill Weinhart."

"What's your point?"

"My point is, you ain't got an alibi."

"Do you?"

"I'm not an Ezkeemo."

"Huh?"

"I don't know nothin' 'bout worms and rituals."

"So?"

"And I wasn't the one out looking for Driscoll by myself," Billy Bob said accusingly.

"I never found him! What do you think, I beat myself senseless with a winch on purpose?"

"Don't know."

"And what about my machine? You think I rigged it to break down on the trip to Davis?"

"Maybe."

"Okay, then what about the body? You were the one who was in the can when it was stolen."

"Don't know about that. You coulda ditched it when you was *stranded*. Nobody ever saw it at the Davis camp."

"Oh, come on . . ."

"I do know that instead of going with us to get Driscoll's body and check out the murder scene, you went off to visit some witch doctor."

"I'm not following you."

"And buried the stuff from your sled."

"It was stolen!"

"Along with the rifle and the *ulu*."

"They're not mine! And I suppose you think I sabotaged my Polaris and almost froze to death just to cover my tracks."

"That'd do it."

Ray swore at the deputy's illogical assumptions. "And Honey, I killed her too?"

"You were the last one to see her alive, Ray."

"Someone else was coming up," he rebutted.

"So you say. But nobody 'members that. Not Fanny. Not even Elvin."

Ray swallowed hard. The accusations were illegitimate, nonsensical, absurd. Still, taken as a whole, they formed a neat, circumstantial trap. He had been at the right place, or at least unaccounted for, during each of the killings.

"What about motive?" he called.

"Huh?"

"Why did I murder three people I never met before?"

"You got me there, Ray. Why did ya?"

"That's what I'm trying to tell you, I didn't."

Billy Bob appeared at the bars, unlocked them and walked past on his way to the can. Thirty seconds later, Ray heard the toilet flush. The water ran for a moment, then the deputy retraced his steps and locked the gate.

"You left the light on," Ray told him.

Billy Bob glanced toward the bathroom. Shrugging, he said, "Maybe you knew them."

"Knew who?"

"The victims. For all I know, they owed you money or somethin'. Maybe you got a real problem with yer temper. Maybe all three of 'em ticked you off."

"Right. Sure. That explains everything. And maybe I'm engaged to marry Cindy Crawford."

"Cindy who?"

"Never mind."

"I thought you said yer sweetie's name was Margaret."

"Did you start the coffee yet?"

Billy Bob left to attend to it. There was a thrashing sound, a cabinet opening, something falling out. "Comin' right up."

Ray stared at the wall, the bars, listened to the faucet leak. Five minutes later, when Billy Bob finally showed up with coffee, Ray asked, "Where were you when Weinhart was killed?"

The deputy stared at him through the bars with a puzzled expression. After unlocking the outer door, he replied, "Right here in the office."

"Anybody with you?"

"Nah. I took the sheriff to the airport that mornin'. I was just hangin' around by ma-self."

"So you could have killed him."

Billy Bob blew air at this. "Could have, I guess. But didn't."

"And when I got knocked out by that hoist in the shop, you could have been out killing Driscoll."

He passed a cup of coffee to Ray. "Guess I coulda. But I didn't."

"You went to the bathroom about the time Weinhart's body disappeared."

"Yep. So?"

"You could have hidden it. And you could have rigged my snow machine."

"Just as easy as anybody else, I s'pose. But I didn't."

"And Honey . . ." Ray paused, thinking. "You could have killed her."

"Nah. You cain't fit me into that one."

"But you see what I'm getting at, don't you?"

"Huh-uh." He shook his head, bunny teeth displayed prominently.

"You can frame just about anybody if you glue together enough circumstantial evidence."

"Frame?" This seemed to perplex the deputy.

Ray sipped his coffee. It was blistering hot, incredibly

weak: amber, boiled water. "Yeah. When I didn't freeze to death after my breakdown, whoever it is that's running this show decided to frame me."

Billy Bob made a face at this. "Wouldn't that mean that a whole buncha people are involved?"

"Maybe."

"Some sorta conspiracy?"

"Maybe."

"Against you?"

Ray shrugged. Spoken aloud it sounded ludicrous. Who would care enough to frame an Inupiat cop from Barrow? "What if we were getting close and we spooked the murderer?"

"So he frames ya?"

"Yeah."

"What about me?"

"What about you?"

"If they got rid of you, there's still me to deal with," Billy Bob protested.

"That's the beauty of the frame," Ray suggested. "It takes me out, supplies a perp, so you'll stop looking."

Billy Bob weighed this, then retreated, relocking the outer door.

"It's possible. Don't you think?"

"I think you should try to get some sleep," the deputy advised. Seconds later a radio came to life, country music making its way through the static.

"Makintanz has something to do with it," Ray thought aloud. "I'm not sure what, but . . . And Salome. Whoever she is, she fits in, somehow."

"What was that?"

"Nothing," Ray groaned. Then, "I don't have a motive."

"Yeah, I heard ya before."

"But I don't."

"Sure ya do," Billy Bob called back.

"Oh, yeah? What?"

"I don't know. But ever-body's got a motive."

"What?"

Billy Bob showed up at the bars again. "Just about ever-body has got somethin' that really gets their goat.''

"Is that right? And watching police shows on TV makes you an expert in these matters?''

"Nah. I ain't no expert, but I know people. Ever-one's got things that bother 'em.''

"Such as?''

"Ah . . . I don't know. Could be any number a things. In yer case, maybe ya hate white fellas. Let's say yer gosh awful tired of the way we been treatin' yer folks and ya finally had a snoot full. Now yer gonna get us back.''

"Uh-huh . . . sure. That's it. How'd you know?''

"There's lotsa white folks back in Texas that got problems with black folks. Some of 'em downright hate 'em, just cause of the color of their skin. My great granddaddy was a Klansman.''

"KKK?''

"Shore-ly. He thought the blacks deserved to be taught a lesson, on account of the Civil War and all.''

"The Civil War?''

"Hey, now, the South's gonna rise again. Or so a buncha them rednecks would like to think. They're hopin' slavery makes a comeback.'' He shook his head at this, indicating that it was truly barbaric.

"How do you feel about blacks?''

"My Mama's a Baptist. She raised me up to respect folks. Taught me that people deserved to be treated fairly, no matter what they look like or where they're from. We're all God's children.''

"Including *Ezkeemos*?'' Ray asked sarcastically.

"Yep.'' Billy Bob sighed. "I hope you didn't do it, Ray. And I'm gonna make sure you get a fair hearin'.''

"Thanks,'' Ray offered without enthusiasm.

The deputy returned to the office area, leaving Ray to contemplate his fate. He finished his coffee, hoping the caffeine would somehow jump-start his brain and help him think of a way out of the mess. Setting the cup on the floor next to the bed, he called out, "What about the *ulu* I found in back of the roadhouse?''

"What about it?''

"Do you think I'm stupid enough to keep that thing in my pocket? If I used it to kill someone, wouldn't I hide it?"

"Don't know," Billy Bob replied. There was a minute of silence before he added, "Course, if you did do it, pretendin' to find the weapon would be the perfect cover-up."

Ray considered arguing with this warped line of thinking, but decided against it. Instead he asked, "Okay, then what about the gun?"

"They found it with your stuff."

"No. The one I supposedly used on Honey?"

"You musta hid it."

"I hid the gun, but not the *ulu*? That doesn't make sense."

There was no response.

"It seems obvious that I didn't do it."

Billy Bob failed to argue with this.

"Don't you think?"

Travis Tritt was plunking out a tune, yodeling something about a cheatin' heart.

"I'm no more guilty than you are, Billy Bob."

More music.

"I need to make a couple of phone calls," Ray grumbled. "The captain will be thrilled to hear that we've made progress, that a suspect has been apprehended." He punctuated this with a curse. "And coincidentally, I'm it."

Out in the office the front door opened, icy air hurrying back to Ray's cell. He heard it slam shut. Billy Bob said, "Hey . . ." Then there was a dull thud, a clunk—something heavy hitting the floor. This was followed by a metallic click.

The hair on Ray's neck stood at attention. "Billy Bob?"

Travis Tritt finished his song and Reba McIntire took over, describing her man in less than favorable terms. A drawer opened, shut. The floor creaked.

"Billy Bob?"

Someone groaned. There was another thump, the jangle of keys, then steps . . . wet boots on tile, coming in Ray's direction.

➤➤ THIRTY-SIX ◄◄

RELAX. THERE'S PROBABLY a simple explanation. Billy Bob must have opened the front door to toss the last of the coffee out into the snow. Then he must have come back in and started doing something at the desk. Now he's walking back here to . . . Go to the can again? He isn't responding because . . . he's tired of talking. Billy Bob tired of talking? The "hey" wasn't a greeting. It was just . . . in response to a song on the radio, a song he really likes. The metallic click was only . . . a filing cabinet shutting, not a gun being cocked.

The thoughts flashed through Ray's head in the fraction of a second, moving like lightning from his brain to his heart in an attempt to squelch the panic that was already setting in. It was too late. Adrenaline was flowing freely, urged on by an irrational voice that was ordering him to act, to get out, to get away. From what or whom he didn't know. It was instinct, a primitive drive for survival.

He leapt from the bed and made a break for the bathroom. He was halfway down the short hall before his training ordered him to stop. The bathroom was a dead end. If there was someone out there, and if they had a gun, and if they were going to harm him, the bathroom would only make things easier for them. Spinning on his heels, he sprinted back into the cell. He was shaking, sweat streaming from his brow. He bent and rolled under the bunk, pulling the blanket down to cover his hiding place.

This wasn't much better, he decided, struggling to keep his

breathing quiet and even. It might take slightly longer to be discovered, but would lead to the same result. If someone wanted him dead, he wouldn't be in much of a position to prevent it.

He heard boots approaching, heard the keys again. The bolt on the outer door slid back and it creaked open. He caught a glimpse of the boots as they started forward. Sorrels. Like Billy Bob's. Maybe he was suffering an anxiety attack. Maybe there was nothing wrong. Maybe . . .

The series of calming conjectures ended when he saw the barrel of the gun. A rifle pointed at the floor. It bobbed as the boots addressed the cell, turned and began squeaking down the hall, toward the bathroom.

The boots and the gun would return in a moment, Ray knew. They would find him cowering under the bed. And he would die.

Do something! the voice inside commanded with rising authority. Ray could think of nothing to do, other than hold his breath and accept his destiny. According to Grandfather, death was a natural part of the ongoing circle of life, something to be embraced, even welcomed as a transition into another state of existence. But Ray wasn't ready to enter another state of existence, especially not if the vehicle for the spiritual excursion was a slug of lead.

Lifting the blanket, he eyed the outer gate. It was ajar. Though he couldn't see the office area, he knew the front door was just a dozen yards past the bars.

The plan hadn't fully materialized, when he began to roll. An instant later he was on his feet, out of the cell, passing through the gate.

A deep voice yelled, "Stop!"

Ray ignored it, refusing even to look in the direction of the speaker for fear that it might slow his escape. He was halfway across the office, eyes fixed on the doorknob, when the first shot rang out. It sounded like a grenade in the small, confined space, thunder echoing from the hall, to the office, back to the cell. Behind him, on the opposite wall, the carafe of coffee shattered.

"Stop!" the voice ordered again.

Grasping the knob, Ray jerked the door back. There was another explosion, this one accompanied by a flash. Wood leapt from the door frame, chips and dust lifting into the air to form a miniature cloud. Ray caught a glimpse of the office as he launched himself sideways through the door: empty chair at the desk, figure standing wide-legged in the hall, rifle at the shoulder.

A bullet sang past as he flattened himself against the plank porch. Another sought him out as he somersaulted awkwardly into a snow bank bordering the street.

The voice in the office cursed vigorously. The boots began to run, the rifle no doubt accompanying them.

Ray struggled out of the drift and took off at a sprint, directionless. It was dark, the surrounding buildings indistinct. He had run two blocks before the question of where he was going surfaced. Where did someone in trouble go in Deadhorse? The sheriff's office, of course. Where did someone in trouble go when the sheriff's office was out of the question?

Dancing and sliding into a narrow alleyway, he gripped the edge of a featureless building and peered up the street. There was a dull sheen on the road, dim lights reflecting from the compacted ice. But no boots. No movement. Not even any sound, save the rising wind. An engine revved in the distance and a moment later a pickup lumbered around the corner a few blocks north, headlights rudely intruding upon the solemn night. It roared past, pistons chugging against the cold. Patrons from the roadhouse, Ray decided. Driving too fast for the conditions. But whether or not the drunks made it back to camp safely was the least of Ray's worries at the moment.

Ray resisted the urge to make another dash. The rifle was out there somewhere, probably waiting for him to expose himself. Until he could locate his opponent, Ray would stay put. As Grandfather had once taught him, knowing the enemy was half the victory. His eyes darted along the buildings, up and down the street, night vision improving to the point that he could make out signs: barbershop, grocer, bank . . .

Across the road there was a crunch of snow compacting beneath a hard rubber sole. Ray squinted toward it. Purposefully looking away, he thought he detected movement out of the corner of his eye. A moment later a piece of the wall stepped forward like a statue coming to life. Dark parka, boots, mask, goggles . . . gun. Whoever it was, he had dressed for the occasion, ready and seemingly willing to spend some time in the elements in pursuit of his quarry.

Ray, on the other hand, was already terribly cold. Without his parka and gear he wouldn't last a quarter of an hour. He was shivering, the skin of his hands and face burning. The first order of business, he decided, other than to avoid getting shot, was to find shelter or to procure a parka.

Turning, he gazed into the alley. It was like looking into deep space. There was no way to tell if it led anywhere. Jaw trembling, Ray debated his next move. Try the alley and get trapped? Break into the open and get shot? Stay hidden and become an Eskimo Pie? None of the choices seemed particularly attractive. Exploring the alley, however, was the least dangerous of the three.

He took a few halting steps. A Dumpster materialized. Maybe he could hide in that. Sure. And freeze to death in a heap of ice-hard trash. What a way to go. Continuing on, he managed another dozen steps before kicking a garbage can. The resulting noise seemed obscenely loud, as if he were actually trying to signal his foe to come and get him. He hurried forward and found a gate. It was locked. There was a sound behind him: boots on snow. His numb fingers found the top of the fence and as he sent a leg up over it, the night erupted in bullets. Pellets of supersonic steel ricocheted off of the Dumpster and trash cans, others eating away at the fence. Ray fell over it and thudded to the ground.

Surely someone would hear the gunfire and investigate, he thought as he braced himself for another lethal barrage. When it didn't come, he felt his way into some sort of enclosure. Behind him the voice was cursing again. He could hear empty shells hitting the ground, the rifle being reloaded.

His hands found a door. It was locked. He kicked it once, twice . . . It refused to budge. There was another sound. Close and guttural. A growl. Ray swore. Something got up, a tag jingled. The thing panted, then growled again.

"Nice doggy," he tried.

This seemed to make it angry. It started barking at him.

"It's okay, doggy. It's okay." Ray backed away from the fanged phantom and felt something jab him in the back. Another doorknob. He tried it. Locked. Swearing, he kicked it.

The dog lurched forward. A chain jangled against the side of the building.

"Nice doggy." He kicked the door again, again . . .

Fido sounded rabid now, and Ray imagined that the creature was foaming at the mouth, delirious that some idiot had blundered into its domain. He aimed a kick in the dog's direction and felt teeth catch his boot. Cursing, he fought to get it back. When the jaws released their grip, Ray leaned back and propelled himself into the door with his full weight. His shoulder met the wood and for an instant, the pain eclipsed the fact that the door gave. He sprawled to the ground, groaning.

The gunman reached the end of the alley and started over the fence. Fido went ballistic. Turning its attention to the second visitor, the dog began barking as if it hadn't eaten in weeks and a two-legged steak dinner was stopping by for a visit.

Ray slammed the door shut and felt for a light switch. There wasn't one. He wondered at the stench. It smelled like raw meat. He bumped against something heavy. It swung and bumped back at him. He suddenly realized that it was almost as cold in the building as it had been outside. A string tickled his cheek. He pulled it, and a single bulb flicked on, bathing the small room in a yellow glow. Ray found himself standing amidst a small herd of cattle, dressed out and hanging from ceiling hooks. A butcher's freezer.

Approaching a large metal door, he tried the handle. Locked. This was getting to be a little irritating. The handle had a place for a key. He glanced around, thinking that if he were a butcher, he would hide a key in there somewhere, just in case some bonehead locked himself in.

Behind him, the dog continued its growling assault on the gunman. The voice cursed at the animal. A shot rang out. Silence followed. So much for Fido.

Ray ran his hand along the top of the door. "Please let

there be a key," he whispered. The door to the outside creaked. Ray's fingers met something, cold, hard, with a sharp edge: the key. He tried to pick it up, but fumbled it. The key hit the floor, bounced, hit the floor again, slid to the far side of the cramped room.

The door creaked as the man attempted to force it open. Ray reached for the key. His hands were without feeling now. He used them like paws, lifting the key with both of them and aiming it at the lock.

The alley door cracked loudly behind him. Ray clumsily fed the key into the lock. There was another crack as the gunman's body hit the outer door. It seemed ready to give. Ray turned the key and pushed the chrome freezer door open. Behind him the alley door flew off of its hinges, setting the meat swinging in rhythmic waves.

Ray removed the key, slid out of the freezer, and slammed it shut. His pursuer cursed and opened fire on the door. The bullets ricocheted repeatedly, but the lock held. The man swore again before clomping away, back into the alley.

Ray tried to breathe, lungs incapable of processing the air he was gulping down.

He flipped the light switch and stared at the shop's workroom: chrome tables, sinks, an array of knives. He selected a knife, knowing that it would be of little use against a rifle, and started for the door. That's when he noticed the coats. They were hung in a neat row on a series of pegs next to the freezer: thigh length, neon-green, down-filled, with hoods. They weren't Eddie Bauer Arctic Circle parkas, but in a pinch ... Beneath them two buckets offered canvas gloves, rubber gloves, down-filled nylon mittens. Ray pulled on a coat and grabbed a pair of mittens.

Things were looking up, he decided. Given the appropriate shelter, he might not freeze to death. Now if he could just keep from getting blown apart by a bullet.

The front of the shop was dark, and Ray left it that way. He snuck to the windows and peeked out. There was main street Deadhorse, still deserted despite the gunplay. Perhaps because of the gunplay.

Ray glanced toward the sheriff's office. The door was still

standing open. What had happened to Billy Bob? He checked the other direction before unlocking the front door. After a deep breath and a mock prayer to whatever God might be listening, he pulled the door open. It was tempting to hole up in the warmth and relative security of the butcher shop. Relative was the key word, however. The bad guy was on his way to finish the job he had started. As soon as he made it around the block, he would rush the shop.

Locking the door behind him, Ray shut it and sprinted across the street. He had just reached the cover of a low railing when Mr. Rifle emerged from the alley. Ray held his breath, expecting to feel steel piercing his body. Instead, the man walked casually up the long wooden porch and tried the door to the butcher shop.

He hadn't seen Ray!

Finding the door locked, the man raised the rifle and used the butt to break the glass. He reached in and fiddled with the knob.

Ray watched, wondering who this guy was. Not Makintanz. Too tall. Not fat enough. The chief was recognizable simply from his shadow, his girth capable of eclipsing the sun. It wasn't Leeland either. The build was wrong. Too slight. The man was about 5' 10", approximately 175 pounds. Who fit that description?

As the man disappeared through the doorway, Ray came to a startling conclusion: *Billy Bob?* Did the voice have a drawl? Ray wasn't sure. But it was deep, authoritative. *Billy Bob?* No. There was no possible way that it could be. Unless . . .

Ray forced himself to set off down the street, running from railing to fence to alley to Dumpster, headed for an unknown destination.

Unless it was all an act: the dopey expressions, the naiveté . . . Ray had been down this mental road before and turned back. But now . . . *Billy Bob?*

He came to the end of main street and paused. Where to go? The Davis camp? No. Not until he figured out who was after him. Showing up in Bauer's office might be tantamount to jumping into the lion's den. Turn around and head for the

Bradbury? No. Same reason. Until he figured out how Makintanz fit in, *if* he fit in, the chief couldn't be trusted. The roadhouse? Now there was an idea. Enlist Elvin and his buddies to help apprehend the gunman. Maybe even . . .

The brainstorming session came to an abrupt end: a high-pitched whistle, then, pain. His upper biceps was on fire, bitten by an unseen serpent. He wavered, disoriented . . . then he began to run.

He ran away from the street.

Leaving the hard-pack, he stumbled into the snow. He high-stepped from drift to drift, boots plunging into the powder.

He ran away from Deadhorse.

The wind seemed to mock him, blowing as though it had authored this viciousness. Ray swore at it, pushed through it, light-headed, panicked. One sleeve of his jacket was wet, the neon stained black. He was exhausted, still the voice inside bellowed: *Run!*

He ran away from the rifle, from the boots that bore it up.

He ran in slow motion. He ran a hundred miles. He ran a hundred years. Legs carrying him away from the light . . . toward the shelter of darkness.

➤➤ THIRTY-SEVEN ◀◀

A HALF MILE from Deadhorse, snow gave way to frozen tundra. It was uneven, rising and dropping like swells on a black sea, the wind howling across it.

Willing himself forward, losing then regaining his balance a thousand times, Ray decided that he was marooned, stranded in the closest thing to Hell the earth had to offer. It was insane, really, he thought, trying to escape a madman by setting out across the bleakest, most cruel stretch of territory on the planet, with a bullet in his arm. Smart, real smart. A wise man, a man like Grandfather, would stop running, sit down, and prepare himself for death.

Ray paused and looked back. Deadhorse had fallen off the edge of the world. Either that or he had. No lights. No buildings. His legs began pumping again, as if activated by an autopilot mechanism. Where was he going?

His face was frostbitten. The only question was how severely. The wind had first burned then numbed his nose and cheeks. His lungs felt as though he had swallowed a jigger of gasoline, but the wound wasn't bothering him any longer. Both arms were without sensation. It took some amount of concentration just to move his fingers. At least he *thought* they were still capable of moving. Without feeling, it was hard to tell.

An engine rumbled to life somewhere behind him. Far, far behind him. He tried to analyze it over his own labored breathing. The driver gunned it, then the sound fell away, hidden by the moaning wind. When it returned, it was moving, a constant treble note. A snow machine.

Ray laughed at this. Even the nutcase who was trying to kill him wasn't stupid enough to wander off into the night. He was taking up the chase on a snow machine.

What little hope Ray had managed to collect spilled out of him like water from a paper sack as the whine rose, the engine shifted gears, and the machine raced after him. In the absence of light and direction, he had the eerie sense that he was trapped in a sadistic dream: pursued by a giant mosquito, ever running, but not making any progress.

It was only a matter of time now. He would soon be dead.

The morbid pronouncement was still hanging over Ray when his boots began to slide. The terrain seemed to shift beneath him, the ice rolling away, deserting him. There was a brief moment of hesitation, then he was falling, slowly, effortlessly, without violence. And he offered no resistance. Physically and emotionally he was incapable of reacting.

The ground reached up to greet him. Its embrace was soft, comforting. Warm. As if by magic, the wind ceased, refusing to utter so much as a whisper.

Ray was hovering . . . in darkness . . . in silence . . . in absolute peace.

·➤ THIRTY-EIGHT ◄·

THE SEAL DIED without fear or pain. Asleep on the ice pack, its spirit slipped away quietly, ushered heavenward by the razor-sharp point of his spear. The throw was perfect, the stone tip finding its mark, deep in the creature's heart.

Ray freed his weapon, took the tail fluke and began dragging his catch across the floe, toward his hunting camp. The animal would provide his family—his wife, little ones, and aging Grandfather—with sorely needed meat. He smiled at this, happy that he had again fulfilled his role as provider.

Reaching land, he stopped and stared at the snow. It was covered with tracks. Many. Large. Made by the fiercest, most dreaded creature of the Arctic: a polar bear. Several polar bears.

He continued on, pulling the seal at a more energetic pace, eager to put distance between himself and the bears. His right hand instinctively gripped the spear a little tighter, ready to use it in self-defense if necessary.

Moments later, he heard something: feet in the snow, a muffled grunt, sniffing . . . A glance over his shoulder told him that he was alone. His mind told him that he was imagining things. His heart told him otherwise. He began to trot, the dead seal bouncing limply from drift to drift.

Struggling to the top of a pingo knoll, he took another look back. The sight filled him with terror. Just fifty yards behind him was a polar bear. It was big, maybe 1600 pounds. To his horror, he suddenly realized that it was a mutant, with ten legs reaching down from a thick, barrel-like torso.

You're dreaming, Ray told himself. *It's just a dream.*

The observation did little to quell the rising tide of panic. The scenario was too real, the vision overriding his conscious mind. Even if it was a dream, and he was somehow certain that it was, he couldn't deny the emotions that were assailing him. There was no way to disregard the compulsive, almost pathological desire to run.

Dropping the seal, he hurried down the pingo, away from the great predator. Two minutes later, out of breath, strength already depleted, he twisted his head just in time to see the bear reach the seal. It curved its mighty neck toward the unmoving prey, jaws opening to engulf it whole. An instant later, the bear was racing toward him, ten colossal paws prancing along the surface of the snow, refusing to sink into the dry, crystalline powder.

Ray forced himself to go on, to make one last, futile dash toward safety. Flailing forward through a deep drift, he saw two blocks of ice ahead, each the size of a small *ivrulik*. Without looking back, he ran for them, legs burning as he high-stepped through the bottomless snow. Sliding between the blocks, he flattened himself against the back of one, lungs fighting for air.

Maybe the bear hadn't seen him. Maybe it would give up and go away. Or maybe . . .

He snuck a look around the corner of the ice block. The bear was only a dozen yards away, its long neck lifted high, nose sniffing the air, searching for Ray's scent. The beast grunted, almost smiling as it lumbered toward the ice blocks. Ray swore. Holding his spear with both hands, he braced for the assault.

Seconds passed . . . a minute . . . two minutes . . . The wind had begun to blow, ice pellets blurring the frozen landscape. Ray took a deep breath and looked out from his hiding place. The bear was gone. Or, at least, it was obscured by the snow. He leaned forward, squinting into the wind.

A clap of thunder knocked Ray to the ground: the growl of death overtook him. From his seat on the ice he looked up into the face of the bear. It was standing atop one of the ice blocks, jaws open, enormous teeth gleaming down at him. Ray froze, unable to breathe, unable to think, unable to react ... The spear was beyond his reach, a worthless shaft of wood and stone.

The bear growled again, as if confirming Ray's impending fate, then crouched to attack. Suddenly it was falling, seemingly dozens of feet slipping, tangling, tripping ... The bear performed a slow flip, landing on its back with a tremendous thud. Still alive, it began to squirm, legs pulling at each other, muscles trying to untangle the knots its uncoordinated feet had tied.

Ray dove for his spear. He rose, turned, threw the weapon with all of his might. It rocketed through the air and penetrated the bear's heart. There was a throaty groan, the legs quivered, and then ... it was dead.

Kneeling to cut off its feet, Ray was startled to see the beast change color, dull, yellowed white becoming olive. The ten feet merged into two, paws transformed into feet, the neck retreating, long nose receding. Fur became skin, the hard, predatory gaze softened, then took on human form. The bear was now a woman: jet black hair, curving hips, sparkling eyes, mouth bowed up into a smile. It was Margaret.

The ice floe was gone. Ray was in a hazy limbo, confronted by a vision of his fiancée—without clothes or inhibition. He gawked at her, then gasped as she wavered and began to fade.

''Margaret!''

He reached for her hand, but it was too late. She was gone. So was all color and sound. He was alone in the dark. Before he could reflect on this or even entertain the sadness at having seen but not spoken to or touched the love of his life, he saw something else.

Light. Distant but piercing. It grew from a pinprick to the size of an evening star to the size of the sun and continued to expand, blazing with a fury Ray found difficult to endure.

When the light had swallowed the darkness and was poised to swallow Ray, enveloping him in a hot, pulsing, nearly unbearable glow, the hungry entity paused.

Ray was no longer breathing, his entire being paralyzed by

fear and awe. He had the uncanny realization that he was about to die.

The question came without warning, a feeling that asked wordlessly yet unmistakably: *Do you want to live?*

Snapshots of Grandfather, of Ray as a child, as a man, of Margaret, of Billy Bob, of dead bodies, faces, experiences, fragments of memories, joys, and sorrows. A grainy black-and-white montage spilled over and through him, past, present and future merging into a single, desperate cry: *Yes.*

Cold . . . Pain . . . The far away roar of a river rushing over a falls. Ray's arm was throbbing, his fingers and toes tingling with fire. His cheeks were brittle, his nose a thick, flat chunk of ice.

Prying his eyes open, he squinted through the crystals that had formed on his lashes. Black. Nothing else, except the wind. And yet, he was alive. No amount of darkness or wintry evil could take that away.

The momentary sense of relief was quickly forgotten, driven away by a high-pitched whine: the mechanical mosquito was still on the prowl. Ray sat up and peered into the field of black. The snow machine buzzed at him from somewhere off to the right, faded, then buzzed from the left. An Arctic Cat, he decided. He rose stiffly, groaning at his aching, depleted body, then cocked his head to listen. Wind . . . his own heart beating . . . blood rushing through his ears . . . the sound of the snow machine at close range. The guy was driving back and forth, conducting an exhaustive inspection of the area.

A roar came at him from the west. Or was it the east? Normally quite adept at finding his way in the wilderness, Ray had lost all sense of direction. Even the stars above seemed unfamiliar. The roar rose and fell repeatedly before settling into a constant hum, but there was something unusual about it. Familiar. It reminded Ray of turbines spinning. A jet warming up. The airport! Turning his body toward the noise, he tried to judge the distance, but it was hard to determine.

It was time to make a decision. He was alive, but barely.

Another hour out in the elements would kill him, if the madman didn't do the job first. In order to survive, he needed to seek shelter. There seemed to be only two alternatives: plod back to town, or head for the airport. At least the latter had a guiding beacon—the turbines.

He was about to choose the airport, when something caught his eye: light. The head lamp of the snow machine bounced into view a hundred yards behind him, left and right.

Ray willed his lifeless legs to run. Churning through a drift, skating across a patch of frozen, nearly bare tundra, bogging into another drift, his nightmarish dream came rushing back and he was struck by the irony. Instead of fleeing from a ten-footed polar bear, like the one in the fable Grandfather had related to him countless times, he was fleeing from a rubber-tracked Arctic Cat. The driver of the Cat would soon see Ray's trail and move in for the kill. But, unlike the seal hunter, Ray possessed no weapon. And there didn't seem to be any huge ice blocks around to hide behind.

He changed his mind two minutes later. Muscles inflamed by fatigue, the Cat closing on his flank, Ray saw a pair of metal squares: hangars mostly buried in the snow. It was the outskirts of the airport. He sprinted for the buildings with a last burst of strength, legs energized by the thready promise of escape.

Panting, he dove behind one of the hangars. The roaring jet was louder but still a figment in the dark ahead, probably another three or four hundred yards away. Ray tried to think. He wasn't sure he had another sprint in him. And he was almost certain that the Arctic Cat had picked up his tracks. He could hear it approaching.

No weapon . . . No place of refuge . . . No hope . . . ?

He lifted his head above the roof of the metal shed and gazed into the night. The buzz of the snow machine rang crisply, then evaporated, almost as if the engine had been cut. Ray watched, glancing around the corner of the building. Where was it?

In his mind's eye Ray saw the hunter hiding between the blocks of ice as the polar bear mounted one of them to attack.

The picture offered little in the way of practical assistance. Except, what if . . .

Ray removed the butcher's jacket and hunched next to the metal wall, waiting. One of three things would happen now. Either he would be shot as he stood there like a ninny without his coat on. Or he would surprise the gunman, following the example of the hunter's victory over the mutant polar bear. Or he would be overcome by hypothermia and freeze to death. With the wind whipping at his shirtsleeves, he wondered if the popsicle scenario was the most likely.

In reality, there was little if any chance that his enemy would make the mistake of driving his vehicle over the top of the hangar. Unless he didn't see it.

The whine startled him. It was close, doubling in intensity. The snow machine was accelerating, seemingly right at him. Ray looked up just in time to see the Arctic Cat shoot over the hangar, skis leaving the snow, tracks grasping at air. He reacted by tossing his coat straight up. Missing the snow machine, it caught the driver, clinging magically to his head. The man flailed, making an effort to remove the down-filled blindfold. He succeeded, but lost his hold on the Arctic Cat in the process. His body flew sideways, disappearing into the darkness as the vehicle continued on, unabated. Ray's coat was caught on the skis, flapping like a malfunctioning sail before being gobbled up by the rubber tracks. The machine twisted in the air and landed upside down, the parka effectively gumming the traction mechanism.

The polar bear's feet were tangled!

Ray's eyes darted across the area illuminated by the snow machine's still burning head lamp. Where was the rifle?

The question was answered by an explosive boom. A bullet grazed Ray's boot, puncturing a vapor layer. The bunny boot hissed and went flat. Ducking, he slid around the hangar, using the wall to pull himself through the heavy drifts. Without a jacket, without a "spear," this battle would be over in a heartbeat. There was another shot. This sent him swimming further around the building. In the absence of a plan, he made the short climb to the roof. It was icy, slick, raised above the surface of the surrounding snow just enough to make him an easy target. By the time he realized this and was about to scoot back down, another bullet came after him. It pinged off of the roof. Ray flattened himself and closed his eyes, prepared, or at least expecting, to die.

There was a brief pause. Then a curse. Another. Ray could hear the rifle being cracked open. The man was reloading. Ray stood, glanced at the man to verify his activity and distance, and crouched to make the leap across to the other hangar. He would jump to the adjacent roof and make a run for that jet.

The plan was aborted when he slipped. The flat bunny boot twisted beneath him, the tread failing to grip the ice, and he tumbled from his perch, directly onto his foe. The gun, loose shells, the man, and Ray fell into a heap. Instinctively, Ray fumbled for the rifle. He found it just as his opponent grasped the other end. There was a short tug of war as both of them yanked, butts scooting in the snow. Ray kicked, hit something, and realized that he was now in possession of the rifle. He heaved it away, outside of the dim circle of light, with as much strength as he could muster, then rolled and scrambled to his feet, intent upon finding the jet.

Two frantic steps later, his forward progress was abruptly impeded. He felt his head snap backward, his neck emitting a sickening crack, and was suddenly airborne—shadows, hangars, and the still running carcass of the snow machine spinning around him. His ponytail was being jerked from his scalp. In the next instant he was released and rushed at the wall of the closest building. His cheekbone impacted the barrier first, followed by his shoulder, then hip. The result was a riptide of pain as his skeletal system quaked with shock waves. His lungs were empty, seemingly unable to replenish themselves.

He felt his body rise and squinted at his assailant. The masked face offered no expression. The hands that held his shirt were mechanical, void of mercy or care. He was dragged to the snow machine and propped against it.

The man cursed and began hunting for the rifle. When he returned thirty seconds later, Ray was still fighting for air, his body unable to offer the slightest rebuttal. The man fished a box of shells out of a tiny compartment on the snow machine and started to reload.

As he watched, Ray wondered if there really was a God. It was a strange thought, and yet a vital one at that instant. In a matter of seconds, he would find out. He suddenly wished that he had agreed to let Margaret teach him how to pray. No matter what the truth turned out to be, you couldn't be too careful. Maybe there was no God. Maybe it was a fable, just like Grandfather's stories. On the other hand, if there was a Supreme Being, why not make friends with him? Just in case.

Ray reached up and fondled his ponytail. The crucifix was still there.

The man tossed the box aside.

"Forgive my sins," Ray muttered.

The rifle snapped shut.

Ray removed the clasp and gave the crucifix a squeeze. Even with frostbitten hands, the cross hurt. It was sharp, almost dangerous.

The man stepped forward. At point blank range, he raised the rifle, apparently ready to end Ray's life without further delay. Ray jerked forward and jabbed the crucifix into the man's leg. It was impossible to tell if it had penetrated the RefrigiWear suit, until the man yelped and bent to grab at his leg. This brought his face within reach. Ray stabbed him in the cheek, the cross making a jagged gash in the neoprene and coming out tainted with blood. He swung again and caught an eye. The rifle tumbled away as the man howled in pain.

There was a noise off to the right. Another plane? A truck? Ray couldn't tell, and didn't particularly care. There wasn't time to survey the scene. The man was wounded, but would recover quickly.

Ray managed to drag himself to the edge of the circle of light and was trying to stand when he heard the rifle hammer click into a cocked position. He looked back and saw the barrel rise to eye him. The man wavered. Ray held his breath.

Ready or not, God. Here I come.

There was a thunderclap, the sound of breath departing, of

life leaving a human being. The body tensed, relaxed . . . and fell.

Ray stared, dumbfounded. He glanced around, his mind struggling to make sense of what had happened. The throbbing in his arm told him that he was still alive. His eyes told him that the gunman was dead.

Was he dreaming again?

➤ THIRTY-NINE ◄

"Ya okay, partner?"

Ray smiled at the drawl. It was beautiful. Angelic. A voice from heaven.

"Reasonably," he responded.

Billy Bob came crunching in from the shadows. He stepped up to the motionless body, kicked the rifle away, then attended to Ray. "You look like heck."

"I feel like *heck*," he assured him.

The deputy ripped the parka from the limp gunman and wrapped it around Ray. As he did, he noticed the blood on Ray's shoulder. "Yer hit."

"Yeah. It's nothing a few stitches can't remedy, but . . ."

When the hood was on and fastened, Billy Bob helped him up. "Let's getcha in the truck, getcha warmed up."

Ray paused as they reached the body. Bending, he pulled up the mask.

"Reynolds?" the deputy gasped. "Is he . . . ?"

After checking for a pulse, Ray nodded. "You're a good shot."

Billy Bob's shoulders heaved jerkily and he dove away. Ray heard Velcro being ripped apart, then there was the gurgling sound of the deputy expelling his lunch. When his stomach was empty, Billy Bob returned, breathing heavily, and assisted Ray to the Explorer.

"First time you ever shot a man?"

"Uh-huh," Billy Bob grunted. He tweaked the heater controls to high.

"I've never had to do that," Ray confessed. "I can't imagine that there would be any satisfaction in it."

"Nope . . . Shore ain't." He sighed heavily. "Should we load him up?"

"He's not going anywhere," Ray retorted. "The city cops will be here soon, won't they?"

"Supposed to be."

"Let them clean up the mess."

Billy Bob nodded and shifted into gear. The Ford's studded tires began fighting for traction. "Reynolds . . ." he muttered. "Why in the world would he kill three people?"

Ray considered this. He tried to imagine the military-style security guard using an *ulu* to set the spirits of his victims free. He couldn't.

"Musta been a real sicko."

"I don't think so."

"Huh?"

"I don't think he killed them."

"Ya don't?"

Ray's limbs were starting to thaw, causing the pain level to escalate. Grimacing, he said, "He's not our murderer."

"But he tried to shoot ya!"

"I realize that. And he may have been in on the frame-up. But . . ."

"But what?"

"I think he's just a *qaspeg*."

"A what?"

"The shell that goes over a parka to keep it clean."

"Ya lost me."

"Someone else did the killing, and Reynolds was supposed to protect their identity. So he framed me and then decided, or was pressured into, finishing the job."

"Why?"

"Because they were afraid that we might track down the killer."

"Who's they?"

"I have absolutely no idea." Even as the words were tumbling from his still frozen lips, a name materialized in his mind: *Salome*. It was followed by a phrase that Maniilaq had spoken: *She betray him*... The *anjatkut* had presumably committed the murders because Salome had betrayed him. If Salome was a prostitute, who did that make the *anjatkut*? Someone, a Native, according to Maniilaq, with enough clout to enlist others to help him cover it up. Makintanz? But why? Why would he kill Weinhart, Driscoll, and Honey? Why would Reynolds help him cover his tracks?

"You all right?" Billy Bob wanted to know.

It came again: *Salome*. Ray silently cursed the name. What did a phantom prostitute have to do with Chief Makintanz?

She betray him... *dishonor him*... *in beauty. Make much angry.*

They had just reached the haul road and Billy Bob was in the process of coaxing the Ford up onto it when everything inexplicably fell into place.

"Go the other way!" Ray ordered.

"But the camp is—"

"We need to go to the airport."

"Why?"

"Trust me."

"Ya need medical attention, Ray," Billy Bob reminded him.

"I've waited this long. I can wait a little longer."

The deputy frowned at him, shrugged, and begrudgingly twisted the steering wheel. "Yer the boss."

The Explorer bumped onto the road, shocks groaning. "Faster," Ray insisted.

"Why? What's the big hurry?"

"The storm's about over. The airport's opening."

"How do you know?"

"I could hear a jet turbine running."

"So?"

"So that jet will be winging out of here any moment, if it hasn't already."

"So?"

"So I may be totally off base," Ray thought aloud. "It

wouldn't be the first time. But I have a hunch that someone special will be on the first plane out.''

''Who?''

''The person who prompted the murders.''

''Ya sure about that?''

Ray shook his head. ''No.'' Grabbing the radio mike, he tried to reach the Deadhorse tower. Billy Bob stopped him. ''Don't bother. Not the right frequency. Call 'em on the phone.'' He pointed to the glove compartment. Ray fished the phone out, flipped it open, and cursed. ''I don't have any idea what the number is.''

''That's okay,'' the deputy drawled. ''We're here.'' The Ford bounced into a tiny parking area bordering two trailers: the terminal. He slowed to park, but Ray grabbed his arm.

''There it is,'' he said, pointing through the windshield. A 737 was taxiing away, lights blinking, jet fans spinning.

''We're too late.''

''No we're not. Catch it.''

''Catch it? We cain't catch an airliner.''

''Try.''

Billy Bob sighed and shifted, pushing the pedal to the floor. The Explorer sped through an open chain-link gate and onto the ice-encrusted tarmac.

The 737 reached the end of the runway and made a slow, ponderous turn, preparing for takeoff.

''We're too late,'' Billy Bob repeated.

''No we're not.''

''But—''

''Cut it off.''

''You gotta be kiddin'.''

''Do it.''

''You wanna play chicken with a jet air-plane?''

''Do it.''

Billy Bob directed the truck across a shorter landing strip and turned to face the jet. The Explorer skidded, then started down the runway, aiming for the nose of the 737. Undaunted, the plane roared at them and started forward.

''Ya sure about this, Ray?''

''No.''

"Then why are we doin' it?"

"Because we don't have the sense God gave caribou."

"Cari-what?"

Ray swallowed hard as he glanced at the speedometer, 70 mph, then up at the approaching hulk of winged steel. "Is it just me, or is it warm in here?"

"He's not gonna stop!"

"Yes, he is," Ray assured. "Eventually." *After he flattens us into a Ford pancake,* he thought.

"He's not gonna stop, Ray!"

"Yes, he is!"

"No, he's not!"

The cab began to shake, the howling turbines pulsating through their bodies. The nose grew, the wings stretched.

"Okay, you're right, he's not!" Ray conceded.

Billy Bob twisted the wheel, but the Explorer merely slid sideways and continued toward the plane.

Ray swore. Flipping his seat belt off, he yelled, "Get out!"

Before either of them could find a door handle, the gray giant lurched and began emitting a horrid screech: brakes fighting to slow 75 tons of forward-moving mass. The plane lurched crookedly, engines screaming.

What a way to go, Ray thought as he closed his eyes and braced for impact. He had survived a winch attack, the hostile elements, a mad gunman, only to be run down by a Boeing jetliner, under his own orders.

Three seconds later, the opposing objects collided. To their surprise, instead of steamrolling over the Explorer, the jet's landing gear merely tapped against it, crinkling the hood as if it were made of construction paper. The truck and the plane were face-to-face, barely touching.

The underbelly of the Boeing stared at them through the windshield, grotesquely large, like something out of a surrealistic movie.

Ray suddenly sensed pain in the palm of his hand. Opening his mitten he saw the crucifix. He had been squeezing it with such force that it had drawn blood through the fabric.

"Ya shore you ain't Cath-o-lic?" Billy Bob panted.

"I may convert," Ray told him.

"That scared the bejabbers outta me. Talk about close."

"But he did stop. I told you he would," Ray reminded as they climbed out.

Sirens were wailing back at the terminal, a fire truck already rolling toward them, lights blinking. Above them the emergency hatches on the plane popped open and yellow, inflatable slides appeared. Harried, panicked passengers began leaping out, riding down on their backs.

Ray watched, scrutinizing the evacuees. A paramedic appeared at their side. "What happened?"

"Aborted takeoff," Ray said, eyes on the slides.

A sedan pulled up and two men hopped out. "What in blazes do you think you're doing?" one of them demanded.

Ray started to dig out his badge, then realized he didn't have it with him. His parka was back in Deadhorse. "Police matter. Show him your ID, Billy Bob."

The deputy offered it to them.

"I don't care if you're the director of the FBI," the other man argued, "that doesn't give you the right to endanger all these people."

Ray ignored this, his gaze fixed on the hatches.

"Are you listening to me?"

There was a lull. The rush of passengers slowed. The hatches were empty for a moment. A stewardess bailed out. A steward. Ray began to question his theory. What an idiot he would look like if she wasn't on this plane.

"I'll have your badges for this!"

And finally, there she was: well-dressed, attractive even from a distance, parka hanging open to display a curvaceous, toned body. Dark locks lifted away from her shoulders, exposing a glowingly beautiful face as she climbed into the slide.

On cue, a Towncar pulled up and four hundred pounds of quasi-Eskimo got out.

"You'll be fined," the airport supervisor was saying, "and punished, and—"

"Shut up," Ray told him. He walked to the bottom of the nearest slide and stood waiting to receive his charge. She landed clumsily, unladylike, legs sprawled, high heels in the air. Bending to assist her, he greeted, "Salome . . ."

The woman's eyes grew wide, pencil-thin brows rising in an expression of shock.

"That is your . . . *professional* name. Isn't it?"

Her lips quivered, then formed a playful pout as she accepted his hand.

"Isn't it?" he prodded.

Rising, she sniffed at him before turning her attention to the condition of her skirt. The trip down the slide had wrinkled it.

An instant later, Makintanz was at her side, grasping an elbow, overflowing with concern. "Are you all right, darling? Were you hurt?" Out of breath, he seemed to be on the verge of hysteria. The Italian bookends took up position a few yards away, eyes scanning the area, right hands tucked inside their jackets, ready for the worst.

"I'm fine, Daddy," she sighed.

"How's it going, Chief?" Ray asked.

The short, obese man glared at him. "*How's it going?* You nearly killed my little girl! How do you think it's going?!"

"All of the passengers are safe," Ray assured him. "Including your little Salome."

Makintanz glanced at his daughter, then at Ray. "That's not her name."

"That's what the patrons at Fanny's call her."

The chief compared Ray's mother to a half-breed malamute.

"I don't get it," Billy Bob said.

"Deputy Cleaver," Ray said formally, "I'd like you to meet Salome, the most popular 'lady' at the local brothel."

The girl grinned at this, as if it were a compliment, dark eyes sparkling. Makintanz swore, swiveled his immense girth, and took a slow, deliberate swing at Ray.

"Hey!" Ray said, ducking away. "That's not the *Native* way, Chief."

"Stand still and I'll show you the Native way," he threatened.

The bodyguards converged, brandishing their guns.

"Back off," Ray told them. "This is police business."

The men froze, but the pistols remained at their hips.

"Put those away," Ray ordered.

Frick and Frack hesitated, looking at Makintanz helplessly before complying.

"Cuff him, Billy Bob," Ray ordered. He leaned against the fire truck, legs threatening to buckle. The exhaustion that had been chasing him for days was catching up.

"You can't arrest me!" Makintanz argued.

"Just watch."

"What're we arrestin' him fer?" Billy Bob asked as he applied a pair of cuffs to the thick, beefy wrists.

"Three counts of murder one."

"Murder?!" Mankintanz's daughter gasped.

This announcement caused the Italians to retreat to the Towncar.

"You don't have a case."

"Sure we do. A pretty good one, actually."

"I can destroy you both!"

"An *anjatkut* to the end," Ray observed. He blinked at the Chief. The fat man seemed to be levitating off the tarmac. Ray rubbed his eyes. He felt wobbly, drunk.

"A what?" Billy Bob wondered.

There was a distant rumble and they looked up to see a mobile star blinking at them from the horizon.

"City cops," Ray announced with a sigh. He sank to the step on the truck and leaned his head forward to avoid fainting.

"Mind tellin' me what the heck's goin' on?" the deputy asked.

"I haven't figured out the details," Ray confessed, massaging his temples. "But I think it goes something like this: The Chief's daughter was prostituting herself. Why, I haven't a clue. Maybe just to tick old pop off."

"Daddy? . . . Did you kill someone?" she asked. The cocky demeanor was gone, replaced by a mixture of horror and disbelief.

"Adii!" Makintanz bellowed. "Silence," he ordered, scowling at her.

"Okay. So the chief found out and decided to make the johns pay, with their lives."

"Daddy? . . ."

"Weinhart . . . Driscoll, th-they both . . ." Billy Bob stuttered. "With Sal-o-may?"

"I think so." Ray looked to the girl for confirmation. She was breathing erratically, on the verge of tears. "And that violated a number of taboos and traditions. In the old days, if a stranger showed up and took something that wasn't his, you were justified in killing him. Tribes had established territories and kinship networks. In the chief's warped view, Weinhart and Driscoll trespassed, failed to form a kinship pact, failed to ask permission to see his daughter, and therefore deserved to die.

"It's okay to disregard the traditions and be ruthless in business. But family's different. Eh, Chief?"

Makintanz muttered something profane.

"What about Honey?" Billy Bob asked.

"She knew too much?" Ray postulated. "Or he killed her because she talked to me. What was it, Chief?"

Makintanz was examining the ice beneath his feet, head sagging. "You can't prove anything," he mumbled. Over his shoulder the approaching plane was now the size of a small bird, a lantern against the black sky, wings defined by tiny flashing beacons.

"As far as the methodology, I can only guess that the chief considered the 'offenders' to be animals and treated them as such. Either that, or he's just plain crazy."

The chief aimed a vulgar epithet at Ray.

"The part I still haven't figured out is why you used an *ulu*," Ray confessed. "That's a woman's tool. Why not a hunting knife? Be easier to slit the trachea, easier to get the worm out. But maybe that wasn't in the 'How To Be An Eskimo' handbook you got your information from."

This time Makintanz denounced Ray's entire family line.

"Mr. Reynolds . . ." Ray continued, arms propped on his knees. "I'd say he was dispatched to make sure the chief's little hunting expedition didn't come to light before the deal with Arctic Slope Regional was sealed. It could have ruined

Davis. After the deal, they probably would have turned Makintanz in. Let him rot in prison.''

"What about Bauer?'' Billy Bob asked.

"I don't know,'' he answered through closed eyes. His stomach was in on the act now, threatening to send up what little coffee might still be down there. "He's probably in on it at some level.''

"I guess we should have a talk with him.''

"*You* have a talk with him,'' Ray sighed. "You and the city cops.'' He nodded at the 727 that was floating gracefully toward an adjacent runway like a giant hawk. "I've got a previous commitment.''

Rising, he staggered forward into Billy Bob's arms.

"Yeah,'' the deputy snickered, holding Ray up. "With the hospital.''

"No,'' he managed, making a feeble attempt to shake himself free. The faces, the lights, the sirens and shouts, the roar of the 727 as it touched down and reversed engines . . . It all blended into a singular swirling whole. Ray's legs gave way and the entire scene disappeared from view, replaced by a dome of glittering golden stars. As they cascaded down upon him, he whispered, "I need to go home.''

➤➤ FORTY ◄◄

AM I DEAD?

It was his first conscious thought, a question made all the more pertinent by the sensation that he was flying, rising magically into the air, floating, hovering, falling back, then moving forward at great speed.

A thumping sound began to intrude upon his brain. It was distant at first, but quickly picked up tempo and intensity, ultimately becoming a horrendous noise that resonated relentlessly through his chest and limbs. He wondered if it was the beating of his own heart, or perhaps the approach of death itself. Seconds later his eyes fluttered open and the mystery explained itself: glass, glowing readouts and displays, a man wearing a helmet and headset, fighting with what looked like a gear shift that rose up between his legs. A helicopter?

"Take it easy!" a voice shouted above the din.

Ray gazed up into the face of another man. He too was clad in a helmet and radio mike. Attempting to sit up, Ray found that he was restrained.

"Just relax!" the man told him.

"What happened?"

The man lifted a finger and turned to a nearby cabinet. A moment later he produced a headset, slid it beneath Ray's hood, and hooked the line to a dock of plugs.

"You're aboard North Slope Borough Medic-Alert-one," the man explained in a crisp tone.

Ray strained to see out the closest window. The lights of

Prudhoe Bay were retreating into the darkness. Deadhorse, the camps, the scattering of isolated rigs were already reduced to the size of a distant galaxy.

"Where are we going?" he asked.

"Fairbanks."

"No," Ray told him. "I need to go to Barrow."

"Our orders are to take you to Fairbanks."

"What for?"

"Fairbanks has emergency medical facilities."

"So does Barrow. Besides, I don't need emergency medical facilities," Ray argued. "Do I?"

The man shrugged. "We patched your shoulder and warmed you up. Your core temp was down to around ninety. Your vitals are steady now."

"Then why can't I go to Barrow?"

He shrugged again. "It's not our decision. Granted, you're not dying. But you do need to see a doctor."

"They have doctors in Barrow."

"We've got orders to—"

"Who gave you the orders?"

"The sheriff."

"You mean, the deputy?"

"Whatever."

"Well I'm a police officer. Barrow PD. I'm not under the deputy's jurisdiction."

The man held his palms up to Ray. "I don't know what to tell you. We're supposed to go to Fairbanks. So that's where we're going."

Ray swore at this.

"Barrow will still be there when you get released from the hospital," the man consoled.

"Can you patch me through to Barrow PD?"

"Sure. But—"

"Just do it," Ray said. "As a . . . a professional courtesy. One public servant to another."

The man rolled his eyes, then began discussing this with the pilot. Two minutes later, Ray had the captain on the line.

"You're where?"

"Headed for Fairbanks."

"For the ER," the paramedic threw in.

"Do you mind?" Ray asked with a glare. "This is police business."

The man sighed and flipped a switch on his headset, instructing the pilot to do the same.

"Are you all right?" the Captain asked, obviously concerned.

"Pretty much," Ray lied. "Just a little frostbite. Which is why I want you to tell these guys to take me to Barrow."

"Ray . . ."

"Come on, Captain. We caught the killer."

"You did?"

"It was Chief Makintanz."

The captain drew a four-letter-word into two distinct syllables. "You sure?"

"Oh, yeah."

"Talk about a mess . . ."

"A big one," Ray agreed. "Give Deputy Cleaver in Deadhorse a call. He'll fill you in. I'll have a report for you tomorrow."

The Captain swore again, seemingly unable to accept the disclosure. "Makintanz? . . ."

"Right. So in the meantime, have these guys turn this bird around, okay?"

There was a long sigh, then, "Okay."

Ray signaled the two men. "Captain wants to talk to you." He watched as they toggled their headsets, listened, argued briefly, then gave in. The helicopter leaned as the pilot did a 180.

"What time is it?" Ray asked.

" 'Bout . . . six."

"You guys know where Nuiqsut is?"

The man frowned. "Why?"

Ray explained his dilemma—his engagement, the shower, his promise to be there, that Grandfather's presence was required . . . necessary . . . vital.

"You catch that sob story, Bill?" the man groaned.

The pilot nodded. "I could almost hear the violins wailing in the background."

"Guys . . ."

"Think you can find Nuiqsut in the dark?"

"I could find a black cat in a black hole without a flash-light, blindfolded. Question is, why in the heck would we want to?"

"Guys . . ."

"Couldn't be any worse than the missions we used to fly in Bosnia," the pilot quipped.

"Yeah," the paramedic grunted. "At least the Natives don't have SAMs."

"Thanks," Ray smiled. "Could you unstrap me?"

"Don't push your luck," the man said with a scowl.

Less than a quarter of an hour later, they landed in a field of snow in view of Grandfather's *ivrulik*.

"What now?" the pilot asked when the skis were en-trenched in the drift.

"Go over to that house and tell the man inside that his ride to Barrow is here."

"Huh?"

"I'd go, but, well, I'm a little tied up," Ray joked.

The paramedic cursed and began fastening his parka and mask. As he pulled on his snowshoes he remarked, "You owe us big for this one, fella."

"Ray," he smiled. "Ray Attla."

The man nodded. "Jack Harrison." He pointed at the pilot. "That's Bill Swaim."

"I really appreciate this, guys."

"Yeah." Jack groaned.

Ray watched as Jack the paramedic climbed out the door and fought his way across the field, his form illuminated by the copter's high-intensity spotlight. He and Bill sat listening to the rotor blades beat the air.

"Maybe I should cut power," Bill complained five minutes later.

About that time, Jack reentered the glaring light. He was followed by a short, hunched figure in a calf-length fur parka. They ambled toward them in slow motion, Jack waiting as the old man, drum in arms, plodded his way through the snow on a pair of ancient gut snowshoes that were nearly as long as their owner was tall.

Popping the door, Jack assisted Grandfather up into the cabin. The old man was mouthing something, shaking his head, complaining. Ray caught a few Inupiaq words in the exchange. When Jack had strapped him into a seat, he patted Bill on the shoulder and the blades grew frantic, lifting the copter out of the snow.

Once they were airborne, Grandfather looked Ray over. "Ayaa . . ." His creased face was pinched into an expression of disapproval. "You hurt bad?"

"No."

"You no listen Maniilaq," he surmised. This was followed by a paragraph of Inupiaq explaining why the elders should be trusted, why shamans should be held in high regard, their wisdom taken to heart.

When he was finished, Ray asked, "So what do you think of copter hopping to Barrow?"

"No good," he frowned. "Birds fly. Naluaqmiut fly. Tareumiut no fly."

"Well, I'm glad you decided to make an exception."

"For Messenger Feast." He gently placed his hand on Ray's head. "For best grandson."

"Your *only* grandson."

"Only *and* best." With that, Grandfather launched into a chant, invoking the *tuungak* to Ray's aid. He was still singing when they touched down in Barrow twenty minutes later.

Jack unstrapped Ray, then looked at him. "I don't suppose there's any point in sending you to a doctor."

Ray shook his head. "I've got a party to get to."

"A party . . ." Jack laughed at this, passing the remark on to Bill. "Says he's got a party to go to."

"Gonna be a funeral if he doesn't get some medical help," Bill remarked.

"I promise I'll see a doctor, right after the party."

The two emergency workers smirked at him. Jack shrugged and offered a hand. "You're one stubborn Eskimo."

"Inupiat," Ray specified. "And yeah, I guess I am."

Grandfather was nodding enthusiastically. "Much stubborn. Much stubborn."

"Take care of yourself."

"You bet," Ray assured him. "Next time you guys are in Barrow, look me up. I owe you."

"You sure do," Jack agreed. He pulled the door shut and waved them back. The copter rose swiftly and zoomed east, toward Prudhoe.

"Where snow machine?" Grandfather wanted to know. They were standing at the edge of the tarmac at the Barrow airport. The place was deserted, no planes in sight, no people, not even any support vehicles in evidence. Just a pickup idling a hundred yards away.

"At one of the oil camps."

"Where truck?"

"Parked in Nuiqsut."

Grandfather chose an appropriate Inupiaq phrase to describe Ray's lack of planning.

"I'd suggest the bus, but I don't have any money on me."

"We walk."

"Walk? It's gotta be a mile. And I'm—".

"You what? You say you no hurt."

"Well, I didn't mean . . . I just . . ." Ray examined himself: the ill-fitting flannel shirt and the boots the medics had loaned him, the bandages protruding from his collar, decorating his face. He didn't look injured so much as homeless.

"We walk."

"I could call the captain."

"You too much hurt, I carry." He set his drum down and reached to pick Ray up.

Ray took a step back. "No. You're not going to carry me."

"You no think I can? I carry *aklaq*. I carry you."

"The last time you carried a bear was twenty years ago."

"I still strong. Most strong than you."

"Let's walk."

"You no can."

"I can out walk you any day, old man."

Grandfather laughed at this. "We see." He retrieved the drum and set off at a brisk pace.

They arrived at Margaret's place twenty minutes later—at five of seven. Ray was in pain, out of breath, on the verge of vomiting, but, most importantly, he hadn't let Grandfather get the best of him. "Well, we're two hours late," he observed, "but we made it."

"Hope food no gone," Grandfather grumbled.

Ray knocked on the door, waited, knocked again. A woman answered.

"Raymond!" Aunt Edna squealed.

He smiled at her, flinching as she gave him a hug. After the embrace, she gasped, "What happened to you?"

"Long story."

"Are you okay?"

"I'll live."

As they stepped inside, Aunt Edna asked, "And who, might I ask, is this handsome gentleman?"

Grandfather stood up a little straighter, his wrinkled face beaming. "Charles," he told her bowing. "You call Charlie."

"I'm so glad you could come . . . Charlie."

"Much glad," Grandfather gushed. He displayed his drum proudly. "I ready play."

"Good," Edna said, nodding. "Right this way, gentlemen." She led them down a short hall into the living room. It was crowded, the floor space taken up by chairs, all occupied by women. Ray glanced at Grandfather, but the old man was transfixed, mouth hanging open, eyes wide, as if he had just stepped into paradise.

"Aarigaa . . ." he sighed with delight.

At the center of the room, Margaret was seated at a table that was stacked high with boxes, most already open but a few still waiting to be unwrapped.

"Look who's here, ladies," Aunt Edna announced.

Heads turned in their direction. Margaret looked up. When she saw Ray, her face flashed with surprise, then delight, then dismay.

"Ray!" She leapt up and hurried to him, wrapping her arms around him. "What happened? Are you all right? Oh, my poor baby."

Ray responded with a a lopsided smile. The embrace hurt, and yet it felt wonderful. Now *he* was in paradise.

"I'm fine," he assured her. He squinted against the pain as she kissed him on the lips. The women in the audience cheered their approval.

"I was so worried," Margaret murmured. "I thought something awful had happened."

It almost did, Ray thought. "Told you I'd be here, didn't I? A little late but . . ."

She was hugging him again, holding on as if he were a ghost and might somehow slip heavenward and float away if she released him.

The phone rang and Aunt Edna answered it. "Raymond. It's for you." She offered him a cellular.

Ray gave Margaret an apologetic look and took the phone. After a parting kiss, he retreated to the kitchen, sank into a chair at the table and grunted, "Hello?"

"Ya turkey!"

"Who is this?"

"Ya don't recognize my voice? Maybe yer worse off than I thought."

"Billy Bob. How did you know I was—"

"Yer Captain called me and said you wouldn't let 'em take ya to Fairbanks."

"Nope."

"So I figured you'd head right for yer sweetie."

"You figured right."

"Listen, I won't keep you, but I thought you might be interested to know that Makintanz confessed."

"I figured he'd take credit for his handiwork, sooner or later."

"Yep. Soon as the city cops started talkin' to 'im, he just up and said he did it. Said he killed all three of them people. Seemed right proud of it too. And sumpthin' else."

"What's that?"

"Mr. Bauer was in on it."

"I thought so." Ray leaned forward and glanced into the kitchen. Margaret was glowing, eyes sparkling, cheeks flushed, her beauty effervescent, as she slipped the paper off of a box and opened it to find a coffee maker. Behind her, Grandfather was working the room, winking, smiling, showing off his drum, charming the ladies like an amorous old wolf.

"He told the city cops that he was in charge of keepin' a lid on the chief's crimes till after the deal with Arctic Slope was signed."

"What about Reynolds?"

"That's the second thing. Bauer authorized him to cover-up the murders."

"Reynolds rigged my machine, hit me with the winch, stole the body . . . all that?"

"Yep."

"And Leeland?"

"'Cordin' to Bauer, Leeland was outta the loop."

Ray considered this as he gazed at Margaret. "And you relayed all this to my captain, right?"

"You bet. He was right proud of the way you handled yerself. And well he should be."

Margaret caught Ray watching her and blushed. What was it that had so concerned him about getting married? At that moment he could think of no reason whatsoever to balk or even to delay. Spending the rest of his life with that woman, having kids, raising a family, growing old with her . . . He had never wanted anything so desperately.

"I'll let ya get back to yer party now, long as ya promise to see a doc-ter."

"I promise."

"Okay, buddy—"

"Billy Bob. You said three things. What's the third?"

"Oh! I nearly plum fergot. When I talked to yer captain, he said he was lookin' to hire another man for the office there in Barrow."

"Yeah. So?"

"So I was just thinkin', you know, we worked so well together here in Prudhoe and all. Caught us a murderer . . . And I don't really like Deadhorse all that much. Nothin' to do to speak of. And I hear tell the pay in Barrow's real good.

I'd have to clear it with the sheriff first, a-course . . . Not certain what he'll say.''

    ''What are you trying to tell me, Billy Bob?''

    ''I just thought . . . Well, maybe I might apply for that position.'' He paused and chuckled dopily. ''Just think, Ray, if I got the job, we could be partners, ever-day, all the time.''

    ''Wow . . . Just think.''

➤➤ BIBLIOGRAPHY ◄◄

Allen, Lawrence J. *The Trans Alaska Pipeline II: South to Valdez.* Scribe Publishing Corporation: Seattle, WA, 1976.

Allen, Lawrence J. *The Trans Alaska Pipeline III: Emerging Alaska.* Scribe Publishing Corporation: Seattle, WA, 1977.

The Alaska Almanac. Alaska Northwest Books: Seattle, WA, 1994.

Bodfish, Waldo. *Kusiq: An Eskimo Life History from the Arctic Coast of Alaska.* University of Alaska Press: Fairbanks, AK, 1991.

Ellis, William S. "Will Oil and Tundra Mix." *National Geographic*, October 1971, pp. 485–517.

Gavin, Angus. "Wildlife of the North Slope: a five year study, 1969-1973." Atlantic Richfield Company, 1974.

Jans, Nick. *The Last Light Breaking: Living Among Alaska's Inupiat Eskimos.* Alaska Northwest Books: Seattle, WA, 1993.

Langdon, Steve J. *The Native People of Alaska.* Greatland Graphics: Anchorage, AK, 1993.

MacLean, Edna Ahgeak. *Abridged Inupiaq and English Dictionary.* Alaska Native Language Center, University of Alaska Press: Fairbanks, AK, 1980.

People of the Snow and Ice. Time-Life Books: Alexandria, VA, 1994.

Smelcer, John E. *The Raven and the Totem: Traditional Alaska Native Myths and Tales.* Salmon Run Books: Anchorage, AK, 1992.

**Explore Uncharted Terrains of Mystery
with *Anna Pigeon, Parks Ranger* by**

NEVADA BARR

TRACK OF THE CAT

72164-3/$6.50 US/$8.50 Can

National parks ranger Anna Pigeon must hunt down
the killer of a fellow ranger in the Southwestern
wilderness—and it looks as if the trail might lead her
to a two-legged beast.

A SUPERIOR DEATH

72362-X/$6.50 US/$8.50 Can

Anna must leave the serene backcountry to investigate a fresh corpse found on a submerged shipwreck
at the bottom of Lake Superior—how did it get there,
and, more important, who put it there?

ILL WIND

72363-8/$6.99 US/$8.99 Can

An overwhelming number of medical emergencies
and two unexplained deaths transform Colorado's
Mesa Verde National Park into a murderous puzzle
Anna must quickly solve.